STOPPED DEAD

Harry slammed through the door, soaked from the fire sprinklers, gun drawn. There were rows of empty black-and-white patrol cars and unmarked cars in the Hall of Justice basement. The air was thick with the stink of old exhaust fumes and spilled gasoline. His shoes made hollow ringing sounds on the oil-stained concrete, so he slipped out of them.

Where was the shooter? Sitting in one of the cars? Hiding beneath one of them? Either way, Harry was an easy target.

There was just one way out, a ramp on the east side of the building. He crouched behind a concrete pillar and decided to stay right where he was so he could monitor the area and wait for reinforcements to arrive.

Suddenly, he heard the sound of a motor turning over—then revving up. A motorcycle roared by. Harry got off a quick shot and heard it ricochet off the bike's back fender.

He opened the door of the first car in line, a battered black-and-white, and switched on the engine. His stocking-inged foot jabbed the accelerator. The tires squealed as he gunned the motor, heading toward the exit. He was halfway up the ramp when he was blinded by blazing white lights. He jammed both feet on the brake and the car shuddered to a halt inches from the front of an oncoming fire engine. . . .

CHASING
THE
DEVIL

Other books by Jerry Kennealy

The Forger
The Suspect
The Hunted
The Other Eye
The Vatican Connection

The Carroll Quint Mysteries

Jigsaw
Still Shot

The Nick Polo Mysteries

Polo Solo
Polo, Anyone?
Polo's Ponies
Polo in the Rough
Polo's Wild Card
Green with Envy
Special Delivery
Vintage Polo
Beggar's Choice
All That Glitters

CHASING THE DEVIL

Jerry Kennealy

SPEAKING VOLUMES, LLC
NAPLES, FLORIDA
2013

Chasing the Devil

ISBN 978-1-62815-073-5

This one is for the guys and dolls from "The Road"—the only neighborhood in San Francisco where everyone had a nickname and spoke with a New York City accent:

Johnny O, Winky, The Whale, Louie the Barber, Toonder, Jazzbeau Cullen, Dirty Ernie, Tommy T., The Club, The Notorious Landlady, The Dragon, The Duke, The Wheezer, Dodo, Shorty, Tim-Tim-Timmy, The Carnary, Banjo Beak, Chops, and Old Man Sconio and his BB rifle.

Damon Runyon never had it so good.

ACKNOWLEDGMENTS

I greatly appreciate the help so gladly given by Inspector Tom Cleary and Inspector Jim Spillane of the San Francisco Police Department.

Prologue

Brooklyn, New York, May 1973

Detective Tony Fenner massaged his stomach with one hand while he steered the unmarked police car through the dense, slow-moving traffic. It was a warm, balmy evening: star-studded, cloudless sky, the moon a well-honed sickle. He rolled down the window, welcoming the pungent smells of spring: a whiff of Coney Island, the bay, the last lingering effects from the fruit and flower stalls that had closed up shop for the night. He let out a light belch, chastising himself for having that second helping of meatballs. Dino, the cook at Snoop's Bar & Grill in West Brighton, had been eager to please anyone connected to the New York Police Department ever since three wiseguys had strolled nonchalantly into the place and executed a hood by the name of Jimmy McBratney. That took place three nights ago, and Fenner had a lead on the triggerman—a young punk by the name of John Gotti, who, according to Fenner's usually reliable source, had been "anxious to make his bones" by scoring his first kill for the *Familia*.

Now Fenner had a decision to make—go home to his wife, who wanted to see a new movie with Barbra Streisand and some pretty boy named Redford, or go back to the precinct and work on the Gotti hit. It wasn't a hard choice. Fenner loved his job, and making a case against an up-and-coming Mafia hit man was a sure way to get a commendation.

He burped again, then let out a curse when an elderly woman bundled in a loosely buttoned flowered dress lurched into the street, waving her meaty arms for him to stop.

Fenner skidded to a halt and the woman pushed her grizzled head through the open window. Her eyes were small dark raisins in a face that was as wrinkled as a dried apricot.

"Mr. Policeman," she said in a shrill voice, "I just saw a little man. I think he had a gun." She gestured with her hands, holding them shoulder-width apart. "Dis big it was. He went into the alley over dere."

Fenner leaned back to give himself some breathing room. The woman reeked of stale gin. "How did you know I was a policeman?" he asked.

She stuck her head farther into the car. "I may be old, but I ain't stupid, buster. You live around this neighborhood as long as me, and you know. You better get over dere," she said, pointing a gnarly finger over Fenner's shoulder. "A woman was raped and killed right dere a little while ago. Why don't you people do something about it?"

Fenner pulled the car over to an open space by a fire hydrant. He grabbed the flashlight that was clipped to the dashboard, exited the car and slammed the door shut. He ran his eyes over the bird-bombed four-door sedan with a whip antenna and twin spotlights. The old woman was right on target. You'd have to be dumb and half blind not to know it was a cop car.

He thought about calling for a backup. There *had* been a murder in the alley about a month ago. It hadn't been his squeal, but he had been assigned to the follow-up crew, and spent a long night interviewing neighbors and rummaging through overflowing garbage cans.

The victim—a white woman in her forties—had been raped, then stabbed to death. There was something about the victim. What was it? Deaf. That's right. She had been deaf. As far as Fenner knew, the case was still open.

Fenner wasn't a big man—barely five foot nine, with sloping shoulders and a bony chest. What was left of his hair was concealed beneath a creased and stained Borsalino felt hat, a gift from his wife when he'd been promoted to plainclothes detective six years ago.

He tugged at the brim of his hat and hitched up his pants as he approached the alleyway. A chocolate-colored cast-iron streetlight threw a small pool of yellow light onto the grime-smeared sidewalk.

"Dat's it," the woman shouted from across the street. "Right dere."

The old bat was probably half-drunk, half-crazy. What she thought was a gun was probably an umbrella or a baseball bat. Probably.

The alley was too narrow for a car to pass through: rough redbrick walls, lined with open garbage cans and discarded packing cases. Swarms of flies danced between the garbage cans. Fenner knew from experience that there were rats the size of small dogs nesting in the debris. He held the flashlight with his left hand, out and away from his body, washing the beam across the bricks.

"Come on out," he shouted as he waded slowly into the darkness. "This is the police. I know you're in here."

There was a clatter of metal. Fenner reached down for the .38 Chief's Special holstered on his ankle. A black cat leaped from an overturned garbage can and froze, his tail sticking up like an exclamation point.

"Shit," Fenner said, pointing the barrel of his gun to the ground. The boys at the station house would love that. Cop kills cat in alley where woman was murdered.

He heard a small scraping sound to his left. He waved the flashlight beam in the direction of a stack of head-high wooden vegetable crates. "Come out, or I start shooting. Throw the gun out now!"

His finger was tightening on the trigger when a reedy voice said, "I'm coming, sir."

A figure emerged. At first Fenner thought the old woman had been right. A small man. A midget? The flashlight revealed the face of a young boy. He was holding something in his right hand. "Drop it," Fenner barked.

"Yes, sir."

Fenner picked up the weapon, a small rifle—so small and light he realized it was a toy. He dropped it to the ground and pocketed his revolver. Goddamn kid hiding in an alley with a toy gun. He grabbed the boy by the shoulder and dragged him out to the street. "What's your name, kid?"

"Harold, sir," the boy said. "Harold Dymes."

"Are you alone?"

"Yes, sir."

Fenner bent over and squinted at the kid. He looked vaguely familiar. Straight dark hair neatly combed. Strong nose. He'd seen him before. The vision snapped into his memory. The kid and his father had come into the station house to give statements about a murder. They'd been talking to the desk sergeant, Joe O'Malley, who had his solemn I'm-hearing-confession expression plastered on his Irish mug. Jesus Christ. Rose Dymes was the woman who had been murdered and raped in the same damn alley. Her husband had a tailor shop and secondhand clothing store a couple of blocks from where they were standing.

The old woman was waving her hands over her head and smiling. "I told you so," she screamed. "I told you so."

Fenner placed his palm on the boy's head. "Son, what the hell were you doing in the alley?"

"Waiting," Harold said softly. "Waiting for him."

Fenner knelt down, his knees cracking. He looked Harold straight in the eye. "Him? The man who killed your mother?"

"Yes, sir. He did it once. My father said he'll probably do it again."

Fenner straightened up. "That's police business now, kid."

"You're not doing your business very well, sir."

"Oh, yeah? Well, we're doing our best, kid. Better than you could do with a toy gun."

"It's not a toy.

"Stay right here," Fenner said. He did an about-face and went back into the alley. He picked up the rifle and brought it back to the street. It was a Red Ryder BB rifle. "Kid, I'm real sorry 'bout your ma, but this ain't the way to handle it." He shook the rifle at him. "What were you going to do with this? Point it at the schmuck and say, 'Bang, you're dead'?"

"I was going to shoot his eyes out," he said calmly.

"Shoot his eyes out," Fenner repeated. Then he laughed. The little bugger meant it. He had more guts than brains. "You're a beauty, kid. Does your father know you're here?"

The boy fidgeted with his hands. It was the first sign of nervousness he'd shown. "My father doesn't know, and I'd rather he didn't learn about it."

"You'd *rather* he didn't, huh? Hop in the car, kid. I'll drive you home."

The boy stood firm. "Are you going to tell him?"

Fenner rapped the butt of the BB rifle against the sidewalk. "I'll make a deal with you, kid. You promise me you won't come back here again, and I won't mention it to your pop. Is that a deal?"

"If you promise to find my mother's killer."

Fenner shook his head and studied the boy. He was a handsome lad; he stood tall with his shoulders straight, and he looked you right in the eye when he spoke. "How many times you been in the alley waiting for this guy, Harry?"

"Every night for the past two weeks, sir."

Again with the "sir." Fenner had a soft spot for polite kids. Maybe because he didn't run into many of them. "How old are you?"

"Twelve, sir."

"Know what you want to be when you grow up, Harry?"

"All I want to do now is find the man who killed my mother. I spoke to the other policeman, Detective Harlan. He told me to get lost. Mind my own business. This *is* my business. I don't like Harlan. I don't trust him."

"Get in the car, kid." Dick Harlan was a lazy-assed old-timer who didn't put a lot of time into a case, unless it had some juice, an angle that got his face on TV or a line in the newspaper. Fenner held out his hand. "Here's the deal. I'll look into the case. No promises, but I will take a real hard look. And you stay the hell away from here. Okay?"

Harry Dymes's young face scrunched up in a frown. He slowly extended his hand and grasped Fenner's. "Deal. As long as you let me know what's going on."

Fenner squeezed the small hand hard. "Kid, I'm going to keep a close eye on you. The way you handle yourself, I get the feeling that if we're not careful, you'll end up becoming a lawyer."

Twenty-seven days later Detective Fenner arrested Harold's mother's killer. That same day Harry decided what he wanted to be when he grew up—a policeman.

Chapter One

Kiev, Ukraine, March 11, 2002

The sprawling complex of the Science and Technology Center in Kiev had housed fifteen thousand scientists and engineers at the height of the Cold War. Their prime mission was the development of weapons of mass destruction. The population dwindled over the years to a hardcore group of four hundred, who, under an agreement with donor countries—Canada, Sweden, Japan, and the United States—worked in a variety of scientific fields dedicated to converting the former military technologies to "a productive, civilian-oriented environment."

During the Cold War, the STCU had concentrated mainly on nuclear weapons. There was a small group of scientists whose field of expertise involved producing variants of anthrax, botulinum toxins, and nerve gases. The lead scientist in this group was Nicolai Tarasove. He was still considered *the* expert in the field, and he continued his work, presumably in order to identify and destroy caches of deadly toxins that might otherwise fall into the wrong hands.

That was only part of his workload. The majority of his time and energy was spent exploring new DNA technologies, operating on the theory that others were working on similar projects, and it was better to be the first to open one of those treacherous doors in order to prevent future catastrophes.

Tarasove's office and laboratory were in the basement of a two-story stonewalled building separated from the main complex. Tarasove had few visitors. His current project involved a process of isolating venomous genes from poisonous snakes.

Tarasove himself had no difficulty dealing with the deadly reptiles. A lifelong hunter, he relished shooting, and consuming, a variety of game—everything from squirrels to bears. He was a thick-waisted man with graying hair and a round, bucolic face bottomed by a Vandyke.

He toasted the bowl of his battered briarwood pipe with a match and puffed clouds of smoke into the air. The knock on his door coincided precisely with the chimes and bird chirpings from his garish cuckoo clock. Six o'clock on the dot.

Tarasove opened the door wide and ushered the man wearing a dark leather overcoat and clutching a black canvas suitcase into his office. "Come in, come in," he said as cheerfully as a salesman greeting a valued customer. "Has the snow let up?"

Boris Feliks ignored the scientist in his hospital-white smock; his gaze swept the room. He moved to a door and yanked it open, only to find a closet containing nothing more than Tarasove's overcoat and scarf.

"We're alone?" he said.

"Of course," Tarasove responded scornfully. "Neither of us wants a witness to this transaction, do we? Come, come. It's in my laboratory." He pushed a button on the desk and two heavy steel doors retreated into the walls, revealing a large room bathed in bright fluorescent light. There were long tables littered with microscopes, beakers, particle analyzers, rows of test tubes, shakers, and a variety of electronic instruments that were all foreign to Boris Feliks.

Feliks was a husky, heavy-featured man. What hair he had left was a mud-brown color and had been allowed to grow thick and long at the back. His nose had been broken more than once and badly reset. A well-trimmed mustache ran right across his face, cheek to cheek. His whiskey-colored eyes were curtained by thick brows. He gingerly laid the suitcase on one of the tables, then examined the rest of the room.

One wall was lined with glass tanks that housed swarms of snakes. Feliks avoided looking at the beasts as he walked to the far end of the room. He turned the handle of a door, and when it didn't open, asked Tarasove, "What's in here?"

"More of my babies," Tarasove responded with a smile. "A new shipment of cobras. It takes them a few days to become acclimated to the change in climate." He beckoned Feliks with a crooked finger. "Come. Let me introduce you."

Feliks stood his ground. "I'm not at all interested in the snakes. Where's the toxin and the formula?"

"Don't be in such a rush," Tarasove said, placing his pipe into a ceramic ashtray shaped like an otter lying on its back. "I have to verify the money. Take off your coat. Relax."

Tarasove assisted Feliks out of his overcoat. As he hung the coat on a rack, he whisked several hairs from the collar, depositing them into his pants pocket.

Knowing that Feliks, like so many people, suffered from ophiciophobia—the fear of snakes—gave Tarasove an edge, and he always liked having an edge. "Not that I think a member of the Red Mafia would cheat a poor government employee like me. Have a look at this. It's something special."

Tarasove rapped his knuckles against the glass wall of one of the tanks. A glossy black snake lazily lifted his small, snout-shaped head from behind a handful of lava rocks. "This is my favorite. The Inland Taipan from Australia. The most deadly snake in the world. His venom is fifty times more potent than that of a cobra." Tarasove rapped his knuckles again near the snake's head, which quivered a moment, then dropped back onto the sand-covered floor of the glass cage.

"One bite from this little beauty," Tarasove said, "yields a hundred and ten milligrams of precious venom. Enough to kill more than a hundred people."

"The toxin and the formula," Feliks repeated, moving forward, while keeping a cautious distance between himself and the snake tanks. "I'm in a hurry."

"We will have a drink together while I verify the money. There's vodka there, on the table. Pour us both a glass."

Feliks picked up a bottle of Lvivska, a Ukrainian-produced vodka, and studied it closely before pouring two hefty measures into a pair of oversize shot glasses.

"My babies are harmless now," Tarasove said, slowly raising the lid of one of the glass tanks. "They've had their daily meal." He plunged his hand into the tank, grasping the neck of a four-foot king cobra. He held the thrashing reptile aloft and carried it over to a Formica-topped work area next to a stainless-steel sink. "Milking time for my baby," he cooed, reaching for a red plastic stylus the size of a ballpoint pen. He held the snake's head above a wide-mouthed glass vial and pressed the stylus into the back of the cobra's head. The snake immediately stiffened and began spitting up a clear fluid.

"A small electric shock," Tarasove explained, examining the liquid in the vial. "They only give up their precious fluids once every twenty days." He carried the cobra back to the tank, dropped him inside, and lowered the lid. "The process now is to dry the liquid venom into crystals. In the right circumstance, to the right buyer, the crystals could be sold for a thousand American dollars or more per gram." He brought his thumb to his nose and made a loud sniffing noise. "As much as some of those narcotics your comrades deal in, eh?"

"Stop trying to impress me, Nicolai. Count your money, then give me what I came for."

Tarasove acted as if he hadn't heard the instructions. "The Chinese love drinking the blood of a freshly killed cobra. It is reputed to have great aphrodisiac qualities. I tried it once, and do you know what it tastes like? Chicken." He paused a moment, then laughed loudly before saying, "Chicken blood. The toxin is in the Thermos next to the vodka bottle. The formula is in the envelope."

Feliks touched the stainless-steel Thermos lightly with one finger. "How do I know this is not just coffee? And that the formula is correct?"

"Because I'm frightened of you." Tarasove snapped open the suitcase and picked up a packet of crisp American one-hundred-dollar bills secured by a rubber band. He patiently counted the bills—four hundred in a packet. Forty thousand dollars. He spilled the entire contents of the case onto the table and began stacking the packets five high. There were twenty-five packets, totaling two million dollars. He pulled a single bill at random from one of the packets and examined it under a microscope. "I am a coward," he confessed. "A coward with expensive tastes." He examined several more of the bills, then replaced the money in the suitcase. "I'm satisfied."

Feliks picked up the Thermos and the manila envelope. "You had better hope that my clients are equally satisfied."

Tarasove helped Feliks on with his coat, patting him gently on the back and pocketing a few more of the man's hairs in the process, then showed him to the door. The mafioso gave him a hard look and a last piece of advice. *"Khue vye den ki nastal."* If things go wrong, bad things will happen to you.

Tarasove waited until the door had clicked shut before responding, *"Oto idi, a to jebnu."* Get lost, or I'll kick your ass.

He made sure the door was locked, then returned to his laboratory to find FBI agent Roger Dancel pawing through the money in the suitcase.

"You handled that just right," Dancel said.

Tarasove nodded in agreement. "Aren't you going to follow our friend?"

Dancel shook his head. He was in his late thirties, with a pale, moon-shaped face. His stiff, bristly black hair was neatly parted on the left, every comb strand in place. He was wearing a belted raincoat with epaulets on the shoulders. "I have three men along with an army of Russian cops from the MVD trailing him. Besides, we know where Feliks is going. It's who he's going to meet that has us guessing."

Tarasove was thankful when Dancel placed the money—his money—back into the suitcase. Part of the deal for setting up Feliks was that Tarasove would be allowed to keep the money, and would be relocated in America with a new identity.

"The plane is waiting for you at Boryspil Airport, Nicolai. From there you'll be flown to Paris, then on to Washington, D.C."

Tarasove slipped out of his lab coat, bundled it up, and

tossed it into the sink. He picked up his pipe and took a long, last look at the laboratory. At his "babies." The Americans had also guaranteed him far superior working quarters. "Are you flying to Paris with me, Roger?"

"No," Dancel said dismissively. "Agent Citron will accompany you."

Tarasove gave a wide smile. FBI agent Marta Citron, a most beautiful woman. He had hoped she'd be the one. In fact, he'd come close to insisting on it.

Dancel seemed to be reading his mind. "You like her, don't you, Nicolai?"

"Who wouldn't?" Tarasove responded, picking up the suitcase, shaking it so that he could hear the money sliding around inside.

"You'd be surprised," Dancel said, heading for the door. "Very surprised. She's a true blonde, Nicolai. Do you know what blondes say after sex? 'Thanks, guys.' "

Tarasove wrinkled his brow. "That's a joke, no?"

"A joke, yes. You never heard blonde jokes? I've got a million of them." Dancel walked over to one of the tanks and stared into the eyes of a king cobra. "Have you ever been bitten by these bastards?"

"Many times, Roger. I've developed an immunity. A bite that would kill you instantly would only give me an upset stomach, or a headache."

Dancel backed away from the tank. "What's going to happen to them when you're gone?"

Tarasove shrugged his shoulders. "When they get hungry enough, they'll begin to attack each other. The strong will survive. It's the rule of nature, Roger."

Dancel suppressed a shudder. "Let's get out of here."

Chapter Two

San Francisco, California, the Present

Harry Dymes coasted to a stop at Powell and O'Farrell Streets as a cable car screeched to a halt in the middle of the intersection, disgorging a load of shivering tourists in the center of the city's prime shopping area. He tapped his fingers impatiently on the steering wheel of the tiny Honda hybrid gas-electric car that the police department had bought to replace the traditional—and, in Harry's mind, more comfortable and functional—boxy four-door sedans.

Dymes was all for better mileage and less pollution, but trying to stuff two full-size policemen and a handcuffed suspect or a beaten and bloody victim into the little car and still navigate San Francisco's notoriously steep hills was just not feasible—except in the mind of the city's budget czar who, Harry knew, drove around town in a stretch Cadillac.

The cable car clattered off; the tourists gaped at the number of street beggars and set out to buy sweaters and jackets to protect them from the cold, windy summer's day, while Harry made his way across the intersection and into the brick-paved circular driveway of the posh St. Charles Hotel. A black-and-white patrol car was parked directly in front of the revolving glass doors leading to the hotel lobby. He wedged the lime-green Honda between a gleaming silver Jaguar and a butter-yellow Mercedes convertible, then went through the torturous challenge of wriggling his six-foot-plus frame out of the vehicle.

A bellboy wearing a maroon jacket and a matching fez complete with a black tassel ran up to Dymes. He eyed the Honda skeptically before saying, "Are you checking in, sir?"

Harry palmed his inspector's badge discreetly. "Homicide. One of your guests has been stabbed to death in his room. Where's the manager?"

The bellboy peered into the hybrid's interior. "In the lobby, with your buddies. What do you want me to do with this?"

"The keys are in it. Maybe I'll get lucky and someone will steal it. What's the manager's name?"

"Myron Milford. You can't miss him. Look for a guy in a thousand-dollar suit and a twenty-dollar rug."

Dymes pushed his way through the revolving doors. It had been some time since his last visit to the St. Charles, and it hadn't changed: bright yellow swirling leaf-pattern carpet, Corinthian columns covered in snowy-white marble, white oak–paneled walls festooned with bright art deco paintings, and the hushed hum of subdued conversation that's always present in expensive restaurants, at opening night concerts, and in overpriced hostelries.

He spotted a uniformed policeman near the registration desk, arguing with a man in a charcoal-colored suit. As Harry got closer, he could see that the suit was elegantly tailored and would have cost at least a thousand dollars.

He recognized the cop, Don Brady. He patted Brady on the back and asked, "Where's the victim?"

"Room eleven-fourteen, Inspector."

"Has the crime lab shown up yet?"

"Yeah, and the coroner's on the way. This is Mr. Milford, the manager."

Milford had soft, pink skin, an old-fashioned movie star pencil-thin mustache, and one of the worst toupees Harry had ever seen. His hairline was straight as a ruler, the hair inky black. He was tapping his foot nervously on the carpet and glaring at anyone who came within speaking range.

Harry introduced himself. "Just give me a minute, Mr.

Milford." He steered Brady toward the front entrance. "Is that your black-and-white, Don?"

"Yeah. There were two solo bikes parked next to me, but I sent them home."

"What's bugging Milford?"

"The usual shit. He doesn't like cops scaring the customers away."

"Any more uniforms around?" Harry asked.

"Two. One in the victim's room, and one guarding the elevator."

"Good job. You can take off. Radio the coroner to come around to the trade entrance on Post Street." Harry walked back to Milford. "Would you mind accompanying me upstairs?"

Milford fidgeted with his perfectly tied tie for a moment, then said, "Certainly."

He led Harry to an elevator and used a key to activate the bronze gilded doors. "This is a private elevator, Inspector."

When the doors whooshed shut, Harry said, "What can you tell me about the victim?"

"Nothing," Milford responded curtly, as if there were no reason he should have any knowledge of a murdered hotel guest. "All I know is that his name is Paul Morris."

The elevator began moving. Harry pushed the STOP button and smiled at Milford. "I know having policemen all over the place isn't helpful to your business. Let's make a deal. I'll get rid of as many officers as I can and make sure that the crime lab and coroner use the service elevators. I'll try my best to keep the story out of the papers and off TV. I can't guarantee that, but I promise you if it does leak, it didn't come from me. In return, I want you to get me a copy of Morris's billing record, phone calls, credit card information, all of that. Find out if he checked in alone, and if he was here for a convention. I want the names and addresses of the guests who had the rooms on both sides of his." He held out his hand. "Do we have a deal?"

Milford's hand brushed along his trouser leg for a moment; then he extended it. "All right, it's a deal."

Harry pushed the button for the eleventh floor. "Who found the body? The maid?"

"Yes. I'll have her made available for you." Milford ran an eye up and down Harry's suit. "Nice. Italian? Brioni? Or Canali?"

"Brooklyn," Harry responded with a grin. "My father's a tailor."

Milford's eyebrows rose toward his false hairline. "How lucky for you."

A uniformed patrolman was waiting for them when they reached the eleventh floor. He was unfamiliar to Dymes: young, his hat so big for his narrow skull that it practically rested on his ears. Harry showed him his badge, then said, "Any problems?"

"Nah. Nothing going on."

"You can go back to your regular duties." Harry gestured to Milford. "After you."

"Down this hallway."

"Is there a vacant room near the victim's?"

"Yes. The one on the south side. It was vacant yesterday, also. Room eleven-sixteen."

"I'd like to use it for a command post, and, if there's any coffee available, it would be appreciated. I missed breakfast."

"I'll attend to it right away, Inspector."

A bored uniformed cop was leaning against the wall in the corridor. Harry dismissed him before entering the victim's room. A lone member of the crime lab, John Prizir, was methodically going about his business. Harry had worked with Prizir many times before. Like every unit in the department, the lab had been hit hard by budget cuts. They no longer responded to such mundane crimes as burglaries, robberies, or muggings, unless the victim was very rich or politically connected. Harry wondered how long it would be before the great unwashed public became fed up with it all and revolted.

The room was small: a single bed, two end tables, an armoire, a dresser, and one upholstered chair. The body spread-eagled on the bed was that of a naked white male, approximately fifty years old. Harry spoke briefly to Prizir, who looked so very professional as he dusted for fingerprints. Unlike the TV and movie cops, Harry seldom had a case where anything the lab turned up led to an arrest or conviction.

"They cleaned him out, Inspector," Prizir said. "His clothes, suitcase, wallet, watch—whatever he had, they took. Even his shoes and socks. Where's your partner, the big guy, Thorp?"

"Sick leave," Harry said. He took out his sketch pad and began diagraming the room. Despite the popularity of filming crime scenes, when a policeman took the stand at a trial, his personal diagrams were quite often what made or lost a case. Harry then used his personal camera to take photographs. Finally, he took a look at the body. The victim had a good crop of neatly barbered gray hair. His face was diamond shaped, with a sharply prominent cleft chin. His dark eyes were cloudy and fishlike. His mouth was covered with a band of silver-colored duct tape. His hands and feet were fastened to the bed frame with thin wire. Harry examined the wire. It appeared to be from a coat hanger.

Harry checked the victim's hands. No callouses, the nails neatly trimmed and buffed. His torso was dotted with spots of dried blood: chest, stomach, along with his arms, legs, and genitals. Even the bottom of his feet. The killer had used what? An ice pick, Harry guessed.

"Here's your coffee, Inspector. The room next door is open for you and I—" Myron Milford froze in place when he saw the body on the bed. "My God!" His hands began to tremble.

Harry reached for the wobbling tray that held a pot of coffee and assorted pastries. "You might want to wait outside, sir."

Harry placed the tray on the nightstand just as the telephone chirped. He put two fingers to his lips and let out a whistle that could have been heard by a New York cabdriver a block away. "Quiet on the set," he yelled. "Prizir. Is the phone clean?"

"That's the first thing I dusted, Inspector."

Harry gingerly picked up the receiver and mumbled a grunt.

"Kiryl?" a husky voice asked.

Harry gave another undecipherable grunt.

"Who is this?" the voice demanded.

"Inspector Harry Dymes, sir. Are you a friend of Mr. Morris?"

"You're a policeman?"

"Yes. Homicide. Can you tell me—"

"He's dead, isn't he?"

Before Harry could respond, the voice said, *"Ebat 'kopat!"* Then there was a click and the receiver purred in his ear.

"Milford. Can the hotel operator tell me if that was an outside call or if it came from within the hotel?"

"I have no idea," Milford said, his eyes still fastened on the corpse.

"Well, find out," Harry said sharply, handing him the phone.

The lab technician caught Harry's attention. "Who was it? What'd he say?"

"He said 'Oh, shit' in Russian."

"The operator believes it was an outside call," Milford said, "but she can't be certain."

Harry reached for the coffee.

"Mr. Morris's billing record is in the envelope next to the coffeepot," Milford said, before taking a final look at the body, then scurrying out of the room.

Dymes carried the tray to the vacant room next door. The sight of a dead body no longer bothered him, but the smell did. Room 1116 was identical to its neighbor. Harry rapped his knuckles against the wall. Thick, hard. Horsehair plaster. The room was part of the hotel's original construction dating back to the 1920s. It would have muffled any calls for help that the unfortunate Mr. Morris had tried to make.

He sat down on the bed, sipped coffee, chewed on a bear claw and went over Morris's billing record. He'd checked in two days ago, late in the evening, as a single, using a Visa credit card—listing his home address as 9997 Santa Monica Boulevard, Beverly Hills, California, 90212, with a telephone number in the 310 area code. He'd made two local telephone calls from his room, twenty minutes apart, the morning after check-in. There were room service charges for a breakfast, and drinks in the hotel's rooftop bar.

Harry used the phone on the nightstand to call Morris's number in Beverly Hills. A recorded message, an impersonal computerized voice. "I'm out. Leave a message." Brief, blunt, and to the point.

Harry then called the phone company. He identified himself and asked for the names and addresses listed for the Beverly Hills number and for the two local numbers Morris had called.

The nasal-voiced operator lectured him on the phone company's policy. "We cannot provide any information for unlisted telephone numbers to a police agency without the benefit of a subpoena, Inspector."

"In other words, you're telling me the numbers are unlisted."

"Yes, they are," the operator said in a tone that seemed to indicate she was somewhat pleased about that.

Harry dialed the first of the two local numbers.

"Centerfold Escorts, we're here for your pleasure," a seductive feminine drawl said.

Harry broke the connection and dialed the second number. An answering machine recording, a young woman with a statutory rape voice. "Hi, this is Julie. I'm really sorry I missed your call. You mean a lot to me, so leave a message and I'll call you back as soon as I can. Bye for now."

Harry hung up and reached for a jelly roll. Morris calls an escort service. They pass him on to one of the "escorts"— Julie. It would take him a full day, maybe two, to set the subpoenas in motion to obtain Julie's address and to verify the Beverly Hills number. If he went directly to Centerfold Escorts, they'd refuse to release Julie's name and address without another goddamn subpoena. Then there was the credit card. Visa wasn't very cooperative about passing out customer information—even a dead customer's information—to the police without a hassle, and yet another subpoena.

There were many times when Harry thought about his old friend, New York detective Tony Fenner, and how he worried about Harry becoming a lawyer. Maybe he should have done just that, instead of following in Fenner's footsteps.

One of Fenner's first lessons was that there was "more than one way to catch a fish, or anything else."

Harry's way of obtaining confidential information was to

use an outside source. He had an arrangement with Don Landeta, a retired cop who now worked as a private investigator. Landeta supplied Harry with unlisted telephone numbers, credit card data, assessor and civil filing information, in exchange for an occasional Department of Motor Vehicles record, or a rap sheet. It wasn't legal, but it worked well for both of them.

He used his personal cell phone for the call.

"Landeta Investigations," said the man who answered the phone.

"Don, it's me, Harry. Let's do some business. I need the skinny on three phone numbers and some credit card info. How long?"

"The telephone stuff, a few hours. The credit card, a day. Give me the scoop."

Harry did just that.

Chapter Three

Washington, D.C.

Marta Citron's heels made loud clicking noises on the tiled floor of Mahogany Row, the high-security ninth floor of the J. Edgar Hoover Building.

She was wearing a short skirt that switched lazily around. her legs—legs that Roger Dancel, the man she was reluctantly going to meet, once described as looking like they went all the way to her shoulders.

She felt certain that Dancel was monitoring her progress on the surveillance cameras that lined the hallway.

Marta's problems with Dancel dated back to the time she'd been working a deep-cover case involving a drug dealer, Dave Robles, headquartered in Miami. Dancel had been Citron's "Buback"—Bureau backup agent.

The evening before Robles was busted, she'd been left with no alternative but to have sex with him. It had been an awful experience, and to make it worse, Roger Dancel had watched the entire ordeal on the surveillance tape.

The Robles case had been the reason she left deep-cover work, and nearly resigned from the Bureau.

Dancel had tried to "make it up" to her, via a dinner at Don Shula's Steak House in Miami Beach. He'd been in a celebrating mood. Robles had been caught with more than sixty kilos of chunky pink cocaine in the hold of his eighty-four-foot yacht. It's a myth that pure cocaine is white. The best of the best has a pink tinge. The restaurant featured extra-large martinis, huge steaks, and Sinatra. Nothing but Frank Sinatra music. It drove Dancel nuts, but Marta enjoyed it, because it reminded her of long-ago dinners with her parents.

They'd had two martinis each, the second bottle of Chateau Beychevelle Bordeaux was down to midlabel, and Ol' Blue Eyes was singing "The Way You Look Tonight" when Dancel made his move, sliding a hand under the table and latching on to her knee. Her hand quickly covered his and she gave her proclamation: "I don't date married agents, Roger. You know that."

"After what you and Robles did, you don't want to *date* me?"

She'd risen to her feet, poured what remained of the Bordeaux on his lap, and stalked out of the place.

All that was years ago, but not buried in the past as far as Marta was concerned. Dancel was now divorced, and had several promotions, elevating him above her in the FBI's pecking order. She had only worked one assignment with Dancel since the Robles case—Nicolai Tarasove. She feared that that was why she'd been ordered to his office.

Dancel's secretary was not behind her desk. He yelled out, "Come on in" from the adjoining room.

Marta Citron pushed the door wide open to see Dancel smirking at her. Her silk, cream-colored blouse was a perfect match to her skirt. She wore a simple string of pearls around her neck. A tan leather purse was slung over one shoulder. She'd shortened her ash-blond hair since the last time she'd seen Dancel. She wore it jaw length, with the bangs feathered to a fringe.

"This better be good, Roger. I'm knee-deep in a very important project for the EAD."

"I called Stan Cordes and cleared it with him," Dancel said, nonchalantly leaning back in his chair and swinging his feet up onto the desk. Cordes was the Executive Assistant Director, or EAD, for the Bureau's new intelligence unit, and Marta's immediate supervisor.

Citron stood uncertainly for a moment, then gave a big

sigh and settled into the chair directly in front of Dancel's desk. "All right, what is it?"

"Your old admirer, Nicolai Tarasove, wants to see you."

Citron crossed one long leg over the other. "I met with him eight months ago. He seemed fine."

Dancel used the heel of his shoe to nudge a file in her direction. "Consider yourself lucky. I have to go out there with a Pentagon scientist every month to see what he's up to. Hitler would have loved the two of them—merrily chatting away about the possibility of a toxin that could target a particular nationality: Korean, Chinese, Japanese, whatever. No more mushroom clouds, just spray the air with his toxin and the poor bastards get the death flu—a modern bubonic plague. Or dropping a canister of the goop into Lake Tahoe, and eliminating everyone within a radius of fifty miles.

"He called this morning, all in a dither. One of his comrades, Kiryl Chapaev, who was going by the name Paul Morris, was murdered in a San Francisco hotel. Nicolai had set up a friendly meeting with Chapaev. When he called his hotel room, a homicide cop answered the phone."

"Is he—are we—certain that Chapaev was murdered?"

"Yes. I had Tom McNab from the Frisco agency check it out. The cop is a guy by the name of Harry Dymes. That's D-Y-M-E-S. A typical fed hater, according to McNab."

Citron's hand went to her throat, her fingers stroking the pearl necklace. "San Francisco. That's more than two hundred miles from Tarasove's place in Nevada. I didn't think he liked traveling."

Dancel flipped open the brick-colored file and slipped out a photograph. "Tarasove stays at his place most of the time. He hunts—shoots deer, squirrel, God knows what—right from his sundeck. There's a trout stream running through the property, and he fishes it, in and out of season. He hits the casinos at South Shore, and he makes regular visits to Carson City, Nevada. Brothels are legal there. He always requests one particular girl." He handed Citron the photograph. "This one. Wendy. He bought her an ash-blond wig to wear just for him."

Citron examined the photo. The girl was young, with neat, regular features. Her wig was in the style Marta once favored—shoulder length and parted in the middle.

Dancel patted a hand over his neatly combed hair. "I guess Nicolai will have to buy Wendy a new wig, huh?"

"Very funny," Citron said, tossing the picture back onto the desk. "Fill me in on Chapaev. I didn't know him."

"He was a structural biologist. One of Tarasove's buddies back in Kiev. Tarasove insisted we bring him to the good old U. S. of A., so we did. Settled him in Beverly Hills."

"What do we know about the murder?" Citron asked.

"He was wired to the bed, tortured. Cleaned out of everything, including his wallet and laptop computer."

The news disturbed Citron. "Was there anything on the computer that could lead back to Tarasove?"

"Not according to Nicolai. He's certain that Chapaev had no idea of where he's living now. He thinks Boris Feliks is the killer, and I think he's right."

Marta Citron adjusted the hem of her skirt with one hand and rubbed her chin with the other. "Feliks won't give up, will he? How many of Tarasove's old cronies has he eliminated?"

"Five that we know of. Starting with the chemist in Canada, then the woman scientist in Tampa Bay, the computer whiz in Atlanta, and the two genetic engineers in Houston. He must have traced Chapaev to Beverly Hills from one of them. He's a relentless bastard; he won't stop until he has old Nicolai's balls for breakfast."

"Damn," Marta said. "We provide them with new identities, relocate them, warn them not to contact any of their former colleagues, and what do they do? Sit tight for a year or so, then go right back to their old habits, networking with their comrades. Share the knowledge, do some bragging."

"Tarasove is the smartest of the bunch, for what it's worth. I wonder what the two of them were up to?"

"I hope they didn't communicate by telephone."

Dancel pointed to his computer screen. "No. Tarasove's too crafty for that. E-mail only. Tarasove says that he uses three Web filters and that there's no way anyone can trace him through his e-mail address. I checked it out. He's right. I can't bust into his mailbox."

"You don't like him, do you, Roger?"

"He never should have been allowed to keep the money Feliks gave him in Kiev. Two million dollars, for Christ's sake. It could be in a Swiss bank, or buried somewhere in that chateau we bought for him in Nevada. On top of that, we pay him a fortune to develop lethal snake toxins. It's bullshit."

Marta knew she'd hit a nerve. That night back in Kiev, after Boris Feliks left with the bogus formula and Thermos filled with tap water, he'd gone directly to the nearby Hotel Dnipro—four FBI agents and a team of Russian policemen at his heels.

Feliks met with two Asians in the hotel's lobby bar. The Russian cops reacted too quickly. There'd been a shoot-out. One FBI agent and a Russian were killed, along with the two Asians, who had been traveling under false ID. Feliks had escaped through the hotel's kitchen, and hadn't been seen since.

Dancel had blamed himself for the screwup. He'd been the agent in charge. He should have gone along with the men following Feliks, rather than drive Tarasove to the airport. "Homeland Security loves Nicolai," Marta said. "They claim Operation Snake Charmer is developing quite well."

"Tarasove should be locked up in a bunker somewhere. Kept under constant supervision and surveillance. He sold out once, he'll do it again. He could go right back to his old masters in Moscow. They're building up a huge supply of new-tech weapons, and would welcome Nicolai's latest doomsday cocktail. He's probably got a plan in place—a contact he'll use when he gets tired of bilking us and wants to go home, or to some island in the Caribbean. Behind that chubby face and whiskers is an evil man."

"I agree," Citron said. "But it's not our decision."

"This may be news to you. We were able to identify one of those Asians killed in the Hotel Dnipro in Kiev. Turns out he was the favorite nephew of Ying Fai, the Triad's boss-of-bosses for the entire West Coast. Our good friends at the CIA were bugging Fai's yacht in a Hawaii harbor and picked up an interesting piece of information. Fai wants Tarasove bad. He had promised Tarasove's formula to the North Koreans. He's hired a specialist—a Caucasian, *bok wai*, a white devil, to run him down."

"*Bok wai?* That's all we have? No name?"

"I heard the CIA tape. Fai called him Alex." Dancel's face contorted as he tried to stop a sneeze. "I've run that through the computers and come up with nothing solid, just a few thousand possibles." He sneezed loudly, then wiped his nose with a handkerchief. "Fai is reportedly going to meet with this mystery man in Las Vegas in the next few days. Tarasove is all hot and bothered over the death of his buddy, Chapaev, so just go out there and keep him happy," Dancel said with a lopsided grin.

"I'm not a goddamn baby sitter," she said hotly.

Dancel thrust a thumb at the ceiling. "Those aren't my orders. They come from upstairs."

"So you say. Is Tarasove still using the Nick Sennet legend we set up for him?"

Dancel nodded his head. "Yes, no reason to change his name yet. He has a new dog. A ninety-pound pit bull. He calls him Jedgar. Get it? J. Edgar, and the damn hound looks a little like our beloved Mr. Hoover."

"What happened to Shelia, his Siberian husky?"

"A bear ate her, according to Tarasove."

Marta stopped at the door, her hand on the knob. "The San Francisco policeman. Dymes. Is he going to be trouble?"

"No way," Dancel assured her. "He's just a dumb local yokel. He hasn't a chance in hell of linking the body of Paul Morris to Kiryl Chapaev, former brilliant Russian scientist. Give my love to Nicolai."

Citron shifted her purse strap and tucked her arms close to her sides. "I don't like anything about this whole setup, Roger. And if I find out that you had me jerked around just to settle an old score, I'm going to make a formal complaint to the Director. In writing."

"Triplicate, Marta," Dancel called to her when she was halfway out the door. "They like those things in triplicate."

Chapter Four

Harry Dymes was watching the coroner's crew roll Paul Morris from the bed to a gurney when his cell phone buzzed.

"I've got the information on those phone numbers for you," private investigator Don Landeta told him. "The first one is listed to a charming establishment, Centerfold Escorts, at seventeen-sixty Hyde Street. The second number is residential, and belongs to Julie Renton, three-fifty Genoa Place. I haven't gotten the credit card info yet, but the Beverly Hills address and phone number Morris used in registering at the St. Charles—nine-nine-nine-seven Santa Monica Boulevard—are dead ends, pal. They belong to Real Mail, one of those outfits that's used by hookers, drug dealers and wandering husbands. The mail is either picked up there by the client, or forwarded to another address. Morris subscribed to their answering service, too, so all the messages on his phone bounce right back to Real Mail. Your Mr. Morris must have been hiding from someone."

"Not any more," Harry said, as he watched the gurney being maneuvered through the hotel room's narrow door.

"You owe me, pal," Landeta said, before breaking the connection.

Harry spent a long afternoon at the St. Charles, interviewing the maid, the registration clerk, and tracking down the guest who had been in the adjoining room. All to no avail. Not one of them could actually recall seeing Morris, except for the maid, who had taken one look at the bloody body on the bed and run off screaming down the hallway.

There had been three ongoing conventions at the hotel during Morris's stay: the California Science Teachers Association, the Society for Cell Biology and the Academy of Dermatology. He'd spent a futile two hours tracking down the organizers of each organization. Paul Morris was unknown to all of them.

Dymes drove back to the Hall of Justice and ran Morris through the department's database computer. DMV listed fourteen Paul Morrises in the Beverly Hills 90212 zip code, but none to the Santa Monica number, and a hundred fifty-nine in the greater Los Angeles area. Without a date of birth, it was going to be a long process to find the right Paul Morris.

Julie Renton's driver's license showed her as being twenty-six years old, and residing at the Genoa Place address. A local criminal records check on her listed one arrest, for prostitution, eleven months ago.

It was nearing six o'clock, and he was alone in the homicide detail. It was a feeling he was getting used to, and, he admitted to himself, one he was becoming comfortable with. His regular partner, Tom Thorp, suffered from depression. Thorp's idea of a cure was to lock himself in his apartment with a case of cheap vodka, two cases of ginger ale, and a gallon of vanilla ice cream. He'd start with straight vodka, then mix it with the ginger ale, and when that was gone and the shaking subsided, he'd finish up with the ice cream. His latest "run" had been going on for two weeks. Thorp had depleted his sick leave. He'd hired an attorney in an attempt to get a disability pension on the grounds that the depression was caused by his job. If he was successful, Harry figured over half the department would be pushing for disability pensions.

He cleaned up his desk and headed for the elevators. The door to the vice squad was open and he could see Sergeant Bob Dills still at his desk. Dills bore a striking resemblance to the deceased entertainer and later United

States congressman, Sonny Bono. He had developed a habit of warbling "I Got You Babe" whenever he busted a hooker.

Dymes gave Dills a friendly "Hello," then asked, "What can you tell me about an outfit called Centerfold Escorts?"

Dills's cheeks bulged like a trumpet player's for a few seconds. "Centerfold. That's Mother Janey Vayle's operation. She likes her girls to call her Mother, because she's never had any children. Thank God. She's uglier than a mud fence. But she has some very nice ladies working for her. Not cheap, but *very* nice."

"Who does the john give the money to?" Harry asked. "Vayle, or the hooker?"

"Both. Here's the way it works. The customer calls Centerfold, which is strictly an outcall operation. No girls on the premises, just Mother and her cat. If he's a first time caller, he gives Mother his credit card number. She checks it out, and if there's no problem, she gives him the phone number of one of her hookers who she thinks will suit the client's needs. Some of these guys are pretty specific. She has to be a blonde, or redhead, or she has to be short or tall. The one standard is big boobs. All the johns go for that. Mother's girls have to do more than just get the guy off. They have to be presentable in public, know how to hold an intelligent conversation, not look or dress like some Tenderloin hooker. The tariff is three hundred bucks for two hours of *escort* service. No touching. Some of these saps don't even want to sleep with the girls. They just walk around the convention floor with them, take them to dinner. Trophy companions. If the john wants to jump her bones, the girl negotiates a fee, and Mother Janey takes thirty percent of that. She keeps a portfolio on each of her girls, glossy photos, both with and without clothes, so, if the client is really picky, he can drop by Mother's and check them out before he buys. What's your interest?"

"It looks like one of Mother's girls had a date with a john just before he was murdered in his room at the St. Charles Hotel. Julie Renton. Ever hear of her?"

Dills scratched between his eyebrows with his thumb. "Doesn't ring a bell, but these ladies change their names more often than they change garter belts. I've never had a case where anyone from Centerfold got rough with a customer. How did the victim at the St. Charles become room temperature?"

"Strapped to the bed, gagged and used for a dart board," Harry said.

Dills leaned back in his chair and shook his head. "No way one of Mother's girls would handle it that way, Harry. If the guy had died with a hard-on and a smile on his face, I'd say Renton was a suspect, but not that way."

Genoa Place was a narrow street on Telegraph Hill, near the Coit Tower. There wasn't a parking space within a block of Julie Renton's address, not even for the hybrid. Harry bumped the car over the curb and onto the sidewalk adjacent to a fire hydrant. He flipped down the sun visor to display the *POLICE VEHICLE* placard, then walked up the steep hill to Renton's place, a three-story building that had been remodeled recently: new tile steps, fresh beige paint, and a faux-tile roof. Renton's unit was on the top floor. The landing had a view out to the bay— Alcatraz Island, and the necklace of lights on the Bay Bridge leading to the East Bay.

The rail-plank front door featured a lion's head door knocker. Harry rapped it twice, and when there was no response, used his knuckles.

"I'm coming, I'm coming," a sexy voice called from inside the apartment. Harry smiled to himself. Since he was visiting a prostitute, he figured she was either about to open the door, or just working from home.

The door swung open, revealing a buxom brunette wearing gray slacks and a man's style one-button blue blazer— looking like a schoolgirl who had raided Daddy's closet. Only she wasn't wearing a shirt. The gap between the lapels displayed a generous décolletage. Her hair was styled in long, glossy ringlets. She had dark eyes, clear olive skin, a pendulous lower lip and a nicely tipped nose. A black leather purse with the distinctive Gucci buckle was tucked under her arm.

"I didn't think you'd get here so fast, so I—. Hey, you're not the cabdriver."

" 'Fraid not," Harry said, showing her his badge. "But you're Julie Renton."

"Shit," the girl said. She had her hand on the edge of the door, and seemed to be debating the wisdom of slamming it in Harry's face.

He solved her dilemma by crossing the threshold, his shoulder brushing hers as he made his way into the apartment.

"You have no right to come in here without my permission," Renton said hotly. "Or a search warrant."

"Would you rather go to the Hall of Justice?" Harry said amiably. "My car's outside."

Renton slammed the door shut. "Let me see that badge again."

Harry obliged. She studied it closely. "You could have bought this on the Internet. Let's see some more ID."

"I like a careful girl," Harry said. He showed her his department ID card, and, when that didn't completely satisfy her, his driver's license.

A car horn beeped out in the street.

"That's my cab," Renton said. "Do you know how hard it is to get a cab in this town? I'd better go down and tell him to wait."

"Leave the purse, and tell the cabbie to take off, because this may take some time."

She tapped her foot nervously on the Berber carpet, then reached into her purse and extracted a ten-dollar bill. She waved the money at Dymes. "This is for the cabbie. I know exactly how much money is in my purse, so don't try anything."

Harry held his hands up in mock surrender. "I'll be a good boy."

"Where have I heard that before," Renton said sarcastically as she went out the door.

Harry watched her jiggle down the steps. She looked up at him as she pushed the money through the cab's open window. He could read her lips—"Some asshole cop"— before she turned her head away. He took a quick tour of the apartment. He was standing in a combination living-dining room, painted in pale yellow. The furniture was an eclectic mixture: mismatched sofa and chair, a crimson Lava lamp perched on a distressed apple-green cabinet, which held a variety of liquor bottles and glasses. A scratched mahogany table with legs that met the floor with brass serpents' heads, mouths stretched wide, clutching a glass ball. Slick-covered fashion magazines were fanned across a vintage steamer trunk that had been shellacked to a high gloss. There was a framed John Bao pop art print featuring four identical pictures of Audrey Hepburn on one wall, and a Roy Lichtenstein silk screen of a young girl holding a beach ball on the other.

Somehow it all worked. Salvation Army chic.

Julie Renton stormed back into the apartment. The first thing she did was scoop up her purse and rifle through the contents. "All right . . . what do I call you? Policeman? Copper? What?"

"Inspector will do."

She wrinkled her nose. "That sounds like something from an old English movie. What's your name again?"

"Inspector Harry Dymes. And this is about a man you saw last night. Paul Morris."

Renton tossed her purse onto the overstuffed chair, then walked over to the liquor cabinet and selected a bottle of Johnnie Walker Blue Label Scotch and one glass. "Paul Morris. I don't seem to remember anyone by that name. Last night, you say?"

"He had a room at the St. Charles Hotel. The coroner estimates that he died sometime after midnight. What time did you leave him?"

"Died?"

Harry moved over next to her and plucked an old-fashioned glass from the cabinet. "Murdered. We think the killer used an ice pick." He waved the empty glass under her nose. "Do you have any ice?"

Renton rocked back on her stiletto heels. "Christ, you're kidding me."

"Tell me about last night," Harry said, prying the bottle from her hand and pouring both of them a stiff drink.

"I . . . I met Paul Morris through a friend, and—"

"Cut the crap, Julie. I know all about Centerfold Escorts. I have no interest in how you earn a living, so just tell me what happened."

Her shoulders rode up, bringing the tops of her firm breasts into view. "Morris called Centerfold. He had been a customer before, but not with me. He was given my number. We arranged to meet at his hotel."

"What time was this?"

She knocked down half of her drink in one gulp and held out the glass to Harry for a refill. "He called in the morning, and we met at six thirty in the lobby of the St. Charles. We had a drink at the bar. He wanted to go somewhere with live music, so we took a cab to Moose's in North Beach." She dipped into the Scotch again, then wandered over to the couch and flopped down. "We had dinner, then went right back to the hotel. It was about nine, maybe a little after, when we got to his room."

"Did Morris talk to anyone while he was with you?"

"The sommelier, the waiter. That's about it."

"What did he tell you about himself?" Harry wanted to know.

Renton wriggled her rump into the cushions. "His work. He said he was a structural biologist, whatever the hell that is. I tune myself out when they start talking about their jobs. And he asked questions about San Francisco: how it was to live here, what was there to do, stuff like that." She did that raising-of-the-shoulders thing again, drawing Harry's eye. "He spent a lot of the time eating, drinking, and staring at my cleavage. Cleavage is two of the best things a girl in my business can have."

Harry sampled the whisky. "Did he tell you where he lived? If he was married?"

"He didn't mention a wife, but I'm pretty sure he was married. He looked like he hadn't had a blow job in a long time. He said he lived in Southern California, but from his accent, he wasn't born there."

"Accent?" No one at the hotel had mentioned an accent to Harry. "What kind of an accent?"

Renton fiddled with her jacket's one button, rubbing it slowly between her thumb and forefinger. "Eastern European, I'd guess. Maybe German. Guttural, you know what I mean?"

"I do. Could it have been Russian?"

"I guess so. Morris isn't a Russian name, is it?"

"Did he mention anyone by the name of Kiryl?" Harry asked. "The man who'd called Morris's room had asked for Kiryl—it's a popular Russian name, but not used often here in the U.S."

Renton shook her head from side to side, the long ringlets bouncing across her face. "No. I don't think he mentioned anyone's name. One other thing. He seemed to be nervous."

Harry topped off both of their glasses. "How so?"

"He kept looking around, as if he were expecting to see someone. I thought maybe he was worried that his wife would show up, or that she'd hired someone to follow him."

"Was there anyone like that around, Julie?"

Her eyebrows arched, her lips pursed. "When I'm with a date, I give him my full attention. I focus on *him*. He's paying for my time, and he gets it."

"I understand," Harry said. "This is important. Think hard. Whoever killed Morris may have been following him. If so, he saw you. Morris didn't die easily. His killer tied him to the bed, taped his mouth and worked him over. He wanted information. Morris could have told him about you. Your name. Your phone number."

"If you're trying to scare me, you're doing a hell of a job at it."

Dymes sat down next to her. "I'm telling you how it is. Did you see anyone who looked suspicious? Who showed more than an average interest in Morris?"

Julie closed her eyes in concentration. "No one at the hotel that I can remember. At the restaurant . . . no." She popped her eyes open. "I'm used to being stared at. There was one guy at Moose's, a lone diner, sitting right next to us, who flirted a little too obviously, but again, that happens."

"What did he look like?"

"Nice-looking guy, your age, give a year or two either way. He could have easily overheard everything we said at the table."

"Tell me more about Morris. His room was cleaned out. Everything was taken, including his clothes, down to his shoes and socks. How was he dressed? Did he have any jewelry?"

"I can help you there," Julie said. "I'm into labels. He was wearing an off-the-rack business suit, the usual dark pinstripe deal. A nice Hermès silk tie. A lot of guys try to get by with a cheap suit and expensive ties." She raised her left hand and wiggled the ring finger. "One ring. Gold, with a plain black onyx stone. Nothing special. His watch was nice. Cartier tank style, with a crocodile band." She moistened her lips with the tip of her tongue. "Do you have the time?"

Harry shot his cuff. "Twenty after seven."

Renton wrapped her hand around his wrist. "That's a platinum Rolex Yachtmaster. It's not new, but you'd have to pay five grand for it on eBay. And that jacket is cashmere. How does an honest cop dress like you and wear a Rolex, Harry?"

"It's a knockoff."

A phone rang somewhere in the back of the apartment. Renton made no move to answer it.

"Your date must be getting anxious," Harry said.

She twisted the coat button free, exposing a wide expanse of taut, tan flesh. "He's a regular, he'll wait. I'm not in a hurry."

"Tell me what happened when you and Morris got back to his hotel room."

"What do you think happened? He was primed. Foreplay lasted about thirty seconds. I blow, then I go. Simple as that. The hotel doorman put me in a cab and I came right back here. You can check."

"I will," Harry assured her.

"When I left him, he was sitting on the bed, his pants around his ankles, playing with his laptop computer."

"A laptop?"

"Yes, I didn't notice the brand. Is that important?"

"No," Harry said. He should have figured Morris for a laptop, and a cell phone, and probably a pager. He pushed himself to his feet. "You'll have to come down to the Hall tomorrow and give me a formal statement."

The phone rang again.

Harry settled his glass on the steamer trunk. "Where are you meeting your gentleman friend?"

"Liverpool Lil's out by the Presidio."

"Button up, and I'll give you a ride."

Renton's fingers played with her coat button. "I told you I'm not in a hurry."

"I am." He handed her one of his business cards. "Let's go."

She snatched up her purse and followed Dymes out into

the street. When he inserted the key into the hybrid's door, she took a step back. "*This* is your car?"

Harry slapped a hand on the Honda's low roof. "Yep."

"Drop me off a block from the bar. If my date sees me riding around in a piece of junk like this, he'll expect a freebie."

Chapter Five

Lake Tahoe, Nevada

Nicolai Tarasove wrenched the wheel of the sixty-eight-hundred-pound Hummer H2 to avoid the refrigerator-size, moss-covered boulder that he had purposely placed in the middle of the gravel road leading to his chalet. The big vehicle's four-wheel drive churned up dirt and leaves before surging back onto the gravel road.

His purposed meeting with Kiryl Chapaev in San Francisco could have proved fatal. Luck had saved him. He'd made the call to Chapaev's room from Grant's on Market Street, where he'd stopped to buy pipe tobacco. If he had phoned from the hotel lobby, Boris Feliks would have been there waiting for him. He had no doubt of that.

Tarasove slowed the Hummer down as he navigated the speed bumps—half-buried trunks of pine trees spaced every ten yards apart encircling the chalet. A quick right turn around a towering redwood tree, and the two-story, prow-shaped structure was in sight. He hadn't liked the property at first: the long twisting road from the highway, the maze of pines, firs, and aspens that blocked out the sky. The house itself had been too small, but the friendly United States government had done everything he asked, and more: thinned out the trees, built a wraparound deck that now afforded him a look at the cobalt-blue waters of Lake Tahoe, and added on three rooms and a concrete-walled laboratory.

Jedgar, the fawn-colored pit bull, was waiting for him at the entrance to the garage, on all fours, his tongue hanging out. Tarasove pulled the Hummer to a stop alongside the small backhoe he used to clear the property and to bury the remains of the project snakes and mice that had outlived their usefulness, along with the carcasses of the game he hunted.

Tarasove roughed the dog's head and dug his fingers into the animal's sinewy back. Bits of dry leaves speckled his coat. "You're hungry, aren't you, Jedgar? You've gotten lazy. You should hunt for your food when I'm not around."

The dog stared up at him with black, uncomprehending eyes. Tarasove patted him lightly on the head, then punched a code into the chalet's alarm pad. There was a series of light beeps, then the sound of the heavy door lock clicking open.

Tarasove had decorated the chalet in the manner of a hunting lodge he'd once visited in the Crimea. The floor was of wide, random pine planks, the walls of steamed beech, the chandelier made entirely of deer antlers. There was lots of dark, Gothic furniture. Prints of hunting scenes dotted the walls, along with his collection of cuckoo clocks.

He went right to the kitchen, which was in stark contrast to the rest of the house: all stainless-steel appliances, including a forty-nine-cubic-foot freezer, a slightly smaller refrigerator, and a six-burner Viking range. The floor was of dark blue tile. An array of copper-bottom pots and cast-iron frying pans dangled over a butcher-block-topped cooking island in the middle of the room.

Tarasove was a man who thoroughly enjoyed his food, cooking the game he shot and the fish he caught. An herb and vegetable hydroponic greenhouse alongside the chalet provided more than enough for his needs.

The pit bull's nose nudged his leg.

"All right, all right," Tarasove said, opening the refrigerator door. There was an array of leftovers. He took out a soup plate laden with what remained of a small deer he'd shot earlier in the week. He laid the plate next to Jedgar's water dish, put the radio onto a channel that played classical music, then clicked on the computer sitting on the kitchen table. He checked his e-mails first. Just one message, from Thornhill, Roger Dancel's code name: *MC arriving tomorrow at approx. noon.*

Tarasove rubbed his hands together as if he were washing them. Marta Citron. He'd have to prepare a special lunch for her. He checked the refrigerator, but there was nothing that intrigued him. He opened the freezer door, and looked directly into the glazed eyes of the black bear who'd killed Shelia, his Siberian husky. Tarasove had shot the beast and placed the head in a clear plastic bag. There were neatly wrapped bundles of the bear's meat in the freezer. It was too gamey for him, but Jedgar loved it.

He slammed the freezer door shut and went back to the computer. Boris Feliks would have questioned Chapaev thoroughly before he killed him, and a man with his special talents would have made Kiryl tell him everything, including the several meetings he and Kiryl had in San Francisco over the last few months, where the two of them discussed Tarasove's new venture, which he was very near perfecting—the true weapon for all times. Kiryl had dubbed it *Napitak Zlobi*—the Devil's Brew—a combining of Tarasove's snake venom toxins with *individual* DNA characteristics. Everyone had their own unique DNA fingerprint. What excited Tarasove was the capability of narrowing the target down to a single human being: the president of the United States, the chancellor of Germany, the president of Korea. The Americans could have saved billions of dollars, and thousands of lives, by targeting Saddam Hussein. All that would be needed was a sample of his DNA: a strand of hair, a drop of urine, blood, whatever. Once the target's DNA fingerprint was implanted in the Devil's Brew, the target was defenseless. All that was necessary was to introduce the toxin into a home, office building, opera house, wherever, via the air-conditioning or heating system—or simply allow the wind to carry it to the desired victim, and he dies, while all around him, be there dozens, or hundreds, or thousands, they would be unaffected.

Or the formula could be reversed—the person whose DNA fingerprint was introduced into the Devil's Brew would be immune to the toxin, and the only one to survive.

Tarasove had made certain that *his* antidoted DNA fingerprint was inserted into each experiment, so that he was *never* at risk.

He stuffed tobacco into his pipe and lit it, a plume of blue-gray smoke rising languidly into the air. Losing Chapaev was most unfortunate. Boris Feliks knowing about the new project—that's what really concerned him. What would his reaction be? It could only embolden him. Chapaev would have told him that *Napitak Zlobi,* the Devil's Brew, had been kept a secret from the U.S. government—that it had started as nothing more than an intellectual challenge between the two of them, a pushing of the envelope. He stared at the flying windows dancing around on his computer's screen saver. Feliks would have taken Chapaev's laptop, and he would have made Kiryl give him the e-mail address they had used to communicate. He scratched the stem of his pipe against his skull. He had always worried about Boris Feliks. He had an aura of violence about him. Even after the FBI assured him that Feliks would be taken care of, Tarasove had made certain that he had samples of the gangster's hair.

When he learned that Feliks had escaped after their meeting in Kiev and was in America hunting for him, he'd used those hair samples to develop Feliks's DNA, and then used his created samples successfully in the laboratory, injecting mice with Boris's DNA, turning them into little Feliks clones, making sure that if he ever had to use the Devil's Brew on Boris, it would kill only him—swiftly, and silently.

How would Feliks use his newfound information? There was absolutely no way for the Russian mafioso to find him through his e-mail address.

Tarasove settled down into a wood-backed kitchen chair and puffed away on his pipe. There was just one solution: *he* would have to find—and kill—Feliks himself, before he was able to tell the FBI, or anyone else, about the Devil's Brew. Roger Dancel would waste no time throwing him into an American prison, if he knew he'd been tricked—lied to—that Tarasove had held back on this new project. To hell with Dancel, with the entire FBI. They were no better than the KGB, or the Chinese and Koreans, for that matter—all deadlier snakes than the ones he used in his laboratory.

Was there a way to trap Feliks through Kiryl's e-mail address?

He went through two more bowls of pipe tobacco before making his decision. He turned on the computer and accessed his e-mail account, quickly scrolling to his contacts. He put an X next to Kiryl's name and typed the short sentence in with great deliberation: *Why did he have to die?*

Tarasove stared at the screen for several seconds before activating the SEND button.

San Francisco, California

Boris Feliks stretched his mouth wide and peeled the whitening strips from his teeth. He admired the results in the motel's bathroom mirror. A marked improvement, though eventually he thought he'd go for a full set of caps. He smiled at himself. His rough, pocked skin was gone, as were the sagging double chin, the once twisted nose, and the bushy eyebrows. All he really missed was his mustache. He took a comb and carefully parted his hair—his full head of hair—five thousand individual implants done by a production line plastic surgeon in Houston, Texas. His nose reconstruction had taken place in Montreal, the double chin removal and facial lasering in Miami, Florida. He ran his hands down his naked body, exploring the hard muscled chest, the flat stomach, his waist, which, thanks to a surgeon in Madrid, no longer had "love handles." His hand strayed to his semihard penis. There'd been no need for any alterations there. The surgeries had cost a great deal of money—a commodity that was rapidly vanishing. The time spent chasing Tarasove, while avoiding those who were hunting him down—his former good friends in the Red Mafia, as well as the Chinese—had been expensive. He'd been so close to Tarasove. So terribly damn close.

Was the Devil's Brew a reality? Feliks found it hard to believe, but Chapaev, with his dying breaths, vowed that Tarasove was very close to completing the project. Why hadn't he told the Americans about it? Was he planning another move? Another betrayal?

Boris wanted to return home. Sasha Veronin had given him a chance—a slim chance at staying alive. "Find this prick and the formula for his toxin in six months and all will be forgiven, Boris. *Ty moy luchshiy drug.*" You are my best friend. The time limit had long passed, and Veronin was not the kind of man to value friendship over money and power. But if he could deliver Tarasove, and his Devil's Brew, Sasha would call off the hunters—and welcome him back to Moscow.

Above all else, Feliks considered himself to be a realist. If he didn't find Tarasove soon, his enemies would close in on him.

Feliks chose not to blame himself for Kiryl Chapaev's death. Bad luck, that's all it had been. The man appeared to be strong and healthy. The pain he'd inflicted on him was not enough to cause death. But somehow it had.

He foamed his face and began shaving. The radio was tuned to an all-news channel. He had hoped to hear something on Chapaev's—or rather Paul Morris's death. The local police would have a difficult, if not impossible, task in identifying him, unless the FBI gave them a helping hand, and everything Feliks had learned about the FBI indicated that that didn't happen often. It was the same the world over—interagency jealousies, turf protection.

The radio announcer was droning on about traffic conditions. A jam on the bridge, an overturned big rig. He was scraping the razor's blade across the area under his nose where his mustache once grew, when the announcer mentioned another traffic problem. A police action on John Muir Drive, near Lake Merced. The police had found a body in the lake. Drivers were advised to use an alternate route.

Feliks whirled around and threw the razor at the radio. It missed, bounced off Chapaev's laptop computer and fell to the carpet. They'd found Zivon Yudin.

Chapter Six

The motorcycle officer looked quite menacing in his fog-slicked leathers. He tilted the visor on his helmet, revealing a pair of yellow-tinted Ray-Bans. "What the hell is that, Harry?" he challenged as Dymes climbed out of the lime-green Honda.

"Don't laugh," Harry said. "They'll be putting you guys on Schwinns soon. What have we got?"

The officer snapped his visor back in place. "Some nine-year-old kid found a body in the lake. The fire department's bringing it up now. The kid's waiting for you by the fire engine."

Harry hauled his camera kit out of the Honda and surveyed the scene. Lake Merced was actually two lakes, the north and south, separated by a narrow road leading to Harding Golf Course. There were three additional golf courses within a four-mile radius that constantly ranked within the top one hundred in the country. The five-mile paved path that encircled both lakes was a popular area for a myriad of bikers, skaters, joggers and pedestrians of all ages.

The lakes themselves provided food and shelter to local birds—everything from great-winged blue herons to hawks and quail—and were a habitat for thousands of migrating birds. Recreational fishing and sailing were once common activities, but the underlying aquifer had been drained by the bordering golf courses and bedroom communities, resulting in the lakes dropping their water levels to half of what it had been just a few years ago.

The sun had driven away most of the fog. There was the usual array of bystanders gawking at the firemen as they went about their work—carrying a mesh stretcher down to the dense tule willows that ringed the lake's perimeter. The water itself was a soupy green color, glazed with gray algae.

Harry sidled up to the white-capped fire chief directing the operation. "How's it going, Chief?"

"We'll have him up in a minute, Inspector. The boy that found him is sitting in the engine cab."

Harry opened the fire rig's door and was greeted by a wide-eyed, redheaded boy with freckles sprayed across his face. He was clutching a bamboo fishing rod tightly in his hands.

Harry introduced himself, and the boy gave his story. He'd been fishing from the lake's pier, and wasn't having any luck. He decided to try the willows. His hook caught something that he at first thought was a log, but when he started reeling it in, he saw a man's head float up to the top.

"I thought I'd wet my pants, Inspector. But I didn't," he added proudly.

Harry took his name and address and advised him he could go home.

"Can't I stay? I won't get in the way. I promise. Are the TV people coming?"

"Sure, kid," Harry said, with a grin. Nine years old and already hungering for his five minutes of fame.

Harry used his camcorder to film the firemen as they huffed-and-puffed the body up the muddy incline to a patch of trampled-down weeds.

The dead man was white, short and squat—a weight lifter's build, muscles that had turned to fat. He was wearing a pair of black boxer shorts and one white sock. A twenty-pound barbell weight was secured to each foot with a length of rope.

Harry passed the camcorder over the body, then used his instant camera for close-ups. The man's body was fish-belly white and blanketed with tattoos: his torso, arms, legs, neck, hands, and even his fingers. Harry had seen a great many prison ballpoint-pen tattoos over the years, but nothing compared to this. There were numerous crosses, daggers, spiderwebs, and either cathedrals or castles across his chest. The fingers on his right hand had crude Cyrillic characters as well as skulls and cardlike diamonds, hearts, and spades.

There were no entry or exit wounds, with the exception of some blood clotting in the canal of his left ear.

Harry couldn't make out all of the wording on the fading tattoos, but they were obviously Russian. He snapped on a pair of rubber gloves, got to his knees and turned the body onto its stomach. Across the man's back was a tattoo portrait of what appeared to be a military general, complete with donkey-size ears and devils' horns protruding from his skull, and a chest full of medals.

He took more photographs and video footage, turning the camcorder in a half circle, taking in the stand of curious pedestrians. On more than one occasion he'd found a reluctant witness by doing so: "I wasn't there that day." Oh, yeah, then why is it I have you on film at the scene. One young spectator wearing baggy pants and a flowered shirt waved and smiled, as if he were being filmed for the five o'clock news.

People walked, skated or jogged around the lake from predawn to post sunset. Why here? when the Pacific Ocean was just a few blocks away, Harry wondered as he went about his work.

The drop from the path down to the lake was some fifteen to twenty feet. If the lake had been full, the body might never have surfaced.

Was there a connection between Paul Morris and the tattooed man in the lake? Someone had called Morris, and asked for Kiryl, then said "Oh, shit" in Russian.

There had been a number of Russian-born criminals whose headless bodies had been disposed of in lakes in the Southern California area over the past year or two. The local band of Russians Harry had contact with were brainless thugs involved in car thefts, extortion, and unsuccessful attempts to take over the gypsies' much more sophisticated scams.

While walking back to his car, Harry spotted a splash of

fluorescent pink paint on the curb. He backtracked to the lake and found two more streaks of the paint, the last not five feet from where the body had been dumped into the water. So the killer had carefully picked his spot, marked it so that he could find it. The lake was most often surrounded by a heavy fog. He'd driven at night, pulled off the road, dumped the body, and was gone in seconds.

All that made sense, except the killer wasn't aware of the lake's shallow condition. He wasn't a local. An out-of-towner.

Boris Feliks watched the tall police detective in the putty-colored raincoat with great curiosity—his face, lean, weather-hardened, dark hair combed straight back from a widow's peak, and long enough to touch the collar of his coat. There was something about that face. It looked Russian to Feliks. He'd bent over Zivon's body, studying those telltale tattoos, as if he could read Russian.

Feliks was wearing sunglasses. He ducked his head, bent his knees and edged behind an extremely large woman wearing a garish black-and-yellow nylon jogging outfit as the policeman turned his video camera on the crowd. He decided that the discovery of Zivon Yudin's body presented no real danger for him. Zivon's fingerprints were no doubt available in some police files. Although an illegal, Zivon had applied for all the welfare benefits the government generously provided. His tattoos would tell his life story, if someone with the proper expertise examined them, but so what. A stupid Russian criminal, no doubt killed by one of his own, would be the police findings.

And Zivon *was* stupid. Feliks had picked him up in Southern California to help in trailing Kiryl Chapaev. Zivon knew Los Angeles, and claimed to know San Francisco equally well. When they learned that Chapaev was flying to San Francisco, Feliks had taken the unsuspecting fool along. Zivon being present when Chapaev spilled his guts had left Feliks with no choice but to kill him.

America. He was still trying to adjust to it. The customs, the slang: Good was bad sometimes, bad was good, the ridiculous "rap" talk—and everyone saying, "Have a nice day." He'd been talking to a travel agent in Houston after a foul-up on a flight schedule. The man told him, "I can see the writing on the wall," and when Feliks turned to look at the wall behind him, the man laughed. "Just an expression," he explained. And new cities were always a challenge: the confusing one-way streets, the lack of parking.

"The lake," Zivon had told him. "We put Kiryl in the lake and no one will ever see him again." They had driven to the area and marked the exact spot to dispose of the body. Zivon had actually picked his *own* grave, and it wasn't a good one. He felt a moment of uneasiness. The ice pick he'd jammed into Zivon's ear was the same one he'd used on Kiryl Chapaev. Who had seen him with Zivon? A waitress or two. A bartender. No one who had paid any particular attention.

The tall policeman was putting his cameras back into the little car. Feliks had a sudden thought. Was there a way to use the policeman to help him find Tarasove? It was worth considering.

Trailing the lime-green car was not difficult for Feliks. He was on the vehicle's bumper as they inched along the congested, smog-shrouded freeway. The car slipped off the freeway and onto a street labeled Bryant. The policeman ducked the car into a basement garage guarded by a battered steel sign that proclaimed *Police Vehicles Only*.

Feliks circled the block. He coasted to a stop in a disabled-only parking area and killed the engine. Another ticket meant nothing, and, if the car was towed away, it was no great loss. Zivon had stolen the dull Ford sedan from a long-term lot near the airport and switched license plates with a car of similar make and color he'd found parked near a fast-food restaurant. That car had been filled with luggage and children's toys. A family going on vacation. The odds were that the driver wouldn't check his plate number for weeks, or months. It was a lesson Feliks had learned early in his career: Most drivers had no idea what their license plate numbers were.

He followed a racially mixed group of people up the steps leading to the entrance of an unsightly box-shaped building constructed of gray blocks. Rust dripped from the metal legend over the front doors: *Hall of Justice*. Another Americanism. Hall. Why not building? Court house? Jail?

The bleak, gray structure somehow pleased Feliks. It would have blended right in, in Moscow or Kiev.

He pushed through the doors and joined a queue waiting to pass through a metal detector. He unconsciously patted his coat. The ice pick was gone, dropped into a sewer grate a block from his motel. He deposited his keys, wallet, and coins into a plastic plate. The uniformed policeman guarding the entrance gave him a cursory glance as he passed through the metal detector. There was a buzzing sound.

"Your watch," the policeman said. "Take off your watch, buddy."

Feliks followed directions, and again went through the detector, this time with success.

Immediately in front of him was a half-glass wall, behind which several police officers milled about, talking on phones, or to themselves. Stenciled on the glass were the words *Southern Station*. A station house within the building itself. That interested Feliks.

The marble-floored lobby was bustling with activity—well-dressed men and women with briefcases talking to scruffy-looking individuals in need of a bath and a night's sleep. Bulky men in sport coats and ties, the coats unbuttoned to reveal holstered pistol butts. "There are times when it pays to advertise," a Moscow cop had once told him. "Let them know you're the law, and they get out of your way."

Where would the policeman from the lake go? A murder. He scanned a directory attached to a wall. Homicide, room 423.

Feliks rode the crowded elevator up to the fourth floor, trying to keep from bumping his fellow passengers, most of whom looked as if they should be on the street, begging for food. Rich man, poor man—that seemed to be the lifestyle of the people who inhabited this cold, strange city.

A couple of the gun-toting men gave him a quick, appraising glance. One, a leprechaun-faced man in a baggy suit, asked, "How's it goin', pal." Did he really care? Feliks wondered. Did he think that I was a fellow policeman?

He walked by the open door to the homicide detail. A receptionist's face was partially concealed by a vase full of velvety red roses.

There was no way to spot the policeman from the lake. He went back to a public telephone booth near the elevator and dialed the number for information, asking for the San Francisco Police Homicide Department's number. He placed his palm over the receiver when he was connected.

"I'd like to speak to the man who is investigating the murder at the St. Charles Hotel," he said.

"That's Inspector Harry Dymes," the receptionist informed him. "One moment, please."

Feliks wiped a sweaty palm on his pants leg. Was the call being traced? Were the San Francisco police that efficient? It wasn't worth the chance. He was about to hang up when a strong male voice came on the line.

"Dymes. How can I help you?"

"You are the man in charge of the murder at the hotel?"

"That's right. What can I do for you?"

"The dead man's name is Kiryl Chapaev, not Morris," Feliks said. He spelled it out, then added, "He is Russian."

"What's your name?" Harry asked him.

"I'd rather not provide it," Feliks said, opening the telephone booth door and rising to his feet.

"Where are you, sir?"

"In your building. Downstairs. By the front entrance."

"Stay right there," Harry Dymes said.

Feliks exited the booth and positioned himself near the elevators. There were hurried footsteps clicking on the marble floor. The policeman skidded around the corner and pressed the DOWN button. He never bothered to look at Feliks.

When the elevator door pinged open, Feliks held back. He felt good. Luck always did that to him. The same policeman for both murders. That was luck. Harry Dymes. An unusual name. What would Harry Dymes do with his newfound information? Draw in the FBI, Tarasove's protectors. Then they would lead him to the bastard.

He sauntered into the next elevator and hummed to himself as he dropped back down to the lobby.

Dymes was frantically looking around for a man who wasn't there. Feliks waited until Dymes had returned to the elevator before approaching the uniformed policeman sitting alongside the metal detector. "Excuse me," he said.

"I was supposed to meet with a detective in Homicide, but he was not there, and I have to get back to work. Can you tell me if the detectives work at night?"

"Not here, buddy. They go home at five o'clock. Only Southern Station is open around the clock. If it's important, leave a message and he'll get in touch with you. Or come back tomorrow."

Feliks sincerely thanked the man, then walked out to the street. As he approached his car he spotted a lovely young woman wearing a red straw hat crossing the street. She took off the hat and raked a hand through her curled hair. Chapaev's whore! The one Chapaev took to the restaurant. She'd caught his eye more than once while he sat at the adjoining table—flirted with him. He pretended to be interested in order to overhear their conversation. She'd seen him, and now she was going to see the police.

Chapter Seven

"I hope you like trout," Nicolai Tarasove said. "I caught these just this morning."

Marta Citron turned to look at Tarasove. He was standing over a triple-burner grill with a long-handled spatula in one hand. An apron displaying two rifles crossed over a red bull's-eye covered his distended stomach. He seemed to have added thirty or more pounds since her last contact with him. His hair was whiter, longer—the Vandyke gone, replaced by a full beard. He looked like an out-of-work department store Santa Claus.

"I love trout," she said, looking out to Lake Tahoe from the chalet's cedar deck. The view was eye-filling. The surface of the lake shone like a polished mirror under a cloudless chamber-of-commerce blue sky. Birds with sickle-shaped wings flashed from tree to tree, and scatter rugs of wild flowers grew between the outcrops of boulders leading down to the road.

She leaned on the railing and stared at a burlap bag nailed to a thick-trunked pine tree thirty yards away. "How's the hunting, Nicolai?"

Tarasove turned to face her, his unlit pipe clamped between his teeth. "Not bad. If you stay for dinner I can offer you some fresh venison."

Marta kept her eyes on the burlap bag. She'd bet her next month's paycheck that it was filled with rock salt—an illegal salt lick to lure deer. "I didn't think hunting season started until next month."

"The fish are done," Tarasove said, ignoring her last comment. "Let's eat." He brought a platter of plump rainbow trout wrapped in crisp bacon over to a redwood table shaded by a dark green umbrella. The table was set with silver cutlery and china plates. Platters of tomatoes, grilled green and yellow squash, and a large bowl of potato salad were spread across the red-and-white checkerboard cloth.

As soon as Marta sat down, Jedgar, the massive pit bull, came over and tried to nuzzle her lap.

"Go away," she said harshly, drawing a low, rumbling growl from the loathsome animal. He'd been sniffing at her since her arrival.

"Bad dog," Tarasove chided. "Go. Go."

Jedgar gave Marta an intimidating look and another growl before backing away and settling down near the grill.

"You must forgive Jedgar," Tarasove said as he pulled a bottle of wine from a Lucite ice bucket. "Neither he nor I have many visitors here. Especially beautiful women. I hope the wine is all right. White with fish, isn't it? I'm not much of an expert on wine." He patted the vodka bottle next to his plate. "I'll stick with this."

"It's fine," Marta said, sampling the cold California Chardonnay. "I'm not that hungry now. I stopped and had a burger at the diner in Sugar Cove." She didn't feel comfortable eating Nicolai's poached game and fish.

"Shame on you," Tarasove chided. "I made this especially for you."

Marta took a bite of the fish. She had to admit it was marvelous. The pit bull stared at Marta, his tongue dangling obscenely from his mouth. Dancel was right. The dog's ugly, wrinkled face did bear a resemblance to the late, unlamented former FBI director.

Tarasove wiped his hands on his apron and helped himself to more of the potato salad.

"I like your new hairstyle. Very fetching. And that blouse. The color is very becoming. Teal, isn't it? Must you leave so soon? I've prepared a room for you."

"Thanks, Nicolai, but I have work to do." Tarasove had given her a grand tour of his chalet, including the spare bedroom, which had a queen-size bed, complete with the cover turned down on one side and a box of chocolates perched on the pillow.

The rest of the chalet had been of more interest to her, especially his laboratory, though she could have done without the up-close-and-personal look at his snakes. There had to be a hundred of the slimy-looking creatures in those glass tanks: rattlers, cobras, God knew what else. What set her nerves on edge was the terrified squeaking sounds coming from the cage of tiny white mice that Tarasove had set within full view of the snakes.

Another point of interest was Tarasove's "game room," full of mounted animals' heads and racks of rifles and shotguns. He'd been careless. One bolt-action rifle was leaning against the wall, a foot-long aluminum cylinder attached to the barrel's end. She'd wondered why Tarasove's neighbors hadn't complained about his off-season shooting. She should have known. Tarasove used a silencer when he shot Bambi from his sundeck.

"Roger Dancel told me of your new toxin, Nicolai."

"Told you what?" Tarasove asked sharply.

"That you're working on something that could eliminate races, nationalities. A plague."

"He exaggerates, Marta. The toxin would be used against armies of other nations, enemies, not ordinary people. And it's a long way off. There is still much work to do. What has Washington learned of Kiryl's murder?" Tarasove asked, after a quick gulp of vodka.

"Nothing yet. The San Francisco police have no clue as to his actual identity. And they never will. I'm concerned about you."

"Not nearly as concerned as I am," Tarasove announced with an air of confession. "I had been led to believe that Boris Feliks would be either dead or in prison by now. In fact, you and Roger were the ones who assured me of that."

"We're getting close to him, Nicolai."

"And he is getting close to me." He leaned back in his chair and belched before pulling his pipe from his apron pocket. "All this worrying about Feliks takes me away from my work. It unsettles me. I need . . . to relax. I need some-one to help me relax," he added with a widemouthed smile.

Marta was having none of it. "Poor Nicolai. Stuck here in this beautiful chalet, with your own hunting preserve. Tell me about Kiryl Chapaev. You had been in contact with him for how long? A month? Six months? A year?"

"Weeks, not months. He was an old friend. I told you I get lonely. For friends. For companionship. Why don't you stay until tomorrow? We could drive to South Shore, visit the casinos. I've been very lucky in poker lately. Then we could—"

The cell phone clipped to Marta's waist beeped. "Excuse me," she said, getting to her feet. She wandered down to the far end of the deck before answering the phone.

"It's me," Roger Dancel said. "Where are you?"

"At Tarasove's place. We're having lunch."

"Are you now? How sweet. Well, we've got trouble. Harry Dymes, the Frisco homicide cop, just sent in a crimi-nal records request to our database for Kiryl Chapaev. How does that grab you?"

Marta watched Tarasove go through the procedure of getting his pipe going. The dog padded over and sniffed the chair she'd just vacated. "How the hell did he come up with his real name?"

"That's what I want you to find out, Marta. Go down there and shake Dymes's cage. Agent Tom McNab will meet you at the San Francisco office. You've worked the city before, haven't you?"

"A long time ago," Marta said reflectively. She'd spent ten months in San Francisco, at the start of her career, as a raw "Breast-fed"—the Bureau's politically incorrect name for new female agents. She looked at her watch. "It's two o'clock. I won't get there until six or seven."

"So be it," Dancel said with little enthusiasm. "I'm off to Las Vegas. We've had word that Ying Fai is going there to meet with the *bok wai* I told you about. Give my love to Tarasove, if you haven't done so already."

Marta let the innuendo pass without comment. "Send me everything we have on Dymes. And I mean everything, Roger, from the day he was born." She broke the connec-tion and wandered back to the table.

Tarasove's pipe was billowing smoke that smelled like cooked fruit. "From the look on your beautiful face, I take it the call was not good news."

"It might be. There's some news on Chapaev's murder. The killer left prints all over the place."

"Feliks's prints?"

"No. But it may mean he had an accomplice," she lied convincingly. "I have to get down there right away, so I'll have to take a rain check on that visit to the casinos."

"Your Mr. Dancel informed me on how Kiryl died. He didn't provide many other details. What did Feliks take from him? His money, I'm sure. The *pidar gnoinyj* must be running out of money."

"You didn't mention before that Feliks was a homosexual, Nicolai."

Tarasove hitched his shoulders. "It's a Russian expression. I believe he is what you call a pitcher and a catcher. He isn't choosey: man, woman, dog, bicycle, it makes no difference to him."

"I have to go. I'll let you know what I find out in San Francisco."

Tarasove made a motion to rise from his chair, but Marta waved him down. "Don't bother. I know the way. Thanks for lunch." She held out her hand, and he took it in both of his and brought it to his mouth.

He planted a kiss and smiled up at her. "Promise me that you will keep me informed, that you will call me tomorrow and stop by before you return to Washington. I want to hear everything directly from you. You're the only one I trust, Marta."

Citron freed her hand, resisting the urge to wipe it across her skirt. "I'll try, Nicolai."

Tarasove waited until he heard the motor of her car growl to life before pushing himself to his feet. He went to the rail, Jedgar at his side. The dog tried to push his wide face through the railings. He watched Citron's car until it was out of sight. What was the American phrase? Prick teaser. All perfume and promises. The first few months after Tarasove's defection, Citron had constantly been by his side. She spoke excellent Russian, and helped him with his English. They had developed what he thought was a true friendship. But she would not go to bed with him.

When he told her he needed companionship, she arranged for him to see women—whores. Citron had become an obsession with him. He vowed to have her. If just once. "Next time, she'll stay," he said to the dog. "Next time, we'll have her." He picked up Citron's wineglass. A half-moon of lipstick clung to the rim. Not a chance of getting her DNA from that. He scowled as he searched her chair and the dishes she'd used, looking for a hair—just one single strand of her beautiful hair— but there were none. He put the bowl of potato salad on the deck for Jedgar, then carried the remains of the trout into the kitchen. He dumped the fish into the disposal, then went to the bathroom Marta Citron had used to "refresh herself" when she had arrived at the chateau. He had prepared it for her: fresh flowers, fragrant soap, and a new, natural boarhair brush that he thought she would find irresistible. He examined the brush under the bright bathroom light, humming as his fingers plucked out several long strands of ash-blond hair.

He carried the hair to his laboratory—to the workbench where he kept his DNA fingerprint files. There was one R.D., for Roger Dancel. He'd collected enough hair samples from Dancel during his visits over the past year to establish a full genetic profile for the overbearing FBI agent. He couldn't foresee a scenario for using the Devil's Brew on Dancel or Marta Citron, but—one never knew. "Better safe than sorry," he said to a particularly large cobra staring at him from inside his glass-enclosed prison alongside the workbench.

Don Landeta braced both hands on the coffee table and slowly pushed himself to his feet. He'd been chasing a bank robber in the Marina District, and had been involved in a head-on crash. The robber escaped, and Landeta ended up in the hospital with a broken neck and back. "Tough way to get a pension," was his standard reply when asked about his injuries. He was in his early fifties, a bachelor, with a long-chinned face, thinning gray hair, bassetlike eyes, and a perpetually mournful, weary look about his features.

"You know what this means, don't you?" he said after Harry Dymes told him of the new developments on the Paul Morris murder case. "Morris was a fictitious name provided by Uncle Sam. Kiryl Chapaev was most likely in some federal witness protection program. I had a hunch it was something like that, Harry. The firewalled address and phone number. Look at this." He waved a sheaf of papers at Dymes. "The credit report turned up Morris's Social Security number, which was issued in California nine months ago. The killer used Morris's credit cards: Visa, MasterCard, and American Express, at three different ATMs within blocks of the St. Charles. Drained them dry, right up to their daily credit limit. Did you run an FBI check on him under the Chapaev spelling?"

"Yes. Nothing back yet," Dymes said. "It'll be interesting to see how the FBI responds to my records request."

"It'll be even more interesting to see what they'll *tell* you they have. The way I see it—"

Harry's phone rang. It was a private, unlisted number that he shared with few people.

"Dymes here," he said.

"This is Special Agent Marta Citron of the FBI, Inspector. I'd like to see you as soon as possible."

Harry palmed the receiver and smiled at Landeta. "Guess who? The FBI. How's that for a response?" He pulled his hand away and asked, "Where are you now, Agent Citron?"

"Parked in your driveway. Can I come up?"

"Give me two minutes," Harry said. He cradled the phone. "There's a Bucar with an agent by the name of Marta Citron parked in my driveway."

Landeta groaned as he leaned over and began stacking the documents on the coffee table. "Never heard of her. She's not local. Don't let her see any of this material, Harry. I'll go out through the garage. Thanks for the DMV stuff. I'll see what I can pull up on Chapaev, but I'm not holding out much hope."

"Okay. I'll let you know what's up later."

Harry stashed the documents in a kitchen drawer, then walked down the fifteen indoor steps leading to the front door. A lovely woman with ash-blond hair and a frazzled look on her face greeted him when he opened the door.

"Dymes?"

"Citron? I'll show you mine, if you'll show me yours."

Marta stared at him with a slack face for a moment. "Okay," she said, pulling her ID from her purse. "Does this get me inside?"

Harry stepped back and waved her in. "You look like you could use a drink, Citron."

"You're right about that," she said, following Dymes up the cantilevered staircase. The house intrigued her. It was three stories high, perched on a hill in the Potrero District. Like most of the residential buildings in San Francisco, it was squeezed into a twenty-five-foot-wide lot, and was situated in the middle of a ridiculously curved one-way street.

"What can I get you?" Harry asked, when they'd reached what Citron assumed was the living room. The floors were carpeted in an off-white shag. A large L-shaped chocolate-brown leather couch dominated one side of the room. There were two paintings on the wall behind the couch, both in orange tones: one she recognized as a faux Rothko, the other a Van Gogh–like depiction of a field of wheat encircling a small whitewashed cottage. A rectangular flat-screen TV was centered on the wall across from the couch. One entire wall was floor-to-ceiling windows. The tone of the room was harshly male, softened by several vases bursting with roses of every color: deep reds, pale pinks, bright yellows, white, and combinations of all of them.

"Vodka on the rocks, thank you."

"Be right back," Dymes said.

Marta walked over to the windows, which looked out over the low-lying Mission District and up to Twin Peaks, at eleven hundred feet the highest hill in the City. Two powerful-looking telescopes were positioned a few feet from each other.

She wandered back toward the couch. On the coffee table sat three swatches of dark blue material. Pinned to the top piece was a note, in Russian. *Kto iz nih poet?* Marta picked it up and read it again. The translation was, Which one sings?

"Do you like those?" Dymes asked, coming back into the room with a glass in each hand.

"The note is in Russian," she said. "You understand Russian?"

Harry handed her the glass. "My father spoke it all the

time. He writes to me in Russian, just to keep me on my toes."

"What does he mean, 'Which one sings'?"

Harry picked up the swatches. "Pop's a tailor. He's making me a new suit. He always claimed that a good piece of material would sing to him if he held it to his ear and rubbed it between his fingers." He did just that with the swatches. "The one in the middle. That's the one that sings. Try it."

Marta went through the procedure with a frown on her face. "I don't hear a thing."

"Then don't go into the tailoring business." Harry laughed. "Sit down. I didn't expect this kind of service when I sent in that criminal check on Kiryl Chapaev. I must have hit a nerve."

"How did you come up with the name?"

The phone rang. "Excuse me," Harry said.

Marta sipped at her drink and studied Dymes. He was a well-tailored one. Light beige slacks creased saber-sharp, a black turtleneck and houndstooth sport coat. Her own clothes were suffering from a long day's wear: the flight from D.C., to Reno, the drive to Tarasove's chalet, then down to San Francisco to meet with McNab. She needed a bath, a good meal, a change of clothes, and a few more vodkas.

"I thought I knew San Francisco fairly well," she said when Dymes was finished with his phone call. "But what was the name of that street I drove down to get here?"

"Vermont. It's the crookedest street in the world," Harry said, settling down on the opposite end of the couch. "Lombard Street gets all the publicity because it's considered a much nicer area. The Potrero is blue-collar, racially mixed, a little rough around the edges. We don't get too many tourists out here."

"The roses are lovely. Your wife must have a green thumb."

"No wife. The roses are a hobby. Tell me about Kiryl Chapaev. Which witness protection program provided him with the Paul Morris AKA?"

"Who told you about that?" Marta queried.

Harry framed his words carefully before replying.

"You've probably seen copies of my report. You shouldn't have, without my release. Someone called Morris's room at the St. Charles Hotel while I was there. Asked for Kiryl. When I ID'd myself he said, *'Ebat 'kopat.'* If you could read my father's note, I figure you know what that means."

"Did the caller give you a last name for Kiryl right then?"

"If you read my report, you know the answer to that is no."

Marta's teeth made a sharp, quick sound. "Inspector, I haven't read your report. I just arrived in San Francisco, and I haven't had time to do much except drive directly here."

"Who told you where 'here' is? Who gave you my home phone number?"

Marta placed a finger on the rim of the glass and ran it around a few times. "You're ticked because I didn't go through procedures, is that it, Inspector? Come on, give me a break. You're a well-known homicide dick—so of course we'd know where you live and how to get in touch with you."

"What's so urgent about Kiryl Chapaev?" Harry said, admiring the way Citron kept her cool.

"That's Bureau business. I can't go into it right now." She crossed one leg over the other and leaned forward. "How did you come up with his *last* name, Inspector?"

"It's a homicide case. I can't go into it right now. Maybe when you tell me more about Chapaev, we can do business."

"Goddamn you, Dymes, you're out of your league on this, in over your head." She bit off the words, making each one sharp and emphatic. "I'll bust your balls on this if you don't cooperate."

"And if I'm a good little boy, and tell you everything you want to know, what then? You're not going to open the FBI's jewel box on this whether I cooperate with you or not, are you? The Bureau has a bad reputation out here, Citron. You're not making it any better."

Marta slammed her drink down on the table. "I heard you were a fed hater."

"You heard wrong," Harry said, getting to his feet as she headed for the stairs. "I'm investigating two Russians who've been murdered in my town. That makes it my business, and I take my job seriously."

Marta swivelled around to face him. "What are you talking about? *Two* murders?"

"Chapaev and another Russian, killed within hours of each other. Coincidence? I don't think so. Did Chapaev have a friend—big, ugly, body covered with Russian prison tattoos?"

"Tell me more about this second victim," Marta demanded.

"Tell me more about Kiryl Chapaev," Harry countered.

She compressed her lips to hold back a curse.

"You scratch my back, I scratch yours, Citron. That's how it works."

Marta slapped a hand against her thigh and glared at him. "I'll get back to you. One way or the other."

"That sounds like a threat," Harry said. "I don't like being threatened.".

"When I make a threat, you'll know it," she promised before hurrying down the stairs.

Harry went to the window and watched the FBI car's headlights as it wound down the serpentine street. Citron wasn't a typical case agent. *Just arrived in San Francisco.* From where? She'd been careful not to say. She'd been careful about everything. He liked that.

The phone call he'd received just after she'd arrived was from Don Landeta. He'd recognized the man sitting in the passenger seat of the Bureau car parked in his driveway. Tom McNab, a real knuckle-dragger of an agent, who'd stomped his size eleven brogues all over a couple of Harry's cases. McNab he couldn't deal with, but Citron, maybe. Just maybe. But he'd make her work for it.

Chapter Eight

Las Vegas, Nevada

"When did they open this place?" Roger Dancel said as John Fong, the Las Vegas FBI agent in charge, led him across a gracefully arched bridge spanning the moat surrounding the Forbidden City Casino and Hotel.

"Three months ago," Fong said. He was a short, dapper man with a round, wrinkle-free face. He wore a dark blue suit, white shirt, muted tie, and seemed to be immune from the oppressive hundred-plus degree evening heat.

Dancel squeegeed the sweat from his forehead with his hand and took in the impressive sight. The black, aluminum-skinned Forbidden City stretched up some thirty stories into the dark, hazy Vegas sky. He spotted several tourists dropping coins from the bridge into the moat's gold-colored water. Two massive iron lions, with one paw raised, bracketed the entrance.

"The lions' paws are resting on a pomegranate," Fong explained. "A symbol of power to the Chinese."

The air-conditioned lobby felt like a wet kiss to Dancel. He was barely inside when an attractive Asian girl wearing a bright red mandarin-styled minidress approached him with a tray full of drinks.

"How may I serve you?" she asked.

Fong waved her away. "Nothing now. This way, Roger."

Dancel followed Fong through long corridors of blinking, buzzing, clattering slot machines, crap tables, roulette wheels, and baccarat areas. The crowd was three deep in most places. Dancel was somewhat surprised at the way the players were dressed: shorts, smudged golf shirts, women pushing baby carriages.

"I thought this was a high roller's casino, John. These people look like they just came from a Wal-Mart sale."

"Not quite." Fong smiled. "The slots are five dollar minimum, roulette ten dollars, and you have to have a five-thousand-dollar line of credit to sit in at baccarat. But you're right. These are the cheap seats. The heavy hitters are over here."

They crossed an expanse of intricate Oriental carpets laid seemingly haphazardly side by side, as if there to cover the desert sand in a Mongol leader's tent. The check-in counter loomed to the right. A line of bellboys, all wearing long-sleeved black pajama-style uniforms, white gloves, and straw coolie hats, stood at mock attention, waiting to help the arriving hotel guests.

Fong slipped a lantern-jawed man wearing a double-breasted tuxedo a fifty-dollar bill. The man examined the money for a moment, then removed the wrist-thick purple rope separating the entrance to the exclusive Players Club area.

"This is where the really high rollers play," Fong said, ushering Dancel over to a rich red leather booth that overlooked the gaming tables. One of the cocktail waitresses, this one a gorgeous platinum blonde wearing a purple mini-skirted dress that looked as if it had been applied with an air brush, hurried over and asked, "How may I serve you?"

"Two martinis up, shaken not stirred, with a twist," Fong ordered with a straight face.

She took the order with a deep bow and gave no indication that she'd ever seen a James Bond movie.

When she left, Fong said, "How would you like to be the guy in charge of hiring the waitresses? I hear the only qualifications are that they need to be knockouts, who can say 'How may I serve you' and suck an olive through a straw." Fong nodded his head toward the nearest baccarat table. "See that neat little sign on the wall? *Mou haan jai.* There are no limits here, whether you're playing baccarat, roulette, fan-tan, *pak kop piu, pai gow,* or Chinese poker. The rich old mothers of Canton who worry that their sons will spend the family fortune have a saying: 'With drink and women nature sets a limit, but not with gambling.' "

The clientele was definitely upscale in the Players Club: mostly middle-aged Chinese wearing business suits, a few in tuxedos, fat Cuban cigars between their lips, trophy blondes at their sides.

"They all go for blondes, don't they, John. Do you know what blondes say after sex?"

Fong was sure he'd heard every blonde joke in the world, but Dancel was someone he had to keep happy, so he said, "What?"

" 'Are you guys all in the same band'?"

The waitress returned with their drinks. Fong silently passed her a twenty-dollar bill, and Dancel sensed she was disappointed with the amount.

Fong took a sip of his martini, then smacked his lips. "The drinks are free, but if you don't tip the girls fifty bucks, they figure you're a loser. I became . . . friendly with a cocktail waitress at the Bellagio. She was bringing home close to two hundred thousand a year, all for bussing booze. Makes you want to have a boob job and sex change operation, doesn't it?"

"When does Ying Fai make an appearance?" Dancel asked.

Fong tilted his head to the side and cupped his ear in order to hear the transmitter better. "Great timing. He just arrived. He likes to put on a show; let's go watch."

Three identical black Bentley limousines rolled to a stop under the hotel's arched entrance. A quartet of beefy Asians, all wearing black suits, exited the lead and rear cars and formed two lines around the center vehicle. The back door popped open and a bald-headed man nearly the size of a sumo wrestler climbed out. He eyed the men in the black suits for a moment, then turned his back, faced the opened door and bowed from the waist.

A slim, elderly man wearing a vanilla-colored suit made

a slow exit from the vehicle. He had slicked-back dark hair and parchment-colored skin.

"That's Ying Fai," Fong said. "Pompous little bastard, isn't he? The big bald goon is Danny Shu, Fai's number one man."

An exotic-looking Asian woman with long raven-black hair, wearing a skimpy red leather bustier, matching shorts, and knee-length boots, stuck a hand out and Shu helped her from the Bentley.

Fai stood for a moment, examining the hotel with a frown on his face. He then nodded to Shu, who snapped his fingers, and a group of the black-pajama-clad bellboys rushed over to start unloading the limousines' luggage.

A series of hotel employees bowed and scraped as Ying Fai strolled leisurely into the Forbidden City.

"Who's the woman in leather?" Dancel wanted to know.

"Rita Tong, an actress. She's pretty big stuff back in Hong Kong. Karate and naked bodies flicks. Nice pair of knockers, but they're store-bought. I've seen earlier pictures of her. Flatter than wine in a saucer. The word is that Ying Fai wanted her to measure up to Marilyn Monroe. One of the many things that Fai collects is movie memorabilia. He has the actual dress that Monroe wore the night she sang happy birthday to JFK. Fai supposedly has plans to bring Tong to Hollywood and make her a star."

"Girls are still falling for that line?" Dancel said, keeping his eye on Danny Shu. He'd never seen a Chinese man that huge.

"It works for me." Fong grinned. "Let's follow the parade."

Dancel was glad to be back inside the air-conditioned casino. Shu acted like a battering ram, the crowd parting at the sight of him, as Ying Fai and Rita Tong made their way like royalty through the casino, Fai occasionally waving a hand at a lucky commoner. They went directly to an elevator with etched panel doors featuring dragons breathing fire. Shu joined them, giving the onlookers a glowering scowl as the elevator doors pinged shut.

"What now?" Dancel asked.

"The elevator goes straight to the penthouse. It's the only elevator with access, so after Fai and his girlfriend are made comfortable, the rest of the goons and the luggage go up."

"Have you got a phone tap in Fai's rooms?"

Fong's eyebrows contorted in a frown. "Are you kidding? Bug a phone or a room in Vegas. Not possible, Roger. The Bureau's been dead in the water here since the sixties when Robert Kennedy bugged half the phones in town trying to get the goods on Hoffa."

"They can't hold a grudge that long," Dancel responded, his eyes on the bellboys stacking luggage in front of the penthouse elevator.

"Oh, no? Kennedy jumped over Hoover's head on that one, but we paid the price. The mob had better lawyers than the Attorney General's office. All the information acquired via the phone taps was thrown out of court. The phone companies who cooperated with Kennedy were sued for multimillions, and they lost big-time. So the grudge still stands."

Dancel turned on his heel and started for the exit. "Ying Fai's men must know you by sight, John."

"Definitely. And they'd have been disappointed if I didn't show up to see Fai's arrival. I borrowed six agents from Kansas City and four men from the Justice Department who *should* be unknown to Fai's people in the casino. We'll get pictures of anyone who goes up to the penthouse. Including this mystery man you believe Fai hired, but I don't think we'll spot him here. He'll wait until Fai goes out tonight. Fai likes to touch base with all the casinos on the strip, let them all know that he's in town." Fong gestured to one of the cocktail waitresses. "I need a beer. You don't have any idea who the guy is?"

"Ying Fai called him Alex—a *bok wai*. That's all I've got."

Fong smoothed his tie and examined both of its ends to see that they matched in length. "*Bok wai*, a white devil. That covers a lot of territory, Roger. What is he? A hit man?"

"From what we've picked up, he's not only a hit man, he's able to locate people we've set up in the witness protection program. The New York Triad raved about him, now Fai is using him. I can't let him get near our asset, a flaky Russian scientist who Washington is in love with."

"Whoever the white devil is, he must be good. The Triads don't like to hire a *ni ma de bi* if they can help it."

"Ni ma de bi?"

"Chinese for *honky*," Fong said, reaching for his money clip when one of the cocktail waitresses approached them.

Ying Fai's hooded eyes watched Danny Shu shake the gloved hands of the bellboys as they left the suite. Shu's forceful handshake caused the men to wince, but their pain was temporary, since Shu transferred a hundred-dollar casino chip with each grasp.

A hundred-dollar bill might well go home in their pants pocket, but the chip would find its way to one of the gaming tables; thus Shu was actually tipping the fools nothing.

Fai toured the thirty-six-hundred-square-foot suite, stopping to admire the Ming and Qing dynasty vases and jades. There was an impressive display of pottery: horses, dogs, tigers, and ancient warriors dressed for battle. He stopped to admire a bronze mirror that had not been there on his last visit, then made for the master bedroom. A short nap was in order before a session with Rita.

He stepped into the bedroom and froze. Spread out neatly in the middle of the king-size bed were black pajamas and a straw coolie hat.

"Shu!" Fai shouted, edging back out the door.

"Relax, Mr. Fai," called a voice from the bathroom. He turned to see a slender woman wearing loose-fitting blue jeans and a shapeless white T-shirt with *The Forbidden City* printed across it. She was brushing her sable-colored hair with one white-gloved hand; the other was positioned behind her back. She had a delicately sculpted face—which was void of makeup—full lips and iris-blue eyes.

Danny Shu thundered into the room, skidding to a halt when he saw the woman. He gave Fai a bewildered look, then started across the room, arms outstretched, his hands clenched into fists.

"Stay right there," the woman said, dropping the hairbrush to the carpet and bringing a small semiautomatic pistol into view. "I'm Alex. You asked to see me, Mr. Fai. Here I am."

Fai's rigid jaw slowly loosened. He brought his hands together in a soft clap. "You are very courageous, Miss

Alex." He nodded his head an inch in Shu's direction. "But you have made an enemy of Mr. Shu."

The woman tucked the pistol into her waistband. "We're all working together on this, aren't we?"

Fai imagined he could hear Shu's teeth grinding. The woman was clever, and it would be a lesson to Shu. He was becoming lax. He should have monitored the number of bellboys who delivered the luggage and then returned to the lobby. "Go," he said to Shu without looking at him. "And have tea sent. Do you enjoy tea, Miss Alex?"

"Coffee, please. And something to eat if it's not too much trouble." She bent down and picked up the hairbrush.

Ying Fai snapped his fingers and Shu left the room without saying a word.

"The patio is pleasant at this time of the evening," Fai said, heading for the sliding glass doors. "We can dine there."

"Inside is better, Mr. Fai. I'm sure the authorities have cameras trained on your patio around the clock. Speaking of cameras, I'd like to see the hotel's videotapes of the lobby, from two hours before your arrival to right now. The casino was crawling with FBI agents."

Fai barked out an order in Mandarin, and within moments servants were setting plates and silverware on the ebony four-seasons altar table situated near the bed.

"You are certain you will be able to locate Nicolai Tarasove?" Fai said as he settled down on a chair.

"Yes," she responded confidently. "The photographs and background information you sent me were helpful. His fascination with snakes—that's very interesting."

"Your mission is to find Tarasove. He must not be injured in any way."

"My fee is the same price whether or not I kill him. I'll have your man in two weeks."

Fai's face hardened. "I will hold you to that, Alex. Two weeks. Notify me as soon as you know where he is. I'll send Danny Shu to give whatever assistance is needed."

"That's fine with me."

"The other man I informed you of, Boris Feliks. He's been hunting Tarasove for some time."

"Then he can't be very good."

"If possible, I want him taken alive. Don't underestimate Feliks. He's a dangerous man."

"All men can be dangerous," Alex replied coldly. "What are we having for dinner?"

San Francisco, California

Boris Feliks dropped the binoculars onto his lap and rubbed his eyes. He'd followed the policeman, Harry Dymes, from the Hall of Justice parking lot to the location he assumed was Dymes's house. Chapaev's whore, whom he had spotted entering the Hall of Justice, had eluded him. He should have known the police would trace her and interrogate her. Chapaev had told him that her name was Julie. He couldn't remember her last name or her telephone number. Just the phone number of the whorehouse madam.

Dymes had had two visitors. The first, a middle-aged man who walked as if he was in pain, had arrived shortly after Dymes pulled the small lime-green vehicle into his garage. The second visitor had arrived later, as it was getting dark—a beige sedan of the type favored by police agencies the world over. The driver was a young blond woman. She talked on her cell phone, then went to Dymes's door, while the passenger, a man, sat in the car and smoked. The first visitor had come out through the garage almost at the same moment that the blond woman entered the house, and slowly made his way up the hill to his car. Ten minutes later the woman hurried out. She appeared angry as she slid behind the wheel and drove off in a squeal of rubber.

Had he wasted his time? Feliks asked himself. Outside of locating Dymes's house, it seemed he'd learned nothing of importance. Which would be more beneficial—getting into Dymes's house, or his office? Obviously the office. That's where he *should* have the files on Chapaev, and the details of his progress regarding the investigation. Feliks sat up and turned on the engine. It was time to plan his next move.

As he goosed the motor, the door to Dymes's garage swung open and the small lime-colored car slipped onto the street.

Feliks waited until Dymes's car had wound its way to the bottom of the hill before starting off after him. He jammed on the brakes as he navigated the hairpin curves. The wheel nearly slipped from his hands as he fought to keep from banging into the concrete wall that bordered the street. Who would think to build such a ridiculous road? His headlights picked up Dymes's vehicle as it turned north onto a broad boulevard. Feliks joined the beaded line of ruby taillights, staying two or three car lengths behind the policeman, who made no effort to see if he was being tailed. Why should he? Who would tail a policeman?

Clement Street had once been a strong Russian enclave in San Francisco; then the Asians had slowly, and efficiently, taken it over. There were still a few Russian bars and tearooms mixed in amongst the myriad of restaurants featuring Canton, Mandarin, Taipei, Cantonese, Szechuan, and Hunan cuisines, along with sushi and Korean barbecue joints.

Dymes was in his fourth Russian bar, Popov's, nurturing his fourth vodka, before he got a nibble on the photographs he'd taken of Morris/Chapaev, and the unidentified man found in the lake.

Popov's was a hard-drinking establishment. They didn't serve Cosmopolitans, Manhattans, or daiquiris. There was no wine list, just a three-liter jug of cheap red or white wine, both of which were kept in the refrigerator. The customers went to Popov's to *nakhuyachilsya vodkoi*—get stoned on vodka. The grime-smeared linoleum was worn bare to the concrete underflooring in many spots. The battered pool table hadn't been used in years and was crammed with cases of empty liquor bottles.

Milan Nikitin, a longshoreman-poet-philosopher, who had had three books published—all of which earned him excellent reviews and very little money—was camped on a stool in the middle of the long oak bar. He was a stocky man with immense, heavy-veined hands. He squinted through the smoke from the cigarette stuck between his lips as he examined the photographs. "Both dead, no, Harry?"

"Both dead, yes."

Nikitin lifted his empty glass and said, "We should drink to their journey to a better place."

Harry waved the bartender over and pointed at Nikitin's glass.

"Not the shit in the well," the old Russian said. "To toast our dearly departed friends, Cristall, the best vodka in the world."

"You're a poet," Harry said, dropping a twenty-dollar bill on the damp, zinc-topped bar.

"In Russia, all tyrants believe poets to be their worst enemies." Nikitin hefted his now full glass to the smoke-grimed ceiling, then drained it in a gulp.

The sad-eyed elderly woman sitting alongside Nikitin gave a chest-rattling smoker's cough. Though there was a city ordinance against smoking in bars and restaurants, it wasn't enforced in Popov's. Nearly every one of the thirty-plus men and women were puffing away on cigarettes.

"The pictures, Milan. Do you know these men?"

Nikitin lit a cigarette from the dog end of his old one. "No. But the ugly one with the tattoos. I've seen him." He pounded his fist on the bar. "Right here."

"When?" Harry wanted to know. "Was he with anyone?"

Nikitin leaned forward and viced his head between his hands. "Thirsty work, Harry. I'm trying to remember."

Another shot of the expensive Russian vodka seemed to jolt his memory. "It was months ago. Four, maybe five months. He was drinking with a woman, over there." Milan pointed his cigarette to a wood-backed booth near the jukebox that was playing Russian gypsy tunes.

"Who was the woman, Milan?"

Nikitin upturned his palm and ran a finger across it. "The witch who reads hands."

"Lana? The fortune-teller?"

"The witch. I hope she screwed him good. He tried to beat me in arm wrestling. Rolled up his sleeve and showed off all of those tattoos." Milan laid his elbow on the bar and brought his hand down in a crash. "No one beats Milan Nikitin in arm wrestling," he boasted. "At least not in this dump." He leaned toward Harry and gave a knowing wink. "He was a *pedic,* Harry. Did your father teach you that word, *pedic*?"

"I don't think so, Milan. Tell me about it."

"A man who is used as a woman in prison. All those

tattoos. They think it makes them look pretty." Nikitin laughed deeply. "Nothing could have made that one pretty."

"Did you get a name?" Harry asked. "Where was he living?"

Nikitin jammed a heavily calloused finger in his empty shot glass and raised it up to eye level. "Ask the witch, Harry. I had nothing to do with him."

Harry slid his untouched vodka over to Milan. "He spoke Russian?"

Nikitin accepted the glass and nodded his head. "Yes. The only thing he said in English was, 'Fuck you.' Is being a policeman hard work, Harry?"

Harry patted Nikitin on his burly shoulders. "Not as hard as unloading bananas on the docks."

"No one should be afraid of hard work, Harry. We had a saying in Moscow: 'If you beat a Russian hard enough, he can do anything, even make a watch.' "

Dymes glanced at his wrist. "I'll remember that when I need a new watch."

He walked back out to the street, which was filled with late-night shoppers. Skinny, orange-glazed ducks dangling from greasy string cinched around their necks filled the window of one market. Double-parked trucks unloaded fruits, vegetables, and wooden crates jammed with live chickens, ducks, and rabbits. The aroma of day-old fish and rotting produce hung in the air.

Madame Lana's street-level studio was located two blocks from Popov's. The windows were covered by purple drapes. A hand-painted sign with an eye centered in a pyramid advertised Lana's skills:

Palm & Tarot Card Reading.
I can reunite you with your loved ones, help you achieve success in love, marriage, and business.
Your past, present, and future are on your palm.
Senior discounts.

Harry rapped on the door, but there was no response. He slipped one of his business cards into the mailbox and started back to his car. A low fog rolled across the pavement like a gas attack. He felt an icy chill across his shoulders—a chill he hadn't felt since the first Gulf War in Iraq. Someone was watching him. He slowed down, then turned around and dropped to the sidewalk as if to tie his shoe, his eyes searching the fog. He stood up and made his way to the Honda, which was parked in a bus zone. A parking ticket was stuck behind the windshield wiper. Whoever had written out the ticket hadn't paid any attention to his *Police Vehicle* sticker.

Harry rolled the ticket into a ball and tossed it into the backseat. The chill hit his shoulders again. He scanned the street again. The FBI agent—Marta Citron. She hadn't been at all happy when she'd left his house. Would she follow him? Or would she have passed that chore along to Tom McNab, the local agent? Either way, it was a dumb move. But that was why, in too many cases, FBI stood for Fucking Bumbling Idiots as far as Harry was concerned.

Chapter Nine

Lake Tahoe, Nevada

The four bears lumbered slowly toward the bags of dry dog food Nicolai Tarasove had positioned twenty yards from the chateau. A mother and three cubs, the cubs four to six months old, he estimated. The mother made soft grunting sounds as she sniffed her way closer to the food, while the cubs were voicing mild, squealing noises.

It would be forty minutes before the sun rose, and the forest was dark, but Tarasove had no difficulty following the bears' progress through the night-vision infrared scope attached to his air rifle.

"Mama is hungry," Tarasove murmured softly. "And so are the cubs, Jedgar."

The dog couldn't see the bears, but he could smell them. He ground his nose between the deck railings, his mouth open, his tongue dangling inches above the floor.

The big bear stood up on her hind legs for a few moments, her massive head turning back and forth, snout up in the air.

Tarasove knew the beast sensed the danger. But the thirty-five-pound bags were too tempting. She dropped

down to all fours and edged closer to the food, finally raising an arm, then sending her clawed paw across one bag
in a vicious swipe.

The three cubs scurried forward, eagerly digging into the
chicken-flavored nuggets that Jedgar turned up his nose at.

Tarasove centered the scope's crosshairs on the mother
bear's chest. No, he decided. The cubs would never survive
without her. He sighted in on the head of the smallest cub,
the one that sat back and let the others eat first. The piston-
powered air rifle was whisper smooth—there was no need
for a silencer. The featherless, dry-ice dart, tipped with his
latest snake toxin, entered the cub's forehead. It stiffened
for a second, then fell over without a sound.

The mother bear sniffed her cub, then rose to her hind
feet again and began clacking her teeth, a sign that she
was frightened.

Tarasove switched on the outside halogen lights. Jedgar
began barking wildly. The cubs started squealing and running away, the mother following, nervously wheeling her
head around every few yards.

When they were gone from sight, Tarasove opened the
deck gate and Jedgar bounded off, rumbling down the steps
and over to the dead cub.

"No," he shouted, when the dog began licking the dead
cub's face. Some of the toxin could have leaked from the
wound. The whole purpose of killing the bear was to determine if the toxin cells destroyed themselves, removing evidence of the poison; thus the cub—or a human target—
would appear to have died from unknown causes.

If Tarasove were to leave the animal on the ground, its
universal death scent would attract insects and within minutes green flies would appear, eat, and lay eggs. Twelve
hours later, the eggs would hatch into maggots that would
feast for the next few hours. They'd be replaced by beetles
hungry for the drying skins, followed by scavenging spiders
and millipedes.

A pathologist could analyze the insects to reveal the time
and cause of death with surprising accuracy.

What Tarasove was working on was a bonding of potassium with the snake venom. The cells of the body are
rich with potassium. Once death occurs, the other cells start

to break apart and flood the bloodstream with potassium—resulting in a postmortem *rise* in potassium and an obscuring of any poisons.

The potassium in vitreous humor, the fluid in the back of the eyes, rises much more slowly than in the bloodstream. Thus, if a forensic pathologist were to examine a sample from there in time, traces of the poison would be found.

Tarasove had studied the subject thoroughly. In America, the average cost of an autopsy was a thousand dollars. If toxicological tests were requested, the costs skyrocketed—thus the tests were performed only when there were suspicious circumstances. And since Tarasove's dry-ice dart left barely a mark, there would be no such circumstances. The victim died from acute cardiac arrest. Case closed.

"Jedgar! Come. We'll take care of it later."

Boris Feliks had a massive headache. He gulped down four aspirins, then flicked on Kiryl Chapaev's laptop and checked the e-mail, hoping to find a message from one of Chapaev's comrades who could help him locate Tarasove. As a precaution, he changed Chapaev's password on a daily basis.

There were three new messages: one advising him of ways to increase the size of his penis so that he could "break her walls down"; another from a liquor store in Beverly Hills promoting the arrival of French wines; and the third from *khokho*, Nicolai Tarasove's e-mail address!

Feliks had to grin at Tarasove's choice of an e-mail name. *Khokho* was an old Russian word used to describe a greedy Ukrainian. He opened the e-mail, his breath coming in slow, steady streams: *Why did he have to die?*

Feliks got to his feet and picked up the cup of coffee that he'd brewed in the pot provided by the motel. The original plan had been to take Chapaev to the lake and kill him there. Carting a dead body from the hotel had not been an option—there was no way to do so without being noticed. Before he died, Chapaev had told Feliks that he was scheduled to meet with Tarasove at ten o'clock the next morning in the St. Charles lobby-level restaurant.

Feliks returned to the hotel the following the morning, but all he saw were policemen swarming around the lobby.

As he had feared, Chapaev's body had been discovered, and Tarasove never showed up. Or had the crafty old fart been frightened away by the sight of the police?

Feliks carried the coffee into the small bathroom and dumped the contents into the sink.

He paced back and forth near the bed, then made his decision. He clicked the e-mail REPLY button.

I had not intended for him to die. He had a heart attack. He told me about Napitak Zlobi—the Devil's Brew. What will the FBI do when they learn of it? I have a buyer who is very interested. We can make a deal. I know the Americans forced you to trick me in Kiev. It was not your doing. Let us work together on this.

He pushed the SEND button and the message disappeared from the screen, on its way to God only knew where. God and Nicolai Tarasove. And, if things went as Feliks hoped, those two would be meeting very soon.

He stared at the computer screen for a long time, hoping for an instant reply from Tarasove. The foxy old bastard would no doubt make him wait, dangle in the wind, while he plotted his next move.

Feliks decided it was time for him to move. He began packing his belongings, his eyes flicking back to the computer screen, anxious for Tarasove's reply. Could he be right here, in San Francisco? All of his meetings with Chapaev were in the city. If not here, somewhere very close by.

He took his time, using a bathroom towel to wipe his fingerprints from the fixtures, coffeepot, light switches, everything he'd touched. He gave the room a final look before closing the door. He was satisfied he'd left no trace of himself—and soon there would be no trace of Nicolai Tarasove.

He drove to a store four blocks away that offered a variety of services: check cashing, money orders, Western Union, keys made, notary public, mailboxes, and phone cards for "India, the Philippines, anywhere in the world."

The bearded and turbaned man behind the counter kept one hand out of sight. And on a gun, Feliks suspected.

"A phone card, please. I want to call Russia. Moscow."

The man raised both hands and leaned his elbows on

the counter. "Ah. Moscow. How many minutes, my friend? Twenty, thirty, an hour?"

"Thirty minutes should be more than enough."

The man took a narrow box from under the counter and flipped through the contents until he found an embossed plastic card with a photograph of a tulip-shaped tower on Red Square.

"Moscow. You have family there? You are calling your parents?"

"I wouldn't describe the person I'm calling as family," Feliks said, reaching for his wallet.

Harry Dymes's four-day on-call shift, where he handled all the homicide incidents that came in, was over. The annual number of homicides hovered around ninety, so there were times when not a single incident took place during his on-call shift. He treated himself to a late morning's sleep and arrived at the Hall of Justice close to noon, handing a bouquet of bright yellow, long-stemmed roses to Carlotta, the diminutive detail receptionist.

"Ooooh, I like these, Harry. What are they called?"

"Midas Touch."

Carlotta buried her nose in one of the roses. "Ummmm. How many varieties do you have on that roof of yours?"

"Too many," Harry said. "Any messages?"

"No. But you had visitors. The FBI, early this morning. Lieutenant Larsen handled them."

Harry made his way to his cubicle, placing a single rose in an hourglass-shaped vase. The office had been completely remodeled in the last year. Previously, the entire room was open, the inspectors' desks butted up against each other. It had been noisy at times, but at least he could see his fellow cops, talk shop, exchange department gossip, get a feel for what was going on. Now the cubicle walls reached near ceiling height, cutting off interaction with anyone but your partner. And Harry's partner, Tom Thorp, was still off sick.

"Hey, Harry, who was that lovely young lady you had in here yesterday?" Homicide Lieutenant Ric Larsen asked. Larsen, a well-built man with thick, dirty-blond hair, held his hands in front of his body and shook them up and down, as if he'd just touched a hot stove. "She was a real beauty."

Dymes slipped into his chair and looked up at Larsen.

"Julie Renton. A hooker, who was with the victim from the St. Charles Hotel the night before he was murdered."

Larsen perched his butt on the edge of Harry's desk. "Was she of any help?"

"Not yet. Carlotta tells me the FBI was in this morning."

Larsen sucked in his lower lip. "Yeah. Another looker, Marta Citron, and that dummy Tom McNab. How the hell does he keep his job?"

"His brother is a congressman from North Dakota. What did they want?"

"Your balls," Larsen said. He stood up, stretched, and knuckled his scalp. "They say you're not cooperating."

"I'm not," Dymes admitted. "According to Citron, I'm in way over my head."

"Are you, pal?"

"Not yet, Ric."

Larsen pulled at the knot on his tie and unbuttoned his shirt collar. "You know the problem with Citron and McNab, Harry? They forget that the FBI is a civil service job, just like ours. Of course, if they screw up, they get transferred to Icebutt, Alaska, or Shitbrick, Wyoming. Unless we kick the mayor in the balls, in front of witnesses, all they can do is move us down the hall to a new detail, or ship us out a few miles to a district station. They can't fire us, and they can't demote us, without having the union jump all over them, so don't sweat it. I told Citron that 'I'd look into it.' Now I have."

Larsen started for his office, then turned around. "I talked to Tom Thorp's doctor. Tom's filed for disability pension, but it will take a while before all the paperwork is finalized. There's no way I can put anyone in his spot until he's officially retired. Can you handle being on your own for a few more weeks?"

"No problem, Lieut." Harry watched Larsen walk away. Good man, the kind you'd like to have with you when the going got tough. But Citron and McNab wouldn't stop with Larsen. They'd push the captain of detectives, who, unlike the laid-back Larsen, had ambitions to be chief one day, and was definitely "nervous in the service." Not cooperating with the FBI would not go over well with the captain. Harry figured he had two days at the most to get to the bottom of the Chapaev case before the screws were turned deep enough to reach him.

Dymes surveyed his bare desk. A word processor, but no computer. Not one of the homicide inspectors had access to a computer—thus, no e-mails or entry into the Web. He'd been on the phone with a cop in Ukiah, a town a hundred and twenty miles north with a population of fifteen thousand, who wanted to e-mail Harry a six-page attachment on a case involving a slain teenager who had been known to visit San Francisco. The guy hadn't believed it when Harry told him that SF cops had no access to the Internet. Harry could have added that they had no department-issued cell phones either—just a pager, and the use of a portable communications radio, if the batteries were working.

The detail cameras, video and vocal recorders, were so outdated that Harry used his own. There was one computer dedicated to police-only databases—FBI, CI&I, the state-wide criminal files, and DMV records—which Harry intended to use. Private investigator Don Landeta had given him a list of DMV checks he wanted in exchange for the material on Morris/Chapaev. Harry was about to get to his feet and run the DMV checks when the phone rang.

"Dymes speaking."

"Inspector. Dr. Phillips here. Is it too early for a little glass of formaldehyde?"

The coroner's office was located in the basement of the Hall of Justice. Assistant Coroner Alvin Phillips was a favorite with most of the homicide inspectors. He was a middle-aged bachelor, a thin, birdlike man with a ready smile.

Phillips shook Dymes's hand warmly. "I missed you at the autopsies. Those two stiffs you sent me were interesting."

It was no longer mandatory for the investigating officer to be present during an autopsy, and Dymes saw no advantage in watching the gruesome ordeal of a body being sawn apart, its organs weighed, and then stitched back together again.

"I always aim to please, Doc. What's so interesting?"

"Come on into my office, and I'll show you."

Phillips's office wasn't much bigger than Harry's cubicle: a single gray metal desk piled high with files, stacks of photographs and notepads, two matching file cabinets, card-board boxes strewn around the floor, a cabinet jammed with books and medical binders, an old-fashioned water dispenser. On one wall was an etched glass mirror with a

Latin phrase Harry had seen in one form or other in numerous coroner's offices: *Hic locus est ubi mors gaudet succure vitae.* This is the place where death delights to serve the living. An old refrigerator whose door was littered with hot pepper magnets crouched in the corner of the room.

"I had company this morning. A *very* pretty FBI agent."

"Marta Citron."

"That's the one," Phillips said, opening the refrigerator. "She wasn't nearly as shy as you are, Harry. She went over the St. Charles Hotel and Lake Merced cadavers very thoroughly." He retrieved a flat plastic bottle filled to the brim with an amber-colored fluid. The bottle's label showed *Imperium Super-Concentrated Embalming Fluid.* He took two cups from the watercooler's holder and poured them both a drink.

Harry took a sip without qualms. Phillips was well known for hiding his stash of premixed Manhattans in the embalming fluid bottle. He just hoped that one of the nighttime janitors didn't get wise and make a switch one day.

"A libation on the altar of friendship," Phillips said, just before taking a deep sip of his drink.

"Cheers," Harry responded. "What did Citron find of interest?"

"First of all, the cause of Mr. Morris/Chapaev's death." Phillips drained his cup, dropped it into the wastebasket and patted his chest. "Heart failure. The gentleman suffered from dilated cardiomyopathy, a disorder that causes the heart to be become enlarged to a point where it can no longer pump blood efficiently. He could have had a fairly normal life with the proper medication. His death probably came as a surprise. I doubt if his attacker was aware of his condition."

"The weapon, Doc. An ice pick?"

Phillips widened his eyes and rubbed them, as if they were very tired. "Ice pick, a sharp pointed instrument of some kind. The wounds were superficial, barely penetrating the flesh in some instances." He rummaged through the files on his desk and came out with a folder of eight-by-ten photographs. "I took these of the John Doe from Lake Merced, Harry. Agent Citron wanted a copy of them. I said that I would have to have a release from your office before so doing. She wasn't pleased about that."

Harry examined the sharp, clear close-ups of the dead man's tattooed torso.

"None of the gentleman's body art was professionally applied," Phillips said. "And some of them appear to be quite old."

"How old was the John Doe?" Harry asked.

"In his late forties to early fifties, I would think. He had led an interesting life. There were scars on his back, one across his neck, and a few on each of his legs. He suffered from cirrhosis of the liver, and there were numerous genital warts in his anus."

"No wonder you have a stash of Manhattans. I wouldn't want to change jobs with you."

"Not many people would," Phillips admitted. "But at least I have no complaints from my subjects. John Doe suffered a fatal wound to the upper cervical spinal cord, caused by an instrument, such as an ice pick, being inserted into his left ear."

Harry dropped the pictures back onto the desk. "The same ice pick in both murders?"

Phillips swept a hand leisurely across one of the photos, as if admiring its glossy finish. "I couldn't say for sure. I doubt if I'll ever be certain, Harry. But the odds are pretty high that it was the same type weapon." He shuffled the photographs into a neat bundle and handed them to Dymes. "Miss Citron seems to be a competent agent. The persistent type."

"I think you're right, Doc," Harry said, squashing the empty paper cup in his hand and dropping it in the wastebasket. Which meant that he might have less time then he originally thought.

"Do you see that, Frida?" Madame Lana said excitedly, trailing a long, scarlet fingernail across the elderly woman's palm. "Right there, where your line of destiny meets your line of heart, that is *very* interesting."

"Why?" Frida asked anxiously, patting her free hand on her wooly cap of gray curls.

Lana slowly dragged her fingernail across the woman's palm again. "The line of destiny rising from the Mount of the Moon, right there, tells me that your earlier life was influenced very strongly by someone of another sex."

"Yes. That's true. My husband was very strict. Very . . . controlling."

Lana paused for a moment, as if marshaling her thoughts. "Yes. It's all there. See these tiny lines crossing the line of health. Your life has not been easy, has it?"

Frida curled her fingers inward. "No. No, it hasn't."

Lana took a small, chunky green stone from the folds of her sleeve and pressed it into the woman's hand. "This is malachite," she said. "It has great powers over love and protection. Hold it in your hand day and night. It casts a love spell. Your line of heart tells me that you will meet someone new. Very soon. Someone who will—"

Lana's head snapped up. She could see the figure of a tall man through the beaded curtain. She got to her feet and parted the beads. The smiling face of Harry Dymes looked her square in the eye.

"A moment," Lana said, leaning over Frida's narrow shoulders. "I have to end our session. A client with an urgent concern, I'm afraid." She patted the woman's back lightly. "Do not worry. You will not be charged for today. And tomorrow, I'm certain that I will have some wonderful news for you."

Frida gave Dymes a nervous glance as she exited the shop. Lana reached for the string of brass bells attached by a wire cord to the top of the front door, shaking them angrily. "How the hell did you get in here so quietly, Harry?"

"An old gypsy taught me that trick." Dymes laughed. "It might have been you."

Lana sighed theatrically. She was a tall, full-figured woman. Her below-the-shoulder dark hair was streaked with jagged white lines, much like lightning bolts. She was wearing a sweeping, multilayered purple dress. Silver hoop earrings dangled from her ears and the gold bracelets on her wrists jangled with her every move. Each finger on both hands held at least one ring.

"You're looking good," Dymes said.

"You should have seen me twenty years ago, Harry. When I was a belly dancer." She raised her arms above her head and gyrated her stomach suggestively. "I was hot."

"You're still hot." Harry knew that Lana had started her criminal career as a prostitute, then pickpocket, before settling into gypsy scams. He grimaced and shook his head. "'The line of destiny rising.' What scam are you pulling on that poor little old lady?"

"Poor," Lana scoffed. "Her husband died, leaving her a ten-unit apartment house on California Street. She's lonely. I'm just trying to find her a soul mate."

"A gypsy soul mate, who'll end up with the apartments and everything she has in the bank."

Lana clasped her hands to her chest. "You do not have a romantic soul, Harry. You do not believe that the lines on your hand can lead the heart to love."

"The first time we met," Harry reminded her, "your hand had led to the wallet of a Japanese businessman, who wanted to send you to jail."

"No one is perfect," Lana said with a chuckle, and then the chuckle grew to a hearty laugh. "Even you, Harry. What is it you want? You know I haven't dipped a wallet in years."

"I want to show you some dirty pictures."

"Ah. Good." She spread the beaded curtain with both arms. "Come into my spell room."

The walls and ceiling of Lana's spell room were covered with shiny, wine-red cloth, giving it a tentlike look. A shelf was lined with burning candles and incense burners in the shape of a dancing bear. The overpowering smell of lavender caused Dymes to contract his nostrils. In the middle of the room was a green-felt-topped table, on which sat a large, lavender-tinted crystal ball.

"Sit, sit," she said, placing the crystal ball on the floor.

As if he were laying out a deck of playing cards, Harry began slapping the photographs of the body found in Lake Merced onto the table. "I'm told you knew this man."

"Hmmph," she said, snorting through her nose. "Why would I know such a man? And why do you come to me with these?" She batted her heavily mascaraed eyelashes at him. "I am usually paid for my time, Harry."

"These are unusual times. Look at the pictures. Tell me his name, and tell me about the tattoos."

She shifted uneasily in her chair and picked up one of the photographs. "Who told you I knew Zivon?"

"Zivon? Is that his first or last name?"

"Zivon Yudin. A *balfasz*. A mark, a sucker. He came to me suggesting that I work with him. The idiot proposed that I give him the addresses of my clients, and he would break into their houses when they were in my spell room." She twisted the amethyst ring on her pinkie finger and smiled. "I pretended to be interested. He was a believer, Harry. I read his palm, and told him that he had great skills as a gambler, and that his line of destiny showed that he was in a *very* lucky period of his life. I steered him to a friend who runs a *devynake* game in his basement. You are familiar? Russians love it. It's like baccarat, but played with thirty-six cards. Yudin's luck was very bad. That was four months ago. I haven't seen him since. Someone said that he had gone to Southern California, that he had friends in the Russian Mafia there."

"Where in Southern California?" Dymes said.

Lana jangled the bracelets on her arms. "Who knows? I don't know where he lived when he was here, Harry. He was probably sleeping in the park. He smelled like a donkey." She picked up the photographs. "Look. See the dagger across his shoulder blades. That indicates that he was a rapist." She picked up another picture. "The Cyrillic characters on his fingers. See the number of skulls. Six. They symbolize the number of people he killed. And this one, the portrait of the general with horns coming out of his head. That's Brezhnev. Prisoners believed that the guards would not shoot at the tattoo of such a leader. His forearm, the spider crawling up the web, indicates a drug addiction. And here, the church with the spires. Five spires, meaning he'd been to jail five times. He bragged to me about being in a forced labor camp in Western Siberia, and escaping into the Vishera River."

Lana leaned back in her chair and it creaked, like elderly arthritic joints. "There. I have provided you with much information, have I not?"

"You have," Harry agreed, waiting to hear how she'd pitch him for full payment.

Lana stretched her arms across the table and cupped Harry's left hand. She stroked his wrist, pushing his shirt and coat sleeves back. "All those little scratches. A cat? A very passionate woman?"

"Roses," Harry told her.

"Ummm," she said, as her fingers caressed his watch. "I always loved this watch, Harry. Who gave it to you?"

"A dead man."

She smiled wickedly. "A rich dead man. The best kind." She turned over his palm and made clicking sounds with her tongue, like the kind used to settle down horses. "Your line of life and line of Mars are very interesting."

Harry withdrew his hand and reached for his wallet.

"No," she said. "Not money. But I do need a favor. A friend, Camlo Tobar. He was arrested. A mistake, he is innocent, of course."

"What's the charge?" Harry asked, getting to his feet.

"Burglary. He is in the county jail. He's a very pretty boy, Harry. They won't treat him kindly. Can you do something?"

"I'll try, Lana. But I can't promise anything."

"I know," she said, bending down and scooping up the crystal ball. "But please do your best."

"Zivon Yudin. Did he have any friends? Did you ever see him with anyone else?"

"He was a *szopo 'ssza 'ju'*, my handsome policeman. Men didn't like him. Women didn't like him. Dogs would piss on his leg. No one will mourn him. You should not waste your time on him."

"He was murdered in my town, Lana." Dymes placed a photograph of Kiryl Chapaev in front of her. "So was this man. Have you seen him? He's Russian also."

She cocked her head as she studied the picture. "No. Never. Is he important?"

"Everybody's important to someone. Even Zivon Yudin," Dymes said, picking up the photographs.

"Two dead Russians," Lana said, clicking her nails against the crystal ball. "The person who killed them, is he valuable to you, Harry?"

"Yes. If you find out anything, call me, Lana. Be careful. These are dangerous people," Dymes warned her.

Lana gave a vulturelike smile. "Gypsies are not afraid of danger."

"Gypsies bleed like everyone else," Harry said bluntly, heading for the door. "I'll get back to you tomorrow on your pretty friend, Tobar."

"I will find something on your mystery man," Lana promised. "And then perhaps you can find a dead man to give me a beautiful watch, too."

Chapter Ten

Ying Fai watched Rita Tong putting on her makeup with all the precision of a surgeon performing a delicate operation. The magnified mirror exaggerated every minor blemish on her golden-skinned face. She was wearing a pair of black panties and a strapless bra that seemed to be defying gravity by staying in place.

"How long are we going to be in Las Vegas?" Tong asked, tilting her head to one side as she applied liner to her collagen-enhanced lips.

"As long as I deem necessary," Fai said dryly.

Danny Shu's impressive bulk appeared in the doorway. He coughed lightly into his hand before saying, "She drove to the airport. My men believe she took a plane to New York City."

"Who?" Rita Tong asked, blotting her lips before adding, "The skinny white bitch?"

"I wouldn't call her skinny," Fai said with a light smile. Every room in the suite was under the scrutiny of a miniature camera, and he had watched Alex with great concentration as she in turn continued to monitor the casino videotapes for the hours before and after Fai had arrived.

Alex, who had never removed her gloves during the time she was his guest, donned the hotel bellboy uniform she had magically appeared in, thanked Ying Fai for his hospitality, and left, with a promise to be in touch very soon.

Fai had little hope that Shu's men would be successful in following her for long. He waved a forgiving hand at Shu. "You did as well as expected."

Shu stiffened as if he'd been slapped in the face.

Rita Tong began working on her eyebrows. "I still say she was skinny. When are we going to Hollywood?"

Fai crossed the room swiftly. He picked up Tong's lipstick and slashed it across her face several times. "If you don't learn when to close that beautiful mouth, I'll have Shu stitch it shut." He drew a line from her quivering chin down her neck. "Go. Now!"

Tong got shakily to her feet, then ran out the door without looking back, nearly bumping into Danny Shu.

"If I didn't have so much money invested in that *ji nee*, I'd give her to you," Fai told Shu. "You observed the woman, Alex. What is your impression?"

Shu rubbed the palms of his hands along his trousers. "She is clever, there's no doubt of that."

"She made you look like a fool, Danny. Twice. Getting in here, and then at the airport. 'My men believe she took a plane to New York City.' Your *men* have no idea where she went."

Shu held his ground. "She can't be as good as you think she is."

"It's not *I* who thinks she's good," Fai countered. "She came with a very high recommendation from our people in New York, who in turn learned of her though the Italian Mafia, or what's left of it. What did you make of her obsession with the casino videos?"

"She was looking for FBI agents. If we are to believe her, there were more than there usually are."

"True," Fai agreed. "And what does that tell you?"

Shu smiled a mirthless smile. "That they have nothing better to do. I saw at least four of them follow us around the Strip last night. A useless exercise."

"Wrong," Fai said sharply. "It means that the FBI knew that Alex was coming to meet with me in Las Vegas. And that means that our security was breached. The Italians are arrogant and stupid, that's why they're in the condition they are now. I won't allow that to happen to me. Somehow my conversation regarding Alex was overheard. The FBI, or another American agency, had my phones tapped. Have that looked into right away."

Fai rubbed his chin and sighed. "The woman studied the videos looking for agents, all right. Agents she knew by sight, not just through their predictable actions. What does that tell you?"

Shu took a few seconds to respond. "That she was, or is, an agent herself."

Fai clapped his hands silently. "Exactly. She kept her gloves on the entire time, so as not to leave fingerprints. And her face. Not remarkable, but one that could be disguised easily with a little makeup. Now to continue the exercise, what does all this mean?"

This time Shu's response was quick. "That we'll have to eliminate her as soon as she's finished the job."

Fai affirmed the conclusion with a nod. "She could be a valuable asset in the future, but she is too arrogant. I *despise* arrogant women."

The view from the office Marta Citron commandeered on the twenty-second floor of the San Francisco FBI headquarters on Golden Gate Avenue faced southeast, overlooking sections of the downtown area, SBC Park, and the South Bay. If she had one of the powerful telescopes positioned in front of Harry Dymes's windows, she could no doubt zero in on the obstinate policeman's house.

She admitted to herself that she'd handled the meeting with Dymes badly. She'd been too confrontational. Tom McNab had briefed her on Dymes: "A hot shot. The newspapers love him."

Marta reached for the cigarette pack at the corner of the desk. She allowed herself five smokes a day. She drew her hand back. No smoking allowed in a federal building. The muscles in her neck and shoulders were drawn into knots. She stretched her hands over her head, took a deep breath, then went back to the sparse FBI file on Harry Dymes. Born in Brooklyn, mother Rosalie, deceased, father Peter, believed to be alive. She thought of updating the file. The senior Dymes was not only alive, he was tailoring his son's suits and sport coats. Dymes entered the military, was discharged in San Francisco. Joined police force. He was called back to military service in 1990 for Desert Storm, in Iraq.

Married and divorced twice—from the same woman: Eva Ferranti. Why was that name familiar?

Dymes made a quick jump from patrolman to sergeant, then to inspector. He'd worked fraud, burglary, and now homicide. Conviction rate high. There was a note penciled in the margin: *especially for Frisco.*

She picked up the cigarette pack, repositioned it, stood it on its side, then tipped it over with a fingernail. Who had added the note? Tom McNab? From her first impression of McNab, she could imagine him being petty and annoying—a "brick" agent, short on smarts, long on patience, which made him ideal for surveillance cases.

The FBI file listed a San Francisco police inspector's base pay at ninety-seven thousand dollars a year. With overtime, Marta figured Dymes could be taking home a hundred and twenty to a hundred and forty thousand dollars a year. More than she was making!

But was it enough for Dymes's lifestyle? The fancy house and expensive furniture. And the watch on his wrist—a Rolex. San Francisco was a notoriously high-priced place to live, and Dymes seemed to be thriving.

She picked up a pencil and began making notes: *Check Dymes's bank accounts. Possible outside income? Why divorced twice from same woman? Eva Ferranti: Who is she? And who told Dymes about Chapaev?* She tapped the pencil nervously on the desk. It certainly wasn't Tarasove. Had there been something in Chapaev's hotel room with his name on it? Some memento the man couldn't bear to part with?

A loud knock on the door caused her to drop her pencil.

"There's an e-mail for you from Roger Dancel," Tom McNab said, strolling into the office. "I printed the attachment."

The printout looked to be at least fifty pages. Marta straightened up in her chair and adjusted her skirt, wondering if McNab had read the attachment. She didn't trust the man. He had a sullen, pinched-in face and wore shabby Brooks Brothers suits, invariably partnered with a blue button-down shirt and knit ties. McNab had tried to be subtle during the drive to Dymes's house, staring out of the corner of his eye at her with a scowly smirk on his face.

He leaned against the desk and scanned Marta's handwritten notes. "Eva Ferranti. You don't recognize the name?"

"It rings a bell," Marta said, trying to keep the anger from her voice. She hated anyone seeing her notes without her permission.

"She's a fashion designer," McNab said. "Makes all those slinky dresses for anorexic models with no chests."

"Thanks," Marta replied curtly. She should have known. Ferranti created a top-notch line of clothing sold through Bloomingdale's and Bergdorf Goodman.

McNab had that smirk on his puss again. His eyes flicked from the file on the desk to her hemline. "Is there something else?" Marta asked pointedly.

"Yeah. The guy I spotted coming out of Dymes's house when you went visiting. I knew I'd seen him before. He's Don Landeta, a retired Frisco cop. He works as a half-assed private eye now. I was thinking of paying him a visit, shaking him up. Want to tag along?"

"No. You handle that," Marta said, putting some authority in her voice. "But be discreet. I don't want Landeta calling Dymes and making him any more obstinate than he already is."

"I know just how to handle him," McNab said, hitching up his pants. "See you later."

Not if I see you first, Marta thought, sighing thankfully as McNab closed the door after himself. Men could be so stupid, so obvious—though, she admitted to herself, the worst agents she'd crossed swords with in the Bureau were women. Something about the job turned them into bitches.

She wet a finger with her tongue and flipped through the material e-mailed from Roger Dancel. The cover letter was brief: *Las Vegas trip a bust—no sign of the* bok wai. The next page was headlined: *PERSCOM, Army Personnel Command. Subject—Harry Dymes.* There was a detailed phychological profile. One word jumped out at her: Sniper.

Harry Dymes noticed that there was a new addition to the door leading to Julie Renton's apartment—a fish-eye peephole. He knocked on the door and stood back to give Renton a good view of his face.

When the door opened he took another step backward. Renton's forehead was covered with sweat. She was wearing a denim shirt with the sleeves rolled up above her elbows and cutoff jeans, the knees whitened and worn to the underfabric. Her hair was tied back by a blue print bandana. In her right hand she held what appeared to be a motorcycle chain.

"Am I interrupting a session?" Dymes asked.

Renton looked at the chain and grinned. "Sort of. Come on in. Fix yourself a drink, if you want. I could use one."

A battered and scarred walnut table with wobbly Cabriole legs was set over a carpet of newspapers in the front room. Renton raised her arm and gave the table a good whack with the chain.

"I picked it up at the Goodwill for ten bucks. It's not distressed enough yet," she said, wiping her elbow across her forehead. "A few more whacks with the chain, some cigarette burns, a rough sanding, and a crackle-finished paint job in . . . oh, maybe avocado or apricot, and it will sell for five, maybe six hundred bucks."

"Not to me," Dymes said, settling down on her couch. "Take a look at these." He laid out the photographs the coroner had taken of Zivon Yudin.

Renton dropped the chain and peered down at the pictures. "God. Now I really need a drink. Who the hell is that?"

"A Russian gangster. I have reason to think that he was involved in the death of the man you . . . dated. Paul Morris."

Julie went to the liquor cabinet and poured them both a Scotch. She settled down next to Dymes. "I never saw him before. Not that night. Not ever. It's not a face you'd forget."

Harry gathered up the photographs and tapped them into a neat stack. "It was just a thought. Putting in a peephole in the door was a good idea."

"Yep. And I'm adding another lock." She undid the top two buttons on her shirt and began toying with the third.

"Is there something about buttons that you don't like?" Harry asked sarcastically.

"They're slower than zippers," Julie shot back. "I've been thinking about that night with Morris, when we had dinner at Moose's Restaurant. The man sitting next to us. He was *too* close, and seemed *too* interested in what we were saying. Do you want to see his picture?"

Harry almost knocked his drink over in his haste to get to his feet. "You've got a picture of him?"

"Well, sort of," Julie answered softly. "A computer composite drawing." She crooked a finger. "Come into my office."

Dymes followed Renton's streamlined hips past a small, well-designed kitchen and into her bedroom: a double bed with a faux–white fur cover, walls covered in gray silk. The carpet and single, oversized chair were a similar shade of gray. A computer, printer, and fax machine sat on a brushed-steel table positioned against the window.

Renton flicked on one of the ladybug halogen lamps next to the computer and turned the machine on.

"I'm surprised you didn't do this at the police station," Julie said, as she moused into a file. "I see the cops do composite drawings on TV all the time."

Harry saw no point in telling her that the department didn't have access to computer composite drawing software, and that the one real live composite artist in the department was off on disability leave.

"Here he is," Renton said. "What do you think?"

A face appeared on the screen: a detailed drawing of a dark-haired man, looking much like a mug shot—staring straight ahead, no smile on his face.

Julie used the mouse and worked on the nose, making it a tad narrower. "That's the guy."

"Print me a copy." Dymes watched her as she went about the task. "Why does a girl in your line of work have access to composite software, Julie?"

Her cheeks dimpled as she handed Harry the printout. "I'm not going to be in this 'line of work' much longer. I'm studying to be an interior decorator. The software allows me to design a room, a house, an office, all in 3-D." She stretched her arms over her head, then fell backward gracefully onto the bed. "Want to see some of my work?"

"I just did." Harry studied the printout. Middle-aged, not bad looking, a lone diner in a restaurant. Why wouldn't he want to sit next to a beautiful woman and eavesdrop on her conversation?

"I'm not doing anything the rest of the day," Julie said, running her fingernails through the phony fur bedspread.

"I am. Thanks for this."

Julie used her elbows to push herself into a sitting position. "I thought maybe we could go to Moose's for a drink, and then—"

The phone rang and Julie gave it a disgusted look.

"Looks like you're working after all, kid." Dymes tucked the printout into his coat pocket. "I'll let you know if this leads to anything. Be careful. They say it's a jungle out there."

Chapter Eleven

"How long are you going to be in Ess Eff?" asked Jed Dewey, an old man with a gnarly gray ponytail pulled back from his bald, sunburned scalp, as he opened the door to the small cottage situated at the rear of his Victorian house on Diamond Street.

"I'm not sure," Boris Feliks said. "I'm just getting settled down here. Any chance of renting it by the week?" The advertisement in the newspaper described the shingled cottage as being "vine-draped in an herb garden setting." The reality was a dreary-looking shack, surrounded by knee-high weeds, that looked as if its original use had been to store gardening equipment. There was one knotty pine-paneled room, a gray-brown industrial carpet, a Danish modern futon and a faded green chenille chair with fringed pillows. Sunlight barely pierced the cobwebbed windows. A bentwood rocker sat in front of a TV set that was built in the days when they used heavy wooden cabinets, complete with rabbit ears.

"The kitchen and bath are behind those curtains," Jed said, putting his hands in the back pockets of his pants and rocking back and forth on his feet. He was a potbellied man in his sixties with a face that was soft and puffy, like a badly fitted rubber mask. Thick glasses magnified his milky-white eyes. "Sorry about the dust. It's been vacant for 'bout six months. My woman got real sick, then died on me a few weeks ago. She used to keep it fixed up. What'd you say your name is?"

"John Kagel," Feliks said, wondering if the old man was going to bother to check his identification.

"Where you from, John?"

"Canada," Feliks said, pushing the curtain aside to find a chipped enamel sink, a two-burner gas grill and a turquoise-colored refrigerator. A raw pine door opened to the bathroom. Feliks took a quick peek. "Ontario."

Jed took a cigarette from the pack under the sleeve of his tie-dyed Rolling Stones T-shirt. "I saw the Stones up there in September of nineteen-seventy-seven, or eight. Kind of a cold place, as I remember it."

The refrigerator door opened with a soft, sucking sound. "It can get cold," Feliks said. "My company is thinking of opening a branch here in San Francisco."

"Then you might settle permanently?"

"It's possible. I'll be scouting locations. God, the traffic. I've rented a car, but parking is impossible."

"You're telling me," Jed agreed. "There's only one way to get around Ess Eff. A motorcycle. I've got my Harley-Davidson Fat Boy. Classic bike. Do you ride?"

Feliks turned on his brightest smile. "I ride great, Jed. Maybe I can rent your Harley for a couple of days."

A frown creased the rubber mask face. "No one touches my Hog but me. I can let you have the cottage for a week. I gotta get it fixed up, then it's going to be leased by the year. Seven hundred for one week, then if you like it, we can maybe negotiate for a month or two."

Feliks reached for his wallet. "Cash all right?"

"Never turn down cash." Jed laughed. "If you need it, I'll write out any amount you want for your expense account. What kind of business are you in?"

"I'm a headhunter. We specialize in industrial engineers. Sorry to hear about your wife. Do you have any children?"

"Not me. She did. Wimpy kid. Died of that AIDS shit." He took a kitchen match from his jeans pocket, scraped it across his butt and lit his cigarette. "You don't look like no fag."

Feliks dropped Kiryl Chapaev's laptop onto the couch. "Neither do you."

Jed coughed out a stream of smoke. "Damn right, I ain't. But we're surrounded by the suckers. This used to be a workin' man's neighborhood. All the work those boys do is on their knees. My woman used to tell me that I hadta look at things from the 'gay perspective.' I told her the only perspective those fellas have is the floor or the bedpost when their lover boys are jackhammerin' their asses."

Feliks wasn't sure if the old man was serious or making what he thought was a joke. He peeled seven one-hundred-dollar bills from his money clip and passed them to Jed. "There's a week's rent. Do you find it lonely, now that your wife is gone?"

"Nah," Jed said, backing out the door. "I like livin' alone. I want a woman, I don't have no trouble getting one. You can bring all the girls you want back here. Don't bother me none."

Feliks waited until the obnoxious old man was out of sight before opening up the laptop. Still no response from Tarasove. Nicolai was taking his time, letting him sweat. Or is he waiting for his friends in the FBI to find me first? Feliks wondered. He couldn't allow him that time. He had to find a way to apply more pressure on Tarasove. Through the policeman, Harry Dymes?

Last night Dymes had visited a Russian bar, spoken to a drunken old man, then stopped at a fortune-teller's parlor. It had to have something to do with Zivon Yudin. Maybe she'd been Zivon's lover. The gypsies would do anything for money. Even sleep with someone as repulsive as Yudin.

Feliks was certain that Dymes hadn't spotted him last night, but the policeman had sensed something. He would have to be very careful in trailing him from now on. He upturned his hand and studied his palm as he planned his next move. The gypsy, or the policeman's office?

Harry Dymes slipped the computer composite drawing Julie Renton had provided into the case folder. Carlotta, the homicide detail receptionist, had laid out three yellow Post-its across his desk blotter. He'd had two phone calls from Marta Citron and one from Lana Kuzmin. He was reaching for the phone when it rang.

"Harry Dymes."

"Double dozen," a man's voice said; then there was a click and the buzz of a disconnected line.

The San Francisco Giants were on the road, in Philadelphia, so SBC Park was empty except for a line of tourists who were paying for the privilege of touring the ballpark. Dymes leaned against the base of the larger-than-life statue of Willie Mays, the Say Hey Kid, seemingly following the flight of a ball he'd just hit over the centerfield wall. Willie Mays, Number Twenty-four. Double dozen. It became a code word for a meeting there between Harry and Don Landeta.

"What do you think Mays would be making if he was playing now?" Landeta asked, when he came up behind Dymes.

"There's not that much money left in baseball, Don. What's up?"

Landeta swivelled his head around before saying, "I had a visitor this morning. FBI agent Tom McNab. He asked me a lot of questions, Harry. About you. About our *relationship*."

"What'd you tell him?"

"That we're engaged, but the date hasn't been set yet." Landeta scanned the area again. "Let's walk."

They wandered over to McCovey Cove, the basin behind right field where fans in everything from inner tubes, to kayaks, to million-dollar yachts waited for a home run ball from the likes of Barry Bonds to splash into the freezing bay water.

They stopped to watch two young boys fishing for perch from the pier. "McNab is a mental midget, but he's dangerous, Harry. All those FBI jokers are dangerous, and you know why."

Dymes didn't bother giving an answer. Local and state police agencies envied the Bureau's seemingly unlimited budget. They had all the latest "gee whiz" gadgets, and no difficulty calling in extra manpower, and, despite all the recent embarrassing disclosures, still had the best centralized crime lab and criminal statistic database known to man.

"Just what did McNab say, Don?"

Landeta had given up smoking right after his near-fatal accident, but that didn't stop his hands from unconsciously patting his jacket pockets when he was nervous. "Just hints. 'You and Dymes. Are you doing business together? Is he supplying you with confidential records, Mr. Landeta? What are you providing him in return?' Stuff like that. Hell, anyone who's ever watched an old *Rockford Files* episode on TV figures that every private eye has at least one cop who gets him rap sheets."

"Did he mention anyone's name?"

"Kiryl Chapaev. The FBI won't be able to trace my credit card requests, or the phone numbers I pulled for you—I've got too many firewalls in place. I was so pissed at McNab that I put him through the database wringer, hoping to find him in trouble somewhere, but he's squeaky clean. Married, two kids, lives in a townhouse in Walnut Creek. Saturday night dinners at some Italian restaurant over there. Pretty damn boring."

"Isn't it dangerous looking into an FBI agent's record, Don?"

"Nah. Databases don't care if you're a cop, a priest, or a United States senator. You use a credit card, open up a loan, they've got you—and so do I. That name you gave me early this morning, Zivon Yudin. I didn't get a chance to run anything on him."

Harry handed Landeta three driver's license–records printouts. "Lay off of Yudin for now. We had better stop playing Rockford for a while. You may be able to hide behind your firewalls, but if the FBI decides to audit the department computer I've been using to pick up those criminal and driver's records for you, I'm in a heap of trouble."

"I agree." Landeta quickly pocketed the printouts, then said, "McNab thought he was being cute, Harry. He asked me a couple of times if I knew about your army record. 'Did Dymes get rich in the army?' He mentioned something about you and a sergeant, what the hell was the name? Winsoki, Winocki, something like that. What was he talking about?"

One of the young boys let out a loud yelp and began reeling in his line. His buddy leaned over the pier with a net and, using both hands, pulled up a three-foot thrasher shark.

"McNab's just fishing," Harry finally said. "I'll let you know when things have cooled down."

Harry Dymes drove straight home, his eyes flicking to the rearview mirror every few seconds. He stowed the Honda in the garage, checked the answering machine, slipped out of his suit coat, then took a cold Anchor Steam beer from the refrigerator. He carried the beer up to the terraced rooftop. The clear fiberglass fencing protected his myriad of rosebushes from the full force of the wind.

The gravel flooring was covered with redwood decking, on top of which sat dozens of rosebushes in wine barrels and all shapes and sizes of clay pots.

As a child, Harry had reluctantly helped his mother with her rooftop roses, thinking of it as a chore, something to get over with as quickly as possible, so that he could get out on the streets and play ball. After her death, he had continued to care for the roses, more for his father's sake than anything else. The sight of the blooming buds every spring seemed to bring back those happy days for his father. Surprisingly, at least to Harry, he'd grown fond of gardening. It was one of the reasons he'd bought the house on Vermont Street. The roof was perfect for roses.

Harry rolled up his sleeves and used a pruning shear to groom the bushes, sipping the beer as he did his "chores," and thinking of Sergeant Joe Winocki. Winocki was a regular army Special Forces master sergeant who'd been raised in the tough Hamtramck Polish section of Detroit. Thicknecked with a hooked nose and walrus mustache, at first he hadn't taken to nursemaiding a called-up reservist like Harry during their stint in February of 1991 in Scud Alley, near Al Qaim, in the northern section of Iraq. But they soon grew close, the way men in combat do.

They were a team, whose mission was to go in ahead of the troops, map the area, locate missile launchers, fixing the location by bouncing signals off a satellite from their handheld transmitters, then relay the data back to U. S. headquarters, which sent a screaming F-15 to bomb the launcher and anyone within three hundred yards to smithereens.

The winter weather had surprised Harry—high fifties during the day, dropping down to the mid-thirties at night. They carried all of their gear in a special dune buggy that could do more than sixty miles an hour in the slippery Iraqi sand. Winocki was fluent in Arabic, a result of his Detroit childhood and army language courses.

It had been late afternoon when Harry spotted the lone car speeding down what passed for a highway in that section of Iraq. He'd handed the binoculars to Winocki. "A stretch Mercedes, Joey. Let's take it out."

Winocki screwed the binoculars into his eyes. He scanned the desert and then the cloudy gray skies. "I don't see any protection. But that don't mean it's not there."

Harry lay down in the sand and adjusted the telescopic sight on the .50 caliber Barrett semiautomatic sniper rifle. "Who knows who's in the car? It could be Saddam himself. Intelligence claims that he likes to get out and visit the troops."

"Army Intelligence," Winocki scoffed. "The oxymoron of all times. You believe what those assholes tell you and you'll never live to get your pension."

"I say we take it out," Harry said. "That's what we're here for, isn't it? To destroy the enemy."

"Yeah, and to keep our asses in two pieces. We hit the limo and a thousand camel jockeys come humping out of those sand dunes and fall in love with us. An ugly old guy like me, Harry, they'd probably take one look, skin me alive, slow-roast me over the coals for a couple of days, then feed me to the dogs. But a good-looking guy like you, they'd be poundin' your swollen colon till next Christmas."

Harry clicked the scope's lens until the hood of the Mercedes was centered in the yellow-lined crosshairs. "He's a mile away, Joe. I've got about ten seconds to make the shot. Yes, or no?"

Winocki scraped at his week-old beard. "It *could* be Saddam. Or one of his cuddly sons. I've heard they deliver money, gold, Swiss watches to the troops, instead of medals, to keep up their spirits."

"Who told you that?" Harry asked, his index finger caressing the rifle trigger.

"Your buddies in Intelligence. They could have some chow on board, too, Harry. I'm sick of those so-called ready-to-eat meals. And coffee. Thermoses of hot coffee. And some *real* intelligence documents about what these shitheads are up to."

"That's good enough for me," Harry said, curling his finger back.

The muffled crack of the 2.5-inch armor-piercing bullet echoed off the sand dunes. The bullet impacted the Mercedes with the force of a small rocket, causing the big car to swerve around in a tight hundred-and-eighty-degree turn. Harry fired again, and the Merc jerked sideways, than rolled over, landing on its side.

"Let's go, partner," Winocki yelled, running for the dune buggy.

The odd thing about that whole incident was that nearly everything he and Winocki had joked about turned out to be true. When they'd arrived at the Mercedes they found two dead men—the driver, a skinny youngster in the uniform of an Iraqi private, and a portly middle-aged man in a gray suit. The crash had killed them both. It had also torn the center of the stretch limo apart. Under the white Carrara marble floorboard was a cache of twenty-seven gold bars.

Gray Suit's hefty briefcase held several folders marked *Safqa*—an Arabic word that meant *secret arrangement*. There were also hundreds of gold coins—Chinese "Pandas," Krugerrands, Saudi Arabian guineas, U.S. gold eagles, more than a dozen Swiss watches, a picnic basket of food and a large Thermos of coffee.

The two of them had loaded the gold bars and briefcase into the dune buggy, the vehicle's tires sinking into the sand under the weight of the gold, then sped off into the vast, desolate desert.

When they were miles away from the Mercedes, they parked and, for the briefest moments, considered themselves filthy rich.

Winocki used the tape measure etched onto the blade of his assault knife to measure the gold bars: 7 inches, by 3.6 inches, by 1.75 inches. It wasn't until they were back in Saudi Arabia that they learned the correct terminology was *bricks*. They had no way to weigh the bricks, but their estimate of thirty pounds was pretty close: twenty-seven and a half pounds per brick—four hundred troy ounces.

Their celebration was short-lived—how the hell were they going to get them back home to the good old U. S.

of A.? The coins were easy enough to conceal in their canteens and various assault packs and rucksacks. Dymes had settled on one watch, a Rolex Yachtsman, while Winocki had braided a half dozen watches on each arm, from wrist to elbow.

They finally used a survival kit hacksaw on four of the bricks, slicing the gold into one-inch slabs, and taping them to their bodies. Two bricks each—fifty-five pounds of gold. The rest they buried. "That's one thing the army taught me well, Harry. How to dig holes."

Winocki vowed that they'd come back—together—after the war, and dig them up.

Harry knew that was never going to happen. He was damn near certain that they'd never get out of Saudi Arabia with the gold on their backs, arms, legs, chests, and stomachs.

The pilot of the MH-53J Pave Low rescue helicopter that picked them up two days later made a crack about them looking like they'd put on weight. "You guys must love those MREs. Either that or you've been eating camel meat."

Back at the base in Kuwait, Winocki went to work. They had four days of leave before they were due to return to the desert. The price of gold then was three hundred and seventeen dollars per ounce. Dymes never asked how, but the master sergeant was able to move all the gold they had brought back with them: fifteen hundred and eighty-six ounces, at a price of two-hundred forty American dollars an ounce. A total of $380,640.00. Payment was made with a cashier's check, which Winocki deposited in a newly opened account in the Saudi-Holland Bank. After a ten-thousand-dollar transaction fee that Winocki paid for with some of the gold coins they'd taken from the Mercedes, the money was transferred to an offshore bank in Barbados.

Despite his doing all of the work, Winocki insisted that he and Harry split the money right down the middle—which—with the addition of the money made from selling the coins, totaled slightly over two hundred and ten thousand dollars for each of them.

A great deal of money, but Harry didn't think it was enough to risk a general court-martial, jail time, and loss of his civilian job. He regretted everything, except the medal he and Winocki were going to be awarded for bringing in the battle plans found in the briefcase.

Winocki had watched him like a hawk, and Harry felt that he could end up on the wrong end of a fragging incident—a hand grenade rolled into his quarters, or a bullet in the back of his neck.

The morning they were due to go back on special patrol, Winocki suffered an attack of appendicitis. At least that's what Harry was told. He was assigned a new partner, and his patrol area was shifted several hundred miles from where the gold bricks were buried.

Two weeks later the war was over. Three weeks after that Harry Dymes was back working as a San Francisco policeman. There'd been no word from Joe Winocki, but Harry wasn't really worried. Winocki was not the kind of man who would make an enemy of a trained sniper.

It was a Saturday when the thick package arrived from FedEx. Twenty-one nicely wrapped, ten-thousand-dollar packets of hundred-dollar bills, and a hand-printed note:

Harry: went back to where we had that picnic, but the food was gone. Someone beat us to it.

Harry had been smart with the money—slowly feeding it into his checking and savings accounts, taking trips to the gambling casinos in nearby Reno and Lake Tahoe, establishing large lines of credit, so that if questioned, he could always say that he'd gotten lucky at the crap tables. He was in the midst of his first divorce from Eva at the time, so she knew nothing about it. He used part of the money to put a down payment on the house on Vermont Street, doubling up the mortgage payments every month.

Everything had gone perfectly smoothly until fourteen months ago when a young, not very bright lieutenant from U.S. Army Intelligence had stopped by the homicide detail to ask questions about Master Sergeant Joseph Winocki, Retired, who had died in a boating accident in Lake of the Woods, Minnesota. At first this was of little interest to the army; however, when Winocki's estate was found to include two solid gold bricks in his safe-deposit box and a portfolio worth close to three million dollars, their interest increased.

Harry had given a written statement declining knowledge of Winocki's off-duty activities, and that had been the end of it—he thought. Now the FBI was sticking their upturned noses into it.

Harry drained what was left of the beer and made his way downstairs. He'd have to be much nicer to Marta Citron from now on.

New Orleans, Louisiana
National Finance Center

"Well, well, well, look who has decided to grace us with her presence," Howard Hughson said, twisting around in his swivel chair to smile at Trina Lee. "God, how I envy you. How often do you come to the office? Twice a month? Less than that?"

Hughson was a disheveled man with mud-colored hair and an egg-shaped paunch. He was technically Trina's superior at the NFC, but he treated her, and everyone else in the office, in a lighthearted manner that endeared him to the majority of his fellow workers.

Trina wasn't part of that majority. She distrusted anyone who found contentment in being a low-level bureaucrat, although Hughson's nonchalant management style suited her perfectly.

"I was here two weeks ago, Howard. Haven't my reports been arriving in a timely manner?"

"Most timely," Hughson said, turning his attention back to the computer. "I just wish I could lie in the sun and do my work like you do." He gave Trina what he thought was a charming smile. "I like the suntan. Where was it this time? Hawaii? Miami Beach?"

"My sundeck at home," Trina said, parking her laptop on the edge of Hughson's desk. It was ten minutes past five o'clock, and the twenty-plus workers in Hughson's domain had left for the day.

She had monitored Hughson from the hallway, and waited until he was alone before making her entrance. He had a habit of sticking around fifteen to thirty minutes at the close of the business day.

"You may envy my working conditions, Howard, but remember, I don't have any of your perks: sick leave, paid vacations, and fantastic retirement benefits."

Trina was one of the growing list of independent contractors the federal government had hired to cut down on expenses. She filed her work through what the government considered a totally secure e-mail gateway.

The NFC, a part of the U.S. Agriculture Department, was the nation's largest bookkeeper, keeping tabs on payroll deductions and vacation time for many of the government's largest agencies.

"Poor Trina," Hughson said dryly. "Somehow I think you'll make do. You know, you really are a chameleon. Every time I see you, you look a little different. What is it this time?" He ran his eyes over Trina. "The hair—lighter, isn't it? It looks good."

He started to log off from the computer, but Trina laid a hand on his shoulder and said, "Do me a favor, Howard. Stay online, so I won't have to go through all that rigamarole of logging in. I'll just need thirty minutes or so to post the data on the new payroll withholding forms you asked for."

Hughson shrugged his shoulders. "I guess that's okay," he said, getting to his feet and slipping on his suit jacket.

"Anything new going on?" Trina asked, sliding into his chair.

"More work. The NFC is taking over the payroll for the Department of Homeland Security. You know what that means—another half-million employee records. I've been working on the new software. Do you have any idea how much some of those DHS people are being paid? We're talking two hundred thou a year for the middle management."

Hughson stuffed a sheaf of paper into his battered leather briefcase. "That's more than your former colleagues in the FBI are making." He snapped the case closed. "Tell me the truth. Aren't you ever sorry you left the FBI?"

"Never," Trina answered truthfully. Her time at the Bureau had been rewarding in many ways, especially when she realized that she could access the records—and locations—of those individuals the Bureau had placed in the Witness Security Program. "I was just a glorified accountant there. Like I am here."

"Come on," Hughson coaxed as he headed for the exit, "tell me where you really got that tan."

"Las Vegas, Howard," she said, though the truth was that the sun-kissed color had come from a bottle. She'd left Vegas—as Alex—under a coating of pale makeup. Losing Ying Fai's men at the airport had not been difficult; she'd slipped into a restroom, donned a blond wig and bright red stretch jersey that had been secreted in her baggy pants, and took a cab back to the room she'd booked at the Forbidden City.

There she'd sipped bottled mineral water and listened in on the "day bugs" she'd sprinkled around Ying Fai's penthouse suite.

The bugs, tiny silicone marvels the size of peppercorns, transmitted a weak signal for up to twenty-four hours, then simply ran out of juice.

Trina's main concern was that one of the hotel maids would vacuum them up before she was able to hear Fai's plans. She had to listen to the comical moans and sexual encouragements mouthed by Fai's girlfriend Rita, but was rewarded when Danny Shu returned to the penthouse and admitted he'd lost Alex at the airport. Fai's chilling reply, to get rid of her—*I despise arrogant women*—made Trina's next decision an easy one. She'd find Tarasove for the Triad boss, take his money, and disappear.

"Have a safe ride home, Howard," she said. "I'll see you in a week or so."

He waggled a finger at her. "I'll take that as a promise, because I believe you owe me a lunch."

Trina settled down at the computer and posted the information Hughson had requested.

When she was finished, she stood up, stretched, and walked to the sealed-in windows, looking out at the parking lot, making sure that Hughson's dark green Volvo station wagon was gone from its slot.

She hurried back to the computer and quickly navigated her way to the NFC's files relating to the FBI travel system and transportation chits.

Spotting Roger Dancel at the Vegas casino had been a mixed blessing. She recognized him right away, but what was a senior Bureau official doing on what should have been a routine surveillance job? It could only mean that the Bureau had penetrated Ying Fai's organization, that they knew that she—Alex—was going to meet with Fai.

Back in the days when she was working for the FBI, Trina had spent a long, sweaty weekend with Dancel at her Alexandria, Virginia apartment.

Dancel had been a bore, as well as a lousy lover; however, she had decided to cultivate him, because he was in charge of the Witness Security Progam—WSP—in the government's alphabet soup of agencies.

Dancel had fallen into a deep sleep after a long night of kinky sex, drinking, and smoking some excellent dope that he'd brought, allowing Trina the opportunity to gain entree to his laptop, which enabled her to learn the identity of the majority of the two hundred-plus agents working for him, as well as the names of the people in the witness protection program.

The minor league defectors were provided with a new legend—name, Social Security number, papers, an income stream—then patted on the back and told to behave like good little boys and girls.

A prize like Nicolai Tarasove was an entirely different project. First, he'd be taken to one of the half-dozen FBI camps sprinkled around the country, and thoroughly debriefed. Only then would he be given his new legend and residence.

There had been times when Trina was successful in tracing the subject simply by following the FBI babysitters' expense chits and travel vouchers. On other occasions she'd had to dig deeper—tracing them to a town, a neighborhood, then relying on the subject's profile to lead her to her prey. Whether the target was a foreign defector or a New York Mafia turncoat, they all had their individual personalities—their appetites, be it for sex, reading material, hobbies, or favorite foods. Things that they simply couldn't do without.

Trina had once tracked a New York City hit man the FBI had relocated to an Atlanta suburb through his penchant for a daily meal of beef brisket on a potato pancake with gravy and applesauce. Trina had found the one deli in the suburb that served the brisket—and sure enough, he had strolled through the deli's front door on her first day of surveillance.

A Russian defector resettled in a farming community outside of Des Moines, Iowa—his downfall had been his love of beluga caviar. He was the only person in the entire area who ordered the expensive fish eggs in one-pound tins.

From what Ying Fai had told her, Tarasove was an ardent hunter, compulsive gambler, and womanizer. His work involved snake venom, so he'd be provided with a complete laboratory and supplied with all of his needs. And, most importantly, he'd be monitored on a regular basis.

The WSP was stocked with specialists who handled the subject by his or her language and ethnic needs: Chinese, Latin American, Eastern and Western European, and, of course, Russian.

Howard Hughson's computer had access to sites Trina simply could not access via her laptop. She was careful not to venture into any FBI files that would catch a "watcher's" attention. Her focus was on Dancel's travel vouchers and Bureau credit card charges, which were so up-to-date that they included his travel expenses to Las Vegas and a just-booked flight to San Francisco, California.

She scrolled through the data, finding a thread of travel that interested her. Nearly every month for the past two years, on the fifteenth day of the month, Roger Dancel flew from Dulles Airport to Reno, Nevada. A turnaround flight. Dancel rented a car at the airport, never staying the night.

Trina modemed over to the NFC's computer library tape and searched for Dancel's travel records at the time of Nicolai Tarasove's abduction from Kiev. There were four additional agents with Dancel at the time, including one who died in the hotel shoot-out. One of the agents was a woman—Marta Citron. Dancel had bragged to Trina about all of the female FBI agents that he'd seduced. She went back to the travel and credit records and entered Citron's name. Just a few days ago, Citron had taken a flight to Reno from Dulles. A rental car at the Reno airport, which was turned in at the rental agency's downtown San Francisco location.

Marta Citron. She'd come across the name before, but she couldn't put a face to it.

Trina printed out the latest travel vouchers and credit records for both Dancel and Citron. While the printer was spitting out the reports, she leaned back in the chair and pictured a map showing the distance from Reno to San Francisco.

A thought suddenly occurred to her. Ying Fai hadn't gone into specifics regarding Tarasove's scientific projects, other than to say that his work required a great number of poisonous snakes. Where did the Russian get his snakes? What did the reptiles eat? Mice? Rats? Who supplied those?

She leaned forward and was about to put those questions to the computer when a voice startled her.

"You gonna be here long, ma'am?"

Trina bolted to her feet, assuming a *jodan no kamae* stance, her hands in a clawing position.

The heavyset cleaning woman stumbled backward as she held a mop up in front of her in self-defense.

"I'm so sorry," Trina said. "You scared me coming up like that."

"Not as much as you scared me, ma'am," the woman said breathlessly.

"I'm just leaving," Trina said, exiting the computer and removing the paper from the printer. "It's been a long day."

"My day's just starting, ma'am, and you ain't making it any easier."

Chapter Twelve

Moscow, Russia

Sasha Veronin stirred a spoonful of raspberry jam into his cup of tea and strolled to the window looking out on Tverskaya Street—Moscow's Broadway, according to the tourist guides. His eye wandered over the wedding-cake structures dating back to Stalin's era, then to the modern skyscrapers housing the Marriott and Sheraton Hotels, and the posh buildings filled with stores that rivaled those of any of the capital cities in America.

Ah, capitalists. He blessed the fools who had rushed in to establish a so-called free market after communism fell and Boris Yeltsin came to power. They had neglected the one sacred covenant of a true free market—it needed the rule of law to survive. And there were no rules, no laws, at least none that could rein in a man such as he—the most powerful Mafia figure in Russia, the undisputed head of the *Organizatsiya.*

Sasha was a florid-faced man with drooping shoulders and a bulging stomach. There were balloons of scar tissue over each eye. He wore his gray-brown hair in a lion's-mane style. He had come to power in the way that men like him had always done: inflicting pain, spreading terror.

He'd worked his way up from a *fartsovchik*—a young black-market dealer—then made his first fortune in *loshadka*, the drug trade. During the chaos of the early Yeltsin years, he had turned his terror on the city's wealthiest bankers and businessmen. The profits were enormous, but once you looted a company or bank, what did you have? A dead company—an empty bank. He had become familiar with the ways of the West—earning money in dividends and the increase in the company's stock value. Gangster capitalism.

Still, there were times when he missed the old bare-knuckle days.

There was a tap on the door and his hatchet-faced secretary told him he had a phone call. "A most disagreeable man. Boris Feliks. He insists on speaking to you, Mr. Veronin."

Sasha waved her away and crossed to his desk quickly. He snatched up the phone. "Boris. *Ty moy luchshiy drug. Otkuda ty?*"

"I'm glad you still think I'm your best friend, Sasha. I'm calling from America. I won't be more specific than that."

"Come home," Sasha said. "I miss you."

"All is forgiven? I think not. Your men barely missed me with pistol shots in St. Petersburg. I'm close to Tarasove. Very close."

Sasha flopped down with a *whoosh* into an overstuffed easy chair. "You know what we used to say on the streets, Boris. Close is good with hand grenades. The man isn't important. His work is."

"His work has been perfected, Sasha. He calls it *Napitak Zlobi*, and it is indeed a devil's brew."

"How do you know all this?"

"I have spoken to one of his comrades—who is no longer able to speak to anyone."

"What is so special about this 'devil's brew'?" Sasha wanted to know.

Feliks relayed the information that Kiryl Chapaev had provided him on Tarasove's unique DNA toxin.

Veronin listened intently for a minute, then began scribbling notes on his desk notepad.

"He's tested it on lab animals. Think of the power you'd

have with such a weapon, Sasha. A magic bullet, unstoppable. And I'm the one who can get it for you."

Sasha whistled through his teeth. "Yes. I want Tarasove. Alive. Back here in Moscow."

"There are . . . complications," Feliks said.

Sasha stirred in his chair, as if to relieve a cramped muscle. "Let me guess. Money."

"Exactly."

Veronin's voice turned cold. "End the bullshit. What do you want?"

"Ten million American dollars. And the dogs called off."

Sasha stuck his index finger into the pot of jam and licked it slowly. "And if I don't agree to this?"

"You would break my heart, old friend."

"I will break more than that if you fuck me again, Boris. I have a prospective client, with money, and it isn't that Chinese prick, Ying Fai. When can you deliver Tarasove?"

"A few weeks at the most. I'll contact you soon, but I don't want to use the phone again. Do you have an Internet address?"

"Doesn't everyone? Internet, e-mail, cell telephones— how I wish we had them when we first got into this business. Remember those nights, Boris? Me breaking into a building, you outside freezing, waiting, watching for the police. And if you saw them arriving, the best you could do was beep the car horn as a warning. You can reach me at *bugor*@sitek.ru."

"*Bugor*, how appropriate," Feliks said. The translation was *the boss*—used mostly in prisons to describe the man who controlled the other criminals. He gave Sasha an Internet address he'd opened on Yahoo! that very morning. "I'll be in touch in the next few days."

"*Vesgo nailuschshego!* I wish you the best," Sasha said before breaking the connection. He stuck his finger back into the jam pot. *Ten million!* His time in America had rotted Feliks's brain. A word came to his mind. A word he hadn't used in too long: *razborka*. The settling of accounts. It was time for Boris to pay for his sins. And Sasha knew just the man to provide him with the necessary help—and the money.

Washington, D.C.

"Yes, sir," Roger Dancel said for what must have been the tenth time since he'd settled his rump in the chair in front of Deputy Director James Bartlow's desk.

Dancel felt in his heart of hearts that their positions should have been reversed—he sitting behind the desk and Bartlow coming to him for assistance.

To Dancel, Bartlow defined everything an FBI director should *not* look like: bald, double-chinned, with pendulous rose-colored lips that he'd used expertly to kiss the asses of anyone in the Bureau or Congress who could help him move up in the Bureau's hierarchy.

"The whole Las Vegas trip seems to have been a waste of time, Roger, don't you think?"

"Not necessarily. I'm certain that Ying Fai met up with Alex, but—"

"You still don't have a clue as to what Alex looks like." Bartlow steepled his fingers and looked at Dancel over the tips. "It's rather embarrassing. We've spent a tidy sum of money on this operation, and have come up with diddly-squat."

"We know Alex exists, sir," Dancel insisted. "And we have pretty solid information that Alex was the one who eliminated Gravini, Checco, and Noel Wong."

" 'Pretty solid information' just won't do, Roger. Gravini and Checco were both Mafia targets. Any number of *cugines* or buttons could have clipped them."

"True," Dancel said, unimpressed by Bartlow's attempts to include Mafia slang in his conversation. A *cugine* was a young punk trying to become a made man and wouldn't be trusted to handle a hit on two important mob informants, while a "button" was already there—a true wiseguy. "No one in the mob had the smarts to track them down. Gravini had been living in a Miami suburb and Checco in Denver."

"And Noel Wong in Seattle," Bartlow said. He licked his fat lips, then continued. "Wong had no mob connections—the New York Triad was after him."

"I think we've got a meat eater, sir," Dancel said, relishing the look of confusion on Bartlow's face. *Meat eater* was mob talk for a corrupt cop. "Alex is a freelancer, working for the mob, the triads, anyone who will come up with enough money. We've also lost four Russian defectors, who were provided with impeccable new identities, in the last two years. Two disappeared, the others appear to have suffered accidental deaths."

Bartlow pinched the bulge under his chin. "Meat eater. You mean—"

"Someone working for us is moonlighting as a contract killer, sir."

"But . . . how could one person develop addresses for all of them? Each had a different team set up their new profiles."

"It's a mystery, sir. That's why I wanted to draw it to your attention. If Alex is a meat eater, we have to work fast to catch him before he gets to Nicolai Tarasove."

Bartlow groaned out loud. "The Director himself has spoken of Tarasove's importance to the nation's defense. Why would anyone, the Russians, the Chinese, want Tarasove killed?"

"They wouldn't kill him until they made him give up the details of his toxin formulas."

Bartlow surveyed his fingernails. "Who do we have working Tarasove now?"

"I visit him every month, but the only one he really trusts is Marta Citron. She's in San Francisco, looking into Kiryl Chapaev's murder."

"I read your report." Bartlow sighed. "You're certain it was Boris Feliks?"

"It seems logical. And the fact that Feliks has gotten this close to Tarasove is disturbing." Dancel nodded at his report sitting in front of Bartlow. "That's why I suggest that Tarasove be moved someplace where we can control him, and monitor his work on a day-to-day basis. It's ill-advised to allow a man with his expertise to be completely on his own, sir. He was meeting with Kiryl Chapaev without our permission. I've ordered a team in Los Angeles to check out what Chapaev has been up to."

Dancel admired his choice of words: *ill-advised*. If the shit hit the fan, he'd be on record as having been on the side of the angels.

"I don't disagree with your suggestion," Bartlow said. "However, we can't just kidnap him and lock him up."

"Why not?" Dancel asked, his voice dropping down to a confidential whisper. "If Tarasove were a terrorist, a danger to the country, we'd sweep him up in a second. He could make a deal with some Mideast crazies, or with the Chinese or Koreans, or go back to Russia. The GRU would forgive him for past sins and welcome him with open arms, just to get their hands on his formulas."

Bartlow opened his mouth, then snapped it shut. He thought for a moment before saying, "Tarasove is . . . fond of Agent Citron, isn't he?"

"Very fond." Dancel's report had included the fact that Tarasove went so far as to frequent a prostitute who looked like Marta. "Very fond indeed."

"Until we can find Feliks, and Alex, Agent Citron should stay with him at his place in Lake Tahoe. Around the clock, twenty-four/seven."

Dancel gave a tight smile. "The last time I spoke to Agent Citron she specifically told me that she did not want to be a babysitter for him."

"Citron's performed babysitting roles before. It goes with the job. I want you out there, supervising this, Roger. If Citron gives you any trouble, have her contact me. Do whatever you have to do. If worse comes to worst, we may have to relocate Tarasove. Whether he likes it or not."

Tom McNab popped his head into Marta Citron's office. "You've got a phone call. Someone calling himself 'Snake Charmer.'"

Marta turned her back on McNab to keep him from seeing the look on her face. "Thank you," she said nonchalantly, picking up the phone.

Nicolai Tarasove sounded as if he'd been drinking. "Marta. You never called. How are things going there? Have you found Feliks?"

"Not yet. You shouldn't be calling me. When there is something to report, I'll contact you. Roger Dancel told me that you and Kiryl Chapaev had been e-mailing each other. That means that Chapaev could have given Feliks the address. Have you been monitoring your mail?"

"He would never try e-mailing me," Tarasove protested quickly.

Too quickly? Marta wondered. She heard a loud howl in the background.

"That's Jedgar," Tarasove slurred. "Like me, he misses you. Call me soon."

Citron put the telephone gently back on its cradle and sat staring at it. Was Feliks monitoring Chapaev's Internet address? Would he make contact, and to spook him, lure him into a trap? Was there a way that she could turn the tables on Feliks?

She was reaching for the phone when it rang. She picked it up, said her name, and was somewhat surprised when Inspector Harry Dymes invited her out to dinner.

Zivon Yudin squinted under the bright lighting as he hunched over the ATM keypad. He studied a piece of paper in one hand, looked off to his right, and cupped his ear. He then nodded his head and punched the keypad again. Moments later he stepped back and said, *"Sotnya grina ni za khuy sobachy—podi khuevo,"* as the ATM tray began filling up with money.

"Do you have any idea what he just said, Inspector?"

Harry Dymes turned to look at the bank manager who had been good enough to let him view the ATM videotape from the night of Kiryl Chapaev's murder—without having to use a subpoena. "He said, 'To get money for nothing— cool, isn't it'?"

Harry watched as Yudin pocketed the money, smiling at someone off camera. Someone wise enough to be well out of camera range. It was a replay of what had taken place at the first two ATMs Yudin and his accomplice had hit that night—Yudin reading off of a piece of paper and slowly, painfully punching in Morris's PIN, collecting the money and moving on.

"Do you think you'll catch him, Inspector?" the manager asked as he ushered Harry out of the bank.

"Oh, yes. I'm certain we will. Thanks again for all your help."

Dymes stood on the corner of Mason and Geary Streets, observing the early evening pedestrians. One of San Francisco's infrequent heat spells was in the process of warming up to the mid-nineties. All of a sudden the tourists didn't look so out of place in their Bermuda shorts and floppy Hawaiian shirts—it was the natives in their business suits, long dresses, heavy sweaters, and Windbreakers who were suffering from the Tarzan heat. Tempers flared as the temperature climbed: small arguments became knife fights; minor fender benders turned into road rage battles; elderly men looked up into the smoggy yellow air and claimed it was "earthquake weather" and begged for San Francisco's natural air conditioner—the fog—to stream back through the Golden Gate and blanket the town in a cool, gray mist.

Harry took off his suit jacket and draped it over his shoulder. He now had a definite connection between Yudin and the murder of Morris/Chapaev, but nothing on the man who Yudin was working for—no doubt the man who killed him.

He was a careful one. He'd let Yudin face the bank's cameras. And didn't speak loud enough to be overheard. A true professional. Except that he had hooked up with an oaf like Yudin. Why?

Dymes turned into Lefty O'Doul's, a *hofbrau* decorated with photographs of legendary baseball players. He found an open stool at the bar and nursed a draft beer as he tried to put the pieces in place—at least the pieces he had in hand. One of his father's "secret pleasures" was reading detective stories, especially Rex Stout's Nero Wolfe series. Harry had read them too, enjoying the New York scenes, and the byplay between Wolfe and his sidekick, Archie Goodwin. Usually, Wolfe didn't know who the murderer was until the final few pages of the book. Before that he was referred to as "X."

Harry marked an X on a cocktail napkin. Then he penciled in what he knew of his X. Speaks Russian. A pro. Killed Morris/Chapaev by accident—according to the coroner.

Harry stared at his reflection in the bar mirror. X came here to kill Morris/Chapaev. Lana Kuzmin, the fortune-teller, said that Zivon Yudin had left the city months ago. So X used Yudin for a reason—because Yudin was familiar with the city. So X is a stranger here. That could be good. He'd have to rely on maps, tour guides, or find another Yudin. Was X still here? Maybe killing Morris and Yudin completed his mission. Where would he go?

Harry turned the napkin over, and scribbled: *Did X call me at the Hall of Justice? Give me Morris's real name?* He looked at himself in the mirror, seemingly expecting the image to reply to the question. I know X killed Morris/ Chapaev. I'm betting he killed Zivon Yudin, too. Why give me Morris's real name, if he was the killer?

He crumpled up the napkin and drained the remains of his beer. It made no sense. At least not yet.

Harry glanced at his watch. Almost five o'clock, which gave him time to go home and change for dinner. And water the roses. The heat was hell on his roses.

Chapter Thirteen

"This place is known as the vegetarian's antichrist," Harry Dymes said after the waiter had seated him and Marta Citron at a comfortable table in the rear of the dining room at Ruth's Chris Steak House.

Marta looked around the room: dark wood walls, dim lighting. "I'm tired of Lean Cuisine, and in the mood for a good steak, Caesar salad, and a Bombay Sapphire martini," Marta said. "That's why I picked this place."

"Sounds good, but let's reverse the order," Harry said, calling over their waiter, a tuxedoed middle-aged man who had introduced himself as Brian. He had the confident, easygoing manner of someone who knew his business, and made a good living because of it.

"The Bureau is paying for this," Marta told Harry as she snapped her napkin and settled it neatly on her lap.

"I can live with that." Harry admired the way she looked, her hair slightly windblown, her makeup kept to a minimum. She wore a black jacket and skirt, white silk blouse, accented by an off-the-shoulder zebra scarf. Businesslike, professional. But there was no way for her to tone down her sexuality.

The waiter brought their drinks, and Harry raised his in a toast. "To your expense account."

"To our mutual cooperation," Marta said pointedly, before sipping her drink.

"I'd be a lot more cooperative if you'd call off the tail you have on me," Harry said, plucking the lemon twist from his glass.

"Tail? You've got to be kidding. It's not us. A jealous husband?"

Harry let the crack pass. "I like your outfit. Is it a Ferranti?"

"A poor agent such as myself couldn't afford to buy your ex-wife's stuff. And my father was a career diplomat, not a tailor." Marta ran her hand across her jacket's lapel. "I have to rely on dear old JCPenney." She held up her arm and waved her wristwatch at him. "This came from Penney's too, and it's not Swiss."

"Diplomat? For which country?" Harry said, enjoying the sparring.

"We're from the heartland. Kansas. My dad was a junior diplomat, and held some pretty interesting postings: Paris, Berlin, London. He was overworked and underpaid, but it provided me with an interesting education."

Marta told Harry of some amusing incidents that took place during her childhood: the constant traveling, being uprooted from schools in midterm—and, as she matured, learning how to fend off passes in five different languages.

She signaled to the wine steward, and the two of them took their time before she ordered a California Cabernet. "Bring the wine and let it breathe," she said, "and while we're waiting, another round of martinis."

"What did you think of my army service record?" Harry said, working on his first drink.

Citron's eyes narrowed. "What makes you think I've seen it?"

"Your boy McNab mentioned the name of an old army buddy of mine to Don Landeta. Joe Winocki. That could only have come from my army jacket."

"That dumb fucker," Marta said, loud enough to cause an elderly woman dining at an adjoining table to snap her head around and glare at her.

"I'll go along with that description. McNab leaned on Landeta pretty hard. For no reason. Don and I are old friends, nothing more."

Marta dove into her martini before responding. "Believe me, I had nothing to do with that. I was sincere when I told you that we should cooperate on this. Your file was marked for my eyes only, but obviously McNab chose to ignore that. Unfortunately, he's not under my control. I'm a visitor here, but I'll make sure the right people hear about it."

The fresh drinks came, giving them both time to marshal their thoughts.

"Okay," Harry said. "I received a phone call two days ago. I was at my desk. A man's voice. No noticeable accent. He told me the real name of the murdered man in the St. Charles Hotel was Kiryl Chapaev. You saw the coroner's report. There was nothing at the crime scene to provide any identification on Chapaev. All I had was the Paul Morris name from the hotel records."

"Did you tape-record the call?" Marta asked.

"No can do. We're not equipped. Unless someone leaves a message on my answering machine, it's not possible to tape incoming calls."

Citron did that narrowing-of-the-eyes gesture. "I kid you not," Harry assured her. "We're a few eons behind the times when it comes to electronic equipment."

"Could you make a guess as to the caller's age?"

"Not a kid, not an old man. Anywhere from thirty to fifty is as close as I can come. He told me he was in the building. The lobby pay phone. I told him to wait for me." Harry began buttering a slice of sourdough bread. "When I got there, he was gone. If he was ever there in the first place. Any ideas on who the caller was?"

Citron sipped her gin thoughtfully before responding. "Chapaev was a former Russian scientist. We placed him in Southern California, and gave him the Paul Morris cover. Somehow, someone penetrated that cover."

"How valuable was Chapaev's work as a structural biologist?"

"Who told you that?" Citron asked sharply.

"Chapaev dated a hooker, Julie Renton, just before he was murdered. They had dinner at a restaurant in North Beach. He told her he was a structural biologist. She hasn't a clue what that means."

"I want to talk to this woman."

"It'll be a waste of your time," Harry said. "I'll give you a copy of her statement. She had dinner with the man she knew as Paul Morris. They went back to the hotel, she did her duty and took a cab home. I've verified all of it."

"I still want to talk to Renton," Marta insisted.

Harry shrugged his indifference. "I've been thinking about the man who called me. Why call and run away like that? What if he is the killer? He gives me Chapaev's real name—for what reason? Because he wanted to see what the policeman who was investigating the case looked like."

The waiter brought their Caesar salads. After he had performed the mandatory pepper mill grinding, Marta said, "Why would that be of any interest to him?"

"So he could follow me around. If you're telling the truth, and it wasn't McNab or another FBI agent trailing me, it could have been X."

"X?" Marta said with an amused grin.

"The murderer. He wanted to see what I'd do with the information on Chapaev."

Marta shifted in her chair. "I don't buy it. Did you actually spot a tail?"

"No. It was just a feeling. But I trust my feelings."

"Do you think you're still being tailed?"

"Not since last night. I've made sure of that."

Marta speared a crouton with her fork. "Did you get those feelings when you were a sniper in Iraq?"

"When it's just you and a buddy surrounded by thousands of bad guys, you develop a sixth sense, or you don't last long."

"Why a sniper, Harry?"

"It was the army's decision, not mine. It turns out I'm what the military calls a natural shooter. A sergeant at boot camp saw my target scores and the next thing I knew I was sent to Fort Bragg in North Carolina for special training."

"The army put you through a thorough psychological profile."

"Which you've read," Harry said, tasting the salad. When Citron didn't respond, Harry said, "Tell me about myself. Or at least the army's version."

"They considered you a loner, natural marksman, physically and mentally tough. And motivated. There was a notation about your mother, who was deaf, being murdered in an alley when you were a young boy in Brooklyn. That had to be awfully traumatic for you. Was her killer ever caught?"

"Yes. A hype who had been paroled two weeks before the incident. A New York cop put a lot of effort into it. All of that was before DNA and crime lab miracles. He used old-fashioned legwork."

Marta frowned, hesitated, and for a moment seemed to be searching for words. "The army sent you to a CIA training base at Harvey Point, Connecticut. That intrigued me, so I checked it out. You went there to learn lipreading. Have you kept up on it?"

"It's come in handy. My mother was an expert at it." Harry kept his lip-reading skills low-key—not many of his fellow policemen even knew about it.

Marta glanced to her left. "Two tables over. The older man in the blue blazer, talking to an attractive silver-haired woman wearing a yellow dress. They seem to be having a heated conversation. What's it about?"

Harry studied the couple for a few minutes. "His name is Arnold, hers is Irene. He's a stockbroker who wants her to buy an annuity. She's not interested."

Marta's eyebrows knitted. "How do I know you're not making that up?"

"I guess you just have to trust me."

"Someone once said, 'Trust, but verify.' I'll be right back," Marta said, getting to her feet.

She approached the table with a smile. "Excuse me. But you look so very familiar. Is your name Irene?"

"Yes," the woman said, rather flustered. "I'm sorry, but I don't—"

"Irene McCarthy?"

"No. My last name is Blakely."

Marta tapped her fingers against her forehead. "I'm so embarrassed, but you look so much like my friend."

The woman accepted the explanation with a weak smile, while the man in the blue blazer held out his hand. "Arnold Talbot. Nice to meet you."

When Marta was back at their table she gave Harry a condescending bow of her head. "Very impressive."

He decided it was time to change the subject. "Why did you join the FBI?"

"Why not?" Marta said. "I was young, eager, ready to serve my country. But I didn't want to join the military."

"I had a partner when I joined the homicide detail. Nina Javiera. A beautiful woman—absolute stunner, and a damn good cop. Guys hit on her constantly: fellow cops of both sexes, district attorneys, crime lab techs, suspects, witnesses, you name it—hit, hit, hit. One bastard kept posting her unlisted phone number in phone booths. Next to the number was a notation on just how much she liked doing kinky things. I found out who it was, a sergeant she wanted nothing to do with."

"What happened to him?" Marta asked. "Internal Affairs?"

"They wouldn't have done anything. I kicked the hell out of him. You have to protect your partner. Nina knew that if she slept with just one cop, the word would be all over the department the next day. She told me when she was really horny, she'd drive to Reno, Tahoe, or down to Carmel. Meet some lucky guy who knew nothing about her and screw his brains out. She finally got fed up and quit the job. She's selling real estate in the East Bay now, and making a fortune."

"I'm sure she's still getting a lot of unwanted attention, Harry."

"Yeah. But from a better class of people. The fact that she was a homicide cop—working a man's job—seemed to make her a target for the scumbags of this world."

"Did you ever hit on her?"

"I was a happily married man," Harry said. "For the second time."

Marta ran a finger around the edge of her wineglass. "Since when does being happily married prevent cops from hitting on women?"

"It prevented this one. I just brought Nina up because I figure you're in the same boat. Are you married?"

"Been there, done that, as they say."

Harry sampled the wine, then said, "You must have a suspect in Chapaev's murder. Am I going to get a name?"

"Not yet," Marta said, noting the sparks of anger in Dymes's eyes. "I have to clear it with my boss in Washington. Harry, this is complicated. Really complicated."

"Chapaev wasn't the big target, was he? His killer was

after someone else. Someone Chapaev could lead him to. That's why he called me, hoping I'd stir things up, spook the man he's really after."

The sizzling steaks arrived and they both concentrated on their food for a while.

Finally, Citron said, "What about the other homicide victim? The man with all the tattoos."

Harry cut off a piece of the porterhouse and chewed slowly. "Zivon Yudin. He was definitely involved in Chapaev's death. He used Chapaev's credit cards at three ATMs within blocks of the St. Charles Hotel. I've seen the bank's videos of the withdrawals. Yudin is talking to someone off camera."

"Your Mr. X?" Marta said.

"Our Mr. X." Harry took out one of his business cards and printed Yudin's name. "I couldn't pull anything on him locally, though I have a contact—a gypsy who saw Yudin in San Francisco a few months ago. He reportedly took off to Los Angeles, which is where Chapaev had his Paul Morris addresses."

"I appreciate your cooperation, and I will try and give you everything I can. But I've got to clear it with Washington first. The person that X is after is a very important man."

"Another Russian scientist, who lives in San Francisco, or close by?"

"I can't tell you that."

"You just did," Harry said, rolling his napkin up. "I'll send Julie Renton's statement to you. Keep McNab away from my friends." He pushed his hand across the table. "Deal?"

"Deal," Citron confirmed with a firm shake. She opened her purse and rummaged around for her credit card. "I think we can stick Uncle Sam with a dessert, coffee and a brandy."

"A brandy sounds good."

Marta placed the order, then said, "The army was very interested in what they found in your friend Sergeant Winocki's safe-deposit box after his death."

"An intelligence officer interviewed me." Harry gave a tight smile. "But that must have been in the file."

"It was. The investigating officer had a theory that you

and Winocki found a cache of gold bricks when you were working together. Somehow he was able to smuggle some of them back to America."

"If I had been in on it, I wouldn't be working as a cop. I like my job, but if I were rich enough, I could live without it."

"There was a report of you and Winocki taking out an Iraqi unmarked vehicle. A Mercedes, loaded with intelligence reports."

"And two dead men. I didn't see any gold. Even if there had been a stash of gold bricks, there would have been no way to get them out of the desert."

"Unless you buried them, and went back after the war."

"You're making all of this sound like a grade B movie plot, Marta. The army must have checked my passport. I came back home and stayed here after the war."

Citron held the brandy snifter to eye height and studied its color. "Well, it's none of my business anyway. The army thinks your buddy got away with it, and had fun spending the money before he died."

"Sergeant Winocki was the kind of guy who knew how to have a good time."

Marta paid for the meal with her credit card, then, after their brandies, Harry offered her a ride back to "wherever you call home now," but she declined. Her temporary apartment in the Opera Plaza on Van Ness was only a few blocks from the restaurant, and she felt like she needed a short walk.

Marta followed him out to the street. As they walked their hips bumped together. Suddenly Dymes wrapped his arms around her waist and turned her around, his lips brushing hers.

She pulled her head back. "What the hell do you think you're doing?"

"I had that feeling that I'm being followed again," Harry said.

Their faces were inches apart. "You expect me to believe that?"

"Believe what you want," Harry said. He kissed her lightly on the nose.

"Are you hitting on me?" she asked somewhat breathlessly.

"Damn right," Harry responded, his lips moving closer to hers.

Marta hesitated a moment, then kissed him hungrily, her tongue dueling with his. When they broke apart, she leaned back and said, "That was nice. But not very smart. This isn't going to work, you know."

"It may not work for a lifetime, a year, a month, or a week. But for twenty minutes we could have a hell of a good time."

Marta laughed lustily. "You're nuts. I like that." She ran her hands across his chest, then down his sides.

"Come on home with me. I'll show you my rooftop roses."

Marta stepped back. "Really. We can't. Not now. When the . . . investigation is settled. Okay? I'll call you tomorrow."

"Sure you don't want that ride?"

"I'm sure."

Harry said a husky, "Good night," before turning on his heel and walking away.

Marta watched his back. A cool customer in his perfectly tailored beige linen jacket and crisp white shirt—just the thing for the heat spell, while she felt stifled in her black knit outfit. She'd brought enough clothes for only two days, and now it looked as if she'd be stuck in San Francisco for a week or more. She wondered where Dymes carried his gun. According to McNab, San Francisco cops were issued .40 caliber Beretta semiautomatics. A gun that size made a bulge no matter how well tailored a jacket was.

Dymes had offered her the information on Zivon Yudin in exchange for getting Tom McNab to leave his buddy Landeta alone. Were Landeta and Dymes in business together? If so, it was *their* business as far as she was concerned. Marta wasn't above swapping FBI information to other agencies for a look at their files. Information was currency in the intelligence game, currency that changed value every day, just like the stock market.

Dymes's Mr. X. It had to be Boris Feliks. Had Feliks been tailing Dymes, or was Harry just edgy about the FBI rattling Landeta's cage and digging through his old army files?

Solid gold bricks. Was that how Dymes paid for his lifestyle, his divorces? And if so, how could she use that information to her advantage?

The kiss. Kisses. He was damned attractive. That story about protecting his ex-partner, horny Nina. Was it just a story? A way of softening her up, proving that he was a good guy. Not the type to kiss and tell. Marta felt empathy for Nina. She'd made those weekend trips herself, going someplace where she was unknown, where there wasn't an FBI agent within miles, and having a fling with some guy she'd never see again.

How long had it been since she'd been with a man? Two months? Three? Too damn long. She still had a policy of not dating fellow agents, but that made it hard to find a nice "normal" guy. Once a date found out her background, he backed off, intimidated by her job, by the gun in her purse.

She lit up her fifth—and final—cigarette of the day when she stopped for the traffic light on Post Street and wondered what it would be like to make a living selling real estate.

Lake Tahoe, Nevada

"Hey, Santa baby. You got some good cards this time?"

Nicolai Tarasove kept his eyes focused on the two cards he'd been dealt. A nine of hearts and a nine of spades. In Texas Hold 'em poker, that was an exceptional draw. He'd been fascinated with the game since moving to the area. The rules were really quite simple. Every player was given two cards. Bets were made, then the dealer turned up three cards in the middle of the table, the "flop."

Each player used those cards in making his hand. A round of betting, then another upturned card. More bets, then the fifth and final up card, and the final round of betting. Simple. A child's game. The skill came in the betting.

Nicolai looked up and smiled at the man in the dark glasses and cowboy hat at the end of the table. "I hope so." He edged out five thousand dollars worth of chips in front of him.

The cowboy, who used the name Sundown, tilted his

head back, grinned widely and called the bet. "Santa baby's got some cards. Let's play poker, boys and girls."

There were five additional players at the table. Two folded; three called the bet.

The dealer performed the flop: six of diamonds, nine of hearts and the king of diamonds. Nicolai had three of a kind! He kept his face passive, his hands cupped around his cards.

"You gonna bet 'em?" Sundown asked. "Or you gonna fold like you usually do?"

Nicolai peeked at his cards again, tapping his fingers on the felt cloth tabletop, looking like a man who was making a difficult decision. He seemingly reluctantly pushed ten thousand dollars worth of chips onto the table.

"I like a man with guts," Sundown said, shoving out two stacks of chips. "Raise you twenty. Let's see if you got some spine under all that fat, Santa."

Two more players dropped out, but the third, a slender, elegantly dressed woman with dark-rimmed eyes, matched the pot.

They were playing a "killer" game, a hundred thousand dollar buy-in, no limit table stakes. A crowd began gathering around the table as the stakes increased. Nicolai leaned back in his chair, scratched his beard, then reached out and nudged the required chips from his pile. "Call," he said softly.

The dealer upturned the next card: the eight of clubs. No help to Nicolai, but it didn't seem to be a card that helped his opponents either.

"Still your bet," Sundown growled, tugging at his earlobe.

It was just the signal Nicolai was looking for. He'd played cards against the loudmouthed *govno* more than a dozen times in the last few months, and every time he bluffed, he tugged on his tear-shaped right earlobe.

This time Nicolai was quick and decisive. He pushed a stack of chips piled in front of him toward the center of the table. "Thirty thousand dollars."

"Then I call, Santa. How about you, darlin'?" Sundown asked the woman with the dark-rimmed eyes.

She picked up the single stack of chips in front of her and got to her feet. "I should have got out last time."

The dealer turned the final card over. The two of clubs. "Last bet," the dealer called.

Nicolai knew the pot was his right then and there. The only question was how far he could push the cowboy. He'd been on a terrible losing streak of late, and now was his time to recoup. The man was rubbing his earlobe again.

Nicolai pushed his remaining stacks of chips into the pot. "I'm all in."

Sundown quickly followed suit, matching the bet.

"Read them and weep," Nicolai said confidently, turning over his pair of nines and beaming at the cowboy.

"Goddamn it," Sundown cursed, tugging furiously at his earlobe. "And all I got is this." He flipped over his hole cards with a polished fingernail and Nicolai stared at the king of spades and king of clubs. "Where I saddle up, three kings kicks the living shit out of three nines, Santa." He let out a loud, braying laugh, then slowly tugged at his earlobe. "You let this fool you, didn't you, Santa? Thought you found my tell, huh? My tipoff. Boy, I've been living off amateurs like you all my life. No hard feelings, though." He picked up a five-hundred-dollar chip and tossed it across the table. "Buy yourself a beer, buddy."

The casino manager came up behind Nicolai, bent over and whispered in his ear, "Would you mind coming to my office, sir?"

Chapter Fourteen

Boris Feliks remembered to remove his watch this time as he passed through the Hall of Justice metal detector. He retrieved his wallet and keys from the plastic tray, stuffing them into his pockets as he observed the lobby. It was much less crowded now than it had been during the daylight hours. He'd made two visits that afternoon, touring each floor of the block-long building. The lobby housed a small district station. The uniformed officers were sealed off from the public by a double-glassed partition. There were several courtrooms and a small kiosk selling candy, newspapers, coffee, and ready-made sandwiches. The second and third floor were dominated by more courtrooms.

The fourth floor had been his point of interest. All of the detective bureaus were located there, including the homicide detail. He'd studied the men walking the halls. Most wore sport coats, a shirt and tie, the tie undone. No hats—that was a major difference between American and Russian detectives. All the Russians wore hats.

Several of the men had eyed Feliks briefly, then nodded their heads and said, "How's it goin'?" or "What's doin'?" as they hurried by, not expecting an answer.

Feliks had knelt down as if to tie his shoe, as he examined the lock on the door leading to the homicide detail.

He had to assume the door would be locked at night. A key-in-knob single-cylinder deadbolt, that he could easily pick; but getting his tools through the front entrance metal detector would be difficult.

He exited the building and toured the perimeter. There were several doors, but all were locked, or guarded by a uniformed policeman. When Feliks tried entering, he was sternly told to "Use the front entrance, buddy."

Feliks finally found the solution to his dilemma. On the north side of the structure was an interior stairway. The door leading to the stairwell had a faded sign, *Exit Only*. A fire door, he realized. To be used in case of an emergency. But the door was scratched, the area around the knob grimy with hand marks, indicating it was in constant use.

He waited some twenty minutes, and was finally rewarded when a burly man wearing a sport coat used a key to gain access through the door. Minutes later two middle-aged women came out the door, chatting to themselves, taking no notice of him. Secretaries? Woman police officers? It didn't much matter. Employees of some type who found it more convenient to use a fire exit than go through the hassle of using the front door.

He hurried to his car and retrieved a small plastic bag which contained a set of lockpicks, torque wrenches, and a roll of adhesive tape, then returned to the fire exit. The wait was shorter this time, less than five minutes. The door swung open and a frail-looking man in a rumpled business suit stepped outside.

Feliks moved quickly, catching the door before it closed. The frail-looking man turned back to look at Feliks.

"How's it goin'?" Feliks said with a smile.

The man nodded his head slightly, then said, "Hello, Inspector," and continued on his way.

Feliks made his way up the stairs to the fourth floor again, walking directly to a men's room. One of the stalls had an *Out of Order* sign on its door. He taped the plastic bag containing his lockpicks to the underlid of the toilet tank, then left the building, deciding he'd earned himself a few hours' sleep and a decent meal.

The meal had been less satisfying than he'd hoped, but Feliks felt confident. The hard part was over. He'd been monitoring the front entrance to the Hall of Justice for more than an hour. The fire exit he'd used earlier in the day was not an option now. He might wait all night and not see anyone use it. The building would be empty, except for the district station in the lobby.

He checked his watch. Five minutes past ten. Finally he spotted a group of unkempt individuals climb the front steps—young girls with dirty, matted hair and mean eyes, and older, shabbily dressed, sad-faced women—there to file reports of beatings, robberies, burglaries, stolen purses, he assumed. Or were they janitorial staff? He melted into the group, and once again went through the metal detector without a problem, without a question from the uniformed woman officer sitting next to the detector, so engrossed with a paperback book that she barely looked at him.

Feliks recalled a particular visit he'd paid to a district police station in Nizhny Novgorod, a small city some six hundred kilometers north of Moscow. Two of his colleagues had been under arrest for selling heroin. The drugs were stored in the station's basement evidence room. He'd gone in at night, pretending to be a narcotics officer who had left his keys home in his overcoat. The janitor, after a drink from Feliks's flask, let him into the evidence room. He'd pocketed the heroin and strolled out into the freezing Russian winter air. The next day his two friends were released from their cells by a furious magistrate, due to lack of evidence.

The group of women walked directly to the glass window of the stationhouse.

Felix ambled slowly behind them, then turned quickly and made for the nearest stairway. The building was eerily silent. He climbed up to the fourth floor, and, seeing it was empty, returned to the men's room and retrieved his lockpicks. He tore off ten small pieces of the adhesive tape and applied them to his fingertips in lieu of surgical gloves, which caused his hands to sweat profusely. Besides, he knew of two occasions where members of the Red Mafia had earned stiff jail sentences when they'd stupidly dropped the gloves near the crime scene, the police later finding the men's fingerprints on the *inside* of the latex gloves.

There was a humming, swishing sound when he cracked the men's room door. He peered out to see a janitor polishing the marble floors with an electric buffer. He waited until the janitor had moved on, then tried to put a swagger into his walk as he made his way past doors with stenciled notations: *Fraud Detail, Sex Crimes Detail, Hate Crimes Unit.*

Finally, he was in front of the door to the homicide detail. He tried the knob. Locked. He rapped his knuckles lightly on the glass. No response. The sound of the electric buffer seemed to be getting closer. He selected a pick with a half-round tip he'd made out of a steel bristle from a street-cleaning machine, then a torque wrench he'd constructed from an eightpenny nail.

Feliks closed his eyes and concentrated, imagining he could see the two makeshift tools go about their tasks. He let out a *whoosh* of air to relieve the tension when the lock clicked open. He wasn't sure how long the job had taken—thirty seconds, two minutes?

Feliks quickly entered the room and closed the door behind him.

A wall of windows let in enough light for him to make out the reception desk, the large vase of flowers, and the first two cubicles. Which one belonged to Inspector Harry Dymes?

Feliks resisted the urge to turn on the ceiling lights. He moved slowly, going from one cubicle to another, stopping to click on a desk lamp, examine the files, go through the drawers.

He'd found an unexpected bonus in the bottom right-hand drawer of one desk—a holstered pistol. He hesitated a moment before slipping the weapon into his waistband, then moved on.

He'd been through seven desks, and was beginning to show the signs of frustration: riffling through the files, rummaging through the drawers. Where was Dymes's desk?

A single rose in a narrow glass vase sat on a shelf next to the desk in the next cubicle. He clicked on the desk lamp and slowly eased the center drawer open. There were neat stacks of pencils, paper clips, various sizes of envelopes and a box of business cards. He picked up one of the cards and smiled. *Harry Dymes, Homicide Inspector.*

The light on Dymes's desktop answering machine was blinking. There were two files on the desk: one marked

Morris/Chapaev, the other Zivon Yudin. Feliks flipped the top file open and saw a drawing. Of himself!

He slid into Dymes's chair and studied the drawing. The nose was too wide, the hairline too high, the eyes not quite right, but it bore a strong resemblance to him. How had a San Francisco policeman obtained a drawing of him? He pawed through the files, speed-reading through the reports on the murders of Zivon Yudin and Paul Morris, which contained nothing that would get him any closer to Tarasove.

There were handwritten notes indicating the date and time of Feliks's call alerting Dymes that Paul Morris was actually Kiryl Chapaev. Scribbled on the inside jacket of the folder was the name *Marta Citron, FBI*. But nothing to show how Dymes had obtained the drawing.

Feliks pounded his hands on the desk in frustration.

How? It had to be the whore. He went back to the file, finding Dymes's report of his interview with Julie Renton. He noted her address. He'd sat next to her and Chapaev in the restaurant. Why had she taken such notice of him? He stared at the blinking answering machine light, then pushed the PLAY button. A woman's accented voice: "Harry. I have some information for you on Zivon Yudin and his new friend. Come see me, darling. Bring a donation and I'll read your fortune again." The woman ended the conversation with a loud, kissing sound.

The fucking gypsy! Zivon must have gone to see her. Told her about him. She must have made the drawing of him, with Zivon's help.

Feliks pushed the answering machine's ERASE button and had positioned the file in the middle of the desk and clicked off the lamp when the fluorescent ceiling lights stammered to life.

"You're working late, Inspector. Sure like to get me some of that overtime."

Harry Dymes waved a friendly hand at the janitor. "No overtime, Charlie, I just do this because I love the job."

"Same with me, Inspector. I'd polish floors all day and night if I didn't have to catch an hour's sleep now and then."

Harry was feeling a buzz from the gin, wine, and brandy

he'd consumed at dinner. He should have passed on the brandy. The alcohol hadn't seemed to have affected Marta Citron. Maybe one of her long, shapely legs was hollow.

He clicked on the lights. The first thing he noticed was that the roses he'd brought in for Carlotta were already wilting. He started for his desk, pausing when he saw that the desk lamps were burning in three of his coworkers' cubicles.

He stood stock-still for a moment. That creeping feeling between his shoulders came back. There was a crashing sound, then pounding footsteps.

Harry ran toward the door. The vase of roses was over-turned. Charlie, the janitor, was backed up against the wall, his hands outstretched, the mop lying at his feet.

"That man's got a gun, Inspector."

Harry reached for the Colt .38 snub nose Special hol-stered at his ankle, then ran toward the elevators. He got there just in time to see the door leading to the stairwell glide to a close. He pushed through the door and was greeted by the blast of a pistol shot, the sound amplified by the thick concrete walls. He ducked instinctively, rolling to the floor, and came up with the Colt cocked and pointed at an empty stairwell. There was the swishing sound of a door opening.

Harry got to his feet and took the stairs two at a time, kicking the open door leading to the third floor, sweeping the revolver in front of him.

He opened his mouth wide to keep the sound of his heavy breathing from affecting his hearing. The long hall-way was completely empty. The man with the gun couldn't have had time to make it to the end of the hall.

Harry walked on tiptoes. There were ten courtrooms lin-ing the hall, each with a pair of double doors guarding the entrance. He paused at the first door, testing the locks. The door creaked open to reveal a darkened courtroom. He'd testified in numerous court cases in that very room. Ten to twelve rows of cushioned seats for spectators. A hip-high wooden bannister in midroom, beyond which were tables and chairs for the defendant, his or her attorney, and the district attorney. At the far side of the room, the raised judge's bench. A small desk for the court reporter. Jury seats to the right. An exit door leading to the judge's chambers behind his bench. Now all he could see was a dark blur.

His left hand groped for the wall. A light switch. There had to be a light switch.

The sound of the gun discharging wasn't as loud as the first shot had been, but it seemed to swell up in Harry's ears. He dropped to the ground, crawling blindly. A slice of gray light from the back of the room. Thudding feet again. He leaped to his feet and blundered ahead, bumping into seats, the separating bannister, and finally the judge's bench before reaching the exit door.

Another dimly lit hallway—narrow, carpeted. A smudged, shadowy figure thirty yards away. Another shot. Harry could see the muzzle blast, feel the force of the bullet as it whined past him. He snapped off two quick shots, then dropped to the carpet. The impact jarred the snub nose free. By the time he'd picked it up, the shooter was gone. He fast-crawled for ten yards, then got to his feet, stopping at a door leading to another courtroom. Sweat streamed down his forehead as he cracked the door open. The bark of the gun, the sound of the shooter running.

Harry wondered why someone hadn't heard the shots—hadn't sent a posse.

Another gunshot, then the honking of a fire alarm. Harry bumped his way through the darkened room. A ceiling sprinkler was spraying water in all directions. He could just make out a dark coat, dark hair. The shooter careened off a wall and raced toward the stairwell.

Harry gave chase, getting drenched in the process. He transferred the Colt to his left hand, using his right to grasp the iron handrails, taking the steps three at a time now, past the second floor, the main floor, down to the Hall of Justice basement. He plunged through the door into the underground garage in a crouch. He could hear sirens. The fire department responding to the fire alarm? Where the hell were all his fellow cops?

There were row after row of empty black-and-white patrol cars and unmarked cars, including his lime-green compact. The air was thick with the stink of old exhaust fumes and spilled gasoline. His shoes made hollow ringing sounds on the oil-stained concrete, so he slipped out of them.

Where was the shooter? Sitting in one of the cars? Hiding beneath one of them? Either way, Harry was an easy target.

There was just one way out, a ramp on the east side of the building. He crouched behind a concrete pillar and decided to stay right where he was, so he could monitor the area and wait for reinforcements to arrive.

Suddenly, the sound of a motor turning over, then revving up. A motorcycle roared by. Harry got off a quick shot and heard it ricochet off the bike's back fender.

He opened the door of the first car in line, a battered black-and-white, and switched on the engine, his stocking foot jabbing the accelerator. The tires squealed as he gunned the motor, heading toward the exit. He was halfway up the ramp when he was blinded by blazing white lights. He jammed both feet on the brake and the car shuddered to a halt inches from the bumper of an oncoming fire engine.

Zhukovka, Russia

Colonel Edik Savelev had to smile at the irony of the exercise—private guards armed with machine guns encircled his car, while another guard crawled around the Lada two-door coupe with a mirror, checking for bombs.

The massive iron-grilled entrance gate and high cement walls surrounding the luxury dachas bore a resemblance to a prison camp.

One of the private security guards grunted something unintelligible and waved his arm to indicate that Savelev was free to drive into the compound.

Savelev motored along the winding, neatly paved road, bordered by towering pines and walls of flowering oleander, occasionally catching a glimpse of a tiled rooftop or chimney of one of the elaborate dachas that had formerly been used as summer homes for Soviet generals or high-ranking politicians. Most of them were gone now, replaced by the new Russian elite: oligarchs, bankers, stockbrokers, and Mafia figures.

Most, but not all. General Burian Kilmov, head of the External Intelligence Service, or SVR, had purchased the largest dacha in all of Zhukovka—for what was described to Savelev as a bullet in the back of the head of the former tenant, and a small pension for his widow.

Savelev turned into the graveled entrance leading to Kilmov's residence. The two "gardeners" who greeted him were less obvious than the guards at the gate, but much more thorough, insisting that he hand over the 9mm Yarygin pistol secreted inside the passenger seat's headrest.

He drove close to a quarter of a mile, passing over a chiseled stone bridge, before the main house came into view—three stories of varnished pine logs topped by a swirling shingled roof.

Savelev parked his Russian-made compact among a cluster of luxurious Mercedes and BMWs. Twin black Dobermans bounded down the brick steps and bracketed him as he climbed up to the house.

The front doorway was high enough to ride a horse through. A squat-figured man in a black suit greeted him formally.

"The general is on the patio, having breakfast with his granddaughter. This way, please."

"This way" took Savelev through the formal dining room with an elaborate silver-leafed ceiling, then out to the brick-paved patio.

Burian Kilmov was sitting in a bentwood armchair, a blond, curly-haired child of five or six on his lap. The redwood table was set with silver and crystal. The smell of fried bacon perfumed the air.

Kilmov glanced at Savelev, and told the girl, "See how big and strong Edik is. That's because he eats all of his breakfast, every morning."

"Yes, Papa." The girl looked up at him with bright eyes, then wiggled in her grandfather's lap.

"I don't want anymore, Papa. I want to watch TV."

Kilmov grunted with the effort it took to get to his feet with the child wrapped in his arms. He held her over his head for a brief moment, then placed her on the lawn.

"Go. Watch. But you must promise to eat all of your lunch."

The girl hugged his leg, then turned and ran back to the house.

"Women," Kilmov said. "They are trouble no matter

what their age." He was in his early sixties, a short man, barely five foot three—two inches taller than Stalin had been, as he liked to point out. He was wearing highly polished knee-length riding boots, which elevated his height to that of Savelev's. No one in the general's inner circle stood taller than he. Savelev had seen high-ranking members of the Russian parliament and war-decorated generals hunch their shoulders and bend their knees when in Kilmov's presence, so as not to offend him.

Kilmov snapped his fingers and the two Dobermans loped off down the sea of emerald-green lawn which led to a set of tennis courts.

"Well, Colonel. What is it that brings you here in the middle of my vacation?"

"I hated to disturb you, General," Savelev responded sincerely. He had wrestled with the decision over whether to come to the dacha or wait until Kilmov returned to Moscow next week. "I received an e-mail from the American agent, Alex. He claims that he has come across information that could lead him to Nicolai Tarasove. Tarasove is the—"

"I know who Tarasove is," Kilmov said irritably. "I'd like to know who Alex is, but so far your investigation has produced nothing."

Savelev didn't argue the point. After Alex volunteered—for a substantial sum—the location of two important defectors, men the Soviet intelligence agencies had been chasing for years, he'd conducted an exhaustive inquiry into Alex—all for nought. The man remained a mystery. "We believe he's highly placed in the FBI, sir."

"After all the money we paid the *pizd'uk*, you think he would have retired by now."

"He's American. He's greedy," Savelev said.

" 'He's American'." Kilmov responded as a schoolteacher might approve the bright answer of a backward student. "Are you even certain of that, Colonel? How much does he want for Tarasove?"

"Three million American dollars, sir."

Kilmov picked up a piece of bacon from the table and popped it in his mouth. He chewed thoughtfully for a minute before replying. "Why now? We've been searching for that Ukrainian traitor for a long time." He locked his eyes onto Savelev's. "Without result. Now, all of a sudden, we are offered the prick on a plate. For three million American dollars. How is the money to be paid?"

"The same as before. A numbered Swiss account—different from the last two accounts. One-third paid immediately, the second million when he provides a general location for Tarasove, and the final payment when Alex places him in our hands."

Kilmov leaned back and looked upward. There was a solid, porcelain quality to the Russian summer sky. "What was the name of the Mafia thug who pushed Tarasove into the Americans' hands?"

"Boris Feliks, sir."

"What is his status?"

"We believe he's alive, and still searching for Tarasove."

Kilmov surveyed his fingernails, then pointed his index finger to the south. "Two kilometers from here, in a large Tudor house, with an indoor swimming pool, lives Sasha Veronin, who considers himself the most powerful gangster in the world. Feliks was, and no doubt still is, working for Sasha. Did you know that, Edik?"

"Yes, sir."

"He keeps a small zoo of exotic animals. There are rumors, which Sasha doesn't deny, that his enemies are fed to one of his pet tigers. He called—said he wanted to see me about something very important. The timing is curious, don't you think? Why do you suppose Alex came to us with this, Edik? We're certainly not the only ones interested in Tarasove. There are the Chinese, the Koreans, the Pakistanis, Sasha Veronin. The list is endless."

"We paid his request promptly in the past. He must trust us."

"Trust," Kilmov remarked bitterly. "He trusts us as much as we trust him."

Savelev heard the *thwack* of tennis balls in the distance. The general's wife—Ivana, his fourth wife—was a celebrated athlete before their marriage.

Kilmov sat back in his chair, lit a cigarette and said, "All right. Wire the money to Switzerland." He pointed the tip of the burning cigarette at Savelev. "But I want to know who this Alex is, understood? I want to bleed the greedy bastard dry once we have Tarasove back."

A woman yelled out a joyous shout, which was followed by a man's deep braying laughter. Kilmov turned toward the tennis courts. He eyed Savelev's trim, athletic build. "Do you play tennis, Edik?"

"No, sir."

"Good. Too many young men do."

Chapter Fifteen

"I wonder how the perp got in here with a gun?" Lieutenant Ric Larsen asked in a lazy drawl that made him sound entirely disinterested. He was dressed in a pair of khakis, a plaid pajama top under a black golf jacket, and floppy leather slippers.

"I'd like the answer to that," Harry Dymes said. The two men were in Larsen's office, Harry using the desktop word processor to make his report on the shooting incident. His still-wet sport coat was draped over the back of his chair.

"I've got the Southern Station lieutenant working on it," Larsen said. "How many shots did he take at you?"

"Four. Then there was the shot he took to set off the fire alarm."

"The janitor didn't get a good look at the guy, and he's not sure what kind of gun it was. All he knows is that it was 'a big mother.' How many shots did you get off?"

"Three," Harry said, typing that information into the report.

"Are you carrying that old thirty-eight peashooter on your ankle?"

"Yes. My last shot nicked the motorcycle he took off on. Any news on the bike?"

"Not yet." Larsen took a sip of coffee and grimaced. "'Nothing in life is so exhilarating as being shot at without result.' Do you know who said that?"

"You. Just now."

"Winston Churchill. Back in the days when he was soldiering for the British Empire. You were lucky this asshole didn't hit you." He sampled the coffee again. "I wish someone would open a Starbucks on this floor. Captain Sanborn is going to have a shit fit when he hears about this." Larsen looked at his watch. "Which will be in about eight hours." He yawned widely. "I'm gonna sneak home for a shower and a few winks. I suggest you do the same."

"As soon as I finish this," Harry responded.

Larsen lowered the half-filled cardboard coffee cup carefully into a wastebasket. "What's your gut telling you, Harry? You're sure the door to the office was locked, right?"

"Right. I used my key."

"I was the last one to leave last night, and I'm certain I locked the door. So, the perp picked the lock. Why? What's in this office that's important to him?"

Dymes patted the two manila folders next to the word processor. "These, the Morris/Chapaev and Zivon Yudin files, were sitting on my desk."

Larsen rubbed his temples with his fingertips. "Maybe the perp was interested in *another* file. Joe McGee and Barney Ford are working on that Chinatown shooting; Ralph Gowan has that case involving the TV weatherman who was stabbed to death in his bedroom, all decked out in a wig and negligee. High profile cases, Harry."

"True," Dymes admitted. "But you asked for my gut feeling. I think he came in here to see what I had on these two cases."

"The ones the FBI is so interested in." Larsen slammed the heel of his hand against his forehead. "Jesus Christ. You don't think the FBI was stupid enough to send someone in here, do you?"

"No. I had dinner with Marta Citron a few hours ago. She's savvy, a player. No way she'd be involved in anything like this."

"There's always Tom McNab. He's dumb enough to try anything."

"The shooter was bigger than McNab. This man isn't a virgin, Ric. It took brains, careful planning, and guts to get into this office. He's handy with a weapon—he came damn close to hitting me. Activating the fire alarm to confuse things, then making his getaway with a police motorcycle showed ingenuity—he's a real pro."

Larsen wiped his lips with the back of his hand. "Okay. Let's go with it your way. The perp comes in to look at your files. Is there anything in them that works for him? Anything that jeopardizes a witness?"

"One. Julie Renton, the hooker who dated Morris/Chapaev. Her name and address are in the file." Harry flipped open the file and showed Larsen the computer composite drawing. "Renton made this up for me. It's the man who sat next to her and Morris at Moose's Restaurant a few hours before the murder."

"He sat next to them? So what? Did he say something to make her suspicious?"

"Nothing. She's just trying to be helpful."

"You better let Renton know about this. If the guy is the killer, and he saw the drawing, she could be a target."

"I sent a car from Central Station to her apartment to brief her, with a suggestion that she get out of town for a few days."

The door to Larsen's office squeaked open. "Hi, Lieutenant. What's doin', Inspector? I hear you guys had a party here tonight."

Harry looked up to see John Prizir of the crime lab staring at him with sleepy eyes. "You better have your whole crew working on this one, John." He pushed himself to his feet. "Come on, I'll show you where all the action took place."

It was a little after two in the morning when Harry Dymes steered the lime-green Honda into his driveway. He slammed on the brakes when he saw a Yellow Cab parked in front of the house. When the cab's rear door opened, Harry reached for the .38 holstered on his ankle; then he realized he hadn't reloaded it after the shooting incident.

"Hi, Harry," Julie Renton called as she hurried over to his car. She was dressed in black slacks and a purple exaggerated turtleneck that looked like an Elizabethan ruff.

"What are you doing here?" Dymes said through the open window.

Julie rested her hands on the car roof, leaned down and grinned at him. "The cops you sent said I should go somewhere safe tonight. What could be safer than your place?"

"How did you know where I live?" Harry asked angrily, as he squirmed out of the Honda.

"You showed me your driver's license, the first time you came to my place."

"And you remembered the address?"

Julie's cheeks dimpled. "My mother always told me everybody has a photographic memory. Some folks just don't have film."

"Very funny," Harry said, approaching the cab. The motor was running. The driver, a dark-skinned man with a thin stubble of white hair across his scalp, gave him a mournful smile.

"How long have you been waiting here?" Harry asked.

" 'Bout half an hour."

"With the meter running?"

The man's smile turned cheerful. "I know the lady. We worked out a deal."

Julie Renton yanked open the cab's back door and retrieved a suitcase. "Thanks, Asad."

The cab surged away before Harry could block it. He stood with his hands on his hips watching the taillights corkscrew down Vermont Street.

"Aren't you going to invite me in and tell me what's going on?" Julie asked, holding out the suitcase to Dymes. "What happened to your coat? It's all wet."

"Julie. You can't stay with me."

"Why not? A man may be trying to kill me. I feel safe with you."

Harry grabbed the suitcase and opened the front door. "A cop having a person who's involved in a homicide case over at his house is not a good idea, believe me."

He snapped on the lights, and Julie stepped in front of him and hurried up the carpeted steps.

"Ooooh, I like this," she said, when she saw the living area. "Too much beige, though. You need more color, Harry. Some print chairs. Softer paintings. I could really fix this place up."

Harry tossed her suitcase on the couch. "I'll get you a blanket. You can fix up the couch. In the morning, you're out of here."

Julie pulled her sweater over her head and surfaced, like a swimmer breaking water, revealing a skintight white nylon tank top. "Are you hungry?" she asked. "I make a great omelet."

"All I want to do is go to bed."

"Me too, Harry," she said, sidling up to him.

"Alone."

Julie pouted. "You don't like me."

"You're gorgeous, bright, and with your personality, you could sell milk to cows. But nothing is going to happen between us."

"Because I'm a hooker? You're worried about catching something, but—"

"No buts. Go to sleep." Harry opened a hall closet and withdrew a blanket and pillow. "On the couch. I hate to seem unchivalrous, but I'm taking the bed."

Julie's voice turned serious. "Is someone really trying to kill me?"

"It's possible," Harry said, handing her the blanket and pillow. "I'll tell you all about it in the morning."

"That's what they all say," she said, the mischief back in her voice. "I'm too wound up to sleep. I think I'll watch some TV. How do you like your coffee in the morning?"

"In the car, on the way to work. Good night, kid."

Julie watched him walk down the hall. "Better lock your door, Harry."

Dymes shook his head and laughed. He suddenly felt exhausted, with barely enough energy to climb out of his clothes. He had pulled the bedspread back and was about to dive into the sheets when he went back to the door and sheepishly clicked the lock. "Maybe there's something wrong with me," he told himself as his head hit the pillow.

Chapter Sixteen

Lake Tahoe, Nevada

"Stay," Nicolai Tarasove said to Jedgar, as he pushed the button that opened the steel doors to the laboratory. It was an unnecessary command. Jedgar wanted no part of the snakes, and was content to wait patiently for his master's return—outside the lab.

"Hello, all," Tarasove said to the group of thirty white rats in a pillow-size wire cage. The cage was separated into three compartments. Twenty-nine of the rats were huddled together in one compartment, quivering from hunger and thirst. The thirtieth rat, with *BF26* in red marking ink on its back, was alone in an adjoining compartment, and looked just as hungry and thirsty as the others.

"Feeding time soon," Tarasove said. He filled a bowl with tap water, then, from a long rack of test tubes, selected the one marked *BF24*. He carefully poured a minuscule drop of the clear liquid from the test tube into the bowl, stirring it with one gloved finger, then carried the bowl back to the cage, carefully placing it into the unoccupied compartment.

Tarasove slid open the gate leading to the lone rat's compartment. The rodent scurried over to the water bowl, lap-ping at the water for several seconds before keeling over on its side.

Tarasove then opened the gate for the others, who raced to the water bowl in a frenzy, climbing over the corpse of their fellow rat.

After a couple of minutes watching the rodents quench their thirst, Tarasove murmured to himself, "Project Boris Feliks twenty-four is another success—an unqualified success."

There had been enough toxin in the tap water to kill all thirty of the rats. Or three hundred. But only one died—the one that had been programmed with Boris Feliks's DNA fingerprint, and the only one that didn't have Tarasove's DNA antidote.

He peeled off his gloves, sat down on the stool, and opened the folder of autoradiographic film images.

He selected the image marked *BF-Boris Feliks*, slipped it under a microscope and studied the series of black strips that showed the banding pattern of Feliks's radioactive DNA molecules. The fingerprint had been developed from the hairs Tarasove had taken from the Russian mafioso's overcoat in Kiev. Tarasove had held onto the dandruff-flaked hair, even though Roger Dancel had assured him that Feliks would be killed or captured and rot in jail for the rest of his life. Which was a lie, of course. How many other lies had Dancel and Marta Citron told him?

The other DNA film images were works in progress on a variety of individuals whom he had no real plans of eliminating—a waitress at a nearby coffee shop who had mocked his accent, the nosy post office manager, and a blackjack dealer who Tarasove was certain had cheated him.

Obtaining samples of their hair had presented a challenge to Tarasove, but where there was a will, there was a way. Everyone loses fifty to a hundred hairs a day. The waitress's scarf was always left hanging on the restaurant's coatrack, as was the postal manager's cap during her twice-a-day visits to the coffee shop. The cheating blackjack dealer often went directly to play at the casino poker tables after his shift, draping his sport coat over the back of his chair.

Tarasove started to work on developing a DNA finger-print for Marta Citron from her hair samples.

"How's everything in Washington, Roger?" Agent Tom McNab said as he stowed Dancel's luggage into the car's trunk.

"God, I hate those red-eye flights. We stopped in Chicago and sat on the runway for an hour. I thought I'd find some decent weather here," Dancel complained as he slipped into the passenger seat. "It's hotter than back home." He ran his fingers across the unfamiliar dashboard. "Where's the air conditioner?"

McNab waited until he was behind the wheel and had maneuvered the car into the heavy airport traffic before punching the air conditioner up to high. "The heat waves usually last about three or four days, Roger."

"Just my luck. How's Marta treating you?"

"Treating isn't the right description. She's a . . ."

"Bitch," Dancel volunteered. "Is that the word you're searching for?"

McNab lowered the sun visor as he merged into the traffic on the airport ramp. "It fits. She had dinner with Inspector Dymes last night."

"Where?" Dancel wanted to know.

"A steak house on Van Ness Avenue, close to where she's staying."

"She has a thing for steak houses," Dancel said, remembering his last dinner with Citron. "Did she take him back home with her?"

"I don't know. I didn't bother sticking around to find out." McNab turned to face Dancel. "I don't think she'd appreciate it if she found out I was tailing her all night."

Dancel adjusted the air-conditioning vent so it blew directly at his face. "Our Marta doesn't appreciate much of anything. Do you think she's screwing Dymes?"

"I don't know. The night she arrived, we drove straight to his house. She was only in there for a few minutes, and she wasn't a happy camper when she left."

"I've got enough on Dymes to bury the guy. Why waste time having dinner with him?"

"Beats me," McNab said, accelerating down a straight

stretch of road that led to the Bayshore Freeway. "There was an incident last night."

"Tell me about it, damn it. Don't make me guess."

"Apparently, after dinner with Citron, Dymes returned to the Hall of Justice. He surprised someone in the homicide detail. Shots were fired. Whoever it was got away."

Dancel narrowed his eyes and studied McNab. He had to have messed up somewhere, violated "the Three Bs," the three things most likely to get an FBI agent in trouble—booze, broads, or smashing up a Bucar—because with his political connections, he should have been a bureau chief by now. "Was Dymes the target? Was it an escaped prisoner? What?"

"We don't know yet, Roger."

Dancel slumped back in the seat and laced his fingers across his stomach. "Who's Dymes's superior officer?"

"The homicide lieutenant is Ric Larsen. Another loser. I know that Dymes is dealing confidential reports to a private eye, an ex-cop by the name of Landeta."

"Good. More ammunition. We own the guy. Where's Marta now?"

The morning commute traffic caused McNab to slow down to loitering speed. "Probably in bed, in her apartment."

Dancel thought of the videos of Marta in bed with the drug dealer in Miami, and her breaking his balls when he suggested that the two of them slip between the sheets. "Do you know why God gave women orgasms, Tom? So they'd have something else to moan about. Let's stop by and roust her from her beauty sleep. I've got some news for her that's going to make her real unhappy."

There were no police in the area. Boris Feliks was certain of that. He tapped a knuckle on the weather-blistered door. "Come in," a woman's voice called to him.

A string of bells hanging from the door announced his entrance.

"You are Victor?" Lana Kuzmin asked from the beaded curtain leading to her spell room.

"Yes," Feliks replied softly, his eyes scanning the room. "Are we alone? I am a little embarrassed. This is the first time I've been to a . . ."

"Fortune-teller," Lana said, pulling back the beaded curtain. "There is no reason to be shy. A handsome man like you. We are completely alone. Come. You must have many concerns to call on me this early."

Boris settled in the chair and laid his left arm across the felt tabletop, his right hand dropping unseen to his lap. "My friends would think I am foolish coming here. They are not believers."

"Then that is their misfortune." She picked up his hand in both of hers. "My, my. You have some very interesting—"

Feliks dug his fingers into Lana's hand and slammed it on the table, his right hand coming out from under the table with an ice pick. He stabbed the pick into her hand, pinning it to the table, and, in an astonishingly quick move, got to his feet and moved behind her, encircling her jeweled neck with a thin piece of nylon cord. "Tell me about your policeman friend and Zivon Yudin, you filthy whore."

"Idy na khuy," Lana croaked as she tried to free her impaled hand.

Feliks tightened his fingers. "Oh, I'll get fucked, but not by the likes of you. Talk, witch, and I'll let you live."

Lana watched the blood stream from her hand and puddle around the crystal ball. For the first time in her entire life, she could actually see someone's fate in the crystal. Hers.

Chapter Seventeen

Captain of Detectives Lawrence Sanborn cleared his throat and asked, "Where is your weapon now, Inspector Dymes?"

"Right here, sir." Harry reached down and slipped the .38 revolver from its ankle holster, breaking the cylinder open before sliding it across the captain's desk.

Sanborn picked the weapon up with his thumb and index finger and dangled it over the desk as if it were a dead rodent. "That is not the weapon that we issued to you."

"I prefer this one, Captain."

"I didn't ask you what you *preferred*. Where is the forty-caliber Beretta that the department provided you?"

"At home under lock and key, Captain."

Sanborn was the highest ranking African American in the department. He was a tall, fastidiously dressed man, with the kind of face that mirrored nothing and rarely displayed a change of expression. His skin was the color and texture of an old saddle. His head was completely shaved. "Bald as a prick's tip" was the way that Lieutenant Larsen described it, though certainly not when Sanborn was within hearing range.

Sanborn's high, intelligent forehead wrinkled. "We give you a gun, Inspector, we expect you to carry it."

Harry merely nodded his head. There were advantages and disadvantages in everything in life, and the choice of a weapon was certainly one of them. The department-issued Beretta semiautomatic had a ten-round clip, compared to his five-shot revolver, and a lot more stopping power. But the fact that a round had to be cocked into the chamber before firing the semiautomatic, compared to his revolver's simple point-and-shoot technique, made the choice easy for Harry. Most policemen rarely fire their gun in the line of duty. Harry knew several cops who studiously avoided trips to the firing range. Their weapons hadn't been fired, or cleaned, since joining the department. The range master had told Harry that three young men in a recent recruit class had balked at shooting their guns. Pacifist police officers, who believed the word was mightier than the sword. "I'd rather talk a man into surrendering than have to shoot him," one of the recruits had said.

Harry wondered what the kid's reaction would be when a two-hundred-and-twenty-pound crackhead came at him with a baseball bat.

The shooting incident in the Hall of Justice was only the second time Harry had fired his weapon in the line of duty, the first being two years ago when he wounded a homicide suspect fleeing down the fire escape of a downtown hotel.

The fact that his .38 had been given to him by New York detective Tony Fenner, after Fenner had retired, also had a bearing on his choice.

"You're sure the Beretta is at your house, Inspector?" Sanborn said in his dry, raspy voice. "Because the bullets the lab retrieved from the wall in the courtroom were from a forty-caliber gun."

"It wasn't my gun, Captain."

Sanborn stuck a blunt-tipped finger into the revolver's trigger guard and turned it in a circle. "Judge Dutil was not at all amused when he learned that the courtroom and hallways were used as a shooting gallery."

There was a rap on the door and Sanborn barked, "Come in!"

Lieutenant Ric Larsen cleared his throat. "Captain, regarding the forty-caliber bullets, there's a possibility that the weapon belonged to Inspector Barney Ford. He left his gun in his desk drawer last night. It's now missing."

Sanborn ordered Larsen to sit down. "What kind of a detail are you running, Lieutenant? Dymes doesn't carry the proper weapon, and now you tell me the man who was shooting at him may have been using Inspector Ford's gun, which was left in an unlocked drawer. The newspapers are going to have a field day with this."

Harry caught Larsen's eye. Sanborn considered himself the logical choice to be the next chief of police, and his enemies in the department would certainly use this incident against him.

"Ford was attending a promotion dinner for Deputy Chief Gloria Perret," Harry said. "He knew he'd be drinking, and didn't want to violate department regulations by carrying his firearm."

"Really?" Sanborn said sarcastically. "If every homicide inspector subscribed to that bullshit theory, none of them would ever carry their guns! Lieutenant, I want written statements from everyone in your detail as to the location and condition of their weapons. And I want those weapons put into use." He turned to glare at Dymes. "Including yours, Inspector."

"Yes, sir," Harry said, reaching for the revolver on Sanborn's desk.

"I'll take care of that," Sanborn informed him.

"The crime lab wants to test it to verify the thirty-eight slugs found in the hallway, Cap."

"Have the results sent to me immediately," Sanborn said, handing Harry the gun, then waving the two of them angrily out of the room.

"Touchy guy," Larsen said when they were walking back to the homicide detail.

"I'll be glad when he's anointed chief," Harry said, "so he'll be out of our hair. After he becomes the chief of the department, all he'll worry about is the budget and keeping the mayor happy. Real police work will be the last thing on his agenda. They should just hire an accountant for the job, and be done with it. What about the motorcycle the perp drove off with?"

"They found it in an alley down on the Embarcadero. Someone had stripped it bare—probably not the guy who shot at you, just some punks who found an unexpected treasure."

"How much trouble is Barney Ford in, Ric?"

"Plenty. The perp not only picked up Barney's gun, he got the holster and spare clip. I'm glad you made up that line about Barney going to Gloria Perret's retirement dinner. Gloria is probably the last person standing between Sanborn and the chief's job. Now he thinks Barney's a buddy of hers, so he'll tread lightly. Speaking of buddies, you had a call from the zipper-melting hooker, Julie Renton. She's moved in with a friend, and left you her new phone number. What's your next move on the case? How are we going to find this nutcase that came close to killing you a few hours ago?"

"I'm going to get the FBI to help us on this one, Ric—whether they like it or not."

Boris Feliks stood at the entrance to his "cottage," cursing, one hand resting on the butt of the pistol he'd taken from the policeman's desk drawer. Jed Dewey, his landlord, was an unbelievably stupid man. The strands from the carpet that he had wedged into the doorjamb were lying at his feet. His suitcase was a good five inches from where he'd positioned it under the bed. The thin film of talcum powder on his suitcase locks was smudged, and the faded plaid bedspread that he'd stretched smooth bore marks from the case and someone's butt. *"Da ty sovesm okuel!"* Feliks muttered. The useless old man was crazy.

He crossed the room to the TV cabinet and used the screwdriver blade of his pocketknife to remove the fiberboard back panel. His stash of cash and second set of passport, driver's license, and credit cards were in place.

Feliks had devised what he believed was a foolproof method of obtaining identification documents. He paid for everything in cash whenever possible; however, there were times when he was forced to use a credit card, or present a driver's license or passport to a border guard, an airline ticket counter agent, or a hotel desk clerk.

To obtain the ID, he first placed an ad in the "Help Wanted" section of the major newspaper wherever he happened to be:

International bond firm needs man to deliver important documents worldwide. Must have current passport and be free to travel at moment's notice. Send résumé and photograph to the listed postal box.

The responses were always numerous. One such ad in Houston had produced more than three hundred applicants—many of them highly overqualified individuals desperate for a job, others morons who could barely spell.

Feliks would select a man who was in his general age group, then set up a personal meeting in the lobby of a prestigious hotel. He'd size up the victim—one who had no family life, no real ties to the community—someone who wouldn't be missed if he disappeared. Which is exactly what happened. After Feliks thoroughly interrogated him, made certain that he had no criminal record or outstanding warrants, he'd strip the fool of his money, identity cards, and precious Social Security number. Then it was a simple process of informing the state driver's license agency of a change of address—a private postal service with a street address, not a postal box. When the new address was in place, he'd go to the motor vehicles office, claim that he'd lost his license, and obtain a new one, which now carried *his* photograph. Then it was simply a matter of telling the friendly United States government that he'd lost his passport, which they provided after examining his new credentials.

The whole process took several weeks, but was well worth the effort. He paid off the credit card charges promptly with a cashier's check.

John Kagel was the hapless former carpet salesman whose identity he was now using. He removed the Ziploc bag and thumbed through a stack of money and his backup ID, a Canadian passport and international driver's license that had formerly belonged to a man by the name of George Becker.

Becker's headless, handless body had been found in the St. Lawrence River several weeks after Feliks murdered him. The famed Royal Canadian Mounted Police had better things to do than to check the DNA on every decomposed corpse that floated to their attention.

Feliks dropped the pistol onto the bed, then went to the cramped bathroom and splashed water on his face. As he dried off, he studied his features. The whore's drawing of him—he'd left it in the file on the policeman's desk. It would have made Dymes suspicious if he'd found it missing. He was sure that Dymes hadn't gotten a good look at him last night, and neither had the janitor—he'd dropped to the floor and covered his head with his hands as soon as Boris pointed the gun in his direction. How long would it take for Dymes to put the puzzle together?

Luck had been on his side for a long time, but now he could feel it slipping away. He patted his dark hair. A change of style and color was in order. Blond? Reddish? Trim the eyebrows. Blue contact lenses. Glasses. That would buy him some time.

The laptop computer was lying on the floor, attached to its charger. He settled on the bed and clicked it on, impatiently tapping his fingers on the titanium case as the machine warmed up. He went directly to Kiryl Chapaev's mailbox. Six messages: two offering Viagra prescriptions at a discount, the others more junk. When was Tarasove going to make his move? Contact him again? His fingers played with the keyboard; then he made up his mind. He typed in the message: *My client is interested in the Devil's Brew. All past sins are forgiven. This is a business transaction. You will be suitably rewarded.*

Roger Dancel was disappointed to find that Marta Citron had left her apartment early and was already at her desk at FBI headquarters on Golden Gate Avenue.

She looked fresh, rested, a bloom in her cheeks, like she'd just been laid. The homicide cop—Harry Dymes? She wouldn't let a decent, hardworking fellow agent like himself get near her, but she meets up with a local fuzz and after dinner tells him to climb aboard. He looked over at McNab, who was leaning against the doorjamb, his thumbs stuck in the back pockets of his pants.

"Tom. Get me some coffee. And poached eggs, crisp bacon, and rye toast."

"I'll call the deli," McNab said.

"Do me a favor. Go down and get it, will you?" Dancel rubbed his stomach. "I'm starving."

McNab hesitated a moment, then turned on his heel.

Dancel walked over and slammed the door shut. "Does he give you the creeps or what? I don't trust the little prick."

Marta crossed one long leg over the other and said, "His brother's a congressman in South Dakota, Roger."

"A Democrat, who won't win his next election. He's pro–gun control in a state where everyone hunts, fishes, and watches old John Wayne movies. What do you hear from Tarasove?"

"He's worried about Boris Feliks."

"He has reason to be worried," Dancel said, easing himself into a hardbacked wooden chair.

Marta scratched an ankle with her toe. "We believe that Feliks has Kiryl Chapaev's laptop. And it stands to reason he pried Tarasove's e-mail address out of Chapaev. What if *we* send him a message—saying we're Tarasove."

"Saying what? Come on up to Tahoe for fresh venison steaks?"

"No. Saying that Nicolai wants to make a deal. The formula for leaving him alone, or we can say he wants more money, or wants to go back to Russia."

"All of which is probably true. But Feliks wouldn't be dumb enough to fall for it."

"What have we got to lose, Roger?"

Dancel watched Marta's bare toe rub against her ankle. No nylons. An oversight? No time to shop? What else wasn't she wearing? "I'd have to think about it," he said. "How was dinner last night? Did Dymes pick up the check?"

Marta clicked her teeth shut to cut off a sharp reply. "I think I made some progress with Inspector Dymes. He obtained Chapaev's last name via an anonymous phone call, which could only have come from Boris Feliks, and he gave me the name of the tattooed man I examined at the morgue—Zivon Yudin. Dymes thinks—and I agree with him—that Yudin was working with Feliks. I haven't gotten the records check back yet from Washington. Dymes is going to drop off the statement of the hooker, Julie Renton, who had dinner with Chapaev just before he was killed." She looked at the slim watch on her wrist. "It should be soon."

"Maybe not. McNab tells me there was a shooting incident at the Hall of Justice last night. Dymes was involved."

Marta sat upright in her chair. "Was he injured?"

"I don't know. You're close to him. Why don't you call and find out?"

Marta picked up the phone and did just that, dialing Dymes's office number. She left a terse message on his answering machine, then dropped the phone onto the cradle and stared at Roger Dancel. "Do you suppose the shooting has something to do with our case?"

"You never know. When you talk to Dymes, put the squeeze on him."

"He is cooperating, Roger. There's no sense in riling him up."

Dancel unwound from the chair. "I want the jerk riled up. I want everything he has on Chapaev, and I want it right away. These guys always hold something back." He started for the door, then pulled up, looking at Citron over his shoulder. "Oh, by the way, Deputy Director Bartlow wants you to go up to Lake Tahoe and babysit Tarasove until we have Feliks dead and buried."

"Screw Bartlow," Citron said, immediately regretting her choice of words.

"He'd probably go along with that."

"This was your idea, wasn't it?" Marta challenged.

Dancel held his hands up as if he were about to surrender. "No way. I told Bartlow you were indispensable to the investigation, but you know him. Once he makes his mind up, that's it. Find out about that shooting incident before you start packing, okay? I told Nicolai you'd be there soon. He sounded happy about that."

Chapter Eighteen

When Harry Dymes returned to his desk, he found a phone message from Marta Citron: "Please call me as soon as possible. Thank you."

Harry played the message back, listening to Citron's tone of voice—all business, not the same voice he'd heard in the restaurant last night. He picked up the phone and dialed the given number. Citron answered on the first ring, with that same tense voice.

"Stay where you are for five minutes. I'll get right back to you."

When Citron called ten minutes later, she started by saying, "Is there someplace where we can meet right now?"

"I've been trying to find time to call you; it's been hectic over here."

"I heard there was a shooting incident. Are you all right?"

"Yeah," Harry said, looking at the pile of reports he had to fill out as a result of firing his weapon. "According to Winston Churchill, I should be feeling exhilarated. What I am is pissed. Are you in your office?"

"Churchill?"

"I'll explain later."

"I'm at a pay phone," Citron said. "Can we meet somewhere private? And can you bring the Julie Renton statement?"

"Sure, sure," Harry said, thinking about the fact that she hadn't used her cell phone. That interested him. Was she afraid someone was monitoring the call? Cell phones were notoriously difficult to trace, but easy to listen in on if you were in the right distance range and had the proper equipment. And the FBI was loaded with proper equipment. "There's a restaurant down the street, alongside the Flower Mart. I'll be there in twenty minutes. I want to show you a composite drawing of a man."

"I'll be there," Marta promised.

Harry picked a table with a view of a stall lined with buckets of multicolored gladiolas, frost-white Shasta daisies, orange-petaled marigolds, and brightly hued daffodils. The Mart supplied the city's premiere florists, restaurants and commercial buildings with their floral needs. After nine in the morning, the general public was allowed access.

"Tell me about the shooting," Marta said, as soon as they were seated.

Harry gave her an abbreviated version, leaving out, among other things, the fact that the suspect had stolen a fellow policeman's gun.

"Did you get a look at him?" Marta asked, after ordering a cheese omelet, toast and coffee.

"White male adult, thirty to forty, dark hair, dark clothes. I didn't get a look at his face." He opened the folder he'd brought, and passed the computer sketch Julie Renton had made over to Citron. "I think it was this guy."

Marta bulged her lower lip with her tongue as she studied the sketch. "I . . . I don't know this man, Harry. Who made the sketch? You said you didn't get a good look at him."

The waiter delivered her order and Harry's coffee. "Julie Renton, the hooker Kiryl Chapaev was with before he died. This man sat next to them at a restaurant. Julie said he seemed to be paying a lot of attention to what they were saying. I didn't think it was very important at the time, but after last night, I'm not so sure."

Marta studied the sketch again, and Harry had the feeling that there was something about it that had caught her interest. "Do you always eat like this?" he asked, wondering how she kept her figure with such a voracious appetite.

Marta gave a tight smile, adding pepper to the omelet. "No. Only when I'm under a lot of stress. There are days of very little bread and lots of water."

"Here's Renton's statement. She's a bit of a nutcake, but she's very observant."

Harry sat back and watched the activity in the parking lot as Marta read the statement. An attractive middle-aged woman was trying to lower a towering rubber plant through the sunroof window of her Mercedes sedan. A burly truck driver came over to give her a hand. When the plant was safely put away, the driver turned to the woman and said something that caused her to stiffen, and brought a flush to her face. Harry thought the man said, "You owe me now, baby," but he wasn't sure. He was certain that he'd read all of the lady's reply. "Fuck you," she'd said, before slipping into the driver's seat.

"You're right," Marta said, drawing his attention back to the table. "Not much there." She picked up the sketch again. "This isn't what I'd hoped to see."

"Tell me more about the man you hoped to see."

Marta tested her coffee. "All I can tell you is that he's an assassin. A professional."

"So was the man who shot at me last night, Marta. Who's his target?"

There was an uneasy pause, after which Marta said, "A man the United States government has offered its protection to."

"Like Kiryl Chapaev," Harry said. "A Russian defector. A scientist of some kind, who was relocated here, in San Francisco. The assassin is after him. And in the process he's killed Chapaev, a Russian thug by the name of Zivon Yudin, and came pretty close to shooting me last night."

Marta jabbed her fork into the omelet. "You can't be certain it's the same man, Harry."

"You're stalling me. I'm giving you everything I have, and getting nothing back."

"I'm doing the best I can. My supervisor, Roger Dancel, is in town. He's . . . sending me on another assignment."

"Back to Washington?" Harry asked.

"No. Not there."

Harry picked up a piece of her toast and took a big bite. "Let me make a guess," he said while munching on the toast. "You're going to provide protection for the defector. Take him away from here, to some FBI safe house, until the assassin is dealt with."

"I can't verify that," Marta said. "Can I keep the sketch? Maybe one of my colleagues will recognize him."

"You studied it a long time," Harry said. "Are you sure he didn't ring a few bells?"

"I'm not certain. Listen, if I can—" She broke off her sentence when a man with long dark hair and a mustache approached the table. "God, he looks just like Sonny Bono."

Harry smiled and made the introductions. "Sergeant Bob Dills of the vice squad, meet FBI agent Marta Citron."

Dills gave Marta a firm handshake, then said, "Harry, how did you make out with Julie Renton?"

"Just fine, Bob."

Dills waved at an exotic-looking Asian woman wearing a tight-fitting emerald-green pantsuit sitting at the counter. "One of my informants." He leaned down and lowered his voice. "Didn't you know the fortune-teller, Lana Kuzmin?"

"I know her very well."

"She was one of the first hookers I ever sang 'I Got You Babe' to. That was a lot of years ago," Dills said. "I just heard that she was murdered early this morning out in the Richmond District."

Marta could see that Harry was shaken by the news. His eyes narrowed, forming crow's-feet. "Thanks for letting me know, Bob."

"Tell me about Kuzmin," Marta said after Dills slid onto a counter seat next to the woman in green.

Harry took out his wallet and dropped a twenty-dollar bill onto the table. "She gave up hooking a long time ago, and worked as a fortune-teller. She knew as much about the local Russian community as anyone in town. She was a good woman—what the Russian's call *byl dushoj obschestva*—full of life. She met Zivon Yudin when he was living in San Francisco months ago. She was going to try and find out all she could about him for me. I saw her two nights ago. That's when I first got the feeling that someone was following me, Marta. I led him right to her, for Christ's sake! The killer, your assassin. He called me, gave me Chapaev's name, hoping I'd dig around and maybe turn up something linking Chapaev to the Russian you're protecting. He came to the Hall of Justice to go through my files. He saw the sketch and Renton's statement. Tell Dancel that he's in my town, and he'd better start opening up to me, or—"

"You'll kick him out of town, Sheriff," Marta said. "Be reasonable, Harry."

"Shooting at me, killing Lana. That makes it personal."

"I'll do my best to get Dancel to cooperate. Just give me some time." She reached out a hand for the sketch and statement.

Harry pushed his chair back and rose to his feet. "Call me when you've got something to offer."

"Hang on a second. I've got to clear this with Dancel. Look. Is there an outdoor café close to the FBI offices?"

"I'm not in the mood for lunch."

"Neither am I, Harry," Marta said in a forced tone. "Do I have to draw a picture for you? Outdoors, people talking, moving their lips."

"The Asian Art Museum on Fulton has a cafeteria with seating outside."

"I'm going to ask Dancel to meet me there at one o'clock. I'm sorry about the fortune-teller."

Dymes rolled the sketch and statement into a tight roll, and for a moment Marta thought he was going to give them to her. Then he said, "Maybe I'll see you there."

Marta watched him stalk out of the restaurant, nearly knocking over a teenage boy wearing a baseball cap backwards in the process. The sketch. Could it be Boris Feliks? The Bureau had anticipated him changing his appearance—perhaps undergoing plastic surgery—but the sketch bore no resemblance to the photographs they'd taken of Feliks that night in Kiev when he walked off with Nicolai Tarasove's bogus toxin formula.

Tarasove. She dreaded the thought of "babysitting" him at his chateau in Lake Tahoe. There had to be some way to get out of the assignment. She sipped her coffee and stared out the window. A bright green truck was unloading crates of long-stemmed roses. They made her think of the flowers she'd seen in Dymes's house.

What if Harry was right, and Feliks *had* trailed him to

the fortune-teller's place? Could he have been there watching the night she and McNab dropped by Harry's house? If so, Feliks now knew what she looked like. He'd do anything to get to Tarasove. That thought didn't please her at all.

The waiter came with more coffee. He noticed her nearly untouched omelet and said, "Is everything all right, ma'am?"

"I lost my appetite." She handed him the twenty-dollar bill Dymes had left. "Keep the change."

Max was a cadaver-thin man in his thirties, with a deeply tanned, pear-shaped face and eyes that nearly closed when he smiled. He wore a black-and-blue striped T-shirt, with a red-and-white polka-dot scarf knotted at his throat. His platinum blond hair stood up with the firmness of a garden broom.

"I wouldn't go blond," he said, holding a color chart in front of Boris Feliks's face. "Too drastic." He ran a hand slowly through Feliks's hair. "*Very nice* transplant. Your natural color is close to blue-black. Of course the gray is starting to show. No, I recommend something like this. Toasted Chestnut." He tapped a long nail against another swatch. "Or Coffee Bean. If it has to be blond, then I'd say Bold Gold would be as light as you should go."

Feliks studied the hair colors. He'd noticed several young men on Castro Street with obviously dyed hair, and asked them all who was the best stylist in the area. Max won the poll hands down. His shop window had numerous framed photographs of movie actors: Clint Eastwood, a gap-toothed Arnold Schwarzenegger, Sylvester Stallone, and Harrison Ford, along with a dozen more professionally posed men he didn't recognize. All of the photos were autographed and expressed thanks to Max for a wonderful haircut, or, in Stallone's case, *The best style I ever had. You're my man when I'm in San Francisco.*

The handwriting on each photo showed distinct similarities: the Ms and Ns made with rounded tops, the dots on the Is above and to the right of the stem, the Ts crossed well above the stem. Feliks considered himself to be an adequate—though not expert—forger, and he could see that the signatures were all done by the same hand.

The shop had six chairs, and reeked of chemicals and hair spray.

"I want to look different, but I don't want it to appear obvious," Feliks told Max.

"I know just what you mean." Max's fingers made snipping motions. "I don't know who's been cutting your hair, but he or she should stick to mowing lawns. What I'd like to do is feather-cut everything, get rid of those sideburns, and give you a part on the right side, to accent your strong nose. How does that sound?"

Ridiculous to Feliks, but the man seemed to know his business. "Let's do it."

"Wonderful," Max said, sounding sincerely pleased. "And the color? I think Toasted Chestnut is just right for you."

"Fine. Do it."

Max turned to the sink and began scouring his hands. "John. You did say your name was John, didn't you? May I make one more tiny suggestion? Our tanning booths. You have the kind of skin that's just right for the sun."

"All right. How long will all of this take?"

"Three hours, perhaps a little longer. But you'll be a new man. No one will recognize you. I promise."

A muscular young man wearing a scuffed black bicycle helmet, tight-fitting elastic shorts, and a blue-and-yellow nylon jacket with a Corona Beer ad splashed across the front, walked over to Max and smiled widely. "Are you ready for the games tomorrow, Maxie?"

Max slipped a starched white apron over Feliks and picked up his scissors. "I'll be there. Are you riding, Billy?"

"Hell, yes," the young man said. "And I'm playing rugby, too." He slipped off his helmet and flicked his eyes at Feliks. "Bring your new friend."

"Go, go," Max shushed, as he started trimming the hair at the back of Feliks's head.

"What's that all about?" Feliks asked, monitoring the barber's actions closely in the mirror.

"The Gay Sports Festival is this Sunday in Golden Gate Park. It's really fun. Soccer, bike races, softball. All kinds of music, food, and dancing. We get a real crowd. You're not from here, are you?"

"No. Just visiting."

Max used his fingers as a comb, snipping the hair with

the scissors at a fast and furious pace that worried Feliks. "Come out to the park. They close it down just for us. No cars, no traffic. Just good ol' dirty fun."

Are there a lot of police there?"

"A few," Max said. "But they leave us alone. Unless they want to join in the party. I'm sure you'd have a good time. Maybe make some new friends."

"It sounds interesting. I was looking for a place—out in the open—to met someone who's a little nervous about the police. What's a good spot?"

"Try the food booths by the Dutch Windmill. The firemen have a chili cook-off, and the chili is to *die* for." Max used the scissors on Feliks's eyebrows. "And so are the firemen."

Jedgar made low growling noises as Nicolai Tarasove carved the rattlesnake into bite-size chunks and then tossed them on the sizzling grill. He sipped a vodka tonic and used long tongs to turn the meat over. Jedgar wouldn't touch the raw snake meat, but he loved it well-cooked, as did Tarasove.

When the meat was done, he forked it onto a paper plate and placed it on the table to cool. Jedgar's head snapped around and he let out a deep bark. Moments later Tarasove heard a car's engine. He leaned over the balcony to see a beige-and-white SUV making its way up the hill. As the vehicle got closer he could make out the *Sheriff's Department* lettering on the doors.

"Stay," Tarasove ordered, closing the deck gate before running down the steps to greet the lanky young man climbing out of the patrol car.

"How do you do, Officer?" Tarasove said as he stepped down onto the gravel walkway. The policeman was very tall—six foot five or six, he estimated, with hair cropped so close Tarasove could see the splotches of his scalp.

"Deputy Delgetti. Are you Mr. Nick Sennet?"

"That's right," Tarasove said with a tight smile. "Is there a problem, Deputy?"

Delgetti rested his butt on the SUV's hood. "Do you know a Mr. Homer Rutlidge?"

Tarasove kept the smile on his face. "Homer Rutlidge? I can't say I do."

Delgetti pulled a small spiral notebook from his shirt pocket and flicked it open. "Mr. Rutlidge was known as Sundown. A professional gambler. Does that help you remember him, Mr. Sennet?"

"Ah, yes. Sundown. The cowboy." Tarasove patted the top of his head. "He always wears a cowboy hat."

"That's what I've heard," Delgetti said, flicking through his notebook. "We were told that you lost a great deal of money to Sundown the other night at a casino in South Shore."

"True, true," Tarasove said, shaking his head ruefully. "But I had won at least as much from him in the last few months."

Reading from the notepad, Delgetti said, "We understand Rutlidge lived in his motor home and drove from here to Reno, or Las Vegas, depending on the weather and gambling opportunities. Is that right?"

"I wouldn't know," Tarasove protested lightly. "The only times I see him is at a poker table, Deputy. Is he all right? What happened?"

Delgetti put the notepad back in his pocket, tilted his head back and looked up at the chalet's deck.

Jedgar's paws were hanging over the deck railing, his massive head stretched in an attack mode.

"That's a mighty big pit bull. Don't think I've seen one that size before."

"I bought him from a breeder in Georgia. I'm alone here most of the time, except when my son and grandchildren visit."

"Homer Rutlidge died as the result of a heart attack. The coroner believes the attack was induced by a rattlesnake bite."

"My God," Tarasove swore. "A rattlesnake. I see them all the time around here, but I make sure I keep my distance."

Delgetti stood up and stretched to his full height, one hand resting on the horn-handled pistol in his holster. "Somehow the snake gained entrance to Rutlidge's motor home. Hard to figure out how. There are three steps up to the entrance door. Neighbors say that Sundown always kept the door locked."

Tarasove's shoulders flinched. "Snakes. They give me the creeps."

"How much money did you say you lost to Sundown?"

"I didn't say, Deputy. But I'm sure the casinos have records. It was more than fifty thousand dollars."

Delgetti ran his tongue around his jaw. "That's a lot of money where I come from. Can you afford to lose that much, sir?"

"Yes and no." Tarasove laughed. "I couldn't afford to do so on a steady basis. Over the long run, I make money. But there are always those times when you lose. That's the nature of gambling."

"I hope you don't keep that kind of money in the house, Mr. Sennet." Delgetti turned his head around in a half circle, taking in the property. "Nice place. Must have set you back a pile."

Tarasove tilted his head to the side and frowned. "A pile?"

"A lot of money. You're not from around here, are you?"

"No. I'm from Germany. I sold my business a year or so ago and moved here. Wonderful country. My condolences to Mr. Rutlidge's family. He was married? Children?"

"None of the above. And the money he won from you, sir. That was missing from his motor home."

"Perhaps he deposited it with the casino," Tarasove suggested. "That's what I do. Or then again, he might have lost it in another poker game."

Delgetti hitched up his pants and said, "I guess that's possible. Thanks for your time, Mr. Sennet. I may have more questions for you when we get the results of the autopsy."

"I am at your service," Tarasove said genially. "May I ask, how did you obtain this address?"

"The casino had a post office box address for you at Sugar Cove. The postmistress says you pick up mail and boxes there all the time. She told me where the house was."

"That was good of her," Tarasove said, remembering the day the nosy old woman who ran the post office stopped to give him a push when his vehicle had slid into a snowdrift at the entrance to the road leading to the chalet.

Delgetti opened the door to his SUV and was about to slide into the driver's seat, when he straightened up. "Oh, another thing. We've had reports of bears breaking into cabins around here. They're usually pretty easy to get along with, but something's got them riled up. We've found a couple of dead ones down by the lake. We don't know what killed them, but it wasn't old age." He looked up at the deck again and inhaled deeply. "Something smells good. Chicken?"

"Exactly. Barbecued chicken."

"Be careful about those bears, Mr. Sennet."

"I will," Tarasove assured him. And he meant it. He would have to be much more careful from now on. He had had no intention of killing Sundown, just frightening him, so that the next time they were face-to-face in a poker game he could mention something about snakes, and shake the loudmouthed bastard up.

He'd milked the diamondback rattler of its venom before he slipped it into Sundown's RV window, so that a bite would not prove fatal. A heart attack. That's what Boris Feliks claimed Kiryl Chapaev had died from.

He sighed heavily and used the handrail as he climbed up the stairs to the sundeck, remembering a proverb his mother was fond of quoting—"Death to the wolf is life to the lamb." Perhaps, but he preferred being the wolf.

Chapter Nineteen

Boris Feliks grunted disgustedly when he saw the strands of carpeting that he'd wedged into the doorframe were once again lying on the threshold. He unlocked the door and slammed it behind him. He would either have to move, or take care of Jed Dewey, his nosy landlord.

Feliks checked the back of the television set. The money and ID papers were still in place. He flopped onto the lumpy bed, massaged his aching forehead and stared at the moldy ceiling, thinking of Lana Kuzmin, the palm reader. A strong woman. She hadn't died easily—he respected her for that. The only information she had to give homicide detective Dymes was the address of the apartment Zivon Yudin had rented in San Francisco before moving to Los Angeles. Seemingly useless information, but there was no telling what Dymes could have developed from it. Possibly Yudin's rat-infested Southern California address—or perhaps the bar where they'd first met. Had Yudin bragged to his friends about his new contact, a true Russian gangster who used the credit cards of an American named John Kagel?

He ground his hands into his eyes. He'd been careless—allowing a *balkany* punk like Yudin to place him in jeopardy.

Someway, somehow, he had to end this soon. He elbowed himself to a sitting position and activated the laptop computer.

The mailbox was empty, and he was about to shut off the machine when suddenly the screen rolled and the box indicated one message.

Feliks opened the mail from *khokhov,* Tarasove's e-mail name: *Money is a concern. How much are you offering? There are other interested parties. I have twenty-five million reasons to deal with them.*

Tarasove *just* sent the message. Was he still on line?

Quickly, Feliks tapped in a reply: *My clients value your future contributions to the field of science. You will have your money and a guarantee of safety.*

Tarasove's reply came back in under two minutes: *We have to meet. Where?*

Feliks chewed that over before responding: *San Francisco. As soon as possible. Satisfactory?*

Feliks leaned back on his elbows and stared at the screen. A minute passed. Then two. "Come on, Tarasove," he urged. "Answer."

The in-box changed from 0 to 1. *Agreed. I will e-mail you Sunday, at noon. Have a telephone number so that we can talk before the meeting. Ya by hotyl kogda-nibud posetit Rossiyu.*

Feliks had to laugh at that—*"I'd like to return to Russia some day."* So would I, you piece of shit. You're the reason I am unable to. And the trap you think you are setting for me will swallow you up. He jumped to his feet and reached for the bottle of vodka on the wobbly bed stand. He had taken just one drink, but the bottle was now half empty. Jed Dewey. He picked the bottle up by its throat and swung it around in a tight circle. It was time to buy his landlord a drink.

He exited the cottage and climbed the stairs to the back of the main house and was immediately assaulted by loud music: screeching guitars, jarring drums, distorted wailing that reminded Feliks of his first job as a teenager in Moscow working in a dilapidated steel mill.

He opened the door and walked down a dark, musty hallway, coming to a stop when he spotted Dewey standing in the middle of a large room. His bony shoulders were hunched forward, his head shaking violently from side to side, his hands strumming an invisible guitar, a cigarette hanging from his lips. A rolled-up carpet lay before the grate of a soot-stained redbrick fireplace. Several framed posters of long-haired musicians leaned against one wall. The furniture—a faded maroon couch, some chairs, a few small wooden tables—was huddled together at one end of the room near tall windows. There were shades on the windows, but no curtains. The hardwood floor was scarred with heel marks and cigarette burns. Phonograph albums were scattered everywhere. Dust swam around a burned lampshade centered over a sixties-style hi-fi set.

Feliks walked over and turned down the record player's volume.

"Who the fuck are you?" Dewey screamed.

"Your tenant, Jed." Feliks held up the vodka bottle. "I thought I'd buy you a drink."

"John? What the fuck did you do to your hair?" He lurched over to Feliks, drew deeply on his smoke and said, "I didn't think you were no fag."

"Are you alone, Jed?"

"Yeah. But you got no right coming in here. No right cutting off my music. If I knew you was gay I never would have—"

Feliks walked over to the hi-fi and adjusted the music so that it was even louder than before. He then curled his fingers and snapped a short knuckle-extended blow to Dewey's stomach.

Dewey collapsed in a heap. Feliks grabbed his shirt collar and dragged him over to the maroon couch. He positioned Dewey so that he was lying down, the back of his head resting on a pillow.

"Open wide, Jed."

Dewey tried getting to his feet, but Feliks straddled his stomach. As Dewey attempted a scream, Feliks jabbed the neck of the vodka bottle into his mouth. "*Vo pizdu.* To hell you're going, but at least you'll be drunk when you get there."

Harry Dymes focused the video camera's lens on the man he correctly assumed was Roger Dancel. He and Marta Citron were sitting under a green umbrella on the terrace of the Asian Art Museum's cafeteria.

Marta looked cool and attractive in a white skirt and sunglasses. The man took his suit jacket off and looped it around the back of his plastic chair. There were saddlebags of sweat under his arms.

Marta was positioned so that she was facing Harry, who had melted into a large group of tourists on Fulton Street, at the side entrance of the city's main library. He easily read Marta's lips when she called the man "Roger." The crowd of lunchtime office workers, the homeless, and drug dealers had spilled into the street.

Citron and Dancel kept up an animated conversation for several minutes. Harry picked up a word and phrase now and then. Tom McNab, all sweaty and out of breath, arrived on the scene, but his back was to Harry.

Dancel seemed angry about something, taking out his cell phone and shaking it, then tossing the remains of his hot dog bun down to the grass where it was immediately engulfed by a covey of pigeons.

Harry kept filming until Marta and Dancel got up from their chairs. He pulled the camcorder from his eyes and blinked rapidly to get them back in focus. Marta Citron had made it easier for him to see what she was saying. Roger Dancel's lips were more difficult to read, and he had a habit of biting down on his lower lip after a long sentence. He'd have to study the video closely to decipher their conversation.

He placed the camcorder in its case and watched both Dancel and Marta Citron stroll away from the terrace. He took a step, then jerked his head around quickly. That tingling feeling was back. He looked over the crowd, seeing no one unusual—if you called people with beetroot red hair and shower curtain–size rings through their noses normal. No one resembling the man in Julie Renton's sketch.

Chapter Twenty

"You don't have to feel ashamed, Nicky. It happens to a lot of my guys."

Nicolai Tarasove swung his feet off the small bed and hooked his bare foot into his boxer shorts. "It has never happened to me before," he said as he lifted the shorts so that he could reach them with his hand.

The prostitute gave him a sorrowful look. "I have to charge you the same. Whether you get off or not, I have to charge you." She smiled, her upper lip riding up above stubby, tobacco-stained teeth, revealing pale pink gums.

"I understand, Wendy." Tarasove put on his pants and shirt, then sat down on the bed and pulled on his socks.

Wendy leaned against the door, her arms crossed under her bare breasts. There was a time when those breasts excited Tarasove. But no longer. Nothing about her excited him now. She looked ridiculous in her red fishnet stockings and six-inch heels, her jaws moving as if she were chewing gum. And the ash-blond wig. She'd put in on in a hurry. It was tilted to the side, out of place. No wonder he couldn't perform. It had been like making love to a mannequin.

He wiggled his feet into his shoes, then slipped two hundred-dollar bills from his wallet.

She looked from the money to Tarasove, her makeup-smeared face registering disappointment. "No tip today?"

"I'm a little short. I'll make up for it next time. Could I trouble you for a glass of water?"

Wendy tucked the money under the strap of her garter belt and said she'd be right back.

Tarasove moved quickly, going to the bureau drawer where Wendy kept her "toys." He rummaged through the assortment of dildos, whips, and blindfolds, finally finding what he wanted—a finger-size pink plastic vibrator. He jammed it in his pocket just as Wendy returned with the water.

"You'll have to leave right now, Nicky. I have other clients, you know."

Tarasove stopped at a gas station and washed the vibrator with soap and hot water for a good minute, making sure that the battery compartment stayed dry. He purchased a cup of soda and a pint of vodka from the station's convenience store, then pointed the Hummer's hood toward Lake Tahoe, taking alternate sips from the soda and vodka bottle.

He pulled off the road at a rest stop at the top of a mountain. The parking lot was dominated by enormous trucks and trailers. He took a few more hits from the vodka bottle, then used his high-speed, Third Generation mobile phone, which allowed him wireless access to his e-mail, had software that provided a music recorder, and included a number of games, chess, poker, and blackjack. He dialed a number in San Francisco.

"Consulate General of the Russian Federation," a brisk, feminine voice said.

Tarasove switched the vibrator on and held the tip to the hollow area just beneath his Adam's apple. "I represent a prominent person who wishes to go back to the homeland," he said in Russian. "He will need special help."

"There are forms to fill out, and—"

"No forms. This is a *very* prominent person. I will call back in exactly five minutes, and I want to speak to someone in the FSK."

Tarasove cut the connection, worked on the vodka and lost four straight hands of video blackjack, before calling San Francisco again.

The voice that answered the phone this time was different—a man's voice, the accent coarse, guttural.

"Are you FSK?" Tarasove said in Russian.

"That is correct. I am having difficulty understanding you."

Tarasove moved the vibrator down an inch or two and lessened the pressure on his vocal cords. "What is your name?"

"You may call me Arman," the man said.

Tarasove almost chuckled. Arman—protector. A good choice for an embassy goon.

"Give me a safe number."

"All the phone numbers are—"

"You have no idea who you are talking to. The number!"

There was a slight pause, then Arman fulfilled the request.

Tarasove started up the Hummer's engine and reentered the highway, driving for ten minutes before edging off on the side of the road and making the call.

The phone was answered on the first ring.

"Are you certain this number is safe?" Tarasove said.

"Positive," came the reply from Arman.

"I represent a Russian scientist who was kidnapped by the Americans. He wants to return to his home, or at least to another country. The Americans will do anything they can to prevent this. There will have to be accommodations—money, safety guarantees—but you can be assured your superiors in Moscow will be extremely anxious to talk to my client."

"I will need this scientist's name."

"Tell your superiors he's the snake charmer. They will understand. I will call you back tomorrow. This will no doubt lead to a promotion for you."

Tarasove dropped the cell phone into his pocket and took another hit of the vodka. The call had gone well, he thought. He would be more specific when he called again. Or, if it was necessary to actually negotiate with Moscow, set up a meeting with a consular representative in San Francisco—with someone of a higher rank than the thick-headed Arman. *I will need this scientist's name.* He gulped more of the vodka before edging the Hummer back onto the highway.

Arman Ritokov slipped the minicassette out of the recorder and dropped it into a plain white envelope, upon which he printed the date and time and the word *pyccho-ahrinnckom*—routine work.

He stroked the bristles along the edge of his jaw, making a rasping sound. How many crank phone calls had he handled today? Four? Five? All from idiots who wanted to sell secrets, or turn in defectors. He believed half of the calls originated from American agents who were as bored as he was and thought it would be interesting to play a joke on the Russians.

This last call was the best of the week. *Snake charmer.* And the attempt to disguise his voice, demanding to speak to someone from the FSK—the *Federal'naya Sluzba Kontra-ravedky*, Federal Counterintelligence Service—something he must have picked up in an old spy novel. The FSK was no longer in existence, having been reorganized and renamed the FSB—*Federal'naya Sluzhba Bezopasnosti*, Federal Security Service.

Arman stretched his sleeve and consulted his watch. Three hours until he was relieved of duty. How many calls would he have to listen to before he could go out to dinner?

Roger Dancel's face filled the forty-two-inch-wide TV screen. Harry Dymes studied the shape, movement and rhythm of his lips. He'd run through the videotape he'd taken of Dancel and Marta Citron having lunch on the Asian Art Museum terrace several times, and was getting the "feed" better. Much of lipreading is guesswork; under ideal conditions only about fifty to sixty percent of the speech is retained.

Harry played the tape at super slow motion when Dancel or Marta mouthed a word he had difficulty in deciphering. Several times he'd put the machine on pause, held a hand mirror in front of his face and parroted Dancel's lip movements.

He clicked the TV off, sank back into the couch and studied the notes he'd taken.

He'd had no problem discerning Kiryl Chapaev's name, because he'd been expecting it.

The others weren't as easy, but he was reasonably sure he'd gotten them right. Boris Felix, or Felicks. Marta mentioned Julie Renton's composite sketch: "It didn't look like Boris in Kiev, did it?"

The next name to pop up was Nicolai Tearasof, or Terasove, possibly Tarasove. Dancel saying, "Boris has been hunting for Nicolai for years." Moments later Dancel: "You're going to Nicolai's chalet in Lake Tahoe to babysit him."

Marta's response was interesting: *"I hate his goddamn snakes."* Snakes?

Dancel ripped fellow agent Tom McNab, saying McNab knew nothing about Tarasove, other than his code name— Snake Charmer.

Dancel, agitated, griping about his boss, Deputy Director Bartlow, not agreeing with him about "locking up the Russian traitor for good."

Marta had brought Harry into the conversation. "It's his town, Roger, we need his cooperation."

Dancel's response had been short and blunt: "Fuck him." Then Dancel's hand went to his mouth. Harry missed most of the sentence, but picked up what appeared to be "gold bricks."

Boris had to be the Russian assassin Marta had spoken about at dinner—the man who had called him, given him Chapaev's name, followed him to Lana Kuzmin's place— who came to the Hall of Justice, nearly killed him, and then, the following morning, murdered Lana.

Nicolai—the snake charmer. A Russian traitor, with a chalet in Tahoe.

Harry went to the kitchen and pulled a beer from the refrigerator. He had names, or pieces of names. He carried the beer into his bedroom and settled down in front of his home computer. In a case like this, there was only one place to go for the answers—Google.

He struck out with every possible spelling of Boris Feliks, but hit pay dirt when he entered the three possible spellings for the snake charmer's last name, the one Marta was going to have to babysit. "Bingo," he said aloud, as a half-dozen listings filtered across the screen.

The entrance dates were several years old, but generally described Nicolai Tarasove as a renowned Russian scientist at the Science and Technology Center in Kiev, famous for its work on developing weapons of mass destruction. There were two entries in Russian and Harry had to stretch his knowledge of the language to decipher them. One personal item appeared—Tarasove's love of the outdoors, including hunting and fishing.

There was nothing about a wife, children, or snakes. Why the code name Snake Charmer?

Something had been troubling Harry since the murder at the hotel. How had Feliks gotten on to him? Where was the first contact? At the St. Charles? No, he'd been pretty inconspicuous there—meeting the manager briefly in the lobby, then conducting his investigation from the room next to the murder victim's.

He returned to the living room and slotted the cassette with the footage from Lake Merced into the VCR, forwarding to the scene he'd taken of the bystanders who'd watched Zivon Yudin's body being pulled from the lake. There was a man in sunglasses stooping his shoulders, edging in behind the crowd. Harry froze the picture, just as his cell phone began vibrating.

"Hey, pussy pussy cupcake," a familiar voice said. Dick McKevitt, a fellow homicide investigator. "I'm working this fortune-teller case. I hear you knew her."

"I did, Dick. Lana's murder may tie into something I'm working on. We better get together and talk about it."

"I'm at the coroner's office. Doc Phillips says he has something that might interest you."

"Fifteen minutes," Harry said, turning off the TV and getting to his feet.

The phone buzzed again.

Marta Citron spoke in a hushed tone, as if someone were standing near—someone she didn't want to overhear her conversation. "Roger Dancel wants to set up a meeting."

"Really. Before you go up to the Tahoe chalet and babyset?"

Marta hesitated a beat or two before responding. "I

didn't see you in the crowd. Roger would like Julie Renton at the meeting."

"I'll see what I can do," Harry said, glancing at his watch. "How about seven o'clock, here at my place? And after that, how about dinner? I owe you one."

"I'd like that, but let's see how the meeting goes. See you at seven."

Harry dialed the number Julie Renton had given him and left a message on her machine: "My house at six thirty this evening, if you can make it, Julie. There are some FBI investigators who want to have a chat with you."

Chapter Twenty-One

Homicide Inspector Dick McKevitt was engaged in a conversation with a lab technician when Harry arrived at the coroner's office. One sharp-eyed cop had described him as looking like an itinerant caddie dressed up for a blind date. He was in his mid-fifties, with wispy, brown-gray hair, and reminded Harry a bit of Columbo, the TV cop. Where Columbo had his wrinkled raincoat, McKevitt had a wardrobe that consisted mostly of polyester: suits, pants, shirts. He looked like a time warp from the 1960s, and Harry often wondered where he picked up his outfits, which thankfully, had been out of style for many years.

McKevitt patted the technician on the shoulder and ambled over to Harry. "Doc Phillips is waiting for us in the autopsy room. What's the scoop on Lana Kuzmin?"

Harry gave McKevitt a brief rundown on Lana's tie-in to the Chapaev and Zivon Yudin murders. "The FBI is involved, Dick. It all revolves around a Russian scientist they've got stashed somewhere around here. The killer is after the Russian, and he's not bashful about wasting anyone who gets in his way."

"Jesus, Harry, I hate washing hands in the same bowl as the FBI. Let's go see what Doc Phillips has up his bloody sleeves."

Harry involuntarily tightened his stomach muscles and

contracted his nostrils as they walked into the autopsy room. No matter how much disinfectant was used, the stench of chemicals, blood, and human waste dominated the air.

Phillips was hunched over one of the six stainless-steel dissecting tables. Wrist-thick red rubber hoses were attached to each table, along with a sump pump. Alongside, a rubber-wheeled cart, made of the same surgical stainless steel as the dissecting tables, held an assortment of scalpels, bone saws, rib cutters, toothed forceps and chisels.

Phillips waved a gloved hand in greeting. He was dressed in surgical scrubs: gown, cap, a mask with elastic straps dangling down to his chest. "Hello, boys, come on over and have a look."

A bloodstained sheet covered Lana Kuzmin's torso. Her head lay on a small pillow. Harry noted that the luster was gone from her thick black hair. Her eyes were blessedly closed. A series of narrow bruises encircled her neck, and her forehead, near the hairline, had several scrape marks.

"I haven't started the postmortem yet," Phillips said, tilting Lana's head to one side so that Harry and McKevitt could examine the bruises. "It appears that the killer used a garrote of some type. Too thick for a fishing line, possibly tennis racket nylon or strong industrial cord." His finger trailed down Lana's neck. "Notice how the lines move, sometimes overlapping. My guess would be that the victim was taken from behind, pushed to the floor, then the cord was twisted around her neck. It's just a presumption, but it could be that he—if indeed it was a he—was questioning her." Phillips's fingers stretched the bruised flesh. "Notice the depth of the scoring. I could imagine the killer releasing the pressure, asking another question, then cinching up the cord, moving it an inch or two. It must have been terribly painful for her."

"Kuzmin's place was a shambles," McKevitt said. "Furniture knocked over, her crystal ball smashed, broken glass all over the place."

"Did you find a pointed instrument?" Phillips asked. His eye caught Harry's. "Maybe an ice pick?"

McKevitt shook his head. "No. There was a trail of blood on the floor. The cloth that had covered the table was saturated with blood."

"Was there a small puncture hole in the cloth? And the table?" Phillips wanted to know.

McKevitt thrust his hands into his pockets. "I didn't notice, but I'll take another look, Doc."

Dr. Phillips raised the side of the sheet and extracted Lana's left hand. A nickel-size circle of clotted blood was centered in the back of the hand. Phillips used a scalpel to scrape away the blood. "I would say that a sharp instrument entered here, and exited out her palm. Usually with an ice pick–type weapon, the wound is tiny, circular. But you can see here that the wound on the back of her wrist has an irregular configuration, a Y shape." He turned Lana's hand over. "Yet the exit wound is much smaller, leading me to believe that the hand had been pinned to a hard object, such as a tabletop, and, in her struggle to free herself, she exaggerated the width of the sharp object's blade."

Harry touched Lana's cold naked arm. "She was a strong woman. She would have put up a hell of a fight."

"I'm certain that she did," Phillips said. "But to no avail. A guess, and that's all that it is at this point, is that she was alive for some seven to ten minutes after the hand wound and the assault on her throat." He paused dramatically. "Long enough to do this."

Phillips snapped the sheet back, exposing Lana Kuzmin's entire body. There were bruises on her knees, and a tattoo of a red flower in the center of her stomach, the stem disappearing into her bellybutton.

"What's that?" McKevitt said, pointing to the bloodied scratchings on Lana's inner left thigh.

"Possibly the name of her killer," Phillips said, using a sterile towel to clean the area. "I'm thinking that when she was on her knees, being strangled, she used the tip of the sharp instrument in her hand to scratch out a name." He handed Harry an illuminated magnifying glass. "Take a look."

Harry squinted as he studied the puckered skin. The letters were irregular in height and depth, sometimes broken off completely. He could picture Lana on her knees, her head on the floor, struggling, finally realizing that she had no hope to survive, and using all of her strength to carve a name in her own flesh. "John, that's pretty clear. The second name looks like K-A-G-E-L, to me." He handed the magnifying glass to McKevitt, who accepted it reluctantly before leaning over Lana's stomach to examine her thigh.

"That's it. John Kagel," McKevitt said, straightening up quickly. "Who is John Kagel?"

Harry said, "Doc, I'd appreciate some photos of this as soon as possible."

"Will do," Dr. Phillips said, reaching for a Stryker oscillating power saw. "When I'm through here."

Dick McKevitt was halfway to the exit when he stopped and called out, "Hey, Doc. Any of that special formaldehyde in your refrigerator? I could use a drop or two."

"Help yourselves, gentlemen." Phillips clicked on the saw and revved up the motor. "Unless you'd rather stick around and observe the postmortem."

Harry and McKevitt bumped shoulders hurrying through the door, McKevitt making directly for Phillips's office, while Harry took the steps up to the homicide detail.

He went right to the criminal and Department of Motor Vehicles database computer and entered the name *John Kagel*. There were eight DMV hits. None in San Francisco. He ran each name, then checked the date of birth. Six of the Kagels were in the sixty-five to seventy-two age group; the remaining two were teenagers, sixteen and nineteen years of age. None fit the profile for the man who'd murdered Lana Kuzmin—at least in Harry's mind. Lana's killer had to have been very strong—a professional—like Boris Feliks. Harry asked himself whether Feliks was using the name John Kagel as a complete cover, with driver's license and credit cards, or was it just a name he'd picked out of a phone book?

Harry searched the city and then the entire state for criminal records—no hits. He leaned back in the chair and studied the computer screen, contemplating the consequences of sending a request on Kagel to the FBI. Dancel probably had Harry and the entire SFPD homicide detail flagged for criminal checks—and, without a definite date of birth or Social Security number for Kagel, it was a long shot at best. He used his cell phone to dial a familiar number. "Double dozen," he said, when Don Landeta answered the call.

Zhukovka, Russia

General Burian Kilmov watched the Zvezda military helicopter hover several meters above the lawn leading to his tennis courts. The craft finally settled down, its blades slowly decreasing their rotation, the engine growling to a halt.

Kilmov lit a cigarette, pulling the smoke slowly through his lips and letting it escape just as slowly through his nostrils. He glanced back at the house, nodding in approval when he saw the tips of the assault rifles poking through the third floor windows. He wanted his visitor, Sasha Veronin, the Red Mafia kingpin, to see the weapons, just as Sasha wanted him to concentrate on the helicopter's high-caliber machine guns pointed in his direction.

Sasha climbed awkwardly out of the copter's cabin, keeping his head ducked, though the rotors were still. He moved swiftly, on the balls of his feet, looking as if he were about to break into a run at any moment. A book-size wooden box was clutched under one arm.

For all of Sasha's wealth and power, to Kilmov he still looked like a man who sold things that fell off trucks.

"General, you're looking well." Sasha's eyes scanned the house's windows. "You don't trust me?" he mocked, as he handed the wooden box to Kilmov. "Cuban cigars. Montecristos." He brought his fingers to his lips and gave them a smacking kiss. "The best, my friend."

"You're very kind," Kilmov said, sitting down at the patio table and pouring tea for the Mafia chieftain. "What can I do for you today?"

"Old business first," Sasha said, snapping the cedar box open and helping himself to a cigar. "Examine your gift, please."

Kilmov's fingers worked through the top layer of cigars. Beneath the tobacco were six stacks of one-hundred-denomination Euros. "I trust you, Sasha." He smiled. "I won't count it until you've left."

"Ah, you military men. You all have a sense of humor. Of course, you can always rely on your pension if our business transactions come apart." He leaned forward, his face suddenly serious. "The shipment of antitank rockets was exactly where you said it would be."

"It was unfortunate that two brave Russian army privates were killed in the robbery," Kilmov said, dropping his cigarette to the flagstone patio floor and grinding it under his heel.

"You have more than a million soldiers. Two less won't matter." Sasha dipped a spoon into a crystal jam pot and added two heaping spoonfuls of raspberry jam to his tea. "New business, Burian. Do you remember a little prick of a scientist by the name of Nicolai Tarasove?"

"I remember that you tried to buy his snake toxin for the Chinese, but were duped by the Americans."

Sasha took a loud, slurping sip of his tea, then said, "I hate those cocksuckers."

"The Chinese or the Americans?" Kilmov asked innocently.

"Both!" Sasha heaped more jam into his tea. "Tarasove is in America right now."

"I know that."

Sasha's head snapped up. "Do you know *exactly* where he is?"

"Not yet," Kilmov admitted.

"I have some reliable information on his latest venom project—*Napitak Zlobi*. It is much more powerful, more sophisticated, than before, and he's been holding it back from the Americans."

"How much more powerful and sophisticated?"

Sasha removed a single folded piece of paper from his jacket pocket, and handed it to Kilmov.

It was badly typed, and full of numerous grammatical errors—indicating Veronin had typed it himself.

"It sounds too good to be true," Kilmov said, when he'd finished reading the document.

"Too bad to be true." Sasha bit the end off one of the Cuban cigars. "How much money would your superiors pay for his formula?"

"A great deal," Kilmov said. "I've already authorized a considerable amount of money to the project."

"A considerable amount. That is what I would like the two of us to make out of this. You're holding back on me. How close are you to Tarasove?"

Kilmov twisted the gold wedding band on his finger. "It's difficult to say."

"He won't just offer himself up to you and ask for forgiveness for past sins. The Jew bastard will want money, a new life. All of that will be very expensive. It would be better for us if I bring him and his formula here."

"I didn't know Tarasove was a Jew."

Sasha rolled the end of the cigar in the jam pot, then stuck it between his lips. "All of those scientists have some Jew blood in them." He lowered his voice to a conspiratorial whisper. "There is a fortune to be made from this, Burian. You know something, I know something. Let's work together and not piss it all away."

Kilmov lifted up his pinkie finger and bit off a piece of skin near the nail. "There is a man who uses the name Alex. He has helped me trace defectors in the past. He is a competent assassin, with incredible resources. The defectors were all well hidden by the Americans—yet he found them."

Sasha lit his cigar and inhaled as if it were a cigarette. "I've never heard of him."

"Two days ago, he contacted me, offering to locate Tarasove."

Sasha came to the correct conclusion in a flash, which is why Kilmov liked dealing with the ruthless bastard. He was that rare combination of street thug and shrewd businessman.

"Someone else sent Alex on the hunt for Tarasove, right? He's—what do they say? Playing one end against the other."

"Any idea who the other player could be? I thought it might be you."

Sasha worked his cigar thoughtfully from one side of his mouth to the other. "The Chink, Ying Fai. It has to be him."

"You think so? I know you have a personal grudge against Fai. After all, *you* were going to deliver Tarasove's toxin to him two years ago."

Momentarily caught off guard, Sasha countered with, "That's because I didn't know what a wonderful person you were, my new good friend. Ying Fai is using your Alex, who sees a way to double his money. How much is he asking for?"

"Three million American," Kilmov said. "One million has already been deposited to his Swiss bank account."

"The Swiss. If I didn't have so much of my money in their vaults, I'd hate those bastards too."

"Who is your source for the information about Tarasove and his formula?"

Sasha studied the collar of ash on his cigar for several moments before responding. "I've been after Tarasove ever since the FBI stole him from me. I have someone very close to Tarasove right now—"

"Boris Feliks," Kilmov interjected.

"As usual, you are well informed, General."

Kilmov reached for a cigar. "You were about to inform me yourself, I'm sure."

Sasha grunted, then said, "I'll have Tarasove's exact location in a short time—a week, perhaps two. It will cost, of course. Ten million American." He tugged at one of his sideburns. "That's a lot of money, that should be coming to us, Burian. What if we could arrange for the two of them to cancel each other out? After they've led us to the scientist, of course. And this time I take *him*, not just his notebook and coffee Thermos."

"You're forgetting Ying Fai," Kilmov said.

"I'll never forget Fai until he's six feet under ground. You say that Alex is a competent assassin. Competent enough to eliminate Fai?"

Kilmov turned to watch Ivana, his young blond wife, and her tall, dark-haired tennis instructor stroll toward the tennis courts. She waved a lean, tan arm in his direction. He raised his teacup in a mock toast. "My wife is a perfectionist," he said. "Practice, practice, practice." He poured them both more tea. "I have no reason to think that Alex couldn't handle such a job, but the price would be very high."

"Who cares about the price?" Sasha said. "He's never going to collect. It's a win-win situation, Burian. We get Tarasove and the grateful thanks of your superiors and the people of Russia, along with an enormous amount of money—which we will split exactly down the middle." Sasha leaned back in his chair and puffed rapidly on the cigar, waving the cloud of smoke away with a backhanded paddle motion. "Sometimes," he said contentedly, "despite all of what we've been told, I do believe there really is a God."

Chapter Twenty-Two

Reno, Nevada

Trina Lee rolled the silver Jaguar X-Type sedan to a stop alongside a dust-streaked dark brown cabover van. She opened the door, swung her legs out, and began a series of yoga deep-breathing exercises.

It had been a hectic twenty-four-hour period. She'd flown to San Francisco, rented the Jag at the airport, established a base at a motel near Fisherman's Wharf, then gone about her "shopping chores."

She had no difficulty getting her camera and surveillance equipment through the airport security systems; however, the risks were too high to consider carrying even the most rudimetary of weapons—and that had created a burgeoning network of underground arms suppliers near every major airport in the world. She contacted a man she'd dealt with in Seattle, who—for a fee—had recommended a San Francisco amateur gunsmith, whose place of business was the trunk of his vintage Mercedes sedan.

Trina had selected a .22 caliber semiautomatic with a screw-on silencer from the Merc's well-stacked trunk. The weapon fit snugly in her leather Meridian holster purse, which featured a side-entry, self-contained holster compartment with locking zipper. It was her one holdover from her brief FBI career—nearly every female agent in the Bureau had one just like it.

She was up and on the road by six in the morning for a three and a half hour drive to Reno.

She tilted her sunglasses up to read the printing on the side of the dust-streaked brown cabover van. *We deliver anything, anywhere, on time.*

The van was parked in the rear of Cresta's Delivery Service parking lot. She pushed through the entrance doors to find two empty desks, overflowing waste cans, a watercooler, and walls covered with thumbtacked calendars, San Francisco 49ers banners, and photographs of cowboys roping steers

A wheezing air conditioner helped drown out the sounds of a country and western music radio station. A pebbled-glass door at the rear bore the stenciled name *Robert J. Cresta.*

"Anyone here?" Trina called out, her eyes scanning the windows and door casings for telltale security alarm wires.

"Back here," a gruff male voice answered.

Trina opened the glass door. A lean-faced man with short dark hair was sitting behind a cluttered desk, his scuffed boots resting on a pile of business forms and manila folders.

"Are you Mr. Cresta?"

"Guilty," the man answered reluctantly. "Are you a process server?"

"Hardly," Trina said. "I'm with the *Wall Street Journal.* We're doing several feature stories on small delivery businesses in the area. I was out at the airport, and your name came up."

Cresta dragged his boots from the desk and stood up, offering his hand. "*Wall Street Journal?* I'm about as small a business as you can find, Miss . . . ?"

"Lee. My article will focus on exotic deliveries." She was wearing tight black slacks and a matching sleeveless T-shirt with an industrial-size zipper down the front from throat to bellybutton. "The shipping clerk at the airport said you pick up exotic snakes, and rats, and mice. I find that fascinating."

"I find it profitable," Cresta said. "I just don't get enough of it. One customer." He waved a hand at the papers on his desk. "I can't pay my bills that way."

"Who is the customer?" Trina asked

Cresta wagged his head from side to side. "Sorry. I can't tell you that without his permission."

Trina took off her glasses and slipped them into her purse, her fingers brushing against the trigger of the semi-automatic. She pursed her mouth a moment, debating just how to handle the situation. It wasn't worth the effort to kill the man. Breaking into the office late at night wouldn't be difficult, but judging from the looks of Cresta's desk and dilapidated file cabinets, finding Tarasove's billing records would be time-consuming.

"Okay," she finally said, moving up close to Cresta. She tugged at the zipper on her shirt. It whispered seductively. "Tell me, Robert J., do you get lonely down here all by yourself?"

Cresta seemed startled by the question. "Are you some kind of private eye my wife hired? That *Wall Street Journal* line is bullshit, right?"

"I'm not a private eye, not a process server. Just a girl who needs help on a story." She ran her hand down his shirt, then across the oversize silver belt buckle in the shape of a horseshoe. She unhooked the buckle and the jeans' waist button, then wiggled her hand inside his pants. "What's the name of the snake man, Robert J.?"

Cresta's eyes drifted down to her open shirt. "Sennet. Nick Sennet."

"And where does Mr. Sennet live?"

"Lake Tahoe. By Sugar Cove." Cresta groaned as Trina's hand explored further. "It's hard to find. I'll have to draw you a map."

Trina dropped to her knees and tugged at his jeans. "If you're lying to me, Robert J., I'm going to come back and bite off a piece of you."

Cresta reached a hand out to the desk to steady himself. "Why the hell would I lie to you, lady?"

Trina Lee drove the fifty-four miles from Reno to Sugar Cove in just under an hour and ten minutes. She parked under a towering pine tree, studying the map Cresta had made on the back of one of his billing forms, searching for the unmarked road leading to Nick Sennet's place—"Big joint with a nice deck, but look out for his dog. He's a mean sucker," according to Cresta. The house was on the east side of the narrow highway, 2.6 miles north of the Sugar Cove Restaurant, which featured "Great hamburgers and home-made pies." Cresta also told her that Sennet looked "a lot like Santa Claus," and drove a big black Hummer.

Trina's rented Jaguar sedan was parked in that exact location according to the odometer, but she saw no sign of a road.

She got out of the Jag and began walking, her sandaled feet making crunching sounds on the fallen leaves that littered the roadway. She couldn't believe that the delivery man had lied to her. She *was* going to go back and settle the score with him.

A black Hummer squealed to a halt on the opposite side of the road and a man with a round, white-bearded face stuck his head out of the vehicle's window.

"Did your car break down? Do you need a lift?"

"No," Trina assured him. "I'm just taking a little walk. Stretching my muscles."

The man nodded pleasantly, put the Hummer in gear and drove some fifty yards before turning west and vanishing into a thicket of trees. *West.* Cresta had gotten it wrong. On purpose? Or was it just a mistake? It really didn't matter now. Trina hurried to the Jaguar, made a quick U-turn and pulled over to the spot where the Hummer had disappeared. The road wasn't much—rutted, chocolate-colored dirt, spiraling up a steep grade.

She leaned her head back on the headrest and smiled at the blue sky. She had Tarasove. It had been almost too easy. Now came the hard part—collecting the money from Ying Fai *and* General Burian Kilmov of the SVR. And there was still the matter of Boris Feliks to attend to.

She drove the Jaguar a few hundred yards down the road, took a camera bag from the trunk and started climbing through the trees bordering the road leading to Nicolai Tarasove's sanctuary.

"Quiet," Nicolai Tarasove shouted to Jedgar as soon as he climbed out of the Hummer. He was in no mood to placate the dog. He unlocked the front door to the chalet and made directly for the kitchen, the chastised pit bull following closely behind.

Tarasove yanked open the freezer door and reached for the vodka bottle sitting alongside the bear's head. He poured himself a stiff drink, swallowed greedily, then began coughing.

He waited until the coughing subsided, then drizzled more vodka into the glass and took a sip, swirling the icy liquid around his mouth before swallowing.

"*Khue "vye den 'ki nastali*," he said, glaring at the dog. "It's been a bad day, Jedgar, and I'm taking it out on you."

He leaned down and scratched the dog's head in an apology. It *had* been a bad day, and could get much worse. He'd spent the morning in the Lake View Casino manager's office, assuring the greedy capitalist that his line of credit was not in jeopardy, and that he intended to continue his poker playing. The man could have been a Russian banker: cold, heartless, inflexible. There would be no more credit. Nicolai had exceeded his limit, and would have to come up with fifty thousand in cash within the week, before he could participate in any high-stakes gambling. The two million dollars he'd received from the FBI had all been gambled away, and his monthly stipend was not enough to cover his losses. He needed an infusion of cash to turn his luck around.

There were half a dozen casinos within walking distance of the Lake View, but word of bad credit spread quickly. He'd foolishly tried to turn the three thousand dollars in his pockets into fifty thousand at the crap tables and roulette wheels—only to lose it all.

The casino manager had also made several pointed remarks about the unusual circumstances of the death of Sundown, the gambler. "The sheriff has been in twice, asking questions about you, Mr. Sennet. I hope everything is all right."

Everything wasn't all right. Tarasove drained the remains of his vodka and rubbed the cold glass across his forehead. The only pleasant thing that had happened today was seeing that pretty girl walking along the highway. There was no time to drive down to Carson City for a little relaxation.

"A pretty girl," he said aloud. "That's what we need, Jedgar."

Tarasove often spoke aloud to Jedgar, as he had to Shelia, his Siberian husky, before the bear killed her. When he wasn't talking to the dog, he talked to the snakes, or the mice and rats. It somehow comforted him to hear his own voice. He went to the laboratory, put on a smock, then washed his hands before donning a pair of thick rubber gloves.

He shook two white pills from a prescription medicine bottle and used a mortar to grind them into a clear powder, then carried the mixture back to the kitchen.

"Rohypnol, Jedgar. The date rape pill." He leered at the dog. "Not that I intend to molest you."

The drug was illegal, but widely available in the United States. Tarasove had ordered it on the Internet from a Mexican pharmaceutical firm, and used it in very small doses to calm the native rattlesnakes he trapped for his experiments.

"How much are you weighing now, Jedgar? You're getting fatter than me. Ninety-five pounds? And what does our good friend Marta weigh? A hundred and twenty? Not much more."

He took some venison he'd ground into chuck and mixed the powder into it, then dropped the meat into Jedgar's food bowl.

The big dog's paws slipped and clattered on the tile floor in his haste to reach his lunch.

Tarasove fixed himself another vodka, noted the time on the wall clock, and turned his attention to Jedgar, who consumed the entire bowl of food in less than two minutes.

Tarasove snapped his fingers and ordered the dog, "Come."

Jedgar took a final lick at the bowl, then started toward his master, who turned on his heel and headed for the sundeck.

He leaned on the railing, enjoying the vodka and the view, planning his next move. He was not quite ready to leave America, but there seemed no choice now—Boris on his back, threatening to leak the information he forced from Kiryl Chapaev about the DNA toxin to the FBI. Roger Dancel would be furious when he learned of the gambling debts and the circumstances of the poker player's death. He knew that Dancel resented his lifestyle, and would rather have him locked away in a compound where his every move would be monitored.

Being a scientist involved careful planning, and Tarasove had a backup plan if ever the occasion arose when he'd have to leave the United States in a hurry—a call to the Russian Consulate. He'd settled on a country—Finland, somewhere near Helsinki. There were many casinos in that area, and it was a short boat ride to St. Petersburg. The prostitutes were young, blond Nordic beauties, and hunting in Finland was considered a God-given right.

Jedgar began moaning lightly. His footing became unsure. He slipped to the wooden deck, tried to get back up on his paws, then collapsed and began snoring loudly.

Tarasove checked his watch again. It had taken the drug a little more than nine minutes to put Jedgar into a deep sleep. Rohypnol would work even faster when mixed with alcohol, the results being a blackout of up to twelve hours—often accompanied by complete memory loss for that time period.

There were many fine wines in his cellar. He'd been saving a bottle of Opus One Cabernet, which set him back close to a hundred and fifty dollars, for a special occasion— and Marta Citron certainly was special.

Julie Renton was waiting at the entryway to Harry Dymes's house when he pulled into the driveway, leaning against the hood of a sunburn-pink Miata convertible. She was wearing a coral-colored dress, cut low, with spaghetti straps scoring her bare shoulders. A black leather purse the size of a carry-on suitcase was at her feet, which were encased in stiletto-heeled sandals that added four inches to her height.

"You told me to be here at six thirty," Julie said, looking at her wristwatch. "That was fifteen minutes ago."

"Sorry about that, kid." Harry fumbled for the keys in his pocket. "I had to attend an autopsy. Nice car. Business must be good."

"It belongs to a friend. A *girl* friend, who I'm staying with in Sausalito, until you tell me it's safe for me to go back to my apartment."

Harry held the door open for her. "Come on in. I want you to see a video I made."

Julie stopped with one high heel on the stair. "I've heard that one before. I hope it isn't of the autopsy."

While Harry poured them a glass of wine, Julie peered through his telescope. "Peeking in bedrooms?" she said, after he'd handed her the wine.

"Let me brief you on the two FBI agents who should be arriving any minute. One's a hard-ass by the name of Roger Dancel. Don't let him rattle you."

"Not a hell of a lot rattles me, Harry."

"He'll ask you questions about the time you spent with Paul Morris. Much the same questions I asked you."

"What about the other agent? They're not going to play 'good cop, bad cop' with me, are they?"

"It's a woman. Marta Citron. Dancel will try and pressure you about your profession, confuse you. Just don't take any guff from him."

"You *will* be here to protect me, won't you?"

"I won't let you out of my sight, kid. Just be your charming self, and try not to fall out of that dress. You'll do fine."

Julie ran a hand across her ear, brushing away an errant lock of hair. "Tell me more about Dancel. How old is he? What does he look like?"

"Forty, something like that. Nothing special about his looks."

"And the lady agent. Citron?"

Dymes nodded and headed for the kitchen. "A little younger. She's sharp, but Dancel is the agent in charge." Harry opened the refrigerator door. "I haven't got much for hors d'oeuvres except for cheese and crackers."

Julie let out a long, exaggerated sigh. "I don't think the FBI is going to be interested in your hors d'oeuvres, Harry."

Chapter Twenty-Three

Washington, D.C.

"Is there anything else, Mr. Bartlow?" his secretary asked, looking pointedly at the clock over Bartlow's desk.

"No, you can go, Miss Keaton. And thanks for staying so late." He watched his stocky, dour-faced secretary walk to the door, thinking that, though she had been working for him for nearly two years, he didn't know her first name. Was Keaton married? Children? Grandchildren? He really had no interest in her personal life, but he *did* have an interest in Roger Dancel's. "Oh, one more thing. Bring me a list of the personnel in our San Francisco office."

Keaton nodded her head, her face showing no sign of irritation.

Bartlow's desk was strewn with reports relating to Dancel's allegation that there was a meat eater in the Bureau. He'd run the names of every defector and Mafia turncoat who'd died while in the Witness Security Program over the last six years. The total number was thirteen, four of which were from cancer or heart attacks, the victims expiring while in the hospital.

One of the very few people who had access to all thirteen records was Roger Dancel.

There was something about Dancel that rubbed Bartlow

the wrong way. His snide remarks, his disgusting jokes about women. And his behind the scenes, backstabbing attempts to discredit Bartlow in order to get his job

Bartlow had his own network of Bureau whistle-blowers, and he had determined that the best way to muzzle Dancel was to implicate him in an inter-agency investigation.

He knew that he couldn't pin the meat eater label on Dancel—he was too high profile—but perhaps he'd been careless, allowed underlings access to those oh-so-secret files.

No, Dancel wouldn't fit into the meat eater's shoes; however, he could be cast as a mole, working for organized crime or for the Russians.

Once an accusation like that was made against a high-ranking Bureau official—even if he was completely cleared—there would be a dark stain of suspicion that followed him for the rest of his career.

The entire American public was now under the impression that J. Edgar Hoover was a fruitcake who paraded around in women's clothing. The accusation had been made by the wife of a low-level mafioso with a grudge against Hoover. There were never any photographs, and the place where the woman claimed she'd seen Hoover in drag was a public party, allegedly attended by hundreds of people.

J. Edgar may have been gay, may have danced around in knickers and wigs, but if he did so, it would never have been where he could be seen and recognized.

Miss Keaton coughed into her hand to get Bartlow's attention. "Here's a list of the San Francisco personnel, sir. Good night."

"And a good night to you." Bartlow squeezed his eyes shut, his eyebrows drawn into a straight, connecting line above the bridge of his nose. What he had to do was put knickers and a wig on Roger Dancel.

He opened his eyes and ran a finger down the list of FBI agents working out of San Francisco. Several of the names were familiar, but didn't suit Bartlow's taste. His finger stopped on the name Thomas McNab. Congressman Gerald McNab's brother. He'd met Gerald once, and considered him to be the type of elected official the Bureau should be cultivating. Bringing his brother into a major investigation was certainly one way to do that.

Bartlow pushed the button on his desk that summoned his secretary—then he remembered she was gone for the night. He'd have to place the call to San Francisco himself.

"This goddamn street ought to be a ride at Disneyland," Roger Dancel complained as Marta Citron tooled the Bucar down Vermont Street's torturous curves. "San Francisco. You can have it," Dancel continued. "Where's the cool gray fog and cable-car-to-the-stars crap I've heard about for years? All I see is hot weather, lousy food, and uncooperative cops."

"I don't think you can judge the city's food by one cafeteria lunch," Marta said. She slowed the car down to loitering speed, looking for a parking spot. "We'll either have to park at the bottom of the hill or circle around again."

"Right over there," Dancel said. "The red zone. If you get a ticket, I'll have McNab pay for it."

"You're in a surly mood," Marta said, when the car was parked and they were trudging up the hill.

"I haven't had a hike like this since boot camp. When are you going up to babysit Tarasove?"

"In the morning. It's too late to drive up there tonight. Have you thought about trying to lure Boris Feliks into a trap using Chapaev's e-mail address?"

"I thought about it, but it's a no-go. Feliks is too sharp to fall for a stunt like that."

When they arrived at Dymes's driveway, Dancel pointed to the small pink convertible and lime-green hybrid. "Who is visiting Dymes? Two of the seven dwarfs?"

"The Honda is an official police vehicle."

Dancel gave her an are-you-kidding-me look, then said, "The pink job must be the hooker's. Let's go feel her out. So to speak. Lead the way. You've been here once or twice, haven't you?"

"Once," Marta said coolly, refusing to rise to Dancel's barbs. She rang the bell and moments later the door was answered by Harry Dymes.

"Come on in," Harry said. "Both of you look like you need a drink."

When they were in the living room, Marta made a formal introduction. "Roger, this is Inspector Dymes."

Marta noticed that when Dancel shook Harry's right

hand, his left hand clamped on Dymes's forearm in a show of authority. She was pleased to see that Roger gave a slight wince before his right hand was freed.

The two men circled each other, like prizefighters before the opening bell. Roger, in his bland, travel-creased gray suit, straightening his usually slumped posture to appear taller; Dymes wearing a blue blazer that looked as if it had been put together one stitch at a time, his gaze fixed on Dancel's forehead, forcing the smaller man to stretch his neck to make eye contact.

"I've heard a lot about you, Inspector," Dancel said.

"If you heard it from Tom McNab, it's probably not true," Harry said.

Dancel frowned at the numerous vases filled with roses as he wandered over to the windows. "Nice place. Must have cost a gold brick or two."

Marta watched as a sexy-looking brunette wiggled her way in from the kitchen.

"This is Julie Renton," Harry announced.

"Can I get anyone a drink?" Julie said. "Wine, Scotch, vodka, Harry's got it all."

"Does he really?" Dancel said. "Nice to meet you, Julie. Scotch is fine, but what I really want to know is about that shooting at the Hall of Justice, Inspector. You're lucky you weren't killed. Marta tells me that you think the shooter may be someone we're interested in."

"Someone we're both interested in. I've seen him—so has Miss Renton. Agent Citron wouldn't give me his name. I'm hoping you will."

Julie came in with a tray of drinks.

Marta nodded her thanks for the vodka on the rocks, then said, "I think Roger would like to see Miss Renton's sketch and read her statement, Inspector."

Harry nodded to the coffee table. "It's all right there."

Dancel sank into the couch and gave the sketch a long look, then zipped through the statement. "This is all well and good." He looked up at Harry and frowned. "But not a lot of it sticks to the wall, if you know what I mean, Inspector."

"It's the same man who shot at me, and who murdered Kiryl Chapaev and Zivon Yudin."

Marta studied Dymes over the rim of her glass, wondering why he'd left out the murder of the fortune-teller.

Dancel took a long sip of the Scotch before saying, "You're convinced of that, but I'm not."

"I'll make a deal with you, Dancel," Harry said. "I'll show you a picture of the man, not a sketch. Then you tell me his name, and the real reason he's in my town."

Marta said, "You didn't mention a picture to me."

"It's a video." Harry jutted his chin at Dancel. "Do we have a deal?"

Dancel settled back on the couch. "Let me get this straight. You're going to show me a video of some guy *you* say is the . . . party the Bureau is interested in. What if I don't agree? What if you pull a fast one? Show me a picture of some Frisco cop. You and Julie here may have cooked the whole thing up, as far as I know."

"What have you got to lose? I'm going to find out what this is all about anyway."

Now Marta was confused. What game was Harry playing? Had his lip-reading skills failed him? He had picked up where Dancel called him a loser, but what had he missed? Feliks's name? Tarasove's?

"Okay," Dancel said. "Let's see the picture."

Harry turned on the TV. The tape was cued to the scene where he'd turned the camera on the Lake Merced onlookers.

"Stop it right there," Julie Renton said.

Harry froze the picture.

Julie moved closer to the TV screen. "The guy in the sunglasses. It looks cold and foggy. No one else is wearing sunglasses. Did you notice how he kind of ducked down and stepped behind that blimp in the black-and-yellow jogging outfit? He's the one who sat next to me at Moose's."

"You're sure it's him?" Harry asked.

"His hair is the same. Yeah. I'm certain it's him."

"The killer returns to the scene of the crime," Marta said. "He does look like the man in Miss Renton's sketch, Roger. It could be . . . our man, wearing a toupee, and after some plastic surgery."

Dancel snatched up the sketch and carried it over to the TV screen. "That's a possibility," he admitted.

Harry ejected the cassette and handed it to Marta. "Do I get that name now?"

Marta turned to Dancel. "It's your call, Roger."

Dancel looked pointedly at Julie Renton, who flashed

her dimples and said, "I'll see if there's something in the refrigerator for snacks."

When she was gone, Dancel's voice became official-sounding. "What I tell you is strictly confidential, Inspector, and I hope you'll handle it that way."

When Harry didn't respond, Dancel continued. "The man who may or may not be the one in Renton's sketch, and in your video, is a skilled assassin, a member of the Russian Mafia."

"His name," Harry prodded.

"Ivan Lemkov."

"Lemkov. What are his AKAs? The different names he's used since he came to America?"

Dancel screwed up his face. "I don't know of any other names."

Marta understood now. Harry was testing Dancel—and Roger had failed.

Harry picked up his untouched wineglass and took an audible sip. "What about the man Lemkov is after?"

"What about him?" Dancel challenged.

"*Why* is Lemkov after him?"

"He's a scientist. That's all you need to know."

"Wrong," Harry said. "If you want help in finding the man you call Lemkov, I'm going to have to know something about the target."

Dancel shook the ice cubes at the bottom of his glass. "I can't give you his name, but his work is vital to the United States. It involves weapons of mass destruction."

"Nuclear?"

"No." Dancel managed a wintry smile. "And that's *absolutely* all I can tell you about him, Dymes."

The two men stared daggers at each other for a moment. Marta thought that Harry was going to reach over and hit Dancel.

The tension was broken when Julie Renton returned with a tray in hand. "Cheese and crackers, anyone?"

Dancel placed his glass on the coffee table. "Thanks, but no thanks. I've got work to do. Miss Renton, I'd like to go over this tape with you again later. What's your address and phone number?"

"Harry has them," Julie said. "You can contact me through him."

Marta picked up her purse. "How convenient. Thanks for the drink, Inspector."

Harry held out his hand, and Marta shook it, coming away with a small piece of folded paper.

"Where did you come up with that Ivan Lemkov name?" she asked Dancel when they were walking down the steep hill to the car.

"Lemkov played jazz violin at a joint on West Thirty-eighth in New York City. He may still be there for all I know."

"Do you think it was wise giving Dymes a phony name for Boris Feliks? He won't be able to help us if he doesn't know who we're really after."

Dancel paused to catch his breath when they reached the car. "Why tell Dymes anything?" He took the videotape from Marta's hand. "I gave him a line of bullshit, and he hands us a video of what Feliks looks like right now. I'd say I shafted your buddy pretty good."

Marta unlocked the car, and, as she got behind the wheel, the words to an old Nashville song came to her mind: *You got the goldmine, and I got the shaft.*

Dancel tapped the videotape against his knee. "Julie Renton doesn't look like your average hooker. I'm going to have to talk to her again, but I don't want to go through Dymes. She'll probably shack up with him all night."

Marta started the car and was about to pull away from the curb when Dancel's cell phone rang. He motioned for her to cut the engine.

"Dancel here." Roger nodded his head a couple of times, then said, "No shit," before cupping the receiver. "It's Tom McNab. You got a call at the office from 'Snake Charmer.' Tarasove said that one of his snakes bit him. Nothing serious, but he won't be up to company for a day or so. He told me in Kiev that a snakebite that would kill me, would only give him a headache or upset stomach. He wants you to delay your trip up there. Give him a call."

Dancel turned his attention back to McNab. "Tom, I want you to run down a local hooker by the name of Julie Renton. Here's her license plate number."

As Marta climbed out of the car, a pink convertible whizzed by with Julie Renton, alone, at the wheel. She rummaged through her purse for the cell phone. She found the piece of paper Harry Dymes had handed her. The note read: *Dimitri's Tearoom on Fifth Avenue. Ten o'clock?*

Nicolai Tarasove answered the call, sounding hale and hearty to Citron.

"I'm so glad you called, Marta. There's been an accident. One of my babies bit me."

"Why don't you get to the hospital, Nicolai? Or call a doctor."

"No. I'll be a little sick for a day. No more. I had extracted most of the venom before I was bitten. I'm worried about my baby. He's loose, and Jedgar's going crazy."

Marta's back stiffened. "The snake is loose in the house?"

"Yes. Scared and frightened to death. Don't worry. I'll find him before you come up to see me. Not tomorrow. The next day, that is convenient?"

"Find that goddamn snake," Marta said bluntly, "or you're never going to see me again."

Zhukovka, Russia

"*Panthera tigris altaica* is the correct terminology," Sasha Veronin said with a wide yawn. "Siberian tiger to us plain folks."

Burian Kilmov gazed down at the huge orange-and-black striped tiger. It was dozing between two jagged rocks in the sunken, junglelike setting Veronin had carved out in his massive garden.

"Biggest cat in the world," Veronin lectured. "Twelve feet from nose to tail, weighs nearly seven hundred pounds. And also the rarest. Do you know why, Burian? Because they're delicious. And those crazy Chinks who poach them think that their bones and organs are the ultimate aphrodisiac. Dumb bastards could get better results from a Viagra pill, but they continue to exterminate these beautiful creatures. I've had Zazzat here since he was a cuddly little cub." He stifled another yawn. "But you didn't wake me in the middle of the night to learn about tigers, Burian. What's up?"

"This." He passed Sasha a photograph. "Alex just e-mailed this to me. I thought you should see it right away. Is it Tarasove? I've never met the man."

Sasha snatched the photograph and held it up to his eyes. "That's Tarasove, all right. He's put on weight. Hair's longer. But it's him. Where is he?"

"Alex won't give me an exact location until I transfer the rest of the money to his Swiss account, but he did indicate that I should plan to have someone available 'near San Francisco' shortly."

"Which Swiss Bank?" Sasha wanted to know.

"Credit Suisse."

"I have some of my money there, an excellent bank. Clever *styervo*, isn't he? Nobody's fool. Get the money up front. Can't fault him for that. We can pay him whatever he wants, and then force him to transfer his money over to my accounts. Which I would then split with you, of course." Sasha studied the photograph closely. The view was from the ground, looking up at Tarasove, who was leaning over a wooden deck railing. The background showed the tip of a roof and some tall trees. "There's no way to know where this was taken."

"Or when," Kilmov said.

"What's the plan after you give Alex his money?"

"We send someone to San Francisco to pick up Tarasove."

"I have just the man," Sasha said, his eyes now on the dozing tiger. "Boris Feliks. You want this prick Alex, no?"

"I want him, yes. Alive. I want to break his balls, and find out just how he locates these people." Kilmov slapped a hand on his hip, causing the tiger's head to snap up. "We've been searching for Tarasove for years, and he finds him in a matter of days."

"So we send Boris Feliks, as *our* representative to Alex. Boris told me he was very close to Tarasove. He may be in San Francisco now. Or somewhere nearby. We let Boris handle Alex, and take Tarasove. We've got the fat scientist, Alex, Boris, and their money. Everyone is happy."

"Contact Feliks right away, Sasha. I want to strike while the iron is hot."

"And I'd like to shove that hot iron up Ying Fai's ass." Sasha put a meaty hand on Kilmov's shoulder. "After we have Tarasove, is there any reason we can't sell his formula to the Chinaman? Not the real one, of course. Something that will blow up in his ugly face."

Chapter Twenty-Four

Las Vegas, Nevada

Danny Shu was sitting at the hotel suite's marble kitchen table, devouring a huge plate of french fried potatoes, when Ying Fai strolled into the kitchen. Fai and Rita Tong had been "lifting their little finger," smoking opium in Fai's bedroom.

Fai used opium in the manner of the Mandarins of long ago—as a relaxant, to restore his energy. He considered it nothing to be ashamed of.

Shu knew that, as Fai aged, he provided the drug to those who shared his bed. It insured that they would not remember how sexually inactive the old man had been. Rita Tong had become addicted to the opium, and was no doubt now in a deep sleep.

Shu rose to his feet. "The woman, Alex, called twenty minutes ago. I didn't think you wanted to be disturbed. She said she will have Tarasove very soon."

Ying Fai tightened the brocaded belt on his black silk robe. "Where?"

"She's too smart to give an exact location. She suggested I come to San Francisco right away, and wait for her call.

I told her to contact me at the Jade Dragon bar, in Chinatown."

Fai picked up a french fry, examined it briefly, then dropped it back to the plate. "San Francisco. How convenient. We can take Tarasove to Hong Kong on one of our freighters, or, if need be, charter a boat. I'll attend to that."

Shu meshed his fingers together and cracked his knuckles. "What about Alex?"

"Be aggressive, but don't kill her. It will be interesting to interrogate her, to find out just how she locates these people so easily." Fai tilted his head back and gave a loud yawn. "After that, she's yours to do whatever pleases you." He pushed his robe sleeve back and examined his watch. "Go to San Francisco now. Keep me informed. I want to be there when the arrogant bitch gives us the Russian."

The San Francisco Giants were still on the road, but that didn't diminish the size of the crowd in the stadium's chophouse, a ground ball to second base from the Willie Mays statue.

Harry spotted Don Landeta sitting at a terrace table, hunched over a plate of fresh oysters, a glass of beer in one hand.

The weather was still abnormally warm, and the restaurant was jammed with a mixture of tourists and regular diners.

Harry slipped into the seat across from Landeta. "Hi, Don. Ready for another drink?"

Landeta tucked a napkin into his collar and spread the cloth across his chest. "I just got started on this one." He pushed the plate of oysters in Harry's direction. "Help yourself."

"What did you come up with for John Kagel?" Harry asked, signaling to the waitress that he wanted a draft beer.

"Quite a bit. But let's start with Lana Kuzmin first." Landeta took an envelope from his lap and shook the contents onto the table. "The afternoon and evening before she was murdered, Kuzmin made six calls to numbers in Los Angeles." He thumbed through the pile of pages. "Here they are. Three calls to the same number, which is unlisted and belongs to a Jahloul Reyes, on South St. Louis Street near the Hollenbeck District Station. A lot of gypsies live around there."

"I think that's where Lana came up with the John Kagel name. She'd told me she was going to find out something about Zivon Yudin, the guy who was pulled from the waters of Lake Merced. He had moved to Los Angeles. My guess is that Kagel, who I believe is Boris Feliks, met up with Yudin in L.A. Reyes is probably a gypsy con man Lana knew in L.A., and he passed along the info about Kagel to her."

The bartender brought Harry's beer, and he took a swig before saying, "I'm interested in Kagel. Were you able to pull anything on him?"

Landeta sucked down two oysters before answering. "You know, Harry, there are times when I'm so brilliant I don't believe it myself. Even without a middle initial for Kagel, I nailed him. You told me that he'd probably be somewhere between thirty and forty years of age. You shortchanged him. Forty-two. He has a Houston, Texas, driver's license."

"Houston? You're sure it's the John Kagel I'm interested in?"

"On August fifteenth, Kagel charged two one-way flights on United Airlines from LAX to San Francisco. I haven't been able to find out who his traveling mate was, but—"

"Zivon Yudin is my bet. They flew up to meet with Paul Morris, the man they killed at the St. Charles Hotel."

"If you say so. Kagel used the credit card twice here. Once at the Sands Motel on Sloat Boulevard—that was two days ago—and yesterday at Max's Styling Salon on Castro Street."

Harry whistled softly. "I owe you big-time. The Sands Motel is about a half mile from where we found Zivon Yudin's body. Max's Styling Salon on Castro Street. I wonder what that's all about?"

Landeta brushed his remaining hair with the flat of one hand. "You're asking the wrong person. I've been going to the same barber for thirty-five years. I like him because he has less hair than me."

Sasha Veronin's e-mail message had been short and to the point. *Call me! Very important. Too important for the Internet shit.*

Boris Feliks selected a spacious old-fashioned enclosed

telephone booth in a downtown San Francisco hotel. It took several minutes for the international call to go through. "What is it, Sasha?" he said when they were connected. "I give you two minutes, then I hang up."

"We have a problem, Boris. Someone else has found Tarasove."

"Someone else? Who?"

"The only name I have is Alex. He's a *propezdoloch*, a real smart fucker. Finds men the Americans hide from their enemies—us."

Feliks watched as a heavyset woman wearing a ridiculously wide red straw hat approached the booth. "How do you know this?"

"The person I had intended to sell Tarasove to hired Alex, who sent him a photograph via the Internet. It's the scientist all right—a little fatter, his hair longer, but it's him."

"Who is this person?" Feliks pressed.

"The esteemed leader of the SVR, General Burian Kilmov. He hired Alex, but he doesn't know who the bastard is." Sasha barked out a laugh. "Imagine that. He pays the *propezdoloch* millions of dollars, but doesn't know who he is."

The woman wearing the straw hat rolled her sleeve back, glanced at a diamond-crusted wristwatch and glared at Feliks.

"This is making no sense, Sasha. How do you know it's really Tarasove? Where was the photo taken?"

Veronin's answer startled Feliks. "Somewhere near the city of San Francisco, I assume, because that's where Alex is now."

When Feliks didn't respond, Sasha said, "Is that where you are now too, old comrade?"

The woman tapped on the phone booth door and pointed at her watch. Feliks turned his back on her, trying to retain his composure. "I want to see the photograph."

"I will have my secretary e-mail it to you within the hour," Sasha promised. "Tarasove has a glass in his hand. There are tall trees in the background, but there's no way to tell where the picture was taken."

"Why are you telling me this?"

"*Babki*! Money, of course. The esteemed general and I

are working together on this. He wants to know who this mysterious Alex is, and how he finds people like Tarasove."

There was a tap on the door again. Feliks wheeled around and yelled, *"Poshe "l y pizdu!"*

When the woman stared at him with a slack jaw, he shouted the translation: "Fuck off!"

"Who are you talking to?" Veronin wanted to know.

"Someone wants to use the phone. I had an e-mail from Tarasove. He mentioned the sum of twenty-five million dollars."

"Tell him that's fine. He'll never live to see a dollar, or even a ruble. What I want you to do is snatch Tarasove, and find out everything about Alex. Don't kill him. He could be very valuable to us."

The woman waiting to make a call was speaking animatedly to a man wearing a tuxedo jacket and striped pants. "And how do I accomplish this, Sasha?"

"I have done all the hard work for you. Alex is waiting for Kilmov's instructions on what to do. He will be told to meet with someone. You, Boris, understand? *Kak dva pal 'tsa obossat'.* What the Americans call a piece of cake."

Feliks understood, but he didn't like any of it. "Send me the photograph. I want to see it before I have any contact with this Alex. I have to hang up."

He hurried out of the booth. The man in the striped pants started to approach him, but changed his mind when he saw the angry look on Boris's face.

Chapter Twenty-Five

Harry Dymes spotted Marta Citron at a table near the swinging shutter door leading to the kitchen of Dimitri's Tearoom. The restaurant was decorated with a collection of garage sale cast-offs—art deco paintings, milk glass statuettes, old hubcaps, black-powder rifles, and photographs of the city following the 1906 earthquake. One corner of the L-shaped room was devoted to palm and tea-leaf readings. Lana Kuzmin had read his palm there more than once.

"Sorry I'm late," he apologized.

Marta poked a fork into one of the chunks of roasted lamb on her plate. "I started without you. In fact, I thought you were going to stand me up."

"I'm sure that hasn't happened often," Harry said, settling into the seat across from her. "I had some things I had to do."

"Anything relating to Ivan Lemkov?"

The waiter hurried over and Harry lingered over the menu, stalling for time. The reason he was late was that he'd gone to the Sands Motel. The desk clerk had taken one look at the computer-generated sketch Julie Renton had given him, and said that it looked a lot like the John Kagel who had stayed two nights, and checked out without leaving a forwarding address.

Next, Harry went to Max's Styling Salon on Castro Street, finding it closed. The bar next to Max's was called the Rearender, and the bartender knew that Max lived "somewhere on Dolores Street," and that his last name was Verdi.

There were no Verdis in the phone book, on Dolores Street or anywhere else in the city.

Harry ordered *zharkoye*, a beef stew, and a bottle of Bull's Blood red wine. "Your Roger Dancel is a real charmer. Where did he come up with Lemkov's name?"

"He's not *my* Roger. He has a hard time being honest with people."

The waiter set an opened bottle of wine and two glasses on the table, then disappeared into the kitchen.

"How am I going to find Boris Feliks?" Harry said, pouring the purplish wine into the glasses.

"I wish I knew." Marta sighed heavily, then added, "I'm being sent to the—"

"Chalet in Lake Tahoe," Harry said. "To babysit the Russian scientist, Tarasove, right?"

Marta rested her chin on her hand and smiled lightly. "You're good, Harry. Damn good, I've got to admit that. Yes, I'll be there, looking out at the lake from his deck. Were you able to lip-read everything Roger and I said on the terrace?"

Harry hadn't noticed at first, but Agent Marta Citron of the FBI had a buzz on. He slid one of the glasses across the table to her.

"Not all of it. There was one thing that confused me. 'Snake charmer.' And you said something about being scared of all his snakes. What's that all about?"

"I shouldn't tell you that. State secrets, you know."

"I know that Tarasove is a scientist. I ran him through Google. He worked at some university in Kiev—on weapons of mass destruction. Tell me more. It won't go beyond this table."

Marta took a sip of the wine and grimaced. "This isn't very good." She turned the bottle around so that she could read the label. "Bull's Blood?"

"It's a blend of anything the Hungarians can get their hands on. As the story goes, back in fifteen hundred fifty-two, the fortress in the town of Eger was under attack, and the good guys were badly outnumbered by the bad guys, the Turks in this case. To give themselves courage, the locals consumed large amounts of red wine, which spilled all over them. When the Turks attacked and saw these wild-eyed drunks with red liquid all down their chests, they thought the Hungarians had been drinking bulls' blood, and they ran like hell. Now, tell me about the snake charmer."

"The . . . scientist uses venom from snakes in his projects. A great deal of venom."

A sad-faced violinist wearing a faded velvet smoking jacket came by their table, playing a vamped-up version of "As Time Goes By."

Marta laughed lightly at first, then louder, causing the violinist to scowl and move on to the next table.

"Did I miss something?" Harry asked.

Marta used a napkin to dab her eyes. "Ivan Lemkov plays violin in a New York club. That's where Dancel came up with the name."

The waiter plopped Harry's stew on the table and topped off their glasses. Harry eyed Marta as he took a bite. "I have to know more about Tarasove. Why is Feliks after him? To kill him? Kidnap him and take him back to Russia? What?"

"Nicolai is too valuable to kill. Feliks was—still is, I assume—a member of the Red Mafia. Tarasove sold him a fake formula."

"What was Feliks going to do with the formula, Marta? Who's the customer?"

"Our information is that he was going to sell it to members of a Chinese Triad headed by Ying Fai, who is—"

"I know who Fai is. He runs all the gangs in Chinatown, here in San Francisco, Los Angeles, Seattle, the whole Left Coast." Harry circled his fork in the stew. "We're talking some heavy hitters here. Fai, the Red Mafia. This assassin Feliks. Is there anyone *else* in the picture you haven't told me about?"

Marta started to say something, then took another sip of the wine. "Not to my knowledge."

Harry knew she was holding something back. "I showed you mine—Feliks's picture. How about showing me yours. Tarasove."

"I don't have a photograph. Just think of Santa Claus: big belly, white beard, but with a Russian accent. That's Nicolai."

"What name is he using now?" Harry said.

"I can't tell you that. Dancel would have my head on a plate if he knew what I've already given you."

Harry debated whether or not to offer a trade: John Kagel's name for whatever one Tarasove was using. He decided to hold off. If he gave her Kagel, she'd have to pass it on to Dancel, and he didn't want that to happen right now. "Where in Lake Tahoe?" he asked. "South Shore, Incline?"

"You're pushing too hard, Harry. Why didn't you mention the murdered fortune-teller to Dancel?"

"It slipped my mind, I guess. What's our next move?"

Marta screwed up her napkin. "I had a drink at your house. I had a drink with Dancel near the office. I've had two drinks while I've been waiting for you at this place, and now some of this lousy wine. So either you take me to your place and show me your rooftop roses, or I'm going home to bed."

Harry pushed himself clear of his chair and reached for his wallet. "Your car or mine?"

"Is everything all right, sir?" the nauseatingly cheerful young man with half-lens glasses perched precariously on the edge of his nose asked as he peered over Boris Feliks's shoulder at the computer screen.

"I want to print this photo attachment," Boris said. "Make a half dozen prints."

"Sure," the man said affably. "It will take just a few minutes."

Boris strolled the aisles of the store as he waited for his photographs. Kinko's. The name sounded Russian. There were dozens of color printers in use, and banners over the counter boasted of their business and personal solutions: cards, brochures, video conferencing, digital photo printing, and online access. He'd dropped Kiryl Chapaev's laptop computer into a construction site debris box after the disturbing phone call with Sasha Veronin—Sasha claiming that the man called Alex was "somewhere near the city of San

Francisco." Was there such a man? Or was Sasha playing a game—trying to bring him out into the open? San Francisco. That was the worrisome thing.

Boris knew of no way for Sasha, or the FBI, to trace him through Chapaev's laptop, but there was no point in taking chances. From now on he'd use commercial or public access computers for any Internet messages to Tarasove or Veronin.

The only positive information Sasha had passed on was that he was working with General Burian Kilmov. Feliks remembered Kilmov as a hard-edged colonel in the SVR— a short man with a Napoleon complex, who was very careful when it came to accepting a bribe. Careful men were the kind Boris felt most comfortable dealing with.

The clerk handed Feliks the prints showing Nicolai Tarasove leaning against a deck railing. Feliks passed a credit card across the counter as he studied the photos.

"Is there anything else we can do for you, Mr. Kagel?" the clerk asked as he checked the Visa card before ringing up the sale.

"No. I'm going to have to do everything myself."

There was a coffee shop down the street, and Boris paid nearly four dollars for something called a white chocolate mocha. He sat near the window and studied the photographs. It *was* Tarasove. There was no doubt about it. Who had taken the picture? This mysterious Alex, who was supposed to lead him to Tarasove?

Feliks sipped at the coffee drink, finding it too sweet for his taste. Alex had to be real. Sasha wouldn't waste his time setting up an elaborate trap. Burian Kilmov and Sasha working together. What a pair they made—the possibilities were endless.

He longed to get back home, to Russia, and the only way to do that was to give Sasha what he wanted. Alex. And Tarasove. It could be done. It must be done.

Chapter Twenty-Six

Lake Tahoe, Nevada

"Watch carefully, Jedgar," Nicolai Tarasove said as he picked up the kitchen scissors. He held the edge of his beard in one hand and snipped off a chunk of the white hair, letting it drop to the tile floor.

The dog edged away as more hair followed. "Watch," Tarasove commanded. He wanted the animal to observe the entire procedure, so that there would be no mistaking his new look.

It took Nicolai some ten minutes to snip off enough hair to allow the use of a razor. As he foamed his face, he hummed along with Tchaikovsky's *Sleeping Beauty Ballet* on the stereo. The first swipe of the razor scraped through the beard under his chin. He paid careful attention to his reflection in the magnifying mirror propped on the kitchen table. It had been what? Ten years since he'd been entirely clean-shaven. At least that.

He added more shaving cream, and Jedgar began barking.

"Calm down," Tarasove crooned. "What is it, Jedgar? A little hangover from the Rohypnol? You'll be fine by the time I return from San Francisco."

When the razor had removed the final line of hair from under his nose, Tarasove went to the sink and rinsed his face with cold water.

When he'd toweled off, he beamed down at Jedgar. "Well? What do you think?"

Jedgar tilted his huge head to the side, the wrinkles in his homely face deepening. Finally he let out a series of high-pitched barks.

Tarasove roughed his head. "I take that as a vote of confidence, my friend."

He returned to the table and picked up the mirror, his head snapping back at his own image. There were small patches of hair around his nose and upper lip. His skin was pink-red, and smoother than he remembered it being. He ran a hand over his flesh, enjoying the feeling.

There was an electric razor in the bathroom. He'd use that to remove the spots he'd missed.

"Not bad, Jedgar. Not bad at all." He picked up the scissors again, snapping them at the dog. "Now for a haircut. Watch closely. I want you to recognize me when I come home this evening."

The roar of the vehicle's engine and the crunching sound made by Nicolai Tarasove's Hummer as it drove over the day bugs Trina Lee had planted on the road leading to and from Tarasove's chalet brought her out of a fitful, uncomfortable night's sleep.

She shrugged out of the blanket wrapped around her shoulders. The Jaguar's dashboard clock registered eight minutes after seven. Where was Tarasove going this early in the morning?

Trina had parked the Jag in behind a bird-bombed pickup truck in the Sugar Cove Restaurant's parking lot. She had a story prepared in case a restaurant employee— or a nosy sheriff—rousted her during the night, but she hadn't been disturbed. When the restaurant opened at six a.m., she made a dash for the restroom, then purchased coffee and a slice of apple pie, and returned to the Jag, bundling up in the driver's seat, waiting for Tarasove to make his next move.

The black Hummer flashed by, traveling south. She pulled in behind it. The driver! Not Tarasove! No beard. Shorter hair. Who the hell was he? She edged up to his bumper. Round head. White hair. She positioned the passenger side sun visor so that it would block the driver's view of her, then floored the Jag and zipped around the Hummer.

The driver turned his head for a moment and Trina got a split-second view of his face. It was all she needed. Tarasove! Beardless—but it was him.

She pushed the Jag up to eighty miles an hour, then exited onto a deserted side road, executed a "stunt" one-hundred-and-eighty-degree turn, and was in position to see Tarasove behind the wheel when the Hummer sped by.

Why the shave and haircut? Was he getting ready to defect? On his own? Through who?

The Hummer streamed past the gaudy South Shore casinos, made a left turn onto Pioneer Trail, and after a few miles, turned onto US-50 West.

"Where are we going, Nicolai?" Trina whispered.

Tarasove kept a steady speed, slightly over the limit, and as the morning traffic increased, Trina slipped back a few more car lengths. She monitored the Jag's odometer. They'd traveled a hundred and six miles when Tarasove pulled into a service station.

While he used the self-service pumps, Trina purchased coffee and chocolate bars at the station's adjoining fast-food counter. As she peeled back the wrapper of a Hershey bar, she made a bet with herself. The Russian was going to San Francisco. To meet who? Roger Dancel? Marta Citron? Was the FBI planning to whisk him away from her? To some new location?

No, she decided. If that were the case, they'd have come for him—with a half dozen agents in bulletproof sedans and a helicopter.

Tarasove hopped back into the Hummer.

As Trina strolled to the Jag, a worrisome thought wormed its way into her brain. Was there something in the photo of Tarasove she'd e-mailed to Ying Fai and Burian Kilmov that gave one of them a clue as to where the chalet was?

She'd taken photos of Tarasove when he came out onto his sundeck, drink in hand. She'd examined them all closely before settling on the one that showed his profile best. There was nothing in the picture, she decided. Nothing.

* * *

Marta Citron inhaled deeply on her first cigarette of the day as she walked barefoot over the decking on Harry Dymes's roof. The roses really were beautiful. She couldn't remember meeting a man who'd taken such an interest in gardening.

"Here's some coffee," Dymes said, coming up behind her. "I've got eggs in the refrigerator and bread for toast, if you're hungry."

"Starved, but I'll settle for a piece of toast. I have to get back to work."

"It's Sunday," Harry said. "A day of rest for most people."

"We're not most people." She took a grateful sip of the piping hot coffee. "Dancel will have a few little chores for me."

"When are you going up to Lake Tahoe to bodyguard Mr. Tarasove?"

Smoke from her cigarette drifted into Marta's eyes, making her blink. "I'm not sure. What about you? A day off?"

"No. A few loose ends. We should exchange cell phone numbers in case something comes up."

"Good idea," Marta said, wondering if he was holding something back—as she was. Dancel would have her hide if she told Harry about Alex. "Your roses are lovely."

"Thanks." Dymes scanned the morning sky. There was a thin gauze of orange-sherbet clouds, and not a trace of any fog. "We're in for another day of hot weather."

Marta was wearing one of Harry's dress shirts, and nothing else. "I know I shouldn't ask, but why did you and your wife break up? Twice."

"Eva thought I could do better than being a policeman. She had grand ideas of the two of us being fashion designers—even bringing my father in for a line of men's clothes."

"That might have worked. You have great taste in clothes."

Harry took her into his arms. "I like being a cop." He nibbled lightly on her ear. "And I like your taste."

Marta pulled away. "Last night was last night." She waved her coffee cup toward the sky. "The light of a new day."

"Regrets?"

"Ummm. The coffee could be better. But no regrets. How about I shower first and you make the toast? Then you can drive me back to my car."

There was a ticket flapping on the windshield of Marta Citron's Bucar when Harry pulled alongside it.

"Damn it," she said, as she climbed out of the Honda.

Harry held out a hand. "Give it to me. I'll take care of it. You don't want Dancel to find out that the car was parked in the Richmond District all night."

Harry waited until Citron pulled away from the curb before turning right on Geary, then left on Sixth Avenue. The Sunday morning traffic was sparse, and he made it to the Hall of Justice in a few minutes. In a typical close-the-barn-door-after-the-horse-is-gone mode, there were solo bikes blocking all entrances to the building's garage.

Harry skirted around the motorcycles, parked and hurried up to the fourth floor. He entered the address of Max's Styling Salon on Castro Street into the detail computer's report base and was rewarded with a copy of a burglary incident dated six months ago. The reportee was Maxwell Green. Residence address, 1942 Dolores Street.

The bartender Harry had spoken to told him Max's last name was Verdi—Italian for green.

The house was an ornate, well-kept Queen Anne Victorian complete with turrets, cupolas, dormer windows, a gabled roof and fish-scale shingles.

"It's Sunday morning, for God's sake," the thin, spike-haired man who opened the door complained.

"Are you Max Green?" Harry Dymes said, waving his badge in the man's face.

"Oh, my God. Who died?"

"Quite a few people," Harry said. "Can I come in, please?"

Max cinched the belt on his white terrycloth robe tightly and stepped back from the door. "I guess it's all right. The neighbors are probably spying on us already."

The entry hall flooring was well-polished parquet. The wall paneling and coffered ceiling looked to be all of the same rich walnut. The stairway handrail was elaborately carved walnut, while on the opposite wall a thick piece of lavender-colored rope, strung through brass holders, led the way upstairs.

"Just what's this all about, Officer?"

"Inspector Dymes." Harry took a copy of the Renton sketch from his jacket pocket. "Do you recognize this man, sir?"

Green barely glanced at the sketch. "No. Who is it?"

"Who is it?" echoed the young man in spandex pants coming down the stairway. He was bare-chested, and his smooth, tanned skin looked as if it had been slathered with baby oil.

"The police," Max said disgustedly. "Go back to bed, Billy."

Harry pushed the sketch toward the young man, who smiled at him with sleepy eyes. "Is it someone I should know?"

"You tell me," Harry said.

Billy's eyes bounced from the sketch to Max Green. "He does look a little familiar, but I can't place him. What's his problem? Parking tickets?"

Harry looked Max straight in the eye. "Mr. Green, or Mr. Verdi, whichever name you prefer—that's a drawing of a man who used a credit card under the name John Kagel when he ran up a bill of a hundred and seventy-six dollars at your shop yesterday. What did he have done?"

Max crossed his arms across his chest and stuck out his chin. "I don't believe that's any of your business, Inspector. And, unless you can tell me just what your interest is in the gentleman, I must ask you to leave my house."

Harry took a deep breath, and remembered the advice New York detective Tony Fenner had given him years ago: "When in doubt, bullshit, Harry. And make it a whopper."

"The man in the drawing is wanted by the Houston Police Department for a series of homicides. He is a vicious homophobe, whose victims are always gay. He gains their confidence, then, after-hours of torture, murders them in a horrible manner, then dismembers the bodies with a hacksaw. The papers in Houston have dubbed him the Hacksaw Killer."

"Oh, my God," Max said, reaching out a hand to the staircase to steady himself. "It's him, Billy. It's him."

The young man looked at the sketch again. "You're right."

"What did you do for him?" Harry asked.

"A complete makeover," Max said, lowering his haunches to the steps. "Styled his hair, tinted it in . . ."

"Toasted Chestnut," Billy chimed in. "And he used the tanning booths. He looked wonderful when he left the shop."

Max threw an arm up toward the ceiling. "He said something about wanting to look like a new man, but didn't want it to be drastic. I changed his hairstyle, removed those ridiculous sideburns, and gave him a real nice coloring."

Harry retrieved the sketch from Billy's hands and tried to picture how those changes would look on Boris Feliks. "Did he mention an address? Anyone's name?"

Max's fingers played with the hem of his robe. "No. Not that I remember."

"Me either," Billy said. "What did you mean when you said the Hacksaw Killer 'murders them in a horrible manner'?"

Harry held his hands at shoulder width. "Anal penetration, with long, thick metal objects—crowbars, things like that. The victims die of trauma."

"Oh, my God," Max said again, his hands covering his face, like a child playing peekaboo.

I think I overdid it, Harry told himself. "Is there anything else you can tell me about the man. What was he wearing?"

"Call Wardrobe," Billy said with a wince. "I mean, he really needed help with his clothes. Button-down shirt and dark pants. Boring."

Max pulled his hands away from his face. "He'd had a *really* good hair transplant. Not that toothbrush stuff. Individual hairs. If you didn't look close, you'd never have known."

"Can either of you men draw?" Harry asked.

Billy pointed to a series of three framed Matisse-style ink-on-paper nudes on the wall. "I did those."

"Do you think you can make me something that will show how John Kagel looks now?"

"I can try," Billy said. He turned and started up the stairs, then turned around quickly. "Max. Didn't he say something about going to the park today?"

"What park?" Harry wanted to know.

"Golden Gate," Max said. "To the Gay Sports Festival." He used the handrail to hoist himself to his feet. "He asked me if it was a good place to meet someone. A friend, I think he said. He also wanted to know if there would be many policeman there, because his friend was nervous about being around police. Come on into the kitchen, Inspector. I'll make tea while Billy does his drawing."

Chapter Twenty-Seven

The tall Black man with shoulder-length dreadlocks and a flowing mustache approached the curb cautiously. He tapped the tip of his pointed-toe boot against the front wheel of the late Jed Dewey's Harley-Davidson. "Hey, man, you got some serious meat on that Hog. Whatcha buying, baby?"

Boris Feliks pulled off his leather gloves. "Cell phone."

"You're on the wrong block. Just weed goes here. You want prescriptions—tricycles and bicycles, Vicodin, that Rush Limbaugh shit—you go up to Turk Street. You want some heavy stuff—brick gum, or nose candy—you drive to Eddy Street. But you want e-ah-lectronics, you got to head up to Post Street. Look for my man Rajah. He be in a beat-up VW van, you know, like the ones those hippies used to load up with dumb white bitches. You make sure you tell Rajah that Sweet Jesus sent you, so I can get my cut, right?"

Rajah turned out to be a frail-looking man in his twenties with bulging eyes and alabaster skin. "Sweet Jesus sent you? I thought he was still in Pelican Bay."

Feliks had no idea that the man was talking about a state penitentiary. "He told me you have cell phones."

"He was right. Step into my office."

Feliks climbed into the eggshell-colored Volkswagen,

which was packed with electronic gear, most of it in unopened manufacturers' boxes.

"What's your pleasure?" Rajah asked. "Sony, Samsung, Motorola."

"It doesn't matter. As long as it works, and can't be traced back to me."

"They all work," Rajah said indignantly. "I don't sell anything that doesn't work. The thing is, how long will they work. You know what I mean? The longer you want use of the phone, the more the price is. A few days, a week, a month—that's what determines the price. My advice is buy a week, then exchange. That way you're not going to have any complications."

"A week should be fine. How much?"

Rajah rummaged through a black plastic bag, coming out with a small clamshell cell phone. "Nothing fancy here— no photos, no Internet access—but you can call anyone, anywhere you want for seven days, guaranteed."

"I will have people calling me," Feliks said, holding out his hand.

Rajah dropped the phone into Feliks's hand. "This baby is billed to a phantom number at the international brokerage unit at Wells Fargo Bank. I love screwing those assholes." He took a pen from his shirt pocket and wrote down the cell phone's number on a Burger King paper napkin. "It comes with all the cookies: hands-free headset, extra battery, the works. You can have it for five hundred bucks, fifty of which I'll have to kick back to Sweet Jesus. Come to me direct next time, okay? You can use it for a week with no problems, but after that you'll need another card and number."

"Show me how it works," Feliks said.

After the demonstration, Feliks handed Rajah five of the one-hundred-dollar bills he had originally given to Jed Dewey for the rental of the cottage.

"Here's the charger," Rajah said as Feliks wormed his way out of the cramped camper. "Use it in good health."

Feliks's next stop was the city's main library, which he had verified was open on Sunday.

The library clerk, a man with a turban and unruly black beard, listened impatiently to Feliks's claim that he was from out of town and needed access to a computer for a short time.

The clerk pointed to a row of computers, two-thirds of which were in use. "You have thirty minutes—that's all."

Feliks had no difficulty logging on. He used one of his new e-mail addresses at Yahoo! and sent Nicolai Tarasove a brief message: *Golden Gate Park, one o'clock, this afternoon.* He then added the cell phone's number, and an old Russian phrase: *Poide 'm popizdim.* We'll have a friendly chat.

The sleepy-eyed morgue attendant bent down and gave a tug on the metal body drawer handle. "Sometimes they get stuck," he said.

He tried again, grunting at the effort, and Marta Citron thought how awful this must be when someone came down to view the remains of a loved one.

"Here we go," the attendant said when the drawer finally released and the draped corpse of Lana Kuzmin was wheeled into view. He pulled down the top of the sheet covering the body, exposing Kuzmin's lifeless head.

"All the way, please," Marta told him, leaning over and observing the bruising around Lana's neck. The sutures across her torso were done in typical postmortem style—a Y-shaped incision extending from the shoulders toward the midline, over the sternum and down to the pubis. The stitches resembled those on a baseball.

A phone rang somewhere and the attendant said, "I've got to answer that. We're shorthanded on the weekends. Are you okay here alone?"

"I'm fine," Marta assured him. She touched the firm, icy skin on Kuzmin's arm. What was it that Harry Dymes had called her? *Byl dushoj obschestva.* Full of life. She saw something in Lana's pasty, gray face—wide lips, strong nose, and broad forehead—that seemed to confirm that. This was a woman who had lived life to the fullest, and would not die easily, even at the skilled hands of a man such as Boris Feliks.

Lana Kuzmin's legs were close together. Marta noticed something on the woman's inner left thigh. The doctor who had performed the autopsy was not on duty, and the attendant told her that the victim had been strangled to death.

He hadn't mentioned anything about a sexual assault. Marta used both hands to spread Kuzmin's feet apart. She stared at the name scratched on the deceased's marblelike flesh. "Harry Dymes, you son of a bitch," she whispered.

Nicolai Tarasove used the first available off-ramp on the Bay Bridge. He pulled the Hummer to a stop alongside a gas station and looked at the street sign. He then unfolded a map and found his location.

He had been to San Francisco some ten to fifteen times since moving to Lake Tahoe—usually on shopping trips, to see a concert, or acting as a tourist, when not meeting with Kiryl Chapaev.

He found the city charming, somewhat European, but he was familiar only with the well-known locations. Where would Boris Feliks suggest they meet?

He activated his pocket PC, squinting and holding the machine at arm's length as he carefully accessed his e-mail address. There it was, the message from Feliks: *Golden Gate Park*, and a phone number. According to the map, the park was a huge place. He wrote Feliks's cell phone number down on the map, then made the call.

"*Kak dela*, Boris?" he said when the connection was made.

"I'm in good health, Nicolai. And I intend to stay that way. Where are you?"

"In my car. I'm hesitant about meeting with you. After what you did to Kiryl, and the others—"

"You have no reason to fear me," Feliks assured him. "We both know you are too valuable to have harm done to you. Your genius is your shield. Your protector."

For a vicious, murdering bastard, the man had a way with words, Nicolai conceded. "Where in the park do you suggest we meet? It must be somewhere public, Boris."

"I agree. Kennedy Drive, between the buffalo paddocks and Dutch Windmill. There is a festival of some kind. I'm told the firemen's booth serves excellent chili. There will be many people. You'll be safe. I guarantee it."

"Will I recognize you?" Tarasove asked, his eyes scanning the map of Golden Gate Park.

"I will recognize you."

"Don't be too sure," Tarasove cautioned, rubbing a hand across his smooth chin.

"Come alone," Feliks warned. "If I see your protectors, all guarantees are off."

"Where's Dancel?" Marta Citron asked when she opened the door to Dancel's temporary office, only to find Tom McNab sitting behind the desk. "And what the hell do you think you're doing?"

McNab calmly opened the center drawer and pawed through the contents. "Roger's in Sausalito, supposedly interviewing the hooker, Julie Renton." McNab slammed the drawer shut, then immediately began thumbing through a pile of reports in Dancel's out-basket.

"He's not going to like it when I tell him you've been sticking your nose where it doesn't belong."

"You're not going to tell him." When Marta started to protest, McNab said, "If you want to argue about it, I suggest you contact Deputy Director Bartlow right now." He gave a twitch of a smile. "Bartlow thinks you're up in Lake Tahoe at Tarasove's chalet. If I were you, I'd get my ass up there right now."

Marta tried to make sense of McNab's aggressive manner. Dancel had kept him out of the loop. Now he not only knew Tarasove's actual name, but his location. "What's going on, McNab?"

"Nothing you need to worry your pretty head about. Just go up to Tahoe and keep Tarasove happy."

Marta fought back the urge to slap McNab's smug face. The son of a bitch was more obnoxious than Dancel. Instead, she picked up the phone on the desk. "I'm calling Roger."

McNab lunged forward and clamped his hand over hers. "Don't do that. That's an order. Not from me. From Bartlow."

Marta yanked her hand free, balled it into a fist, then swivelled on her heel and stormed from the room. When she reached her office, she toed her shoes off and sent them flying across the room.

"Bastards," she shouted, including McNab, Bartlow, Dancel, and Harry Dymes in the group. She sat down abruptly and thumped the arms of the chair with her palms, while she tried to figure out what was going on. Why was Dancel suddenly in deep trouble? Tom McNab going through his desk. McNab never would have brought up Bartlow's name if he didn't have his backing. McNab and Bartlow. The two of them. Too little and too late. The combination made no sense. Bartlow was a squeaky-clean career deskman who'd been described as being so cautious he had two seat belts on his chair, while McNab was a loose cannon who never would have made it through the Bureau's training academy at Quantico, Virginia, if it hadn't been for his political connections. Was that it? Bartlow buttering up McNab's brother? Why was he going after Dancel?

Marta was so upset by McNab's actions that she nearly forgot how mad she was at Harry Dymes. She leaned forward and jabbed the name she'd seen on the fortune-teller's leg into the computer database: *Kagel, John*. The computer sat silent for a moment, then responded with a form for entering additional information. *DOB*, date of birth. *SSN*, Social Security number. *DLN*, driver's license number. *KA*, known associates.

She had nothing to fill in the blank spaces. Without some qualifiers, she'd end up with a stack of confusing information on every John Kagel in the United States.

Her cell phone vibrated against her hip. She snatched it up and growled, "What?"

"I'm certain that you didn't get up on the wrong side of the bed," Harry Dymes said. "What's wrong?"

"What's wrong? Do you want me to count them out? For starters, you. You somehow forgot to tell me about John Kagel."

"I knew you'd check out Lana's body. Good job."

"Oh, thank you," Marta said sarcastically. "Do I get a dozen roses for that? Another power breakfast? Goddamn it, Harry. I thought we were working together on this."

"Where are you?"

"In my office, trying to find out something about this Kagel guy, and I can tell you—"

"I'll be in front of the building in five minutes. Kagel is the name Boris Feliks is using. He's changed his looks again, and I think I know where he'll be this afternoon. Can you keep this from Dancel?"

"Definitely," Marta said, looking around for her shoes. "I can definitely keep it from Roger."

Chapter Twenty-Eight

Trina Lee was forced to keep close to Nicolai Tarasove's Hummer, for fear of losing him.

The height of the Hummer, in comparison to her low-slung Jag, was a distinct advantage. Tarasove never bothered looking in the rear or side view mirrors as he plowed straight ahead, as if the road was his and his alone.

She monitored the street signs as they motored through the city: Fifth Street, Mission, Tenth Street, then left on Fulton. At one point Tarasove held up traffic at an intersection while he studied a map. He seemed to be as unfamiliar with the area as she was.

Traffic picked up dramatically when they were abreast of Golden Gate Park. Tarasove drove as far as the road allowed, up to the sand dunes fronting the crashing waves of the slate-gray Pacific Ocean. He slotted the Hummer in a handicap parking zone and exited the car slowly, rubbing his neck before ducking back into the vehicle and coming out with a tan leather tote bag.

Trina parked the Jag in the lone available spot—a red zone marked *Emergency Vehicles Only*. She ran to catch up with Tarasove, wondering about the tote bag. It was too small for more than a hasty change of clothes. Would that be enough if he planned to disappear? To where? With whom? With no one but her, she vowed. She watched Tarasove swing the bag lazily back and forth as he threaded his way through the thickening mob of pedestrians, pausing to admire the neat garden of colorful impatiens and pansies bordering a towering windmill, its blades frozen in place.

The crowd seemed to be predominantly in their twenties and thirties, many in bizarre costumes, their arms braided with tattoos. There was a goodly mixture of teenagers, and a contingent of "Gray Gays" in their fifties and sixties. There was the roar of a caravan of motorcycles—twenty at least. People craned their necks to look. Some applauded. The drivers were all women, muscly specimens in halters and shorts and highway patrol–style glasses. Not one of them was wearing a helmet.

The lead motorcycle had a fluttering black banner protruding from its skull-shaped taillight—*Dykes on Bikes*.

Trina let her eye wander from Tarasove to the throng of racially mixed revelers—openly gay couples in shorts, T-shirts, and hiking boots, some holding hands, kissing, feeling each other up. The showboating drag queens were dressed in everything from elegant evening gowns to rhinestone-studded thongs and leather bras with sharp metal spikes directly over their nipples.

Canvas-roofed concession stands offered a variety of goods: silk-screened clothing, soft drinks, burgers, hot dogs, cotton candy. Men in aprons and leather fire helmets were hawking "Blazing hot chili!" There were tattoo stalls, and piercing stands, and one vendor whose display featured rows of various sized, bullet-shaped dildos and vibrators.

The warmth of the sun and spicy scents of pine, cypress and blue gum eucalyptus trees did nothing to cloak the sweet, earthy, lawn-clipping smell of improperly cured marijuana.

Trina thought she could get high simply by doing yoga deep-breathing exercises.

Sharp-eyed young men in torn jeans and shirts with slogans like *Wake Up and Smell the Weed*, or plain and simple *Druggie*, were everywhere, making eye contact or boldly shouting, "You want it—I got it."

Trina wasn't worried about Tarasove recognizing her from their brief encounter on the road near his chalet. Her hair was now under a pirate-style bandana, and she wore

metal-framed, lavender-tinted glasses with lenses barely
larger than her eyes. She looked like she belonged there.
She edged up to Tarasove, who was shuffling slowly, stopping to examine the merchandise and openly gape at some
of the women, especially the few who were topless.

He took a cell phone from his pocket and tapped in
a number.

Trina was close enough to hear the beeps.

"Boris," Tarasove said. "Where are you? I'm going to
buy chili and beer from the firemen. I'll wait for you."

"This is a zoo," Marta Citron said, looking out at the
unruly crowd clogging the dirt paths of Golden Gate Park.

Harry Dymes bumped the Honda over a rock-strewn
road bordered by thick rhododendron bushes. "You ain't
seen nothin' yet, as someone once said."

A cop on horseback clattered over to them. Harry rolled
down the window and showed the officer his badge. "We'll
be a couple of hours."

The man leaned over in his saddle to peer at Marta, then
shrugged his shoulders. "I hope it's still here when you get
back. In another hour or two this place will be bedlam.
About all we do is stand back and keep out of the way."

Marta struggled out of the seat belt harness and banged
her knee against the dash. "I hate this damn car," she said,
swinging her legs out the door.

"You're just a ray of sunshine, aren't you?"

She gave him a look that matched her mood. It was the
first time she'd seen Dymes without a suit or sport coat. He
was wearing khakis, a black polo shirt, a matching sweater
tied over his shoulders, and a Giants baseball cap. "Let me
take another look at the drawing of what Boris Feliks is supposed to look like now." She paused, then said, "Please."

Harry spread the drawing that Billy, Max's friend, had
made of the man he knew as John Kagel onto the Honda's
hood. "I don't know how accurate this is. The hairdresser
said that Feliks was thinking of coming to the festival to
meet a 'friend.' Do you think it's Tarasove?"

"No. Nicolai wouldn't want to be within a hundred miles
of the bastard."

"Then who?" Harry pressed. "Come on. What are you
holding back?"

Marta had gone through her daily allotment of five cigarettes, but today was a day to break rules. She lit up, inhaled deeply and blew the plumes of smoke through her nostrils. "There is someone else. But I don't think Feliks would consider him a friend. Alex. Another hit man. He's working for Ying Fai."

"How long have you known about this guy?"

Marta slung her purse over her shoulder. "For a while. *He's* top secret, Harry. We don't know anything about him: his looks, where he's from, nothing. Just the one name—Alex. Ying Fai hired him to find Tarasove. Fai called him a *bok wai*. White devil."

Harry rolled up the sketch, then locked the Honda. "And you were pissed at me for not giving you John Kagel's name."

"I plead guilty. If I could have told you, I would have. Dancel will have my butt if he finds out I told you about Alex. Let's call it even, and start all over."

"Let's find Feliks, and celebrate later."

"Do you think we have a realistic chance of spotting him in this mob of whackos?"

Harry watched as four portly middle-aged men, their naked bodies painted silver and wreaths of redberry garlands on their heads, trooped by singing, "We're off to see the Wizard, the wonderful Wizard of Oz." It didn't surprise him that they all had deep, professional, baritone voices. Today's version of a barbershop quartet. "It's the only game in town, and Feliks couldn't have picked a better spot. I didn't tell anyone in the department about this. If he sees a lot of cops, he'll bolt."

"Feliks knows what you look like," Marta reminded him.

Harry donned a pair of dark glasses and pulled the brim of his hat down. "Master of disguise. He hasn't seen you, so let's not stay too close together." He placed a hand gently on her shoulder. "But let's not lose sight of each other."

Nicolai Tarasove admired the variety of sausages hissing on a barbecue grill at the volunteer firemen's concession stand. He purchased a Polish, a bowl of chili, and a tankard of beer, then sat down in a wobbly plastic chair and placed his food on a wobbly plastic table. He positioned the tote bag between his legs, undid the zipper and removed a purple plastic, battery-operated fan-mister that in some ways resembled the windmill near the beach. Its four foam blades fanned whatever liquid was placed in the container—normally water. He'd found the gadget at a sporting goods store. It's intended use was to provide a cooling mist on warm summer days.

Tarasove activated the device and watched the blades disperse a fine mist into the crowd. He took a spoonful of the chili, then dialed Feliks again. "Join me, Boris. I'm alone now. In a brown shirt and hat by the volunteer firemen's chili stand. Do you see me?"

"When did you get rid of the beard?" Feliks asked.

"Weeks ago. It makes me look younger, don't you think? Come. Buy some chili. It's excellent."

Boris Feliks studied Tarasove through binoculars from a distance of fifty meters. The prick did look younger without his beard. *Weeks ago*—which meant that the photograph sent to Sasha by Alex was taken long ago, from who knows where.

Tarasove chewed his food slowly, occasionally fiddling with the silly little fan.

There was no sign of a police presence. Feliks slipped his hand inside his jacket to reassure himself that the pistol he'd taken from the policeman's desk at the Hall of Justice was still safely nestled in his waistband.

He felt a surge of adrenaline as he made his way toward the chili stand. The months of living like an animal, worrying about the police, about Sasha's men, were in the past. He *had* Tarasove. Delivering him to Sasha would not be all that difficult. He had already mapped out an itinerary: drive to Seattle, a ferry to Vancouver, then a boat, a plane, directly to St. Petersburg or Moscow.

"Ty ochen umny," he said as he dropped into the chair alongside Tarasove.

"You think I'm clever? No more than you, Boris. Is it really you? I would never have recognized you. You're a completely different man. It's been a long time, hasn't it?"

"Too long. Let's go. Do you have a car?"

"Yes. Relax. Don't be so hasty." Tarasove picked up his glass of beer. "Before we leave, I want to know who I'm going to be dealing with. And we haven't settled the financial aspects yet."

"We can talk about that in the car."

"No," Tarasove said firmly. "I must know right now, or there is no deal. The Americans are not fools. They will not be pleased when they learn I've deserted them. Who is your master?"

Feliks nearly bit his tongue. *Master*! "The gentleman who will provide you with the money, and a new home, is Sasha Veronin. You know the name?"

"Very well," Nicolai responded. "I don't trust him. My work is of no use to Veronin. He must have a client. Who? Ying Fai again? The FBI told me all about Fai. I don't know if I want my project ending up in his hands." He picked up the mister and sprayed the fan in a circular pattern.

Feliks waved the mist away with the back of his hand. "Put that foolish thing away."

"As you wish." Tarasove pointed the fan toward the chili stand, which now had a long line of waiting customers. "How many people do you think are here today? Thousands?"

"Who cares. Let's get going."

"No. This is important. Within two hundred meters. How many people? Hundreds, at least." Tarasove dabbed his lips with a paper napkin. "Kiryl Chapaev told you of my latest project, but he didn't really know very much. Look around you, Feliks. Instead of being in an open park, imagine you are in a building. Say a bank. Or better, a gambling casino. Filled with wealthy capitalists. The safe overflowing with money. You place my toxin in something like this." He pinged his finger against the fan-mister. "The toxin disperses into the atmosphere, the air-conditioning. In a few minutes, those around begin coughing, clutching at their throats, gasping for air. Then they start to scream, drop to the floor, die in agony, while you—because you have had your DNA profiled into the toxin as an antidote—suffer no effects from the poisonous air. You can empty the safe at your leisure. Strip the corpses of their wallets and jewels, and simply walk away."

Feliks picked up the mister, found the switch and snapped it off. "I say we leave right now."

"A moment, please." Tarasove took a loud, slurping sip

of the remaining beer, then smiled at Feliks. "Or I can alter the formula. Turn it around. *Napitak Zlobi*. Devil's Brew. Chapaev came up with the name. We're back in our casino, but this time we don't want to harm all those innocent people. Just one specific man. I program his DNA into the formula, then disperse the Devil's Brew. He alone dies. Once he's targeted, there's no escape. All I need is a drop of his blood, or his urine. A fingernail." Slowly Tarasove reached into his jacket pocket, coming out with a small glassine envelope. "Or his hair. I've had wonderful results with hair." He dropped the envelope directly in front of Feliks. "Recognize these? I retrieved them from your coat, in Kiev. The two times we met at that nightclub, then the evening you came to my laboratory."

Feliks picked up the envelope. "My hair?"

"Exactly. Your DNA fingerprint is in the mist you inhaled."

Feliks bolted to his feet, one hand going for the pistol.

"Sit," Tarasove commanded. He held a blue pill between his thumb and forefinger, close to his lips. "This is your antidote, Boris. If you don't swallow it within the next few seconds, you will be dead in five minutes. Tell me who else is involved with Veronin."

Feliks's hand turned into a claw. Was the bastard bluffing? He sat down slowly, carefully, his eyes never leaving the pill so close to Tarasove's tobacco-stained teeth. "Sasha is working with General Burian Kilmov, the head of the External Intelligence Service."

"Ah, an unholy alliance. And they are planning to do what? Kill me once they have my formula? The truth! The pill coating is melting. I can't hold it like this much longer."

"No. They will provide you with the money. I am to deliver you safe and sound. I told you, your genius is your shield."

Tarasove dropped the pill into Feliks's waiting hand. "I believe you now."

Feliks gulped down the pill, vowing to kill Tarasove as soon as Sasha had milked him of his formula. "Now, let's go," he said in a dry, raspy voice.

"The Hacksaw Killer!" someone screamed.

Tarasove bumped the wobbly table over in his haste to get to his feet.

"Police! Police! He's a killer!"

Feliks stared at the spiky-haired man pointing at him. It was Max, the hairdresser! He looked to Tarasove, who began running as fast as his fat legs would carry him.

"Help! Police!" Max Green shouted at the top of his lungs.

Someone grabbed Feliks roughly by his neck and tried to wrestle him to the ground. He freed the pistol from his waistband and fired into the man's bare, oil-greased stomach. He rolled free of the aggressor, scrambled to his feet and darted off after Tarasove.

Harry Dymes heard the shouts for "Police!" moments before the unmistakable *ka-pow* sound of a high-powered weapon. The screams that followed confused him for a moment. "Over there," he told Marta, on the run. The crowd was scattering frantically in all directions. Harry spotted Max Green waving his arms in anguish. There was too much noise to hear what he was saying, but Harry thought he saw Max's lips form the words "killed Billy!"

Another gunshot. To his left. A man in a dark jacket, waving a gun—Feliks. More shots. He seemed to be firing blindly into the retreating crowd.

Feliks saw Tarasove's bulky figure melt into a grove of shadowy bushes. Someone clutched at his arm—one of the helmeted firemen. He shot the man point-blank in the chest.

Suddenly Tarasove's voice was in his ear. He'd forgotten the cell phone was still on.

"You didn't think I'd let you get away with it, did you, Boris? Killing Kiryl, and the others. All good friends. The pill was nothing but sugar. You'll die in agony within moments."

Feliks's throat felt like it was on fire. His heart seemed to be trying to burst from his chest. He staggered forward, wildly firing his pistol.

Harry Dymes dropped to one knee, rested the butt of his revolver in the palm of his left hand, and sighted in on Boris Feliks, who was now shooting in his direction. A bullet plowed into the ground near Harry's knee. He pulled the trigger four times, his target inching up from Feliks's groin to his stomach, his chest, and finally his head.

He heard another shot, the weapon no more than a few feet from him. Marta Citron was standing in the approved FBI shooting position: legs spread, arms extended, both hands on her smoking weapon.

Harry reached Feliks first. He kept his revolver pointed at the mutilated body, while he kicked the weapon free from the Russian's hand.

"He's dead, Harry," Citron said between labored breaths.

Harry holstered his .38, then draped his sweater over Feliks. Marta's Glock semiautomatic was still clutched tightly between both hands.

"Put that in your purse," Harry suggested. He used his cell phone to call 911 and report the incident, then said, "Stay here and guard the scene. I'll go check on the other victims."

"I think I shot that woman lying over there," Marta said in a tight voice.

Harry spotted the circle of angry-faced women in leather surrounding a young curly-haired girl who was clutching her stomach and moaning in pain.

Chapter Twenty-Nine

Lieutenant Ric Larsen exited Captain of Detectives Lawrence Sanborn's office and walked over to Harry Dymes, in slow smooth movements, as if he were walking in water.

"You're next, pal. Good luck," he whispered.

Sanborn was sitting ramrod straight behind his desk when Harry entered the room.

"Don't bother sitting down, Inspector. You're not going to be here long. What is it with you? Have you been watching old Clint Eastwood movies on television? You think you're the new Dirty Harry? Is that it? First the shooting right here in the Hall of Justice, then this fiasco in Golden Gate Park. And with the same fucking gun I told you to get rid of." He pounded his fist on the desk, causing a stack of papers to flutter to the floor.

"Two innocent people were killed, Inspector, and a young woman badly wounded." Sanborn raised the fingers on one hand until three were pointing to the ceiling. "Three innocent individuals who had gone to the park to celebrate. To have a good time. Enjoy the sun. And the weapon the shooter used belonged to a San Francisco policeman. A buddy of yours, Barney Ford. That really makes us look like boy wonders, doesn't it?"

Harry stood with his legs apart, his hands clasped behind

his back, and merely nodded his head, which only seemed to infuriate Sanborn.

"Two *gay* citizens of our fair city, Inspector. And then there were the unfortunates who fell and were trampled while trying to get away from the shooting. Do you know how many calls I've received from outraged citizens? From gay civic leaders? You've been around long enough to know how much clout these people have."

Again Harry nodded his head and remained silent.

"What am I supposed to tell them, Inspector?"

"That *I*, along with an agent of the FBI, was responsible for eliminating a professional killer who had murdered three people in the city, in addition to the ones injured in the park, and, if not shot dead, would have killed many more, Captain."

Sanborn bent his eyebrows together. "Someone spilled the bastard's name to the press. They're blaring it all over the radio and TV. Boris Feliks."

"It wasn't me, Cap."

"Your face is all over the TV channels, Dymes."

"All I said was, 'No comment,' Captain."

"I don't want you near the press. Period. Any news release on this will come directly from me. Tell me what you *think* you know about this professional killer."

"His name was Boris Feliks. He was a member of the Red Mafia, who came here to the United States to find a Russian scientist, who is under the protection of the federal government."

"What's your source on his ID?" Sanborn asked.

"The FBI, sir."

"*Who* in the FBI, Dymes? I want names, not initials."

Harry shifted his weight from one leg to another. "Agent Roger Dancel. When you speak with him, Captain, I believe he will deny giving me any information."

"And why would he do that?"

"Dancel is unaware of the fact that he provided me the information."

Sanborn hunched forward in his chair. "Are you telling me that you bugged an FBI agent? That you tapped his phone?"

"No, sir. I read his lips."

Sanford screwed up one side of his face, as if he were

squinting through a telescope. "Who do you think you're messing with, Dymes? Some rag-ass lieutenant who doesn't have the balls to drop you back to patrolman?"

"I read Dancel's lips while he was having lunch, discussing the case with another FBI agent, Marta Citron. It's a skill I developed when I was in the army."

"Citron. The agent who was in the park with you at the time of the shooting. You read her lips, too, Dymes? Up close and personal? Why was she there? And, if you knew that this shooter was going to be in the park, why didn't you alert your lieutenant?"

"I wasn't certain that Feliks would be in the park. One of my informants, a gypsy fortune-teller, was able to develop the name Feliks was using—John Kagel. A man by that name had gone to a local hairdresser who dyed the shooter's hair yesterday. I talked to the hairdresser and he said that he and Kagel spoke of the Gay Sports Festival in the park. There was no certainty that Feliks was going to show up there, but I figured it was worth a shot."

"That's an unfortunate choice of words under the circumstance, Dymes. You were responsible for killing Feliks, from what Lieutenant Larsen told me. How did you come up with the information on the hairdresser?"

"Kagel's credit report."

Sanborn made a catcher's mitt of one hand and a baseball of the other and pounded them together. "Inspector, I'm going to give you until tomorrow morning to provide me with a complete written report regarding your interaction with the FBI, understood? And I hope you had a subpoena for the credit card information. I spoke to the city attorney an hour ago, and he expects that there will be a slew of civil lawsuits against the department because of your actions today. I don't want you within spitting range of a reporter. As of this moment, you're officially off duty—you can make it easy on yourself and take some vacation time, or I'll put you on suspension, it's your choice."

"I could use a few days' vacation, Captain."

"Good, because I don't want you involved further in this investigation until I say so. Turn your weapon over to Lieutenant Larsen. If you disobey my orders, well, you say you can read lips. Read this." Sanborn moved his lips slowly and silently. "Did you catch that, Inspector?"

"Yes, sir. You said, 'You're fucked.'"

Several reporters were stationed in front of the doors to the homicide detail. Harry knew them all, and had a good relationship with two of them, but all he could do was shrug his shoulders and make a zip-the-lip gesture across his face as he made his way past them.

Ric Larsen was in his office talking to Barney Ford, who looked as if he'd just taken a left hook to the stomach from the heavyweight champion. Ford would be the first one Captain Sanborn would throw to the wolves, to keep the heat off himself. And Harry knew that he'd be the next in line.

He settled behind his desk and tried Marta Citron's cell number. This was his sixth attempt to contact her, but again, there was no answer. They'd split up once the coroner had removed Feliks's body from the park.

Lieutenant Larsen patted Harry on his shoulder to get his attention. "Before I saw Captain Sanborn, I had a long session with Max Green. His significant other, Billy somebody, was one of the shooter's victims. Green said you told him the shooter was the Houston Hacksaw Killer. What's that all about?"

Harry gnawed at his lower lip. "Green dyed the shooter's hair. He wasn't very cooperative, until I made up a story about Feliks being a serial killer of gay men in Houston."

Larsen rolled his eyes. "Sanborn will have a shit fit. I'll try and bury it somehow, but it won't be easy."

None of it was going to be easy, Harry knew. He had to somehow keep Don Landeta's name from surfacing. He figured that the FBI would be giving Marta a hard time, too—for not notifying them of the John Kagel ID and the meeting in the park, and for cooperating too closely with a San Francisco cop named Harry Dymes. Hell, he reasoned, Feliks was dead, Tarasove was safe. The Bureau should give her a promotion. Then he remembered the name she'd given him. Alex. Where did he fit into all of this?

He started to work on a report that he hoped would somehow pacify the captain of detectives.

The phone rang and he snatched it up, hoping it was Marta.

"Inspector, you're working me to death—so to speak," Assistant Coroner Phillips said. "Come on down. We have to talk. I think some formaldehyde is in order."

Two small, filled-to-the-brim paper cups were sitting on Phillips's desk, alongside six mushroom-shaped pieces of lead.

"Cheers," Phillips said, picking up his bourbon. "Six bullets, Harry, retrieved from the corpse of the man identified as John Kagel. I'm not a ballistic expert, but I did measure the diameters of the bullets. Four are from a thirty-eight Special round nose load, your brand, I believe."

"That's right. Six? I fired four. The FBI agent shot once, and thought she'd missed the man."

"I removed one bullet from the victim's hypogastric plexus, one from the solar plexus, one from the subclavius—a small triangular muscle between the clavicle and first rib—and the last, this one, the most misshapen, shattered the subject's inferior mandible bone. His jaw bone." Phillips knocked back the whiskey and made a small belch. "Most likely, any one of the shots would have caused his death. But I don't believe they did." He prodded the two mangled hunks of lead with the empty paper cup. "These are twenty-two caliber hollow-points which entered the gentleman's buttocks and ended up in his abdomen."

"He was shot from behind?"

"Apparently. Though from your initial report, the man was whirling about and firing his own weapon."

Harry was stunned. The only other weapon he'd heard being fired was Feliks's—the Beretta he'd stolen from Barney Ford's desk. Which meant the twenty-twos had come from a pistol with a silencer. A professional assassin's choice. Alex? The crime lab would be able to determine the bullet's grain weight and powder load, which would show whether or not the bullet was subsonic. Harry had had a couple of cases where the killer had gone through the trouble and expense of obtaining a gun with a silencer, only to use a supersonic bullet which traveled at eleven hundred feet per second—breaking the sound barrier and producing a normal bullet blast. "Which shots killed him, Doc?"

Phillips fluttered his lips. "This is between you and me for now, Harry. None of the above. I believe that the man died from SCD—sudden cardiac death—mere seconds before he was struck by any bullet."

Harry's eyebrows cocked in a questioning arc. "What are you telling me? That Feliks had a heart attack? That he was frightened to death?"

"I don't think so. He was in excellent health prior to his death."

"What could have caused the cardiac arrest?"

"Bad luck. It kills outwardly healthy people who have no known heart diseases. Tell me what you observed in the moments before his death. Put me in the picture."

Harry rubbed his chin thoughtfully. "It was warm. The park was crowded. I heard shots. Ran over and saw a man with a gun, spinning around, firing wildly."

"Spinning? Firing at someone in particular?"

"I'm not sure. *Lurching* is probably a better description. He was screaming. No words, just a scream. And at one point he grabbed his throat with one hand. His face was—contorted. As if he were in pain. My first thought was that he was high on drugs."

"Drugs could have played a role. An overdose—though there were no visible needle marks, no obvious organ stagnation, and the preliminary blood test shows no trace of alcohol or narcotics. Or he could have been poisoned. When you've been in the business as long as I have, you get a feeling about these things, Harry. This one just doesn't go down right with me. I'm going to have to wait for the toxicology reports before I make an official announcement."

"Have you postmortemed the other victims?"

Phillips widened his eyes and rubbed them as if they were very tired. "Not yet. Tomorrow is another day, Harry. Dying can take a mere second, but determining the exact cause can be a long process. One thing about my clients, Harry. They don't mind waiting for the results."

Harry pushed his chair back and stood up. "Have the toxicologist look for traces of snake venom."

"There are no poisonous snakes in Golden Gate Park, Harry."

"Have them check anyway. I have a feeling about this, Doc."

Chapter Thirty

Trina Lee paused at the door of the bar on Jackson Street until her eyes became accustomed to the darkness. She adjusted the belt on her jacket and pulled down the brim of her hat when she spotted Danny Shu at the end of the bar, flanked by two young girls: one an Asian brunette dressed in a Catholic School uniform—a plaid skirt and white sweater with the letters *MHS* stenciled on the front—and the other a pale-faced blond wearing a see-through white gauze blouse. Trina thought that the brunette would suit her purpose perfectly.

Shu had given her a brief, unfriendly look, obviously not recognizing her, and turned his attention back to the girls.

She was beginning to feel the effects of a long day. After shooting Boris Feliks in Golden Gate Park, she ran back to her Jaguar just in time to see Nicolai Tarasove's Hummer roar off in a yammer of iron-clanging gear shifts. She'd trailed Tarasove right back to his chalet in Lake Tahoe, the Russian making only one stop to use the restroom and buy more gas along the way.

She wondered about the incident in the park. She'd fired at Feliks to protect Tarasove, and in self-defense, after he began firing wildly into the crowd. What had caused a cold-blooded killer to act in such an unprofessional manner?

And the other shooter, the man in the baseball cap. Obviously a police officer, as was the woman standing alongside him. How did they get there so fast? Were they waiting for Feliks? For Tarasove? Was that possible? Or were they just undercover cops, there to monitor the festival? *She* had no idea of where Tarasove was driving to, or the obvious planned meeting with Feliks. It was only when she overheard him on his cell phone, heard him mention Feliks's name, telling him where he was, that she realized Feliks was in the park.

Trina had kept her distance from the two of them while they sat at the table talking, Tarasove eating chili, fidgeting with a fan, until the man with spiked hair pointed at Feliks and screamed something Trina couldn't quite make out. *Killer*—she heard that—the rest was lost in the hum of the crowd.

Tarasove appeared to be celebrating as he drove away, one arm waving in the air like a symphony conductor's, his head bobbing back and forth.

Trina played with the Jag's radio dial, finding an all-news station reporting on the "massacre in Golden Gate Park." The ID of the "crazed gunman" was unknown, according to the reporter on the scene. Anyone with information relating to the incident was asked to call the station's "Hot Line" number.

Trina had done just that, using her cell phone. "The crazed killer is a Russian Mafia member named Boris Feliks. The FBI has been after him for years."

A half hour later, the radio station boasted of having a "confidential source who has informed us the crazed gunman in Golden Gate Park was a notorious Russian gangster."

Minutes after parking his Hummer at the chalet, Tarasove had turned his audio system up full blast. Trina endured twenty minutes of Tchaikovsky's *Nutcracker* before she concluded that Tarasove would stay put for the night and that it was safe to turn the Jaguar around and head back to San Francisco for the scheduled meeting with Danny Shu.

She slipped a ten-milligram Adderall pill under her tongue to combat the fatigue that was beginning to set in. The prescription upper, a combination of four amphetamine salts, would carry her through the next few grueling hours.

She made her way over to Shu and tapped the blonde on the shoulder. "Can I have your seat, please? The gentleman and I have some business to discuss."

Shu's face folded into a sneer; then his eyes widened. "Holy shit. It's you. Alex."

"In the flesh," Trina said, sliding onto the stool vacated by the blonde. "Sorry I'm late."

Shu pushed his elbow into the brunette's sweater, told her to get lost, then said, "Where's Tarasove?"

"Ying Fai liked the photograph I e-mailed him? That's good. As soon as he deposits the money into my Swiss account, I'll take you to him."

Shu stuck a finger the size of a sausage an inch from Trina's right eye. "Where is he?"

"Near the place shown in the photograph," she explained patiently. "One of my men is watching him. There's no way he can get away, even if he suspected that he was being watched—which he doesn't."

"*One* of your men. How many are there?"

"I'd like a Tom Collins, Danny. Two cherries. Do you think the bartender can manage that?"

Shu spoke to the bartender in Mandarin, then told Trina to follow him to an empty booth in the rear of the bar. When they were seated, he said, "How many people do you have working for you?"

"Not as many as Ying Fai." She toyed with the zipper on her blouse. "And none as competent as you. I know your reputation, Danny. You wouldn't want to quit Fai and join me, would you?"

"You have a lot of guts, lady. I'll say that for you."

The bartender brought her drink and a full bottle of Jack Daniels and a clean glass for Shu. Trina took a sip, then held up the glass. *"Gan bei."*

"You know Mandarin?"

"*Gan bei.* Dry your cup, that's about the extent of it"— she lowered her voice—"and a few ways to tell men to go to hell. Call Fai, tell him to transfer the money, then we can have a celebration party."

"First, I see Tarasove. In person."

"First, I make sure the money is in my account. All of it. I've found the second man, too. Boris Feliks."

Shu reached over and snatched up her purse. "Why should we believe you?"

"It's all over the news. I shot him today in Golden Gate Park."

Shu found nothing of interest in her purse except for three hand-rolled cigarettes. He ran one of the smokes under his nose and gave a toothy smile. "Nice stuff."

Trina turned her head and scanned the bar. "Why don't we go someplace after you've contacted Ying Fai, where we can smoke and drink in private? My suite at Fisherman's Wharf has a sunken bathtub big enough for three."

Shu pushed himself to his feet, then walked briskly to the back of the bar and disappeared through a brightly painted orange door.

When he reappeared, Trina plucked one of the cherries from her drink and popped it in her mouth, her lips making slow, exaggerated movements.

Shu placed his massive hands on the tabletop. "The money will be transferred within an hour. You better not try to screw us on this, Alex."

Trina stuck out her tongue. The cherry stem was tied into a neat knot. She removed it and dropped it on the table between them. "There's only one way I would ever think about screwing you." She looked over to the adjoining booth and smiled at the young Asian girl in the school uniform. "She's cute. I like her, too. Think she could join us?"

Shu flicked the discarded cherry stem onto the floor with one of his huge fingers. "You like to play games, don't you?"

Trina plucked the second cherry from her drink and dangled it in front of her mouth. "Only with some people, Danny."

Nicolai Tarasove tilted the bottle in his hand and dribbled a stream of vodka into Jedgar's water bowl. "You must celebrate with me, my friend."

Chuckling, Tarasove took a hit directly from the bottle. The chuckle quickly grew to a stomach-shaking laugh, and he couldn't help spraying vodka from his mouth.

The Devil's Brew had worked perfectly.

Tarasove only wished that he could have seen Feliks's face—his pretty new face—when he informed Feliks that he had only seconds left to live, that there was no antidote, that he had swallowed a sugar pill. It had driven him mad—shooting at anything in sight, like a cowboy in an American movie.

"What is puzzling," he said to Jedgar, "was the man who called Feliks a 'hacksaw killer.' What do you think that was all about?"

The dog sniffed his water and took a tentative slurp.

Tarasove carried the vodka bottle out to the deck. The night sky pulsed with stars, and the forest soaked up every sound of movement. He switched on the halogen lamps, took another nip, then used his cell phone to dial the Russian Consulate's safe number he'd previously called.

"Is this Arman?" Tarasove said when he was connected. "I spoke to you yesterday regarding Snake Charmer. We may be ready to make a move quite soon."

Arman Ritokov stifled a yawn. He'd been napping, having a pleasant dream about a young woman he'd met in a Union Street saloon. "I remember the call. It is still being processed."

"Processed! I want action, immediately. Do you know the name Burian Kilmov? Call him. Now."

Arman kicked the blanket from his feet and sat up. Could this idiot be legitimate? "I will have to have more information before contacting General Kilmov, you must realize—"

"Tell him that Boris Feliks is dead. And that Snake Charmer is ready to negotiate. With him, and no one else. Tell him exactly that. I will call tomorrow, at one in the afternoon, and you had better have the right information for me."

Incompetent fool, Tarasove fumed when he broke the connection. He would demand to talk to Kilmov directly—no intermediaries. His thumb roved over the phone's keypad. Should he call Sasha Veronin? How would he get his number? Or Ying Fai's? There had to be a way.

There was sudden movement in the brush twenty-five meters from the deck. Jedgar bounded past Tarasove, his massive head smashing into the redwood gate.

"Heel, Jedgar. It's just a hungry deer. Not the kind of animal we have to worry about right now."

The landline phone was ringing in the chalet. He returned to the kitchen, a look of concern on his face. Who was calling at this time of the evening? Had he made a mistake contacting the consulate? Had they somehow traced him? He picked the phone up gingerly, holding it away from his ear, not saying a word.

"Have you found the snake?" a weary female voice asked.

"What?"

"The loose snake, Nicolai."

"Ah, Marta. I did not recognize your lovely voice. Yes, he is back in his tank."

"I have some good news. Boris Feliks is not a concern anymore. He has been eliminated."

"Really? What happened?"

"He was shot to death by a San Francisco policeman. I'll give you all the details when I see you tomorrow."

"I can't wait," Tarasove said truthfully, after Marta had hung up.

He noticed that Jedgar's water bowl was empty. He brought it to the sink, filled it halfway, then added a hefty measure of vodka. "Tomorrow, my friend. Tomorrow we finally have her."

Trina Lee crawled over the prone, snoring body of Danny Shu, stopping to lick his ear. When there was no response, she bit down on the lobe, lightly at first, gradually increasing the pressure until she heard a mumbled grunt pour through Shu's blubbery lips.

The jolly yellow giant had consumed an enormous amount of bourbon and dope. Trina swung her legs over the curled-up figure of Jaleh, the seventeen-year-old brunette who had shared the bath and bed with her and Shu. Jaleh was fresh off one of Ying Fai's tankers from Hong Kong, according to Shu; thus no American crime agency had her fingerprints on file.

Trina slipped into her slacks and top, all the while staring at Shu's enormous, Buddha-like stomach moving up and down with each noisy breath. In his clothes, Shu was an intimidating figure, but naked, with his beach ball–size head fast asleep on a pillow, his bloated arms and legs akimbo, he looked extremely vulnerable. For such a huge man, Shu was small where most men wanted to be large. His shriveled penis looked like a worm resting in a bird's nest.

When they had arrived at Trina's motel room, Danny Shu had checked it thoroughly for possible weapons or recording devices. She'd anticipated him doing exactly that, so her gun, camera, and electronic devices were safely locked in the Jag's trunk.

She padded barefoot to the motel door, peeked out, then walked a few yards down the hallway to where the fire extinguisher was attached to the wall. She pulled it free, returned to the room, and closed and locked the door.

Shu was still snoring. Trina pulled the safety pin from the extinguisher, straddled Shu's chest, centered the black plastic discharge nozzle over Shu's nose and mouth and pulled the trigger. The escaping CO_2 made a loud hissing noise. Shu's entire body bucked, as if he'd been electrocuted. His eyes opened and his hands jerked out. Trina ground the nozzle into his flesh, ignoring his flailing arms. The CO_2 packed into Shu's nostrils, his mouth, filling his throat, effectively suffocating him.

She cautiously pulled the nozzle away. Shu's face was burned from the freezing carbon dioxide, giving him a clownlike look.

Jaleh was still asleep, a result of the Mexican red downers Shu had fed her before and during their orgy.

Trina gently wrapped a towel around the girl's sleek, unblemished neck, then used her fingers to find her carotid artery. Jaleh made barely a sound as she passed from this world. To a better place, Trina hoped. Anything would be better than life as a Triad whore. The girls were treated fairly well while they were young. But once they lost the bloom of youth, they were shuffled through a series of whorehouses, finally ending up in waterfront cribs, where AIDS and syphilis were as common as a cold.

Trina quickly gathered her things together, then went to the hallway again, this time to the motel's ice machine. She filled a cardboard ice bucket to the brim and carried it back to the room.

Trina dumped the ice into the bathroom sink, then dragged a chair over to the room's one and only sprinkler head, using the fire extinguisher to spray the sprinkler's glass-enclosed thermostat with freezing carbon dioxide. Then she carried the empty ice bucket over to the sprinkler and methodically bent the edges until the bucket fit nicely into the sprinkler head's recessed housing bracket. She returned to the bathroom with the bucket, refilled it with ice and secured it into place around the sprinkler head.

Finally satisfied, she jumped off the chair and stared up at the sabotaged sprinkler. The ice-filled bucket wouldn't stay in place long, but it didn't have to. A few minutes would be all that was needed for the fire to build up. By the time the heat reached the sprinkler's thermostat, the room would be an inferno.

She used the fire extinguisher once more on the room's smoke alarm, giving it a thick coating of the snowlike CO_2, then covered the alarm with a disposable shower cap. Again, this wouldn't incapacitate the alarm entirely, but it would delay the system from activating.

She carried Shu's pants, which held his wallet and keys, to the bathroom, dropping them on the floor and closing the door. She wanted his ID to be the only things that survived the fire.

She cracked the screw top off a bottle of bourbon and streamed the liquor over Danny Shu's corpse, then poured what was left in the bottle onto Jaleh. She tore a handful of pages out of the room's phone book, rolled them into crinkly balls and sprinkled them around the two bodies.

Trina used Danny Shu's butane cigarette lighter to ignite the rolled-up papers. She watched the flames grow in strength, licking at Shu's flesh. When the bedsheets ignited, Trina picked up the chair and hurled it through the window. Oxygen immediately gushed into the room, intensifying the flames. She hurried through the door and down the stairs to her waiting car.

The flames were shooting out the window as she turned onto Columbus Street. She checked her watch. A little after three in the morning. She'd be back in Tahoe by seven.

Would Ying Fai believe that it was her charred body lying next to Danny Shu's? Probably not. But, she fervently hoped, he wouldn't investigate too thoroughly. It would save Fai an enormous amount of face if he and his associates concluded that she and Shu had simply been burned to death accidentally. If Fai's number one man had been killed by a mere woman, Fai himself would look foolish—and that he would avoid at all costs.

The money Ying Fai had transferred to her Swiss account would be written off as a business loss. Which left Trina with one remaining client—Burian Kilmov.

Chapter Thirty-One

Zhukovsky Airport, Russia

Colonel Edik Savelev followed General Kilmov up the ramp to the gleaming silver Tupolev TU-134SH supersonic passenger jet.

Kilmov realized he appeared much less intimidating in civilian clothes. Without his uniform and boots, he looked like nothing more than a store clerk.

The attractive flaxen-haired flight attendant obviously knew who he was, welcoming him with a wide smile, addressing him by name and rank, and assisting him out of his raincoat.

He was led to a curtained-off area just aft the pilot's cockpit.

"You will not be disturbed during the flight," the attendant told him. "Is there anything I can do for you, General?"

"Bring champagne. Two glasses," Kilmov said, before settling down into a comfortable window seat. He peered out at the fog-dampened tarmac with mixed emotions. He usually enjoyed his visits to the West, but this time there would be no sightseeing or shopping for presents for Ivana.

This time he had to return home with two presents for himself—Nicolai Tarasove, and Alex.

He glanced over at Colonel Savelev in the seat across the aisle. If anything, he was more dashing in his dark blue suit and red-and-white striped tie than in his uniform. Kilmov realized with displeasure that without the insignias and collar bars, an uninformed observer might have concluded that Savelev was the man in charge.

"Take off your tie," Kilmov told him. "And your shoes are too polished. Scuff them. We don't want to look like a couple of American salesmen."

"Yes, sir." Edik undid his tie, then handed Kilmov a computer printout. "The story from the San Francisco newspaper regarding the shooting, General."

Kilmov read the article thoroughly. "I wonder if Sasha Veronin has seen this," he said when he had finished. "Boris Feliks. Sasha spoke of the man as if he were invincible, yet he dies at the hand of a common policeman."

Savelev shifted in his seat, causing the leather to squeak. "I'm not certain about that, sir. We've had another communication from Alex. He claims responsibility for Feliks's death."

"Does he now? What else does the bastard say?"

"That he has Nicolai Tarasove in a box for us. Tied up in a nice ribbon, in Lake Tahoe, which is some six hundred kilometers from San Francisco." Savelev handed Kilmov a map. "I've marked the lake in red."

Kilmov spread the map across his lap. "How large is this lake?"

Savelev had done his homework. "Approximately thirty-five kilometers in length and twelve in width, a hundred-fifteen kilometers of shoreline."

"A substantial body of water. Alex hasn't made it easy for us, has he? Tarasove could be in a hundred different locales." Kilmov studied the map from a military perspective. Savelev had highlighted the land route from San Francisco to the lake in yellow. "Travel time?" he asked.

"Four to five hours from San Francisco, depending on the traffic, General."

That drew a grunt from Kilmov. "Not satisfactory." His finger traced the route. "A bridge here by the city. Not good. If the FBI learned of our plans, they could easily block the roads. Where is the nearest airport?"

"The city of Reno, Nevada—I've circled it. There is also a small airport some twenty kilometers from the south end of the lake."

"The first place the FBI would search. What are these red circles here for?" Kilmov wanted to know.

"The town of Stateline, Nevada. It is on the California border, and contains many large gambling casinos. From what we know of Tarasove's habits, it would be an attraction to him."

"Excellent, Edik." Kilmov's brow wrinkled in concentration as he continued to study the map. "The solution is a seaplane. You can fly such a plane?"

"Yes, sir."

Kilmov buckled his seat belt. "E-mail Alex. Instruct him he's to continue to keep Tarasove under surveillance. Press him for an exact location for the scientist. Tell him we are transferring the money to his Swiss bank, and that there will be a substantial bonus when he personally delivers Tarasove to us."

"Yes, sir. I was thinking about Alex. A single name. But there may be more than one man involved. A gang: three, four, a dozen."

"He may have contacts that he uses, but my feeling is that he's a loner. I've dealt with the type before, though they were not as competent as Alex. He derives a great deal of satisfaction from making the FBI, and people like us, look foolish. But he can't quit, retire, because this is exactly the life he loves. This is his high, his narcotic. He's an actor with an adoring one-man audience—himself—and we must find a way of ending the charade and relieving him of his bank full of money."

The flight attendant returned with an ice bucket and a bottle of champagne. She silently poured both men a glass before disappearing back through the curtain.

"What do you make of the phone calls the consulate in San Francisco received, General?"

Kilmov took a sip of the champagne. "It's Tarasove himself. Why do you think he made the contact?"

"Perhaps he's homesick," Savelev suggested.

Kilmov raised his glass in a toast. "You have a poet's heart, and a soldier's soul. I'm happy to have you on my team. When do we arrive in Vancouver?"

Savelev consulted the Russian-made Vostok watch on his wrist. "The pilot estimates slightly more than six hours. There is a charter plane waiting to fly us directly to San Francisco."

"When is Tarasove due to call the San Francisco consulate again?"

"One o'clock in the afternoon, Pacific daylight time. We'll be there well before then."

Kilmov pulled the champagne bottle from its icy blanket and examined the label. "Arman Ritokov, the man Tarasove spoke to at the consulate. What do we know of him?"

"His father was a sergeant in the GRU, nothing important—a *byki*—bodyguard and driver for low-level officers. He had enough influence to get his son into the consulate services. Ritokov seems to be much like his father—not overly bright, but reliable."

"You informed him he is to speak to no one of this?"

"Yes, General. He is shaking in his boots for not informing someone of Tarasove's initial phone call."

Kilmov gave a light chuckle. "It's a good thing for Ritokov, and for us, that he did not. Life is strange, is it not? A week ago we had no idea where Tarasove was, or how advanced his new toxin is. *Napitak Zlobi.* A magic bullet. Sasha Veronin told me no one has anything that compares to this Devil's Brew, and it seems he's right. What do you think of this Devil's Brew, Edik?"

"I think I'm better off sticking to my job, General, and leaving such matters to you."

The answer satisfied Kilmov. It showed intelligence and discretion. The colonel was just the type of man he needed alongside him. It was a shame he was so tall and good-looking.

"Tarasove is jumping into our lap, but I want Alex, too. When we have them both, the job will be done."

Savelev coughed into his hand. "General. What of Sasha Veronin? How will he react when he learns we have accomplished the mission without his help?"

"Boris Feliks was Sasha's man, and he failed. We'll take care of Sasha when we return home. He's getting much too big for his riding breeches. He thinks that Alex is playing a double game. Attempting to sell Tarasove to Ying Fai, as well as us. He could be right. We will have to be on the lookout for Fai's men, as well as the FBI."

"Your idea of using a seaplane is brilliant, General. I could make the trip from San Francisco in an hour. Land on the lake, then taxi to wherever Alex is. He will no doubt have a car."

Kilmov nodded his head in agreement. "Make sure a plane is at the ready for you. I hope you've made suitable housing arrangements. I don't want Tarasove to be seen anywhere near the consulate."

"A safe house a dozen blocks from the consulate, General. I was assured it is most comfortable, with a view of the famous Golden Gate Bridge."

"Excellent. I'll lure the scientist into our trap at the safe house, while you go to Lake Tahoe. If Tarasove should be there, take him, and fly him back to the city." Kilmov slouched down into his seat. If things worked out as he planned, he just might have time to shop for something special for Ivana after all. "Get some sleep," he advised Savelev. "We're going to be very busy once we arrive in America."

Harry Dymes paced the floor in front of the receptionist's desk at the San Francisco FBI office. His request to see Marta Citron had been made fifteen minutes ago. Every time he questioned the pert, honey-blond secretary, she advised him, "It will be just a few more minutes, sir."

Harry was too wound up to sit and thumb through the collection of FBI bulletins that took the place of magazines as reading material in the L-shaped room.

A series of youthful, athletically built men in ill-fitted suits streamed through the doors leading to the back offices. Several glanced suspiciously at Harry, others going out of their way to ignore him.

The door opened and the angry face of Tom McNab appeared.

"I want to talk to you," McNab said. "Stay right there." He leaned over the receptionist's shoulder and began speaking in hushed tones. Harry watched his lips closely:

"Don't *something* Dancel. Under any circumstances," was pronounced slowly and emphatically, thus easy to read. "I'm going to be *something something* Harry Dymes *something something.*" Then another emphatic, "Under any circumstances."

McNab turned his attention to Harry. "My office, Dymes."

Harry followed McNab down a narrow hallway to a cubicle separated from its neighbor by a flimsy wooden partition topped by a section of frosted glass.

A half-dozen little pink telephone messages were arranged in a straight line on a beige metal-framed desk.

McNab read each note before easing himself into the maroon imitation leather chair. "You're in deep shit, Dymes."

"Where's Citron?" Harry said, careful to blunt any sign of anger in his voice. He couldn't stand McNab when he was trying to be civil. Now the agent was acting like a terrier, ready to fight any dog in the neighborhood.

"She's where she should have been yesterday, instead of playing cowboys and Indians in Golden Gate Park with you. How did you know that . . . the Russian was going to be in the park?"

"His name is Boris Feliks. It's in the morning paper, McNab."

"Answer the question, buddy."

"I've done a lot of dumb things in my life, McNab, but having you as a 'buddy' isn't one of them. Where's Roger Dancel's cubicle? I want to talk to someone with at least half a brain."

McNab's lips gave a twitch of a smile. "Roger's been called back to Washington. I don't believe he'll be returning any time soon. I'm now in charge here. I'm going to be meeting with Lieutenant Larsen and Captain Sanborn in a few hours, so I suggest that you drop your buns into the chair over there and tell me exactly what took place yesterday."

Harry leaned across the desk, and in a soft, reasonable voice said, "I wouldn't tell you what time it is." He paused dramatically and added, "Under any circumstances."

Washington, D.C.

"Congratulations," Roger Dancel said when he stormed into Deputy Director James Bartlow's office.

Bartlow was surprised by Dancel's opening gambit. The man should be wetting his pants, worrying about the sudden summons back to FBI headquarters, not acting like someone who'd just won the lottery.

"For what, Roger?"

Dancel dropped his briefcase on the floor, flopped down into a chair and sighed loudly. "I'm getting too old for those damn red-eye flights. And getting bumped up to first class is damn near impossible, James."

Bartlow's back stiffened. *James?* Dancel had always addressed him by his job title, or *sir.* "What is it you're congratulating me for, Roger? Putting you on a red-eye?"

Dancel crossed one leg over the other, eased off one shoe and began massaging his heel. "Don't be modest, James. Boris Feliks. I'm sure the Director himself has been down to shake your hand for nailing the bastard. It was your operation, you're entitled to the credit. I'm just happy I could play a part in it. There should be enough glory for everyone in this, even Marta Citron. She actually took a shot at Feliks." He slipped his shoe back on and added, "Missed him, and hit some poor woman in the crowd, but you really can't blame her. Feliks was blasting away in all directions."

"I wasn't aware Citron had injured a civilian."

Dancel hunched forward. "You might want to acknowledge the cooperation of San Francisco Police Inspector Harry Dymes. Dymes is the one who actually killed Feliks."

Dancel removed a manila folder from his briefcase and shoved it across the desk to Bartlow. "Dymes had no idea who Feliks was, of course. Feliks murdered a woman, one of Dymes's informants—a gypsy fortune-teller who knew Zivon Yudin, the thug Feliks had picked up in Los Angeles to help him corral Kiryl Chapaev. I examined her body at the morgue. She'd carved a name in her thigh. John Kagel, Feliks's latest AKA. She must have gotten the name from Yudin." He tossed the folder casually onto Bartlow's leather-bound desk blotter. "It's all there in my report. I ran John Kagel's name, and found that he was a drifter in Houston who disappeared a while back. Feliks obviously killed him, because he had a wallet full of Kagel's ID and credit cards on him when he died. Feliks made the mistake you always said he would. He got careless. That's how we nailed him. So, once again, congratulations."

"What in God's name was Feliks doing in a San Francisco park?"

"I figure he had to be meeting someone—an informant, or possibly another Russian gangster. Perhaps he needed help—or money. Or there could be a simple answer, James. There was a gay festival in the park. Maybe Boris was queer, and was looking to get laid."

Bartlow picked up the folder, holding it in his palm as if he was assessing its weight. "You paint a pretty picture of all this, Roger."

"I'm a fucking Picasso when it comes to a report, James. You know that."

There was a timid knock on the door, and Ida Keaton, Bartlow's secretary, entered, carrying a tray with two cups of steaming coffee and a pile of cookies scattershot with chocolate chips.

"Bless you, Ida," Dancel said cheerfully. "Your home-made cookies are just what I need this morning." He helped himself to a coffee cup, and one of the cookies. "How's your husband? Still in the stock market?"

Bartlow squeezed the bridge of his nose between his thumb and forefinger as he watched Dancel's performance. The man knew Keaton's first name, her husband's occupation, and her penchant for making homemade cookies. The woman was beaming at Dancel, telling him about her grandson.

"Thank you, Mrs. Keaton," he said dryly. "You may go now."

"Good woman," Dancel said with a mouthful of cookie. "But you never know, do you, James? Tom McNab told me about your mole theory. You could be on to something. A mole, working with, or for, the meat eater. I don't think the mole would be a high-ranking agent, do you? More likely someone in an office position, a research clerk, a personnel administrator. Or a secretary, like Mrs. Keaton. Not *her*, of course, but someone like her, with access to our most confidential reports. Maybe with a husband, or significant other, in financial difficulties. I know Ida's husband dropped a pile in the market crash a couple of years ago. How many Idas are there in the agency? And the mole wouldn't necessarily have to be working out of Washington. With the interdepartment computer databases that the Director insisted be put in place after Nine-Eleven, the mole could be anywhere. And then there are all those subcontractors we've been forced to use. The investigation will be time-consuming, and expensive. You'll have to put everyone through the mill, lie detector tests, the works. You and I could get the ball rolling by volunteering to take the tests ourselves. If there is a mole, you're definitely the man to find him, James."

"Tom McNab told you about my mole theory?"

"Right," Dancel said, picking up another cookie. "I hate to talk badly of a fellow agent, but McNab's not the sharpest knife in the drawer. He has a booze problem. Two of them, in fact. He doesn't like to buy, and when he has a couple of gins, he starts shooting off his mouth. He antagonized the Frisco cop, Harry Dymes, right off the bat, James. Luckily, I was able to convince Dymes that we were working together on this."

Bartlow poured cream into his coffee and swirled it around with a spoon. "We still have a major concern. Alex. He poses a direct threat to Tarasove, and we have no idea who he is, or where he is."

"Absolutely, he's a major threat. Ying Fai is not going to give up on Tarasove. Marta Citron is babysitting him in Lake Tahoe. Once again, I'd like to suggest that we move him to another location."

Bartlow picked up a cookie and crumbled it into his coffee cup. He'd ordered Dancel back to Washington to ream his butt, put him on the hot seat—not flat-out accuse him of being the mole, but make him sweat, force him to take a polygraph test and go through a long session with a crack interrogation team. Dancel had figured out the motive for his hasty summons back to D.C. and beat him to the punch, *volunteering* to take a polygraph test, and calling on *him* to do the same.

Bartlow had to admit that Dancel's performance was brilliant. Because of Tom McNab's big mouth, he was going to have to perform some serious butt-covering himself, and invest all kinds of time and money into the fantasy he'd created of a mole in the Bureau.

"All right, Roger. I'll talk to the Director about moving Tarasove. In the meantime, you're to return to San Francisco. Monitor Tarasove—and, Roger—find Alex. He'll lead us to the mole.'

Dancel bit into another cookie and waved a friendly good-bye from the door, his stuffed mouth mumbling an incoherent, "There is no mole, you pompous asshole, and we both know it."

Chapter Thirty-Two

Nicolai Tarasove locked Jedgar in the chalet's kitchen, then taped a handwritten note to the front door: *Marta—went shopping. Back in a few minutes.* He didn't want Citron to happen by while he was on the phone with the Russians.

He drove the Hummer three and a half miles to Stateline, parking in the huge lot behind Caesar's Casino, and used his 3G phone to dial the Russian Consulate in San Francisco.

"Arman speaking."

"Have you spoken to Kilmov?" Tarasove said, squirming in his seat as he watched a casino security van make a slow sweep of the lot.

"I have. I will patch you directly to him."

The dark-windowed security van cruised by without stopping.

There was a crackling noise on his phone; then a strong voice said, "Is this the famous scientist himself I have the pleasure of speaking to?"

"You are General Kilmov?"

"Indeed. How are you, scientist? Are you enjoying California?"

Tarasove relaxed. The Hummer was some half mile from the California border. Kilmov was guessing. He had no idea where he was. "Indeed I am. But my landlord has become uncooperative. I am thinking of moving to a new location. However, moving expenses would be quite high."

"How high?"

"Twenty-five million. Dollars, not rubles."

"Is your new project worth that much to us?"

"More. Much more. Boris Feliks must have told you of my work."

"*Napitak Zlobi*, the Devil's Brew. It sounds interesting, but Feliks was not an expert, and the people I've spoken to in Moscow do not believe it is possible. You would have to prove to me that it is viable."

"I have already proven it. To Feliks. He . . . caught a fatal flu from my Devil's Brew, while all those around him were unaffected."

"I know you like to gamble, scientist, but that is a terrible bluff. Feliks was shot to death by an American policeman."

"It was a wasted bullet, because he was already as good as dead."

"How do I know you're not bluffing, scientist?"

Tarasove yanked the car door open and stepped out into the fresh air. "It would be a simple matter to prove. Do you have someone in mind? I need a sample of his blood, hair, or urine. It will take several days to develop the DNA fingerprint. Time I do not wish to waste. Or I could stand in a crowd of a dozen, a hundred, a thousand poor fools, as many as you wish, and eliminate them all. And I would walk away. Would that satisfy you?"

"When can we meet and discuss all this man-to-man?"

Tarasove kicked at an empty beer can that had been left in the parking lot. "I was born at night, General. But not last night. The money will have to be deposited in the numbered account in the Grand Bahamas. And I want a proper new address, where I can continue to work, and live without fear of the Americans kidnapping me again."

"Yes. We certainly wouldn't want that to happen. Give me a meeting place, and I will come to you. Personally, to show my good faith."

"You're here? In America?"

"I came especially to meet with you. There will be no dealing with underlings, this time. Do not go to the consulate. The FBI no doubt has it under observation. I have arranged a safe place for our meeting." There was a rustle of papers. "The address is three thousand sixty-four Vallejo Street, in San Francisco."

Tarasove strolled over to the beer can and gave it another kick, sending it into the side panel of a cherry-red Corvette. "There are certain things I must take care of. Papers I need to pack."

"Give me your number so we can stay in communication."

"No. I'll call you. I will need assurances that I will be left alone, General."

"Your genius is your insurance, scientist. My superiors would feed me to the wolves if I let anything happen to you. You will be provided with the money you so richly deserve. *Do svidaniya!*"

And good-bye to you too, General, Tarasove said to himself as he fast-walked back to the Hummer. My genius is my insurance. Feliks and the general spoke the same lines. But it is true. I am worth far more to Kilmov alive than dead.

General Kilmov settled the phone gently on its cradle, then toasted the end of a Cuban cigar—one Sasha Veronin had given him—with a wooden match.

"Was the conversation satisfactory, General?" Colonel Savelev asked.

Kilmov puffed on the cigar to get it going. "No. It was not. I'm afraid Nicolai Tarasove has developed a God complex. He acts as if he and he alone has control of the world. If Tarasove becomes a problem, we'll have to deal with him harshly." He attempted to blow a smoke ring, but created something closer to a mushroom. "I'm beginning to think that this Devil's Brew of his is a genie that should remain in the bottle. If he doesn't cooperate, shoot the traitorous son of a bitch."

The homicide detail was not the place to be, Harry Dymes decided when he saw Captain Sanborn in Ric Larsen's office, reading the riot act again.

Sergeant Bob Dills was perched on the edge of Inspector Ralph Gowan's desk, the two men involved in a deep conversation. Gowan was wearing a heavy canvas jacket and knee-high rubber boots. Carlotta, the receptionist, hurried over when she spotted Harry. "Two men from Internal Affairs have Barney Ford in one of the interrogation rooms. They were asking about you, too."

"You never saw me," Dymes said, backpedaling out the door.

"Hey, Harry," Dills said, catching up with Dymes in the hallway. "How's it going?"

"Not good. What were you and Gowan discussing?"

"Danny Shu was found torched in bed at a Fisherman's Wharf motel early this morning. Ralph says it looks suspicious. Shu and some unidentified young girl were burned to a crisp, yet his clothes and wallet were found intact in the bathroom."

"Danny Shoe? Who the hell is he?" Harry asked, snapping his fingers together as if that would help jar his memory.

"S-H-U. He is . . . was Ying Fai's number one boy."

"Now I remember Shu. He was a suspect in a Chinatown hit a few years ago. He walked, but I remember we pulled him in for an interview, which lasted all of ten minutes before Fai's attorneys had him sprung. Christ. There's a link between the guy I shot in the park and Ying Fai. Bobby, I need a desk and a phone, and I don't want to use mine. Internal Affairs is looking for me."

"There's an empty desk next to mine. Help yourself."

Harry's first call proved to be disappointing.

"I can't help you," Don Landeta told him. "I mean, I've got to have something to go on. You're sure that this Tahoe property isn't under the name Nicolai Tarasove, right?"

"Yeah. It probably belongs to the federal government."

"Three-quarters of the acreage up there belongs either to the state or the feds, Harry. There are four counties surrounding the lake. The chalet could be in any of them. I could run a list on all properties sold in the last two or three years, but it would stretch from my office to yours. And the title has got to be set up under a fictitious name, so unless you can pull Tarasove's AKA, I can't do a thing for you."

Harry sank back and stared at the dingy acoustical ceiling. He'd once arrested a guy for manslaughter who'd claimed that he kept his sanity in prison by trying to count the number of holes in the overhead acoustical tiles in his cell.

What do you know about this Russian scientist? he asked himself. Real name, Nicolai Tarasove. Looks like Santa Claus, speaks with an accent, according to Marta. Lives somewhere near Lake Tahoe, in a chalet with a view of the lake. And he needs poisonous snakes for his experiments.

"You look like you've got troubles," Bob Dills said, offering Harry a grease-stained paper plate loaded with stale donuts.

"Big troubles, Bobby."

"Well, how about telling your troubles to a cop?"

Marta Citron tilted her head to read the note Nicolai Tarasove had taped to his front door. She grunted her displeasure and headed back to the car. She'd been up most of the night and badly needed a nap, but she wasn't about to enter the chalet, or even go up to the deck, until she knew the location of Nicolai's monster dog.

As if on cue, she heard the beast howling from somewhere within the chalet.

She lit a cigarette and strolled over to the tree where she'd seen the salt lick a few days earlier. The lick was gone, but there were groupings of bullet holes in the thick tree trunk. She imagined the poor Bambis prancing over for a taste of salt while Tarasove plinked at them from his sundeck.

No meat, she vowed. She'd eat nothing but salads and fish for however long she was stuck here babysitting Tarasove. She was fed up with Tarasove, with Tom McNab, Roger Dancel and the entire FBI.

The shooting in the park had deeply affected her. She still wasn't sure if her bullet had hit the young woman she'd seen on the ground, or if Boris Feliks was responsible. He was shooting indiscriminately into the crowd. What had driven him to do that?

Harry Dymes was cool and methodical when it came to aiming and firing his weapon. No wonder he'd been chosen to be a sniper in the army.

The one thing that she remembered from her time spent on the FBI Academy pistol range in Quantico, Virginia, was the range master's stern pronouncement that "once you fire a bullet, you can't bring it back. Always be aware of the background before you pull the trigger."

Marta admitted that she had frozen for a second or two before firing at Boris Feliks. There were too many people behind Feliks. It wasn't until Feliks's gun was pointing in her direction that she'd pulled the trigger. And missed. Was it time for a career change?

McNab had flat-out accused her of misconduct for not reporting the possibility of Boris Feliks being in the park. "Conspiring with local police officials" was the term he'd used. When Marta admitted that she and Harry Dymes had been in contact, and that Dymes had her Bureau cell phone number, her phone was taken away and she was issued a new one, along with more explicit orders: The number was not to be given to anyone other than Bureau personnel.

Until the investigation was completed, she was in FBI limbo. The Glock she'd used in the park was sent to the FBI lab in Washington and replaced by an identical model, which was now in her purse. She was admonished by Tom McNab, with Deputy Director Bartlow's backing, not to speak to *any* member of the San Francisco Police Department unless there was an FBI legal affairs officer with her.

A tooting horn brought her out of her reverie. Tarasove's Hummer bumped its way up the hill and skidded to a stop. Its engine died with a jerk and a loud sigh.

Tarasove popped out of the driver's side door holding a large brown bag.

"Marta. So good to see you. I bought something special for dinner. T-bone steaks and fresh bread. Or would you rather go out for dinner?"

"What happened to your beard? Your hair?"

Tarasove propped the grocery bag on the Hummer's hood and ran a hand over his smooth chin. "I think it makes me look younger. But if you don't like it, I'll let it grow back."

He juggled the bag while entering the alarm code near the front door. The lock clicked and Tarasove nudged the door open with his hip.

Marta could hear Jedgar barking close by. "I'm afraid I have some bad news. There's another man after you. Hired by Ying Fai."

The grocery bag slipped out of Tarasove's hands, falling with a thud to the floor. "Another man? Who? Where is he?"

"Where, we don't know. He uses the name Alex."

"Shliakh trafyt," Tarasove cried out angrily.

Marta knew the words well—a Russian phrase wishing the worst possible fate on an enemy. What she didn't know was if Nicolai was cursing Alex, herself, or the entire FBI.

"Calm down," she said, but Tarasove was having none of it. He kicked the bag of groceries, then took out his anger on the wall, pounding his fists helplessly into the wood paneling. Jedgar was in a barking frenzy, banging his head into the kitchen door.

"How long have you known of this person Alex?" Tarasove said when his breathing had returned to normal.

"A few days. It was decided not to tell you. Not to cause unnecessary concern."

"Unnecessary?" Tarasove scowled. "I thought I'd ended all of this. You, Roger, and the others, all told me that Ying Fai had hired Feliks. Now you reveal he's hired someone else."

"Tell that dog to stop barking. I can't hear myself think."

"Jedgar! Silence!"

The dog's barking wound down like a switched-off siren. Marta took a deep breath. "There's nothing to worry about, Nicolai. We are certain that Alex is unaware of your location. I'll be here with you, until we've found him."

Tarasove dry-washed his face with his palms. "I apologize. I know you're doing your best." He stooped over and picked up the grocery bag. "We will still have that celebration dinner. I've been saving a special bottle of wine for you."

"There's no need to apologize. We're both a little on edge. I was there in the park when Boris Feliks was shot to death."

"You were there?"

"Yes. With Harry Dymes, the San Francisco policeman who killed Feliks. Feliks was meeting someone in the park. We don't know who. It may have been this Alex."

Tarasove's naturally ruddy face turned pale. "I saw the policeman on television. But not you."

"We'll find Alex, Nicolai," Marta said.

"Before he finds me?"

"Yes. You're safe here." Marta shifted the purse on her shoulder. "You haven't been bothered by anyone lately, have you? Any surprise visitors? Strange telephone calls?"

"No. There was nothing like that." Tarasove opened the kitchen door slowly, and Jedgar trotted directly over to Marta.

"Heel," Tarasove shouted. "*Ploho, ploho.* Bad dog."

"Lock him up somewhere," Marta said wearily. "Then make some coffee, please. Better yet, pour us both a stiff vodka."

Chapter Thirty-Three

"Thanks, Sergeant," Harry Dymes said. "I appreciate the cooperation." He dropped the phone on its cradle and glanced over at Bob Dills, who had half of a donut clamped between his teeth and the telephone tucked between his shoulder and neck.

Harry had made a rough map of Lake Tahoe, and he and Dills contacted the departments on the South Shore, California side, circling their way around the lake. He scratched off another law enforcement office from the list.

All the responses had been negative. Harry was down to Douglas County, Nevada, which covered the lower eastern border of the lake.

"Douglas County Sheriff's Office, how may I direct your call?" said a crisp, friendly voice.

"Inspector Harry Dymes, San Francisco. I'm trying to locate a witness in a homicide case, who we believe to be living in your area."

"I'll connect you to our investigation division."

The next voice Harry heard wasn't crisp or friendly; it was gravelly, bored, guarded, and had the raspy twang of a hangover. "Sergeant Rennick, who's this?"

Harry went into his spiel: "Harry Dymes, Homicide,

SFPD. I can give you a number to call if you want to verify that."

"Tell me what it's about, Dymes, then we'll see if it's worth a call."

"I'm looking for a witness, who we're told is living in the Tahoe area, in a large chalet with a view of the lake. He's a WMA, in his fifties. Short, fat, white beard, looks like Santa Claus. He's Russian, and speaks with an accent."

There was a long pause; then Rennick said, "That's it?"

"That's it," Harry admitted, "except for the snakes. He's a scientist, and uses them in his experiments."

"Give me that number," Rennick said.

Harry helped himself to a cup of the vice details's coffee and one of Dills's donuts while he waited for Rennick.

"You're for real," Rennick said when they were connected. "Funny thing, I was about to tell you to take a flying leap when you gave me that Santa Claus line, but then you mentioned the snakes. We had a man die under suspicious circumstances a couple of days ago in a trailer park near the state line. Big-time gambler by the name of Homer Rutlidge, liked to call himself Sundown. Died of a heart attack in his recreation vehicle. The coroner thinks that the attack was induced by a rattlesnake bite. We found the snake in the RV. A Western diamondback, over four feet long, thick as a baseball bat. What makes it suspicious is that Westerns are native to Nevada, but are usually found much farther south, down by McLaughlin. It's a mystery how the snake was able to access his trailer."

"Maybe it came through the front door when the guy was out dumping the garbage," Harry suggested.

"That's a possibility," Rennick conceded, "but not likely."

"Did Sundown happen to look like Santa Claus?"

"Nope. Skinny drink of water, with a wrinkled-up puss. The night before he died, he stripped a guy of fifty Gs or more in a high-stakes poker game, according to the casino manager. I sent Deputy Delgetti over to talk to the loser—man by the name of Nick Sennet. According to Delgetti, Sennett looked just like Santa Claus. And he spoke with an accent. Claimed he was German."

Harry began scribbling notes. "What's Sennet's address?"

"A postal box in Sugar Cove. His house is off Highway

Fifty, a mile or so past the Sugar Cove Coffee Shop. West side of the road, then it's a quarter of a mile or so up a steep hill."

"Did you see the house, Sergeant?"

"No. Delgetti described it as a big place, with a wrap-around sundeck."

"Think it could be called a chalet?" Harry asked.

"Call it anything you want. All I know is that Delgetti said it was big. And he mentioned that Sennet has a huge pit bull. He's off duty tonight, be back tomorrow."

"What about his home phone number?"

"It wouldn't help you. He told me he was driving over to Reno with his wife for the night. Any of this do you any good?"

"Yes. It sure does. I hope I can return the favor sometime."

"How 'bout next month? My wife wants me to take her down to your town to see a play called *Beach Blanket Babylon*. You have any juice for free tickets?"

"Let me know the day, and I'll have the tickets waiting for you at the box office."

"Delgetti is one of those guys who does everything by the book. His report has a hand-drawn map of just where this place is. I can't send you the full report, but if you have a fax number, I'll send you the map."

Harry gave Dills a thumbs-up, and asked for the vice squad's fax number. He relayed it to Rennick.

"Tell you what," Rennick said. "I know the area well, so if you want some backup, just give me a call. I can drive you right to the place."

"I may take you up on that." Harry broke the connection and dialed Don Landeta. "I've got a name for you, Don. Nick Sennet, Douglas County. His house is near a place called Sugar Cove. Get me anything you can, as quick as you can, and buzz me on my cell phone. I'm heading up there now."

"Heading where?" Bob Dills asked, handing Harry the faxed map from Sergeant Rennick.

"Sugar Cove, Lake Tahoe. I found the bastard." He gave Dills a brief rundown of his conversation with the Douglas County sheriff. "I'm officially off duty, Bob. So this is be-tween you and me. You know Chinatown and Fai's operations better than I do, but my take is that Danny Shu ran Ying Fai's Chinatown operations."

"Fai does the running. Shu was just muscle. *Big* muscle. Drugs, gambling, prostitution, extortion. Fai's the *man*, Harry. Be careful if you're messing with him."

Harry tried to fit Shu and Ying Fai into the Golden Gate Park shooting while the Hall of Justice elevator lumbered down to the garage.

Marta Citron had told him that the Chinese Triad leader was in the hunt for Tarasove. Was Shu the man who shot Feliks seconds before he did? Harry remembered that Shu was a huge man. He would be hard to miss. One of Shu's underlings? He massaged his forehead and tried to remember the scene: Feliks wheeling around, gun in hand, his face contorted in pain. Why? Had he already taken a bullet before Harry opened fire?

Marta at his side, the crowd scurrying every which way, bumping into each other. Where had the silenced shots come from?

The Honda wasn't in its usual spot. He went to the garage office and queried the civilian attendant. "Where's my car, Freddy?"

The man did a shrug-and-pout and flex-his-hands-from-the-wrist French gesture. "Sorry, Inspector. They told me you were off duty, and to consign the car to Lieutenant Kelterer in Burglary."

An unmarked car was one of the biggest perks in the job, because it was virtually immune to parking tags—even if a meter maid slapped a ticket on the windshield, it was ignored by the parking commissioner. Harry wasn't at all happy about losing the vehicle, even temporarily, but at least there was some irony in that Kelterer was a six-foot-five former basketball star at UC Berkeley. He'd need a shoehorn to get his frame into the Honda.

A black-and-white patrol car cruised genteelly toward the exit ramp. Harry recognized the driver. "Hey, Jerry. Got time to give me a ride home?"

Trina Lee was beginning to think that the Russians were stalling, asking her to guard Tarasove. She'd found the man, and now she wanted payment, before he bolted. His shaved face, his meeting with Feliks in San Francisco. Then this morning's curious drive to a South Shore casino parking lot, where he used his cell phone to make a call—to who? Why did he leave the house to make the call? She hadn't detected any signs of life at the house, other than Tarasove and his dog.

On the ride back from the parking lot, Tarasove stopped at a supermarket. She'd driven ahead, hid the Jag in some bushes, and hiked up the road to his house. She'd decided to kill the huge dog that she feared had caught her scent, confront Tarasove when he arrived, and hold him for General Kilmov.

Those plans were discarded when she discovered the car parked outside Tarasove's place, and the attractive blond woman pacing around the premises—the same woman who'd been at the park, shooting at Feliks.

Trina pegged the blonde as Marta Citron, FBI, and was proved right when Tarasove drove back and called her Marta. Marta Citron. FBI. Were they planning to pull Tarasove out?

She couldn't let that happen, even if it meant eliminating Citron. She crept up to Tarasove's Hummer and filled its tailpipe with rocks, leaves and dirt, using a small tree branch to push the dirty mixture as far into the pipe as possible, then performed the same task on Citron's sedan, effectively disabling both vehicles. While she worked, she kept a sharp eye on the house and deck, wondering about the pit bull, Jedgar. She heard Tarasove shout out the dog's name several times. Where was the mangy beast? Did he lock it away when he had female company?

She hurried down the hill to the Jaguar and activated her laptop. A message from the Russians: *We are ready. The payment has been deposited in your bank account. Now, a cash bonus. Where in Tahoe?*

Trina quickly went to the bank's Web site, opened her account and found that the third million dollars had indeed been deposited. She went back to the e-mail site and responded: *Sugar Cove. The coffee shop near the boat dock.*

The response came immediately: *Excellent. Your contact is Edik. He will wear a gray suit, red tie. Ask him for the time. Your response—"it's too late." Take him to T—million bonus $ is yours. He will be there at six o'clock. GK.*

Dinosaurs, Trina thought. Still playing Cold War code games: *It's too late.* GK. General Kilmov himself?

She checked the clock in the Jag's burlwood dashboard. Thirty minutes. That meant Edik was already here, at the lake. She didn't have much time. How many Russians would be there in addition to Edik? Was it worth exposing herself to them? She switched on the engine and asked herself a final question: Did she have any other options now? If she was forced to abandon the Russians, she'd find a way to peddle Tarasove to Ying Fai, using a new identity.

"Shall we eat out here on the deck? It's still so nice and warm."

"That's fine with me, Nicolai," Marta Citron said, with little enthusiasm. The man just didn't look right without his beard. There was more to it than just trying to look younger. "Where's Jedgar?"

"Locked up in the back. I know he annoys you, but he means no harm."

Tarasove handed her a brimming glass of red wine. "It's a nineteen-ninety-nine Mondavi-Rothschild Opus One. I'm told it was an excellent vintage." He took a long, slurping sip, then smacked his lips. "Delicious."

Marta held the glass under her nose and inhaled deeply, detecting aromas of cassis and cloves. She took a sip and rolled the wine around her mouth, enjoying the rich fruit flavors. There was a slight bitterness that surprised her. If she had ordered it in a restaurant, she would have sent it back.

"I'm so delighted that you're here, Marta." He quickly topped off her glass. "This is my favorite time of the year. On warm nights like this, I sometimes sleep here on the deck. The night air is like perfume."

Marta had another taste of the wine. Combined with the vodka Nicolai had poured earlier, the alcohol was already starting to affect her.

"Have you ever thought of leaving the FBI?" Tarasove asked, opening the lid of the grill and igniting the coals.

Marta was caught off guard, because she had been pondering that very question. Was she giving off some kind of body language? "I'll have to retire one of these days. Until then I've—"

The cell phone on her hip vibrated. "Excuse me," she said, slipping the phone free.

"It's Roger, where are you?"

"Where I'm supposed to be," Marta responded quickly. She smiled at Tarasove and covered the receiver with her hand. "Dancel." She picked up her purse. "I'll take the call in the kitchen."

"How is the old guy holding up?" Dancel wanted to know.

"Fine. He was a little upset when I told him about Alex, but right now he's pouring expensive wine and cooking steaks."

"Wine and steak. He must know your weaknesses. Keep a close eye on Nicolai, because we're moving him out of there."

Marta leaned against the kitchen cooking island. "When?"

"As soon as I get there. I'm still in Washington. The Director just passed the word. He's finally taking my advice. We'll take Nicolai to Quantico, until we can find a permanent location with lab facilities."

Marta settled the wineglass on the chopping block. "Why the rush?"

"What rush? I've been trying to get this done for months."

"Nicolai's not going to like it."

"But I will. See you soon. Don't drink too much wine."

Marta felt a sudden wave of dizziness. She carried her glass over to the sink and dumped the wine. Tarasove's cell phone was sitting in a charger near the chopping block. She thought of calling Harry Dymes. She hadn't seen or talked to him since the shooting in the park. She couldn't use her cell phone, or Tarasove's landline—both were monitored by her colleagues.

But Nicolai's elaborate cell phone wasn't. Who had he been talking to? She picked it up, her thumb massaging the ON button, and the machine hummed to life. She fiddled with the controls until she found the listing for *Last Dialed*. A 415 area code. San Francisco. She initiated the call.

The person on the other end picked it up after one ring. *"Privet."*

Hello, in Russian. *"Dorbry vehcer,"* Marta responded. Good evening.

"Kto dela?" Who are you?

"Ty govorish po angilyski?"

"Yes. I speak English. Who is this? How did you get this number?"

"From a friend."

There was a long pause, then the man demanded, "Put your friend on the phone. Right now."

Marta quickly broke the connection. She went back to the phone's *Last Dialed* feature and ran through the numbers. Three calls to the same number she'd just been connected to. The next call on the list was also to the 415 area code. The numbers looked blurry. She hit CONNECT.

A woman's voice answered: "Consulate General of the Russian Federation. How may I help you?"

The phone slid from Marta's hand and crashed onto the blue tile floor. She had to put both hands on the chopping block to keep from falling herself.

Nicolai Tarasove strode over and shook her shoulder. "Who did you talk to?"

"Roger Dancel," Marta slurred.

"On my phone?" He stooped down and picked up the phone. He could hear a woman's voice saying, "Who did you want to speak to? *Privet.*"

"Who is this?" Tarasove asked.

"The Russian Consulate. I have—"

Tarasove snapped the phone off and held it under Marta's chin. "What did you tell the consulate?"

"Nothing. Why, Nicolai? You're going back, aren't you? You're—"

Tarasove slapped her across the face. "Why? They've offered me more money. And I won't have people like Roger Dancel looking over my shoulder all the time. What did Dancel want? Where is he?"

"Wassshintoooon," she heard herself mumble. "He's coooming . . ."

"Having trouble talking? You should have been nicer to me, Marta. Much nicer." Tarasove picked up her empty glass and waved it at her. "Don't fret. My Devil's Brew wasn't in the wine. Just a little something to help you sleep for eight or ten hours. You'll live, Marta, but I'm afraid this will be our last meeting."

The dog moved in, nuzzling her hip. Tarasove plucked several strands of her hair and waved them in front of her eyes. "I have your DNA as well as Roger's. Programmed into a Devil's Brew. I can come for either of you anytime. There's no place to hide if I decide to kill either of you. Nowhere."

His fingers roamed down her blouse, ripping at the buttons.

She tried to do something to stop him, but her arms wouldn't respond.

Chapter Thirty-Four

"Thanks, Don," Harry Dymes said, breaking the connection to Don Landeta and tossing the cell phone onto the empty passenger seat of his "weekend warrior," a six-year-old Lincoln Mark VII coupe that had been part of the divorce settlement, Eva having no use for a vehicle in New York City. There were less than twenty-four thousand miles on the odometer, and it was parked in his garage, most of the time. The Lincoln was spacious, powerful, and comfortable, and attracted parking tickets in the city the way picnic baskets attract ants.

Landeta's background check on Nick Sennet hadn't turned up anything significant: a postal address in Sugar Cove, a bank account in Carson City, and numerous everyday credit card transactions.

The Lincoln crawled its way up through soaring granite mountains, pine forests and small villages bordering shuttered ski slopes and rusted highway signs proclaiming *Brake Chain Area.*

Traffic came to a complete halt when he reached the summit, with its breathtaking view of Lake Tahoe. In daylight the lake was a deep cobalt blue. The approaching sunset had turned it into a sheet of polished brass, outlined by the snow-tipped peaks of the Sierra Nevada mountains.

He wondered what kind of reception Marta Citron would give him when he knocked on Tarasove's front door. She knew nothing of the unknown shooter in Golden Gate Park, or the possibility of Feliks having been poisoned. Or of Danny Shu's supposed homicide. Men like Shu don't end up accidentally burning to death in bed. Chapaev, Zivon Yudin, Lana Kuzmin, Feliks, Shu, an unidentified young woman—all killed in his town, and all with links to Nicolai Tarasove.

Harry was going to have a long talk with Tarasove, whether the FBI or Captain Sanborn liked it or not.

San Francisco, California

Arman Ritokov cleared his throat, then said, "General. I've heard from Colonel Savelev. He has arrived at the destination, Sugar Cove, but has not made contact with Alex."

General Kilmov strolled over to the window with a view of the famed Golden Gate Bridge, and studied Arman Ritokov's reflection in the glass. The man was standing against the wall, looking as if he were trying to be invisible.

"Excellent, Arman. Tell me, do you enjoy your duty here in San Francisco?"

"I have no complaints, General."

A good answer, Kilmov judged. No commitment, not a yes, and not a no. Ritokov was nothing special to look at: bland, squarish face, thinning hair, stocky build. And he was not tall—five foot three or four. He'd give him another simple test.

"If you had your choice of assignment, anywhere in the world, which would you choose, Arman?"

"I would be happy to go anywhere I would be of most use to my country, General."

Ah, an even better answer. The man was a kiss-ass, but a clever one. Kilmov turned back to the window, folded his arms across his chest and rose up and down on his toes, a lesson his wife had taught him as a way to strengthen his legs. A vacation, he decided. When he returned home, he and Ivana would go skiing in Switzerland. Serre Chevalier had wonderful snow in the summertime. But first, a stop in Geneva—to visit his bank.

He rapped his finger against the window. "The bridge, Arman. Did you notice? It's not gold, it's orange. Another American lie. If tonight's exercise ends satisfactorily, I might ask you to join me in Moscow."

"I would be honored to serve you, sir," Ritokov said.

And well you should, Kilmov thought. Victory has many fathers, but defeat is an orphan, as the saying went. And if for some reason the Tarasove affair was bungled, Arman would end up serving his country under the frozen ground of Siberia.

Nicolai Tarasove was moving frantically behind the locked steel doors in his laboratory, packing files and removing computer hard drives. He was adamant about not leaving a single piece of information for the Americans. Marta Citron had been the final betrayal. His only regret was that he had not been able to take advantage of her unconscious state. He'd dragged her to a bedroom and started to undress her, but common sense intervened—there was no time to waste, and there would be many beautiful women, more beautiful than Citron, waiting for him in Finland.

In his haste, he bumped into a cage of laboratory mice. The cage clattered to the ground and the mice darted away in all directions.

"Freedom, you think," Tarasove said aloud. "Soon I'll release the snakes, and then we'll see how much you enjoy your freedom."

Marta Citron woke with a taste of cotton in her mouth. She rubbed her face vigorously, and stared at the cedar-paneled ceiling. Her hands groped around, feeling the pillow, the bedcovers. Tarasove! Where was *he*? She sat up abruptly, only to fall back at the onset of a murderous headache.

Marta gritted her teeth and waited for the pain to subside, then began exploring. Her blouse was torn, but her skirt and panty hose were intact. Her purse—she wanted her gun and cell phone. Was it still in the kitchen?

She elbowed herself to a sitting position. She was alone, in the room Nicolai had prepared for her. How long had she been unconscious? She remembered being in the kitchen, Tarasove saying she'd be asleep for eight or ten hours. He'd drugged the wine. Nicolai thought that she'd consumed the entire glass, but she'd only had a few sips before tossing the rest down the drain.

Come on, you're tough, an FBI agent. You've survived worse things than this. Now do something really tough. Sit up.

She slowly pushed herself to a sitting position, then lowered her feet to the floor and took several deep breaths, while grinding her fingernails into the back of one hand, willing the pain to wash away the effect of the drug.

Okay, tough girl. So far so good. Tarasove could be back at any moment, and there was no way she could fight him off in this condition. To your feet! She wobbled for a moment, arms out like a tightrope walker, then took a tentative first step. Then another, over to the door, turning the knob a millimeter at a time. The latch slipped out of the strike box. It was unlocked. Tarasove must have taken off! She pulled the door open wide, only to find the menacing face of Jedgar.

The dog leaped forward as she attempted to slam the door on him. He kept coming, growling, his teeth bared, drool foaming at his mouth.

Marta backtracked toward the bed, searching frantically for a weapon.

Jedgar countered her every move. He was herding her back to the bed! Marta's calves bumped into the mattress. She clutched at a pillow and threw it at the dog, then yanked the bedcover free and used it as a bullfighter's cape as she raced for the bathroom door.

She barely made it into the bathroom, Jedgar howling now, ramming his head into the door.

Marta clicked the door's lock, then sank down onto the toilet seat, wrapping her arms around herself to try to stop shaking.

Chapter Thirty-Five

Trina Lee kept her eyes focused on the cars entering the coffee shop's parking lot. She'd been staking the area out for over an hour, awaiting the arrival of Edik. Gray suit, red tie. Except for the casino pit bosses, he'd be the only man within fifty miles wearing a tie.

The day bugs she'd dropped around the perimeter of Tarasove's house were transmitting choruses of mating crickets, and symphony music from Tarasove's stereo.

God, she was tired. She'd been living on caffeine and uppers for the past two days.

There was a loud roar coming from the lake. She turned to see a small seaplane coasting up to the dock.

A man climbed out of the cockpit, leaped onto the pier and fastened a rope to the plane's wing structure, and another to the tail section. He was bareheaded, wearing a gray suit and red tie. He pulled on the ropes, leaned into the cockpit, and came out with a briefcase.

"Son of a bitch," Trina said to herself. A seaplane. She had to admit that was clever.

The man's shoes rattled off the gangway planks. He had the stiff, shoulders-straight stride of a military man. He paused to get his bearing, his eyes searching the parking lot. He glanced at his wristwatch, then made his way up the steps and into the coffee shop.

Trina edged deeper into the trees, and waited several minutes before joining him. No one had driven into the lot, and no new arrivals on the dock. The man was seated at the end of the counter, which gave him a good view of the shop's entrance. Trina slipped onto a stool two down from his, and ordered coffee and apple pie à la mode.

"The pie's really good here," she said, giving the man a warm smile. He wasn't bad-looking, but in his suit, tie, and buzz haircut, he was as inconspicuous as dog crap on snow.

He flicked his eyes at her briefly, then turned his attention back to the entrance.

"Do you have the time?" she asked, after the waitress delivered her order.

When there was no response, Trina said, "Do you have the fucking time, Edik?"

Savelev's head snapped back as if he'd been slapped. "You work for Alex?"

"No, no," she chided. "You're supposed to tell me the time, and then I say, 'It's too late.' Weren't those your instructions?"

"You *are* Alex."

"Are, work for him, what's the difference? Do you have the money? My bonus."

Savelev pressed both of his hands on the briefcase. "In here. Take me to the scientist, and it's yours."

"We have a saying in America. 'Show me the money.'"

Savelev hunched forward, undid the briefcase's latches, and raised the lid. "Satisfied?"

"Not completely. Are you alone?"

"Yes, I am," Savelev said, closing the case and securing the latches.

Trina took a spoonful of the pie and chewed it slowly. "Well, I'm not. So don't try anything foolish."

"You have my word. But if you are thinking of a trick, if you are working with Ying Fai, there will be no place on earth for you to hide."

Trina stabbed her spoon into the center of the pie. Ying Fai. How much did the Russians know about her arrangement with Fai? "Come on. He's just a few minutes from here."

*   *   *

Harry Dymes flicked on the Lincoln's high beams as he negotiated the bumpy dirt road leading up to Tarasove's chalet. He knew he was on the right road—but there was no notation of the log speed bumps on the sheriff deputy's map. He skirted around a huge boulder and drove cautiously for another few hundred yards before being rewarded with a view of the prow-shaped chalet. There were two vehicles parked close together: a black Hummer and a beige Chevrolet sedan—a typical Bucar.

Harry made a tight U-turn so that the Lincoln was pointed downhill, then beeped the horn and exited the car, slamming the door with more force than was necessary.

Lights on, loud music: a heavy-fingered pianist playing Bach—and Bach was losing.

"Hello. Anybody home?"

No response. Not even a bark from the pit bull the sheriff had mentioned. Harry checked the front door. There was no bell, just a combination touch pad.

He skirted around the side of the house and found the steps leading to the sundeck. He now wished he hadn't followed Captain Sanborn's orders—he was not carrying a gun. He edged up the stairs slowly. "Marta? It's Harry Dymes."

There was the heavy smell of barbecue coals. A wine bottle, a vodka bottle, a plate of potato chips on a picnic table. The side entrance to the chalet was wide open.

Harry stuck his head past the doors. "Marta! Anyone home?"

Marta Citron's eyes were fixated on the hollow-pine bathroom door. The spring lock was designed to keep family and lovers from walking in unannounced, not to stop a ninety-pound pit bull.

Jedgar had been banging his head furiously against the door for what seemed like a very long time. It wouldn't hold much longer. She searched the medicine cabinet for a weapon: a razor, scissors, anything. All she found were bars of soap.

There was no window—just a fan, a shower, a nylon curtain depicting bright red poinsettias.

Jedgar rammed the door again. She could hear wood cracking.

There had to be something! She couldn't fight the beast bare-handed. She yanked the shower curtain open, its rings making a rasping sound on the aluminum curtain rod.

Marta pounded one end of the four-foot rod with her palm and it came away from the wall. She threaded the rod free of the curtain, examined the rounded ends, then placed one end of the rod under the toilet seat and slammed down hard. Once. Twice. A final time. The metal gave way and flattened out to a thin, jagged edge. She had a weapon!

At the FBI Academy, she'd been taught to get down to an attacking dog's level—don't allow him to jump and knock you down. A dog's weak points are his legs and eyes. When attacked, distract and break his leg, try to blind him.

The instructor, padded with so much protective gear that he looked like the Michelin Man, had demonstrated the technique on a German shepherd. *His* German shepherd, who knew the drill as well as his master.

Marta wrapped her arms and neck with towels, then got down on her knees. One quick prayer, then she leaned forward and unlocked the door.

Jedgar didn't leap as she'd expected. He was in full attack mode: head lowered, teeth bared, back slightly curved. He edged his way into the room, his paws clicking when they hit the tile.

Marta crawled back a few inches and made a whimpering sound. Jedgar took that as a sign of weakness and lunged for her. She jabbed the rod into his chest as he leaped forward. The force of the impact caused the rod to slip from Marta's fingers.

Jedgar kept coming, driving the opposite tip of the rod into the bathroom wall, impaling himself as he did so. He was rolling madly back and forth. Blood bubbles foamed from his mouth.

Marta scrambled out of his way, then climbed on his back, riding him like a horse, her fingers digging into his eyes.

Jedgar's legs went out from under him, and Marta slipped back, grabbed his hind quarters and pushed as hard as she could, shoving the animal toward the wall, and into the curtain rod.

Finally Jedgar's body gave one last shudder and was still.

Marta crawled back into the bedroom, using the bed to lever herself to her feet. She stared at her image in the bureau mirror. She looked like hell: hair disheveled, blouse torn, hands and arms smeared with Jedgar's blood. But she was alive. And planned to stay that way. She had to find her gun—and Nicolai Tarasove.

She was wiping her hands and arms on the bedcover when she heard someone calling her name. Harry! "Help!" she yelled. "Back here, Harry!"

"Why are we parking here?" Edik Savelev demanded to know. "Why don't we drive up to the house?"

"Because there's an FBI agent protecting Tarasove," Trina said. It was a crystal clear night, dominated by a harvest moon that threw shadows under the trees.

"FBI? You should have told us that."

"Shoulda, woulda, coulda. It's one agent. A woman. I don't think you'll have any difficulty with her." Trina snapped off the flashlight and said, "Oh, shit. There's another car, that wasn't here an hour ago."

A pistol suddenly appeared in Savelev's fist. "This is not what I expected."

"The FBI must have sent more agents." She'd turned off the bug monitor in the Jaguar when she went to the coffee shop to pick up the Russian. The vehicle was a Lincoln. Not a typical Bucar. Who the hell was it?

The cold barrel of Savelev's gun pressed against Trina's ear.

"Relax," she said. "The FBI monitors Tarasove on a regular basis. They visit, he bullshits them about his experiments, they leave. All we have to do is wait."

Savelev bit down on his lip. "What if they're here to relocate him? Take him away?"

Trina wormed her hand into her purse's holster compartment. "Wherever they take him, I'll find him, so put the gun away, Edik. We're working together on this."

The gun barrel retreated a fraction of an inch. "I warn you, if you're lying, if you're working with Ying Fai, I'll kill you."

Trina's fingers curled around the trigger of the silenced semiautomatic. The Russian's briefcase, with her money, was in her car. She'd done her job. It was time to leave. "Look," she whispered. "On the deck. It's Tarasove."

When Savelev twisted around, she nudged the purse against his back and pulled the trigger three times.

The Russian dropped his gun and sank to his knees, a look of disbelief on his face. She positioned the purse against his forehead. "I lied," she said, before pulling the trigger again.

Nicolai Tarasove had a suitcase loaded with documents, computer hard drives, DNA files, and a half-dozen canisters containing his Devil's Brew. He took a final look at the laboratory to see if he had forgotten something. And he had. His babies.

Tarasove always wore heavy boots when working in the lab, on the small chance that a snake would escape from the tanks. He slipped on his heavy rubber gloves, slid open the tops of the glass reptile tanks, then, using the wooden end of a broom, upended the tanks, sending them crashing to the cement floor.

Some of the frightened snakes quickly squirmed away, looking for a dark hiding place. Others broadened their jaws and hissed, while still others coiled up, frantically shaking their rattles.

He nimbly backed toward the steel doors, picked up his suitcase, then pushed the release button. The doors slid into the wall and a train of terrified lab mice scurried over Tarasove's boots.

He wondered why Jedgar wasn't at his usual post outside the lab door. Then he remembered Marta. Unconscious. Was Jedgar with her? He had time to—

Then someone shouted, "Help! Back here, Harry!"

Chapter Thirty-Six

"What happened?" Harry said when he found Marta leaning against a hallway wall, a blood-soaked towel clutched in her hands. "Are you all right?"

"No time," she said breathlessly. "Tarasove. We have to catch him. He—"

A voice bellowed, "Jedgar!"

"It's him," Marta said, and Harry couldn't tell if she was relieved or frightened. "He drugged me, left me in the bedroom, his dog—"

"Jedgar!"

"That's Tarasove. Where's your gun? Mine's in my purse. It was in the kitchen but I—"

Harry held his arms away from his sides, feeling foolish. "No gun. Who's Jedgar?"

"Nicolai's dog." Marta grabbed Harry's hand. "I killed him. We've got to stop Nicolai. He's gone mad."

Harry wrapped her in his arms. "Take it easy." He pointed to an open bedroom door. "Is there a phone in there?"

"No. In the kitchen."

"Show me."

Something scurried by their feet and Marta let out a scream. Harry jumped back as a small mouse darted past them.

"Calm down. Where is Tarasove? Is there anyone else in the house?"

Marta sucked in a lungful of air. "I'm still a little groggy. I'm not sure where he is." She took a step and started to sag to the floor. "We were here alone."

Harry ducked down, lifted her over his shoulder in a fireman's carry, and started down the hall. "Where's the kitchen?"

He came to an abrupt halt when a snake slithered into sight. A rattler, with its tail up in the air. Snakes. God, he hated snakes!

Tarasove could hear Marta talking to someone. It must be a fellow FBI agent. How had she regained consciousness so quickly? Where was Jedgar? Questions he had no time to seek answers for now. He ran toward his gun room. A small rattler leaped out from behind a door, sinking its fangs into his boot. He shook the snake off, then started running again, looking over his shoulder every few seconds. One FBI agent? More? He shoved open the door to the gun room, and grabbed his favorite weapon—a Weatherby big-game rifle that fired .300 Magnum cartridges, which, like the rest of his arsenal, was kept fully loaded at all times.

Harry Dymes hugged the wall as he crept around the snake. Marta directed him to the kitchen from her shoulder perch. He set her on the table. Her forehead was clammy with sweat, her breathing rapid. He placed a hand on her wrist. Her pulse rate was off the charts.

"There, there!" Marta said, pointing to her purse. "Get the gun!"

Harry draped his coat over her, then grabbed her purse, fumbling through the contents, finding the Glock pistol. "Tell me what's going on."

"Tarasove's going back to Russia, Harry. With his goddamn toxin. We've got to stop him."

Harry scanned the area. Windows over the sink—at least a fifteen-foot drop to the ground. He could handle it, but not Marta. "Is there another way out of the kitchen?"

"No. His gun room is down the hall, to the right. He's a hunter. He has an arsenal."

Harry pushed the table over close to the wall with a phone. He handed Marta the receiver. "Call nine-one-one, get the sheriff and an ambulance."

"Be careful," Marta warned. "Don't let him get away, Harry."

There were three more snakes in the hallway. Thankfully, they seemed to be as frightened of Harry as he was of them, because they slithered away in the opposite direction. How many of the goddamn things were there? He spotted Tarasove, holding a rifle, creeping toward the deck.

"Hold it," Harry shouted.

Tarasove wheeled around and fired. The blast was deafening. Harry dropped to the floor, then, remembering the snakes, scrambled to his feet and fired four rounds in the direction of the rifle shot. He opened a hall door and edged inside. Coats, jackets, rubber boots. A closet. Trapped!

"FBI," Tarasove said, "if you try to stop me, I will kill you. And Marta."

Harry leaned out the door. The hallway light switch was within arm range. He checked the floor for snakes, then flicked off the switch.

"Drop the rifle, Tarasove. You can't get away."

"Oh, but I can, FBI," Tarasove assured him. "I can kill all of you. And everyone within fifty miles of here."

"You're full of shit," Harry said.

The kitchen door opened, sending a slice of light into the hall.

Marta Citron poked her head out. "Nicolai! Stop this. You and I can work it out."

"One minute, Marta," Tarasove shouted. "I give you one minute, then I expose you to the Devil's Brew. You will all die, and I will walk away, over your dead bodies."

Harry ran to Marta, pushing her back into the kitchen.

"He's not kidding, Harry," she said, her teeth chattering. "What he says is true."

"How? He's got a rifle, and—"

"And his toxin. It's like a poison gas, Harry. He'll use it. He's crazy."

"Thirty seconds left, Marta," Tarasove shouted. "It's your choice."

"All right, Nicolai. Go, damn you. Go."

"Send your fellow agent out, Marta. I want to see him give the order."

"Jesus Christ," Harry mumbled. "How does the poison gas work? How does he activate it?"

Marta spread her hands and gestured impatiently. "He could put it in a water supply, disperse it into the air. Enclosed in the house here, we're defenseless."

"What about outdoors? If we get him outside?"

"I don't know for sure," Marta admitted.

Harry scratched the back of his neck with the pistol barrel. "You called nine-one-one?"

"Yes."

"Tell this nut we're going along with him," Harry said, shoving the Glock down the front of his pants.

"You win, Nicolai! You win," Marta shouted.

Harry looked longingly at the kitchen window. They *could* survive a fifteen-foot drop. A broken bone or two maybe, but they'd survive.

"Time's up," Tarasove yelled.

Harry looked at Marta's tear-filmed eyes. "Here goes," he said, before kneeing the kitchen door open.

As soon as Harry's foot touched down on the hallway floor, Tarasove yelled, "Turn the lights back on, FBI." Tarasove's voice had taken on a shrill edge.

Harry groped his hand along the wall, found the switch and clicked the light on.

"Where's your gun, FBI?"

"Marta has it. And she's keeping it."

"Turn around!"

Harry made a slow pirouette. "I'm unarmed." He could hear movement. The scraping of a chair? Then Tarasove said, "How many agents are with you?"

"More than we need. Drop the rifle, Tarasove. You're not getting out of here. You're surrounded. Listen to Marta. She can help you, you—"

"Tell your men to leave. All of them. And not to follow me. If they disobey your orders, if anyone follows me, I'll put a canister of toxin in the lake. Dancel knows what that would do. So does Marta."

Harry cupped his hands around his mouth. "All agents. All agents. Tarasove is coming out. He is not to be stopped.

Not to be followed. Under any circumstances. Repeat. Do not stop or follow the subject."

"Give Marta a good-bye kiss for me, FBI."

"Eb trvoju mat'," Harry said.

"Fuck you, too," Tarasove responded quickly.

Harry was expecting a bullet in the chest. He stood there, muscles tensed, a waiting target, holding a useless phone, trying to remember the words to an appropriate prayer.

The bullet didn't come. He dropped his arms, flicked the light switch off, and crept forward.

There was the sound of a motor turning over, grinding, coughing, then dying. More grinding. A door slamming. A man shouting *"Opesdol!* Dumb-ass bastards!" A rifle shot.

Harry pulled the Glock from his crotch and gave chase, feeling like Indiana Jones as he jumped on a couch and sprung back to the floor, leaping over a coiled rattler in the process.

He skidded to a halt when the biggest snake he'd seen yet suddenly appeared in front of him. Jesus, it was a cobra!—its neck swollen, making a strange *chikachikachik* sound, its lethal fangs exposed.

Harry's gun was down at his side. He feared if he raised it too quickly, the snake would strike. He inched his hand up slowly. The cobra stretched its ugly head up farther into the air and hissed.

Sighting a rifle in on a target through a scope was one skill; shooting from the hip like a cowboy was another— one which Harry Dymes had never practiced.

Chikachikachik. Something in the cobra's beady eyes told him he had no choice. He leaned his weight on his heels and pulled the trigger, catching the snake's midsection, its head wriggling, hissing, fangs snapping out for Harry's legs.

Harry moved faster than he had in his entire life, running for the deck. He spotted Tarasove just before he was swallowed up by the forest.

Tarasove paused to catch his breath. He could hear the pounding of the FBI man's feet on the steps from the chalet's deck. What had Marta called him? Harry. He'd looked familiar. Could he be the San Francisco policeman who shot Feliks? The one he'd seen on TV? She'd said his name was Harry. Which meant he was *not* FBI. Pretending that he was. Why? Because he was alone? There were no other agents? Harry was a lying bastard. He'd disabled the Hummer. If there had been a posse of policemen, they would have cut him to ribbons. Which meant that Harry was Marta's lone colleague.

Nicolai patted the butt of his rifle, his confidence soaring. He knew the land around his chalet—every rock, every tree. It was his hunting ground.

The bright full moon was a curse as far as Harry Dymes was concerned. He could see where he was going, except in the darkest, thickest patches of the forest, but Tarasove would be able to see him. He'd taken part in several night skirmishes in Iraq. The enemy was usually a good distance away, with only small hills and sand dunes for protection. He leaned against the trunk of a towering pine tree, closed his eyes, and focused all of his senses toward his hearing. Movement, to his right, traveling west, down toward the lake. Quiet movement: twigs creaking, low branches rustling. A night animal, or a trained hunter? More noise—from behind. He looked back to the chalet. Heavy feet, snapping sounds. Someone in a hurry. Marta?

Nicolai Tarasove moved swiftly, traveling over familiar ground, spots where he'd killed deer, bear, raccoons, coyotes, gulls, waterfowl. He estimated it would take him twenty minutes to reach the lake. There were cabins with boats, cars, campers. All he had to do was get to San Francisco—to Kilmov's rendezvous—and to do that he'd have to lose, or kill, his clumsy pursuer. Harry, the policeman, who knew nothing of his hunting ground.

He stopped at a favorite spot, a craggy run of granite boulders. He laid the suitcase on the ground, and gently, quietly, placed the rifle's stock between two of the boulders. He regretted not having had time to attach a silencer to the Weatherby. "Come, policeman," he whispered.

Harry was beginning to think that Tarasove had outfoxed him, circled around him. The forest sounds were mostly from behind now. And they stopped when he stopped. He was being stalked. He crossed a small stream, the icy water deep in spots—he was wading up to his hips. His foot turned on a slippery rock, causing him to fall to one knee.

The thunderous crack of a rifle shot, the sheer velocity of the bullet whizzing by, knocked Harry down, into the creek. He half swam, half crawled to the safety of the creek bank, one hand in the air, brandishing the Glock. He remembered army stories of men having their arms or heads taken off by shock waves from a high caliber weapon.

He lay still, his head resting on a patch of wild mushrooms that looked like Lilliputian villages. The shot had come from his left. He imagined Tarasove waiting for a sign of life. Sniper training—shoot and move on. The scientist must be worried, must be in a hurry to get away. Come on. Move!

Harry heard the *click-clack* of the rifle, the chambering of a cartridge. He braced himself for another shot. And it came, the bullet whining well over his head, landing with a *thunk* into a tree trunk. He's guessing, Harry figured. Trying to spook me. Doesn't know if his first shot was a hit or not.

Movement to his right. An animal? Marta? Sirens wailing. The police, ambulance, responding to the 911 call.

Nicolai reacted to the sirens. He draped the suitcase strap over one shoulder, the rifle strap over the other and started down the mountain, the soles of his high-traction hiking boots gripping the rocky soil. A lifetime of cross-country skiing had kept his legs strong.

He paused under a copse of fir trees with long branches spread out like linking hands. There was an open area, a hundred yards or more of steep, tree-barren land, that would save him ten minutes on the journey to the lake. It would also expose him to the policeman.

There were more sirens. He looked up at the clear sky. Helicopters—they'd use helicopters soon.

He started running, not bothering to smother the sound of his boots, moving with a swift, assured urgency, holding the rifle by the barrel, using the butt to steady himself.

Harry watched a dark shadow emerge from the trees. A man's shadow. He started off, feet pounding, blood beating in his ears. Tarasove! He moved like a fat mountain goat in the moonlight.

"Stay right there," he yelled.

Tarasove didn't bother to stop—didn't look back.

Harry rested the butt of the Glock in the palm of his left hand, centered the pistol's fixed sight just above Tarasove's head and pulled the trigger. He had no idea where the bullet ended up, but it certainly didn't deter Tarasove.

Harry went after him, his wet shoes slipping out from under him, causing him to skid twenty feet on the seat of his pants.

Tarasove disappeared into a thick treeline and Harry realized he was now a sitting target. He double-timed it, falling once again, but never losing hold of the Glock.

The deepening shadows turned the trees from deep green to inky black. The undergrowth was thick with ferns, dead leaves, and odd-size rocks.

A tree branch cracked. A single word—*"Hivno."* Shit.

Chapter Thirty-Seven

Nicolai Tarasove groaned and shook his head. He'd tripped over the carcass of a half-eaten deer. Something black, low to the ground, scurried past him. There was a chorus of childlike moans. The rifle had been jarred from his hand. He was reaching for it when he heard a noise that froze him in place—an animal blowing and clacking its teeth. A black bear on her hind legs emerged from the trees.

Tarasove scrambled to his feet. There were four cubs moaning, seeking protection by gathering near their mother. He'd interrupted their dinner. The mother bear emitted a high-pitched, pulsing moan and started after him.

Tarasove snagged the rifle by its strap and started running. He fired a shot blindly over his shoulder, hoping to frighten her. The lake. He was getting close. He could see a dock. Several small boats bobbing in the water.

Another high-pitched moan. The ground seemed to be shaking under him. The stench of the animal reached him. He fumbled with the rifle bolt, attempting to chamber another round. He screamed and whirled around. The bear was inches away. He swung the rifle like a baseball bat, the butt bouncing harmlessly off the bear's torso.

A swipe of one massive claw and Tarasove's left arm was torn loose from its socket, the suitcase sliding into the darkness. Tarasove dropped to the ground, rolling around in pain.

The bear stood over him, huffing, panting, hissing, growling, popping her jaw.

Play dead, Tarasove thought. His only hope. Play dead.

He kept one eye cracked open. The bear stared at him, head lowered, ears laid back. She began slapping her feet on the ground.

Harry Dymes fired a shot in the air to distract the bear who was towering over Tarasove. The animal stiffened for a moment, then dropped down to all fours, searching for her new adversary.

Harry fired again, and the bear's snout tilted upwards, sniffing the air. She began to lumber forward, in Harry's general direction.

Tarasove got to his feet and staggered off, stooped over, his bloody, mangled left arm dragging at his side. The bear shifted her attention back to Tarasove. Her speed surprised Harry. The bear caught up with the Russian in seconds, clamping her jaws onto Tarasove's legs, then raising him in the air, twisting the Russian like a rag doll.

Harry got off four rapid shots, aiming for the middle of the bear's broad back—but with the unfamiliar handgun, the lighting conditions, and the distance of forty yards, he had little hope of hitting his target.

The bear gave Tarasove a final twist, then dropped him to the ground and loped off into the trees.

Harry kept the Glock at the ready as he approached Tarasove. His body was on its side, his legs twisted awkwardly, his neck obviously broken. Harry knelt down, picked up Tarasove's arm and checked for a pulse.

"Is he dead?"

Harry bolted to his feet. A small-framed woman, her hair covered by a bandana, dark eyes sunken into hollow cheeks. Dark clothes, a purse over one shoulder. "Who are you?"

"Ann Davis. I live down on the lake. My husband and I heard shots a few minutes ago. He called the sheriff. Are you a policeman?"

"You're taking a hell of a chance if I'm not, lady."

She edged closer to the body. "I saw you try to save the

man by shooting at the bear. I figured you were a cop. Who's he?"

"Nick Sennet. He has a chalet up the hill. Did you know him?"

"No." She backed away a few feet. "That was some shooting. I think you hit the bear at least twice."

Harry was getting that tingling feeling between his shoulders. "Why did your husband send you? Why didn't he come along?"

"Dan's a paraplegic."

A group of men and women had come out of their lakeside residences and were cautiously approaching. A man in a plaid shirt had a rifle cradled in his arms.

"Stay back," Harry shouted. "I'm a police officer."

"I think the cavalry has arrived," the woman in the bandana said.

There were several men in western-style deputy hats brandishing flashlights, descending down the steep hillside.

Harry slipped the Glock in his waistband. "Miss Davis, stay here. I want a statement from you."

"Sure. What's this?"

Tarasove's suitcase was lying in a clump of ferns.

"Evidence," Harry said. "Stay away from it."

The group from the lake was creeping up the hill—crime scene rubberneckers.

"I'm going to send one of my neighbors to tell my husband what happened. Do you want a cup of coffee?"

"Keep your neighbors away from here. And you stay close."

The first deputy to arrive was a solid, weatherworn man in his early forties with bushy eyebrows. He kept his gun on Harry. "Talk to me in a hurry, mister."

"I'm a San Francisco cop. Harry Dymes. Call Sergeant Rennick. He'll vouch for me."

Harry surrendered the Glock, showed his badge and ID, then stood back while the deputies went about their work. "Don't touch the suitcase," he warned. "It's a biohazard."

A baby-faced deputy with a paunch hanging over his belt spit a stream of tobacco juice within inches of Harry's shoes. "You shittin' us, padna?"

"No. Keep away from it. I left an FBI agent at the chalet. She was in shock. The place is crawling with snakes."

The bushy-eyebrowed deputy said, "She's okay, an ambulance is on the scene. Just back away, Frisco. We'll take it from here. Everyone listen up. Stay away from that fucking suitcase."

Harry wandered down to the group of civilians. The man in the plaid shirt had his rifle lying across his shoulders, his arms dangling over the butt and barrel.

"Where's Ann Davis?" Harry asked him.

"Who?"

Harry scanned the group. "Ann Davis. She lives somewhere right here on the lake. Small woman. Her husband's a paraplegic."

"Never heard of them." The man turned to a woman with a long mane of blond hair that streamed below her shoulders. "Honey, you ever hear of them?"

"Never. And we've been here for fifteen years."

"Hey, Frisco. I've got Sergeant Rennick on the phone. He wants to talk to you."

Harry looked from the deputy to the lakefront. Davis had vanished.

Chapter Thirty-Eight

Zhukovsky Airport, Russia

The stretch Mercedes pulled up to the tarmac just as General Kilmov was exiting the Tupolev supersonic jet. He felt a twinge of concern for a moment. While Colonel Edik Savelev's body had not yet been identified by the Americans, there was a strong possibility that they would do so in the not too distant future. Kilmov had spent the flight back to Russia devising different strategies to deal with the problem.

He relaxed when he saw the blunt, ugly features of his regular driver, Sergeant Filippov, behind the limousine's steering wheel.

The night air was crisp, a chilling wind blowing from the north.

Filippov jumped from the car and had the rear door open and waiting for Kilmov. A Thermos of brandy-laced coffee was positioned on the leather seat.

"Welcome home, General," Filippov said, when he was back behind the wheel.

Kilmov poured himself a cup of the coffee, took an appreciative sip, then said, "Is there anything I should know about, Sergeant? Has anyone from Moscow been to the dacha?"

"No, sir. There was quite a bit of activity close by, at Sasha Veronin's place." Filippov made eye contact with Kilmov in the rearview mirror. "Veronin and six of his men were killed."

"When?"

"Sometime early this morning. Veronin's men were all shot to death. He was not so lucky. They say he was thrown into a pit with his pet tiger. Poor bastard was eaten alive."

Kilmov watched the steam rise from the coffee cup. "Who was responsible?"

Filippov took his hands from the steering wheel and tugged at the edges of his eyes, contouring them to narrow slits. "Before he died, one of Veronin's men claimed the intruders were Chinese hit men."

"Imagine that," Kilmov said. He leaned back and stared out the car window. Ying Fai, a sore loser. Would Sasha's death satisfy his thirst for revenge? "Sergeant. I want the guard patrol around the house doubled. Something like this, happening so close, must have terrified my wife."

Filippov bobbed his head in agreement. "It makes me a little nervous too, General."

San Francisco—two days later

The heat wave had ended. A tongue of fog had settled on Twin Peaks. A light breeze rustled through the rooftop roses.

"I like the deep red ones," Marta Citron said. "What are they?"

Harry Dymes used his hand shears to cut off a long-stemmed rose. "Olympiad. That was one of my mother's favorites. What's the latest news from Roger Dancel?"

"He's on his way back to Washington. There is still an army of our lab people and technicians combing through Tarasove's chalet. I saw the contents of Nicolai's suitcase. He wasn't bluffing. It was loaded with canisters of his DNA toxin. I have twelve days before I go back to Washington, Harry. Let's pretend I'm a tourist. Where would you take me?"

"Let's not pretend. Napa, the wine country. Calistoga. Mud baths, geysers and Chardonnay."

"I think I'll play hard to get. When can we start?"

Harry handed her the rose. He was happy she seemed to have suffered no lingering effects from the drug Tarasove had given her, or the episode with the pit bull. The FBI physician had suggested several days of *psychological detoxification*, but Marta would have none of it. "Two weeks vacation, and leave me alone, or I quit and start selling real estate."

"I'm waiting for a call from Sergeant Rennick. After that, off we go."

The call came in during lunch. Harry put the call on the phone's speaker so Marta could listen in.

"Good news, bad news," Rennick said. "That unidentified WMA we found shot to death near Tarasove's cabin is still unidentified. No ID on him. No labels on his clothes. Fingerprints are negative everywhere. The bullets were twenty-two caliber. We're sending the ballistic reports to your lab for comparison to the ones from the stiff in Golden Gate Park. Get this, Dymes. There were traces of leather in the wounds, as if the bullets had been fired from under a jacket."

"Is that the bad news?" Harry asked.

"Nope. The bad news is that there is no trace of this Ann Davis woman, or her alleged husband. We canvassed the lake for miles in each direction—nada, zip."

"Okay, Sergeant. Thanks for keeping me informed."

"Hey, Dymes. Don't forget about those tickets to Beach Blanket Babylon."

Marta pushed the food around on her plate with a fork, rearranging it, rather than actually eating it. "Ann Davis. She *could* have been a vacationer, not wanting to get involved, unwilling to give her real name."

"No way. She was Alex." Harry reached across the table and picked up Marta's purse. "She had one like this looped over her shoulder. It looked like dark leather. My ex-partner, Nina Javiera, had one, too. She had her hand on a gun while she was talking to me. If those civilians and the sheriff's people hadn't shown up, she'd have shot me, and taken off with the suitcase."

"Roger Dancel is preaching to the choir that the unidentified corpse is Alex."

"If so, who killed him? And who filled the tailpipe on

Tarasove's Hummer and your car with dirt? It's a damn effective way of disabling a vehicle. My money is on the woman being Alex."

"Dancel doesn't believe that a woman could be that smart or ruthless. If you're right, we'll be hearing about her again." She screwed up her napkin. "Come on. Let's play tourists."

United Airlines' Red Carpet Room was filled with the usual array of anxious travelers and bored businessmen taking advantage of the free coffee and pastries while they waited for their flights.

Trina Lee hunkered down on a sofa, her legs crossed, one foot dangling as she skimmed through the *Wall Street Journal*, thinking she really had to focus more attention on her portfolio. The Swiss bankers were notoriously cautious in their investment recommendations.

She'd spent a luxurious day in bed, alone, in a suite at the Fairmont Hotel, sleeping nearly around the clock, and the following day on a shopping spree in the city's famed Union Square.

The bonus money in Edik's briefcase had turned out to be bogus—low-grade counterfeits—which confirmed her belief that General Kilmov had planned to kill her.

She was skimming over the U.S. treasury auctions when someone nudged her knee.

"Remember me?" Roger Dancel asked.

For a second, Trina felt she'd screwed up—that the FBI had found her, perhaps through the San Francisco policeman's description. Then she recognized the I screwed-you-once let's do-it-again leer on Dancel's face, and she relaxed.

"Roger. It's good to see you."

Dancel tossed his laptop and carry-on case onto the couch. "Mind if I join you?" he said, sitting down uninvited. "Tina, right?"

"Trina. Trina Lee."

"Right. How've you been? You left us and went to work for, who was it? Social Security?"

"The National Finance Center. You're still with the Bureau?"

"Till death do us part." He ran his eyes over her and grinned. "You look like you're doing better than okay."

"A small salary and large alimony payments keep me afloat."

Dancel rubbed his hands together like a man anticipating a gourmet meal. "You beautiful women have it made. That's what I want to come back as in the next life. Of course, I'd be a lesbian. Did you hear about the blond lesbian? She kept having affairs with men. Where are you headed to?"

"New Orleans. Our main office is there. I've got an apartment in town."

"I remember your place in . . ."

"Alexandria."

"Black silk sheets. And you had a teddy that looked like a maid's uniform, right?" Dancel looked at his watch. "What time's your flight?"

"A couple of hours. I always get to the airport with so much time to kill."

"How about a drink? Scotch, isn't it?"

"Sounds wonderful."

She watched him as he hurried to the bar. What a pig. He couldn't remember her name, her employer, the town she'd lived in, or that she drank rum, not Scotch, but the sheets and lingerie were ingrained in his memory. She glanced at his laptop, wondering how much information on Alex was on the hard drive.

"Cheers," Dancel said when he returned with the drinks.

His eyes were darting around the room, no doubt looking for a quiet corner where they could have a quickie. "Are you living in D.C., Roger?"

"Yes. You never were over to my place, were you?"

"No," Trina answered softly. Because you were married at the time, you jerk.

"Do you ever get back to Washington?"

"The Finance Center sends me to town once a month or so. I usually just stay a day or two."

Dancel rattled the ice in his glass. "I'll give you my cell number. We can meet for lunch, or whatever."

"I'd like that," Trina said sincerely. She didn't think she'd ever have another chance at examining Dancel's computer files. "Have you been working on anything interesting lately?"

"You wouldn't believe it. I can't give you the whole

story, but since you're ex-Bureau, I'll let you in on the highlights." He drained the remains of his Scotch. "Another drink first?"

"Why not? I've got nothing better to do."